D0929966

SHADOW MUSIC

ALSO BY HELAINE MARIO

Dark Rhapsody

The Lost Concerto

Firebird

SHADOW MUSIC

A NOVEL

HELAINE MARIO

OCEANVIEW (((PUBLISHING
SARASOTA, FLORIDA

ISBN 978-1-60809-450-9

Published in the United States of America by Oceanview Publishing

Sarasota, Florida
www.oceanviewpub.com

10 9 8 7 6 5 4 3 2 1

PRINTED IN THE UNITED STATES OF AMERICA

For my Grandmothers, Ella Berger and Alice Swarbrick,
who survived wars and the loss of children with courage and grace.
Somehow they still had a world of love
for this quiet young booklover.

For my five beautiful Grands, who fill my world with magic—
Ellie and Tyler Danaceau and
Clair Violet, Declan, and Ian Mario.
Always do what you love, and remember to be kind.

And for RJ. After 50+ years, you still make my heart beat faster.

ACKNOWLEDGEMENTS

Once again, I want to acknowledge—and express my heartfelt appreciation for—our servicemen and -women, and their families, for their remarkable patriotism, bravery, strength, and sacrifice. Colonel Beckett and Simon Sugarman could not have "come to life" without their stories and inspiration.

I am most grateful to three people whose thoughtful comments, suggestions, and support made *Shadow Music* so much better: Gail Crockett, Marge Geiger, and Sue Kinsler, whom I have known and loved since birth.

A special thank-you, also, to Stella, the beautiful three-legged rescue dog in Georgia who was the inspiration for Shiloh.

Finally, a very personal acknowledgement to Pat and Bob Gussin, Lee Randall, and the team at Oceanview Publishing for their remarkable publishing and writing skills, and love of books. Thank you for continuing to believe in Maggie's story.

SHADOW MUSIC

"What makes night within us
may leave stars."

—Victor Hugo

PROLOGUE

ONE FINAL FLASH of light caught the faces of the two women hiding in the trees. Then the sun disappeared beyond the hills.

As the air filled with purple light, edges blurred, shadows lengthened. It was the time of day when shapes grew indistinct, when it became much harder to see. It was both a blessing and a curse.

The women crouched beside a tumble of broken stones in a copse of birch trees that stood, close and dark, on the crest of a low hill. Below them, a meadow of waving grasses sloped toward a rushing stream. On the stream's far bank, a curve of dirt road. Remnants of rusting barbed wire and broken electric fencing flashed silver in the last of the light.

Beyond the stream, Austria. Freedom.

Donata Kardos, the younger of the two, lifted her chin to listen. No truck engine. But no beat of horse hooves, either. No searchlight spearing the dusk, no howl of the dogs. This land, so close to the natural barrier of Lake Neusiedl, was no longer heavily patrolled. Now the only sounds were the brush of new April leaves in the evening breeze and the whisper of geese wings, high overhead, coming home.

Home. She searched the meadow, the ribbon of road just beyond the fence, the shallow stream where she had played as a child. Water, swollen by spring rains, frothed over stones covered in moss.

Donata turned to gaze over her shoulder. The burned-out shell of the once beautiful old abbey rose behind her, the ancient stones etched black against the darkening sky. She would never study her beloved theology texts within those thick walls or walk in the shaded cloisters. She would never take her vows there and pray freely in the abbey's now-silent gardens.

Her parents rarely spoke of those fearful days after World War II, when the Soviet tanks had invaded her country, rumbling into the towns, imprisoning their leaders, setting fire to schools and churches and culture and lives. The Iron Curtain had slammed down years before she was born, and her future had disappeared like the abbey's red embers, spinning high into the starless night sky. The Soviets—and Hungary's Secret Police—had closed not only the borders, but so many of the minds and hearts of her countrymen as well. If only—

Strong fingers gripped her arm, wrenching her back to the present.

"Where is the truck, Donata? You said your cousin would be here by now!"

Donata turned to the young woman who knelt on the earth beside her—her closest friend since the age of two, when Tereza and her family had moved into the Budapest apartment next to hers. If she closed her eyes, she could still hear the gorgeous strains of Tereza's father's violin through the thin walls . . .

Now Tereza was just eighteen, so petite and rounded, with waist-length hair the color of rubies. While she was just the opposite—three years younger, tall and whip-thin, her shaggy jet hair cropped short. In the gathering dusk, Tereza's ivory skin was almost translucent, her beautiful blaze of hair hidden beneath a drab gray shawl and her body stiff with growing fear.

Donata put a reassuring hand on her friend's arm. "Pavel will come. Have faith, Reza."

She saw the disbelief in the wide blue eyes, too bright with tension above the long dark coat. Tereza Janos turned away with an impatient shake of her head and shifted to pull the oversized canvas duffel bag closer to her body.

Just hours earlier, in the small bedroom on the outskirts of Sopron, Donata had watched her friend pack and repack that bag, knew it held warm clothing, bank notes, photographs, and the treasures Tereza's father had left behind the night the soldiers came for him—his Guarnari violin, now wrapped carefully in a heavy woolen jacket, and a painted canvas, almost one meter in length, rolled inside a silk pillowcase. She'd had just a glimpse of one small corner—two glowing chromium-yellow stars against a swirling sky of deep velvety blue.

Donata sighed, shifted, returned her eyes to the road. Only fifty meters down the slope from their hiding place, but it seemed like an ocean away. It was so open, so exposed. What if . . .

She forced the fear from her head. Pavel would come.

Still no headlamps. She tried to see her watch in the fading light. The truck was late. The patrol had passed by more than an hour earlier. They would return within twenty minutes. Where was Pavel?

She slipped her hand into the deep pocket of her cloak, gripped the small pistol she had stolen just days before from a mason in the village. Could she use it? Yes, if she had to. She would do anything for Tereza. Please, she prayed. We're ready. Let the truck come. Let—

A small wail broke the stillness.

Both women froze, their eyes flying to the infant nestled in a soft rose-colored blanket against Tereza's breast. The baby shifted, making small breathy sounds in her sleep.

"Hush, Gemma Rozsa, hush," whispered Tereza, holding her child close. Her wide eyes found Donata's, too aware of the danger. Any sound could alert the patrols. Or the Dobermans.

How did we get here, thought Donata. Two frightened girls and a tiny baby with hair the color of roses, hiding from soldiers and dogs as the light falls from the day.

"Come with us, Donata," whispered Tereza against her cheek. "You can take your vows in Austria, become a nun there."

Donata reached out to smooth the child's wispy copper curls. "You know I can't, Reza. There is no easy choice when your country is occupied. Your father understood that. You leave, escape to the West. Or you stay and fight. Change is coming, I know it. Not long now. I hear the whispers."

"Part of me wants to stay here with you."

"Ah, Reza, I know. Because part of me wants to go with you and my godchild. But our church needs me more than ever. I have no choice but to stay. And you have no choice but to leave."

"Your church had to go *underground*, Donata!"

"All the more reason to stay." Donata gazed down at the sleeping infant. "You have to protect my godchild. Her father will not rest until he finds his daughter, you know that. That's why we are here, instead of the border crossing at Nickelsdorf. They are *watching* for you, Reza!"

"Oh, God. I know you're right. But what if we—"

Headlamps!

The two women stared into the dim light as the small truck halted down by the road. The headlights blinked once, twice, then went out. They could just see the shape of a man emerge, waving his arms at them. Then he began to open the broken, twisted fence with wire cutters.

"It's Pavel." Donata bent to heft the heavy duffel bag to her shoulder and held out a hand to her friend. "You can do this, Tereza. For Gemma Rozsa."

Holding hands, with the child clutched against Tereza's chest, the women began to run across the grass. It was almost full dark now, the tall trees standing like sentinels against the last of the fiery sky.

The bright day is done, thought Donata. *And we are for the dark.*

The stream beckoned, sparking silver in the twilight. Fifteen meters. Ten. Five. And then they were at the stream.

The water was cold, the rocks underfoot sharp and slippery. Donata went first, balancing on the stepping-stones. Behind her, Tereza stumbled, pulling her hand away. Donata clamored up the muddy riverbank, reaching the fence just as Pavel tossed a thick rug across the sharp strands of broken wire and held out his gloved hand through the opening in the fence. "Hurry!" he whispered.

Donata tossed the duffel bag to Pavel and turned to help her friend. Tereza had frozen several yards behind her, on the edge of the stream, her head lifted, breath rasping. Her shawl draped like a veil over her head so that she looked like a Madonna in the halo of soft evening light.

What did she hear?

The howl of a dog on the wind.

Terror iced along Donata's spine.

A searchlight speared the air, edged toward them across the grass. Three soldiers on horseback appeared from the shadows, black and indistinct, riding toward them. A shout. A gunshot broke the stillness, startling the blackbirds from the trees. More shots, closer.

"Donata!"

Donata ran back into the water, saw her friend stagger toward her, hunched to shield the child in her arms. In surreal slow motion, one of the soldiers raised his rifle. A flash of fire in the shadows, a deep, agonized cry. *Nyet, nyet!*

Tereza stiffened, startled, shock flaming in the suddenly blurred blue eyes. A bright red stain appeared high on her breast.

"Reza!" Donata lunged toward her friend.

Tereza thrust her child into Donata's arms. "You take her, Donata," she gasped. "Take her to freedom. Keep her . . . from her father. Keep . . . her safe . . ."

"No!" cried Donata. "No, Reza. Not without you. Please, no . . ."

But now the whimpering baby was in her arms, wrapped against her body, and she felt Pavel's strong arms dragging her through the fence. "Come!" he cried. "Get in the truck! You cannot help her now."

A jagged barb tore her arm. As if caught in a nightmare, Donata heard more gunshots, a shout in Russian, the sharp barking of the dogs. She saw Tereza fall in slow motion to the riverbank. So still.

She felt Pavel push her into the truck, heard the gears grind as the wheels caught the road and the truck roared forward. Clutching her tiny goddaughter to her chest, Donata twisted to look out the window.

In the new darkness, the scene in the meadow was dreamlike. The air glowing purple and silver with ambient light. Three soldiers, standing frozen and black against the vast, shimmering sky. Her best friend crumpled on the ground, one slender arm stretched toward the fence, her hair glinting like fire in the last of the light. The gray shawl, fallen beside her, was red with her blood.

And then the truck careened around a bend, and Reza was gone.

PART I

"MAGGIE"

"Like a shadow, like a dream . . . "

The Iliad, Homer

CHAPTER ONE

THE PRESENT
MUSEUM OF FINE ARTS, BOSTON
TUESDAY, APRIL 8

MAGGIE O'SHEA'S FINGERS flew over the piano keys, the final tumbling chords of Chopin's *Heroic Polonaise* soaring, filling the museum's high, glass-walled courtyard with the chords of its glorious coda. Too soon, the last notes echoed. Then silence.

She dropped her head, trying to breathe, her hands suddenly, achingly still. And then the applause began, rising to thunder in the lofty glassed space. Maggie opened her eyes and willed herself back to earth. Back to the beautiful Boston Museum of Fine Arts atrium. Night was falling, and she saw herself reflected in the tall windows, a slender black-haired woman in a tube of charcoal velvet.

Her eyes found the huge atrium's centerpiece—the forty-foot high lime-green *Icicle Tower*, the gorgeous blown glass sculpture by Dale Chihuly. Sometimes, when she played, an aurora of bright colors flew like silken ribbons across her mind. Sometimes the roof disappeared and she felt herself flying high into the star-filled sky. For darker pieces, she found herself wandering alone, lost in deep shadows. And sometimes she simply stepped into the music like a river and flowed with it. Felt it flow *through* her. Today, those lime-green glass crystals had tumbled through her head. What would Chopin have thought?

Amused, she took another breath to center herself once more in the here and now.

Maggie stood, turned to the audience, gave the slightest bow. Faces floated like cameos, light and dark, in front of her. Then the guests rose, surged toward her. She smiled, murmured thanks, clasped hands, answered their questions as honestly as she could. *Yes, Chopin's Polonaise is one of my favorite pieces. No, I won't be soloing with the BSO until later this summer. I, too, find a definite link between color and music . . .*

The number of classical music lovers she met never ceased to astonish her. Some so knowledgeable and educated, many musicians themselves. But others who simply gave themselves up to the sheer emotion and beauty of the rhythms and melodies. It was why she did what she did—because music filled the emotional spaces, resonating long after the room fell silent. The year after her husband's death, when she had been unable to play the piano, was the longest, most terrible year of her life. *Where words fail*, she thought, *music speaks.*

Now, finally, after months of therapy and hard work, she was making music again. At the invitation of the museum, she had performed several short piano pieces this afternoon, all connected, in different ways, to the museum's current exhibit. *Musical Paintings*—an exhibition focusing on the music in art, and the close links between painters and musicians of the late 19th and early 20th century.

Once more her eyes swept the huge glassed atrium, which showcased Picasso's *Three Musicians*, Renoir's *Dancing Girl with a Tambourine*. On the far wall, Degas' *Orchestra Musicians*, Georgia O'Keefe's undulating *Music, Pink and Blue No. 2*, on loan from the Whitney. Today she had played in honor of Paul Cezanne's *Girl at the Piano*, choosing several intimate pieces to complement the dark and light contrasts of his enigmatic oil. She had played three beautiful Liszt etudes, followed by a Debussy Prelude, included because of his Impressionist technique, and—just because the Cezanne stirred thoughts of Chopin within her—the *Polonaise.*

Maggie smiled and shook her head. Time to return to her apartment and music shop in Beacon Hill. But first—her gaze trailed to the modern, open staircase across the atrium. Just one more visit to her favorite gallery. She laid a palm on the smooth dark wood of the Steinway, grateful for its clear, rich sound, before she turned away. *We did good today*, she told the still-warm instrument.

As she moved past a group of men and women in animated discussion, one voice caught her attention.

"How does every Russian joke start?" asked a deep, rumbling voice behind her. "By looking over your shoulder! Ha!"

Who laughs at his own jokes that way?

In spite of herself, Maggie turned. An older man in the group murmured something to a tall, bearded guest and then moved toward her. Maggie found herself looking up into heavy-lidded, burning dark eyes.

"Madame O'Shea?" The accent was Eastern European.

"I am Maggie O'Shea, yes." The man standing in front of her had a broad Slavic face and a thick wrestler's build. His bullet-shaped head was clean-shaven, with a salt-and-pepper shadow across a strong jaw. A heavy gold necklace sparkled against the white cotton of his open-necked dress shirt. An interesting look.

His hand reached to close over hers in a warm, firm grip as he bowed from the waist. "It is not often that someone gets my attention the way you did. I was lost in my thoughts—and then suddenly I heard your music. I looked up, astonished. Who was playing that piano, creating that sound? I had to meet you."

"And now that you have?"

"Now I am more taken than ever. Please allow me to introduce myself. I am Yuri Belankov. Ex-violinist from St. Petersburg." Laughter boomed deep in his chest. "*Very* ex. It was a long time ago. It is indeed a pleasure to meet you."

"And you, Mr. Belankov. I always enjoy meeting a fellow musician. *Ex* though he may be." She smiled at the handsome Russian.

"Your husband was right. You play like no one else I've ever heard." Maggie froze.

Breathe. You never knew when you might be blindsided by the ghosts of memory. She'd learned that grief was like that—quiet for a while, and then suddenly, when she least expected it, it would come roaring back like an ocean wave, knocking her flat. A scent, a voice, a silhouette beyond a darkened window . . .

Just ghosts, she reminded herself. You're stronger now, not the same woman you were. It's okay.

Maggie stepped closer to Belankov. "You knew my husband, Johnny O'Shea?"

"He interviewed me for a story he was doing on Russian businessmen, some twenty months back. September, I think. A sharp man, a brilliant writer, eh? And we played chess twice. He actually almost beat me the second time. Well, of course I could not let that happen." A broad smile. "He talked about you, naturally, assured me that I would never hear anything more beautiful than you playing his beloved Rachmaninoff."

She smiled with memory. "Rachmaninoff was Johnny's favorite composer. I hope you were not disappointed today?"

"Not at all. I brought my old friend Kirov to hear you—" He gestured to the attractive, bearded man in the crowd of guests behind them. "He owns a very high-end art gallery in Manhattan."

Looking past Belankov, Maggie was surprised to see the stranger's light, intense eyes resting on her. *Kirov.* Tall and very handsome, with a dashing, dark clipped beard. In the narrow European suit, his body had an arrogant grace. Did she know him?

"He looks like a Romanov prince," she murmured.

"Ha, he will love that," said Belankov. Looking down at her, he admitted, "Today I was hoping for the sounds of home—a Scriabin prelude, perhaps, or Stravinsky's Sonata. But your Chopin . . . Dazzling. You play as if you know something about loss." He bent closer. "Which, of course, you do. I am sorry about your husband's death."

Maggie felt herself go pale. "Thank you. It's been eighteen months, but I still miss him very much."

The Russian nodded. "I felt it. You allow the music to break your heart."

She closed her eyes. "The heart will always grieve. But the raw grief is gone now, and I'm actually finding happiness again."

"As it should be."

She nodded. "Perhaps next time I can include one of your Russian composers."

Muscular shoulders shrugged. "I learned their music at my mother's knee. She especially loved the *Firebird*." The dark eyes flashed. "She also told me, 'Too many pieces of music finish too long after the end.' Ha!"

Maggie smiled again, relieved to be on less painful ground. "I agree. Your mother was a wise woman."

"*Da*. She taught me to really *listen*. 'Just to hear is nothing, *Lyubov Moya*,' she would say. 'Even a duck hears, eh?'"

His deep, rumbling laughter enveloped her.

Belankov swept two flutes of champagne from the silver tray of a passing waiter and offered one to her. "Will you join me in a toast, then?" His smile was broad, crinkling his eyes.

"Thank you." Maggie accepted the crystal, raised it toward him. "To your mother."

"*Za tee bya*. And to your husband." He raised a peppered brow in admiration as he touched his glass to hers with a small clink.

"May tonight be the best night of all, and the worst of the nights to come."

"Good words." Maggie gazed at him thoughtfully over the rim of her glass. "What story brought you and my husband together, Mr. Belankov?"

"Two things we had in common," he said softly. "Art and music. My colleagues and I run a Think Tank in Washington dedicated to improving U.S.-Russian relations."

"Good luck with that," she muttered.

Belankov shook his head mournfully. "I admit, Mr. Putin does not make it easy. But we take the cultural approach, who can argue with that? Shared art exhibits, ballet company and symphony orchestra tours. At the time we met, your husband was interested in a Raoul Dufy I had acquired. *Red Orchestra*. Exquisite, you would love it. In fact, your husband tried to buy it for you, but I could not bear to part with it."

"That's so Johnny," she said softly.

"*Da*," said Belankov. "And now, I am in the midst of arranging a tour of the U.S. by the New Russian Symphony Orchestra." He handed her a creamy embossed business card.

Maggie took the card, slipping it into the pocket of her dress. "I've heard of the orchestra, of course, they've taken the music world by storm. Maestro Zharkov has made quite a name for himself."

"Valentin Zharkov is indeed larger than life, an absolutely mad talent. Like you." He wagged thick peppered brows at her. "He's conducting in London for the next week, at the Royal Festival Hall."

"I've played at the Festival Hall," said Maggie. "I'm flying to London on Saturday night. Perhaps I can attend one of Zharkov's concerts."

"It's an all-Russian program, Madame O'Shea." Belankov smiled, leaned closer. "Is there any way I could convince you to solo with Maestro Zharkov and his orchestra one night when they come to the States? Please. How could you say no to your husband's beloved Rachmaninoff?"

* * *

"Call me Yuri, please."

In the Boston Museum's soaring atrium, Yuri Belankov gazed at the lovely pianist standing spine-straight in front of him. Up close, she was slight and slender, with a mass of night-black hair caught up on her head and remarkable eyes the deep green of a St. Petersburg river. Her only jewelry was a delicate necklace, its small gold treble clef glinting in the hollow of her throat.

He turned, gestured toward the beautiful contemporary painting on the wall behind him. "Vasily Kandinsky was born in Moscow, did you know that? His *Composition 8* is one of my favorite pieces of art. The richness of the colors, all those flowing geometric forms. Aggressive and still quiet, *da*? Yet it comes together in total harmony. It *looks* like music."

"It *does*," said Maggie slowly, stepping closer to gaze at the swirling shapes. "It's as if the artist translated music into something for the eye."

"And *you* know art, Madame O'Shea."

She shook her head. "Oh, Lord, no, almost nothing. But I crossed paths with a beautiful Matisse this past fall and it reminded me that visual art, like music, can convey powerful emotions. So I've been coming here to the museum whenever I'm in town to learn more."

He leaned toward her. "And to be inspired, for your music."

"Yes." She glanced toward the grand floating staircase that led to several of the galleries. "I have found inspiration here."

"Your Matisse—was it the *Dark Rhapsody*?"

Her brows arched in surprise. "Yes, how did you know?"

"I read about it in the *Times*. A priceless painting looted during World War II, a missing heir . . . a fascinating story. I have a modest art collection myself."

"Russian artists, no doubt?" she said with a smile.

"Except for the Dufy, of course. Popova, Malyutin, Larionov. A small Chagall. Did you know Chagall was born in Belarus?"

"I had no idea."

He bent toward her. "Is it too much to hope that you would tell me the story of Matisse's *Dark Rhapsody*?"

She glanced at the tall darkening windows. "Perhaps another time. It's been a pleasure to meet you, Mr. Belankov. But it's getting late, and I have one more stop to make before going home, so I will have to say goodnight."

"Of course, I understand. The pleasure has been mine. I hope our paths will cross again, *Zvezda Moya*."

She gave a faint, questioning smile as she turned away.

Belankov watched her merge into the crowd, then gestured to his tall, bearded comrade. Nikolai Kirov crossed the room to join him, his light eyes on Maggie O'Shea.

"She is very beautiful," murmured Kirov.

"*Da*," agreed Belankov. "Second thoughts, old friend?"

"*Nyet*. She is a means to an end. That is all."

Belankov put a hand on Kirov's shoulder. "For both of us, Niki. Each of us will get what we want." Leaning closer, Belankov lowered his voice. "I saw you taking a call. Have you found the boy?"

"Not yet," said Kirov, his eyes still on the retreating figure of the pianist. "But I have a lead—a Russian in Hazelton Prison, who was very close to the boy's mother."

"I am a patient man, but not this time. We are partners; we have a deal. My priority is to find the painting. But yours is to help me find the boy. Find him, Kirov."

"I will."

Belankov put a hand on his friend's shoulder. "I have known you for most of my life, Niki," he said. "Something is bothering you; I sense it. What is wrong?"

Kirov shook his head. "Nothing I can't handle, Yuri. For now, just know that my men are searching every inch of Brighton Beach. We will find the boy."

Belankov nodded slowly. "Soon. As my Little Mother always said, *'Nyet cheloveka, nyet problem.'*"

If there is no person, then there is no problem.

Kirov smiled as he turned away and disappeared into the crowd.

Belankov watched him thoughtfully. *We all have a dark side, old friend.*

Then, once more, his eyes found Maggie O'Shea, now at the far side of the grand foyer near the high stairway. Where was she going?

You can leave me for now, Magdalena, he told her silently. But the stage is set. I need to know what your husband told you before he died. Our paths will cross again.

Sooner than you know.

CHAPTER TWO

MUSEUM OF FINE ARTS, BOSTON

MAGGIE MADE HER way up the floating staircase, pausing at the top step to turn and search the atrium below her. There was Belankov, with his handsome Russian friend. Were they looking up at her? *Imagination.*

Irritated with her inexplicable sense of unease, she shook her head and entered Gallery 154. The museum was still crowded, and she was surrounded by a murmuring sea of art lovers. Then the crowd parted and she saw him across the room.

Very slowly, as if drawn by his inner heat, she moved toward him.

The man stood tall and very still, head tilted in thought, his body in deep shadow. Rumpled pants over narrow hips, one leg bent, one sinewy arm behind his back. His silvering hair was covered by a soldier's cap above a face made of blades and broken angles. The cap covered his eyes but she knew they were the color of rain, glinting with intelligence and irony. And pain.

Maggie stood in front of the large Winslow Homer oil of a Civil War trooper and let out her breath slowly. Damn if the soldier in the portrait painted in the 1860s didn't look exactly like her colonel.

Trooper Meditating.

She had discovered the Homer exhibit the last time she'd come to the museum. Stopped in her tracks the moment she'd entered the gallery, as if she'd been hit in the chest by a bolt of lightning. There was Colonel Michael Beckett, standing in a forest of dark trees, gazing down at a cross. It was so . . . him. A solitary, thoughtful soldier who hated war and yet spent his life fighting to bring all those innocent kids home.

Shaking her head, she turned to a second Homer—a watercolor—just to the right.

An older man in a battered hat sat in an old rowboat, his oars still, the suspenders on his woolen shirt askew, turning to look right at her over his shoulder. Surrounding him, a mountain lake reflected the trees that edged the water, blue with twilight. Except for the beard, this man, too, could have been Michael Beckett—a man as stony and rugged as the mountains he loved. The only thing missing in the painting was a dog.

She shook her head, thinking of the colonel's beautiful three-legged Golden Retriever named Shiloh, rescued from a bombed village in Afghanistan.

I miss you, Michael. I miss you both.

Her thoughts flashed on a dark figure towering over her in a Paris cemetery at dawn, near Chopin's tomb. The early light had touched his eyes—silver, hard and cold as river stones. It was the first time she'd laid eyes on Michael Beckett, just nine months earlier, when she'd journeyed to France to search for her missing godson. And the colonel had ordered her, in his gruff, take-no-prisoners way, to go home. He didn't need her. Didn't want her.

So, of course, she had stayed.

Their chemistry had been immediate, tumultuous. Complicated and adversarial. Still was.

It had taken a long time, but he had slowly lifted her from the black fog of grief, and brought her back to music—and to life.

Her thoughts turned to a firelit bedroom in a cabin surrounded by tall mountain pines. Chopin spilling into the night air, the feel of the ridged scars on the colonel's back beneath her fingertips. Michael's face suspended above hers on the creaking brass bed, the sharp planes of his face turning gold in the flickering light, his eyes on her like stars in the shadows. God.

No one had ever kissed her the way he kissed her. Still she heard the whispering in her bones when she thought of him ...

At least they were in the same time zone for a change.

He was probably in Virginia at the ranch he'd just bought to help heal returning wounded veterans.

So why was she suddenly so anxious? Sunrise Ranch was a beautiful, safe place. Rolling hills, tall trees, horses. The colonel had finally left all the danger, the guns and the war, behind him. Nothing could go wrong at a quiet ranch in the Virginia countryside.

Right?

* * *

"She's dead."

In the stable at Sunrise Ranch, Michael Beckett clicked off his cell phone, unable to stop his eyes from searching the shadows for a body he knew wasn't there. He reached down to rub his Golden's ears. "We were too late, boy. She's gone."

Shiloh, Beckett's Golden Retriever, growled, low and deep in his chest. Behind them, a mare stomped nervously in her stall.

Beckett's breath came out. *Okay, slow and easy.* He sank to the hay-covered floor, leaned back against a closed stall door, and looked up at the barn's rough wooden beams.

Irina Davidov. His best friend Yev's only child.

The Brooklyn detective had been brief and blunt. Irina Davidov, found last night in a dark alley near the beach, strangled by piano wire. No suspects, no witnesses. She'd given her lawyer only two contact names. A Russian mobster in a West Virginia prison named Lev Vronsky. And Beckett, as her will's executor.

Beckett closed his eyes.

Piano wire. *Christ.* Beckett felt his stomach lurch. He reached inside his jacket, withdrew the thick white envelope from Irina that had finally arrived at the cabin just yesterday afternoon after bouncing for two weeks from Bagram in Afghanistan to the Pentagon to the cabin in Virginia. I would have gone to Brooklyn as soon as I read her letter, thought Beckett. *This one's on me.*

The Golden hobbled over to settle by Beckett's side, liquid eyes locked on the folded papers. Beckett withdrew the note first and stared down at the words. Just one page, a feminine scrawl, written in a hurry on blue-lined paper.

Dear Colonel Beckett,

I hope this reaches you. We met in Brighton Beach a long time ago, when you came to see me and my mom after my dad died. I know he was your best friend in 'Nam, he wrote about you all the time. He even told me about that night patrol, on the edge of the river, when the VC attacked out of nowhere and he almost lost you. My father loved you, Colonel. That means a lot. You told me that day to let you know if I ever needed help. Well, I'm calling in that promise. I'm in trouble.

Beckett dropped the note to his lap. "Irina Davidov," he said softly, gazing down at the Golden's smooth head. "Her father saved my life in 'Nam. He was still there on tour when she was born. Irina grew up without a dad. She was a wild child, in and out of the gangs growing up. But, God, she was beautiful. And smart, too—a corporate tax accountant for a Brooklyn firm. Liked to party with wealthy, powerful Russians. We lost touch for a long time. My fault,

I was always gone. But I was planning to go to New York to see her one of these days."

Shiloh rose stiffly, circled around, then settled once more with his head and single front paw on Beckett's thigh with a forlorn, knowing expression. Beckett shook his head and once more lifted Irina's note. The words blurred before his eyes.

My life has been complicated, Colonel. Mom died early on, and I had to fend for myself. Maybe I made too many bad choices, but I did one thing right. Had a kid, the sweetest little boy. Yevgeny. Yevgeny Davidov, after his grandfather. Everyone calls him Dov. He's fifteen now, smart and cocky, with a V-shaped scar on his cheek—like a bird in flight. Always wished my dad could have met him. Dov has my dad's eyes. Blue as a Russian lake.

"So, my pal Yevgeny had a grandson. I never knew."
He held the note to the lantern's light, squinted.

These last few years, I've gotten in way over my head with the mob. Seen things I shouldn't have seen, learned things I shouldn't know. No one knows more secrets than an accountant for the Mafia, right? They got scared, framed me for dealing drugs, as a warning, I guess, and I spent nine months in lock-up.

Christ, thought Beckett. She was talking about the Russian Mafia. Ruthless sons of bitches, bodies inked with roses, thorns, and daggers. Mean as snakes in a bag. Made a bad day a whole lot worse.

Of course I lost my job. The social worker took my boy away from me and put him in foster care. Two days ago I got out—but Dov had disappeared from his last foster home. That night I was attacked outside my old apartment. I managed to get away, I'm hiding now, in a room above the Tatiana Nightclub on the Boardwalk. Someone wants me out of the picture. I know too much. No person, no problem, right? So I just have to find Dov and get away. I've been calling him, texting too. Told him to meet me at the Tatiana. But so far, no word. I'm scared for him, Colonel. Please come. Help me find my boy, help us start over, somewhere safe.

Beckett glanced down at the return address on the envelope. "Mailed from a Russian neighborhood in Brooklyn," he said to the Golden. "Brighton Beach."

But just in case [Irina's pain spilled across the page] *I'm sending you the key to my safe deposit box, and my will. My lawyer has your name. Everything's for my son. Money for Dov's college, his future.*

She'd included her lawyer's name and phone number. Just an hour earlier, the lawyer had put him in touch with the Brooklyn detective in charge of her murder.

Beckett unfolded the second packet of papers, glanced down at the endless legal paragraphs and the small silver safe deposit key she'd taped to the first page.

The last words of Irina's letter were seared on his brain.

Dov is all I've got now, Colonel. I'm all he's got. But I'm in trouble, the kind of trouble that could put my kid in danger, too. I've got to find him, keep him safe. There's no one else—his grandparents are gone, his father died years ago. Please, you're my only hope. Maybe Dov's only hope. You've got to help me find my boy before they do.

"They . . . Who the hell are *they*?" The Golden raised his head to stare at Beckett, as if he knew what was coming. For a moment,

Beckett pictured Maggie's face. What was she going to think about all this?

Help me find my boy before they do.

The kid was in danger. He nodded at the dog and spoke into the stable's flickering shadows. "I'll find out what happened to your son, Irina. I'll find Yev's grandson for you. I owe your dad; it's what he would have wanted. I won't let either one of you down."

And Beckett knew it, just as the Golden knew it.

I'm going back into the darkness.

CHAPTER THREE

BROOKLYN, NEW YORK

THE SOUND OF his body crashing down the stairwell filled his head.

He could still feel the brutal kick of the boot, that sickening sense of falling through air as he tumbled down the cement steps. The lightning bolts of pain. The sure knowledge that his attacker was going to kill him.

The cold fear as he lay curled on the landing—his backpack twisted beneath him, the straps cutting into his shoulders—waiting for the man to come down the steps and finish the job.

And then . . .

A door opening, a shaft of spilling light, a shout.

The Russian thug at the top of the stairs froze, then turned and disappeared into a dark hallway.

"Hey! What's happening here? You okay, kid?"

Somehow, he'd dragged himself to his feet and staggered toward the exit.

Now, it was dark. He'd lost track of the time, the unfamiliar streets, as he ran.

The boy turned a corner and stopped. He stood still, bloody chin lifted, listening.

Quiet as a cemetery. He gazed around. Well, look at that. It was a kind of cemetery, wasn't it? A car graveyard.

He counted to sixty. Okay. He'd lost him. *Maybe.*

Frickin' A, that creep who attacked him at the Rec Center had been hired to *kill* him. Someone wanted him *dead*. And he knew why.

Alert for any sound or movement, he moved slowly, quietly, among the pile of wrecked autos, searching for a place to hide. Just for the night.

Never stay in one place too long. He'd head to a new place in the morning. Somewhere he remembered from the past. Find a safe place, lie low for a while, until he got stronger.

Until he could track down the man who'd killed his mom.

He stopped in the shadows of a burned-out SUV, leaning against the door to catch his breath. The pain in his ribs stabbed at him, and there was a hot rock pulsing where his right kidney should be. At least he thought it was a kidney; maybe he'd missed too many Bio classes. Whatever. The heavy boot had caught him in the back and sent him flying.

If only I'd had a bat, he thought, I could have—

He stopped, eyeing the car on his left. An old junk of a Chevy Impala, front crunched like an accordion. He peered through the driver's-side window. No bloodstains. Good, no way he'd sleep in a death car. He angled his head. The back seat wasn't too bad. If he could just open the rear door, then—yeah, baby! He eased the metal door open, leaned in, sniffed. Another jab in the ribs, but the car smelled like night air, not dead things. Probably because the windows were smashed.

We have a winner.

He tossed the heavy backpack across the seat, bit back the groan of pain that rose in his throat as he slid into the car. Closed the door softly, sank to the torn leather. Head down, out of sight.

It was so cold in the car that he could see his breath. He clutched the thin sweatshirt around him and pulled his knees up to his chest. Felt the heavy rocks he'd stuffed in his pockets, pressing against his hip.

They'd do, if his attacker came back. And in the morning, he'd search the junkyard, find some sharp metal, maybe a long shard of jagged glass. Use what you got, right?

He wiped a hand across his forehead. It came away wet with blood. Jesus.

He closed his eyes and tried to disappear into the car's shadows.

His eyes flew open.

No. Don't sleep. Sleep brought the night terrors.

He shook his head to banish the images, but they flew like bats into his mind.

He'd heard from his mother, gone to find her. And he'd found her, all right.

The shadowed alley. His mother's body sprawled on the filthy stones. So still... And then—the man's face, lit for an instant by the single streetlamp, staring back at him. Then a quick turn, and the man had disappeared into the shadows.

His chest heaved with grief. *Don't go there.*

He blinked, focused on the Chevy's broken window. From this angle, he could see the night sky, a few stars winking. His mother used to sing him a song about stars, the words in the soft, lilting Russian of his childhood.

He lay in the dark, trying to remember the words. The sound of her voice.

Keep it safe, tell no one, until we can be together again. I love you. Those were the last words she'd spoken to him, the morning she'd left for prison. The morning she'd given him the small blue envelope holding a thumb drive. He touched his backpack, where the drive was hidden. *Keep it safe. Tell no one.*

So far so good. All he had to do was get through the night. He'd heard they were offering hot breakfast at the church. He'd kill for pancakes.

You can't risk it.

His stomach clutched. Don't think about food. Think about B-ball, the cool sneakers he'd scored at the Salvation Army, that cute girl who hung out with some of her friends at the Coney Island gym.

Eyes wide open, the boy huddled against the old leather car seat, staring up at the stars and listening to the night sounds through the shattered windows. Cars speeding by on the overpass, the wind moaning through the broken pile of metal around him, the distant barking of dogs.

The dead silence in that alley.

The last thing he saw as sleep claimed him was the face of his mother's killer, frozen in the light of the streetlamp.

CHAPTER FOUR

BEACON HILL, BOSTON

"LONG DAY'S JOURNEY into night," murmured Maggie.

Clad in leggings and an oversized blue sweatshirt that said, *Musicians Paint Their Pictures In Silence*, she stood in the shadowed music shop—quiet, now, at the end of the day.

As always, the sign on the bright blue door made her smile—*Bach Tomorrow, Offenbach Sooner*. She'd purchased it the day she'd bought the Beacon Hill brownstone, so many years earlier, with its cozy upstairs apartment just right for a single mother and her young son. And now Brian had a tiny son of his own. Child of my child . . .

The light from the old-fashioned iron gas lamps on Charles Street fell through the purple-paned bow window, spilled like gold water on her mother's Steinway grand piano, and scattered patterns of light and shadow across the worn Persian carpet.

Maggie clicked on the green-shaded library lamp and stood still to listen. Yes, Luze—her close friend and business partner—had gone home for the night. And by the scents drifting from the back room, she'd left a still-warm lasagna. Suddenly hungry, Maggie shook her head. When had she eaten last? Yesterday? Luze knew her too well.

Maggie turned on the radio, found a harp concerto, and gazed around the large, high-ceilinged room. Named after her son's huge orange cat, Gracie, The Piano Cat Music Shop was lined with oak bookcases and glass cabinets that held an exceptional collection of musical scores and books. Another click, and the Tiffany lamp cast a pool of light on the library table and illuminated the soft watercolors of Martha's Vineyard gracing the walls. Close to the window, two deep red leather wingchairs faced each other across her husband's carved chess set, still ready for a game.

Checkmate, Lass. And now, time for bed.

Johnny O'Shea's low voice flew like a ghost into her mind. Maggie let out her breath. For so many months, she had been unable to look at those empty red chairs, knowing she would be ambushed by a vision of Johnny. He'd be sitting back, gazing at her with those electric blue eyes, a full glass of his favorite Macallan's single malt scotch whiskey in hand.

I may be Irish, Maggie-mine, but there is nothing like three fingers of good Scottish whiskey at the end of the day, whether my writing was very good—or very bad.

She smiled. Now, more than eighteen months after Johnny's death, on some days she was able to think of him and actually smile. Think of him without dissolving into tears—or worse, body crumpling to the floor, the way it had been in those first raw days of her grief. The days and nights when all she could see when she closed her eyes was his white sailboat exploding on a black storm-tossed sea so far from home.

She turned toward the tarnished mirror above the table, searching for his image.

It's been a while since we've talked, Johnny. The nightmares are gone, mostly. I no longer see sorrow every time I look in the mirror. Time softens grief, I've learned.

Was that his face, taking shape in the wavering shadows?

You'll be happy to know that I'm finally ready to take on Rachmaninoff's Piano Concerto No. 2 again, Johnny. I wasn't ready the first time. But now I think I am. You always believed I could play it.

The faintest shimmer, wavering in the dark glass. His voice, so low and close.

The Rach 2! It's the most beautiful concerto I've ever heard, Lass.

I remember. I'll always associate that music with you.

In need of solace, she wandered to the library table. There, set among a handful of music awards, were the silver frames that held the faces she loved. Her son, Brian, with his wife and her new grandson, Ben, smiling at her from a Cape Cod beach. Her godson, TJ, his favorite red kite in hand, blowing a kiss to her from the French vineyard where he lived. And there—her parents, Lily and Finn, standing in a leafy Yale courtyard and smiling into each other's eyes. How would her life have been different if her mother had lived?

Three more frames were set, like a triptych, at the end of the table. First, Michael, with Shiloh by his side, one booted foot on a paddock fence. Eyes shaded against the glow of a setting sun, crooked smile unmistakable. She reached out, touched a gentle finger to the face smiling back at her. Her eyes moved on to the center frame, a candid shot of herself on the Carnegie Hall stage—caught in a shimmering halo of spotlight as her fingers flew over the Steinway's keys, eyes closed, head lifted, her whole being totally lost in Chopin's Ballade.

Do I really look like that when I play music?

She reached for the final frame, set on the far side of her own. Her husband, Johnny O'Shea—a prize-winning investigative journalist with the most impossibly blue eyes she had ever seen. Johnny, with his soft red beard and rumbling voice. His passion for politics and baseball, classical music and chess, modern art and good scotch. The man who had stormed into her life at a Red Sox game and asked her to marry him on a freezing Vineyard beach, the man who had loved her and her son for more than a decade, until the night he'd kissed her goodbye and flown off to Europe to search for her missing godson. And never returned.

Maggie stared at those last three photographs. Her photo was in the middle, flanked by the two men she loved. Her past. And her future.

She turned away with a sigh. Johnny had drowned when his sailboat exploded off the Mediterranean coast. She still suffered from those damned if-only moments, still wondered what if—

A man's low voice caught her attention, scattering her thoughts. Just as well. The harp concerto had ended and now the PBS classical music host's voice spilled into the shadows, introducing Prokofiev's Third Piano Concerto, conducted by Valentin Zharkov and the New Russian Symphony.

Zharkov.

Yuri Belankov had mentioned the conductor and his orchestra, the New Russian Symphony, only hours earlier. She remembered, suddenly, the business card he had given her, and found it on the desk next to her phone.

Moving to the light, she settled the new tortoise reading glasses on her nose and read the inscription on the heavy vellum.

Yuri Belankov
*Krasnaya Zvezda * The Red Star Group*
Washington, D.C.

Red Star. It was vaguely familiar, but why? Belankov had said he met her husband just months before his death. What was the story that Johnny had written about Yuri Belankov and his organization? She would search for it. It had to be one of the last stories Johnny wrote before he died.

And what had Belankov called her, at the museum? *Zvezda Moya.* She gazed down at the business card. Clearly, *Zvezda* meant "star." So Belankov had called her "my star." As if he expected a reaction. What was it about the man that unsettled her so?

Too tired to think about it now, Maggie slipped a CD of Franz Liszt's Consolation No. 3 into the small player on the desk and curled into her husband's red wingback chair, letting the leather wrap like warm arms around her. A flash of orange fur as Gracie appeared from the shadows and leaped to her lap.

Maggie stroked the purring cat and let the soft cords of Liszt's piano, so beautiful, poignant, and filled with longing, flow into her head.

God, Johnny, it's been a hell of a few months.

For so long, she'd believed his death was a terrible accident, blamed herself for sending her husband to Europe. But then—

I learned in France that someone had ordered your death, Johnny. I think it was a man named Dane—a vicious murderer who set the bomb on your sailboat. But now I'll never know for sure.

She shuddered. Dane was a brutal, disfigured killer who had crossed her path after her husband disappeared. Don't think of his wolflike face, those cruel cold eyes.

I was there when Dane stopped breathing, Johnny. Then the EMTs rushed in, the ambulances took us to different hospitals. I never saw him again. But he always hinted that he knew some terrible, huge secret about me. Why do I feel as if he still, somehow, can hurt me? Why am I still so afraid?

The antique clock on the wall began to chime. Maggie started, felt the cat leap to the floor. Nine o'clock already?

Her eyes found the shivering mirror, heard her husband's voice, soft as a whisper against her cheek. *Some things can only be seen in the shadows, Lass. But if you ever need me, I'll step out of the shadows and come to you . . .*

Maggie stood, moved across the room, reached her hand toward the mirror. But there was no image wavering now in the dark, smoky glass. Her husband had seemed so close tonight, as if she could have reached out and touched him.

She closed her eyes. And thought she heard the faint last notes of Rachmaninoff's Piano Concerto No. 2 echoing in the streaming night shadows.

CHAPTER FIVE

BEACON HILL, BOSTON

BLOOD EVERYWHERE. SCREAMS.

Yellow wolf's eyes, staring into hers.

A woman on the floor, sobbing in shock.

Help me, please! Help my baby!

Maggie bolted up from the chair. Heart hammering, frantic, her eyes searching the shadows. Where, where was the baby? She flung out her hands. Air.

Then she saw the bow window filled with night sky, the gold reflection of streetlamps. Desk, sheet music, library table, grand piano. The soft scent of spring flowers. The music shop. She'd fallen asleep in her husband's old wingchair.

And dreamed. No, it was a nightmare.

Shivering and drenched in sweat, Maggie switched on the table lamp and pulled a knitted throw close around her. Just before she'd fallen asleep, she had been thinking about Dane—the vicious killer with the wolf's eyes who quoted Shakespeare and had terrified her for so many months.

She'd been there when he had stopped breathing. He was gone. *Wasn't he?*

Tonight, there had been a woman in her dream. She closed her eyes. Yes, there had been a young woman there that night. A girl, really, who was in love with Dane. She was expecting his child. He'd called her Beatrice. Maggie had helped her, made sure she and her baby were okay. But when Maggie finally had awakened in the hospital, after her surgery, Beatrice was just . . . gone.

The clock on the wall showed it was still early, just before ten. Maggie stood up, wide awake. No way she could go to sleep now.

Coffee. Or a glass of wine?

She was pouring the Pinot Noir when the question flew into her head.

What had happened to Dane's woman?

* * *

Some five thousand miles to the east, a distant church tower clock chimed the five-a.m. hour. A young woman stood on a terrace high above a sea the color of aged port, unable to sleep, staring up at the last winking stars. In the distance, a faint orange glow streaked along the horizon. Below her, the black cubed shapes of the village spilled down the steep hillside—homes that in just moments would catch fire, burn bright white in the morning's first sunlight. The air was fragrant with night blooming jasmine as the months turned from winter to spring.

Her left hand clasped her abdomen as the familiar pain washed through her. She should have been almost seven months pregnant by now . . .

Biting her lip, she swallowed the tears. She had to be strong. Ready.

On the tiled table by her side was the carved box she had taken from the villa's safe. She lifted the cover and gazed at the contents— two damaged photographs, a sheet of paper, a gray-velvet pouch the length of her hand. And a dagger.

The words on the paper were written in the strong, heavy script of the man she had loved—Dante. It described his years-long search for a missing oil painting, worth millions, and a baby girl who disappeared, along with the painting, during the Cold War. The last words of the letter said, simply—"Where is the child now? Find the child, she will lead you to the art."

A message, photographs. And a missing child. She touched her flat, empty abdomen and could not stop the sudden tears that scalded her cheeks.

She set aside the small, heavy gray pouch and lifted the tooled-leather scabbard that held the *Laguiole*, the razor-sharp French knife Dante had favored. She slipped the blade from its casing, held it high so that it flashed in the first rays of the sun.

So be it. She would do what she had to do.

She set the knife down carefully and reached for her cell phone. A United flight left Athens for New York tomorrow morning, with a connecting flight to Boston. She ordered a first-class ticket.

Then she turned and walked toward a man who sat motionless, staring out at the sea, on the far edge of the terrace. A pair of forearm crutches rested within reach on the blue flagstones. As the Aegean turned from deep gunmetal to sapphire, the new light caught his scarred face and touched his mirrored aviator glasses with gold.

His long fingers rested on the heavy book in his lap—a well-worn volume of Shakespeare's tragedies.

CHAPTER SIX

THE VIETNAM VETERANS MEMORIAL,
WASHINGTON, D.C.

"I HAVE A confession to make."

Michael Beckett, alone in the darkness, stopped speaking abruptly and leaned back against the cold black granite with a shake of his head. He could feel the tears welling, stinging in his throat.

"I haven't been here in a while, I know," he said, his words raw. "It's too damn hard to come here, Yev—you left a huge hole in my life. Mostly when I'm in D.C., I go to the cemetery in Arlington instead, talk to all those green kids so they're not so alone."

It was very late, going on midnight, cold and quiet, with only a scattering of stars in the vast sky. The only sound was the distant whoosh of tires on Constitution Avenue and—somewhere—the plaintive, lonely call of a night bird.

Beckett raised his head to listen. "McCartney was always your favorite, wasn't he, Yev?" The words, long forgotten, rose from a distant past. "*Blackbird singing in the dead of night. Take these broken wings, and learn to fly . . .*"

His voice cracked. Beckett took another swallow of the bourbon he'd brought in the small silver flask, shifted on the cold ground, and turned to run his fingers once more across the name etched on the wall.

Yevgeny S. Davidov.

Behind the name was a small carved diamond, the symbol of confirmed death.

The Vietnam Memorial—The Wall—was so highly polished that it reflected his own pale face back at him like a mirror. His eyes—still alive—wavered against the names of all the missing and fallen. All the dead. More than fifty-eight thousand.

The past, and the present.

"We were just green kids, too, Yev," Beckett murmured. "Boys, just out of high school, moving silently through the wet green jungle. Pretending to be brave."

He swallowed, rubbed a hand across his eyes. There was no solace in memory tonight. The bourbon wasn't helping, either. Yet.

Sensing his pain, the Golden brushed his thick left paw against his thigh. Beckett's hand found the warm fur, stroked. Held on.

Taking another long swallow of whiskey, Beckett pulled the old leather bomber jacket more closely around him. A soft gray mist was swirling against the black stone.

Just tell him.

"Your daughter's gone, Yev. Irina's gone. Maybe she's with you, now. I want to think so." He looked up at the black sky. "I don't know what happened to her yet, but I will, and I'll come back here to tell you. Count on it." A breath. "I'm so sorry, man."

He swallowed more bourbon, squinted at his watch. Almost midnight. Almost April 9.

He touched the cold stone. "I know how you feel, Yev. I get it. I know about losing a kid. My son was only four years old when that damned sickness swooped down out of the dark and took him away from me. Christ, he was so still. I told myself he was just sleeping..."

He looked down at the Golden. "My boy would have been turning nineteen in just a few minutes," he said in a shaky voice. "Sam. Sam

Houston Beckett. We would have stayed up late, had a cake with candles. Maybe even a glass of Jack Daniel's together."

What would he have looked like? Tall, fair like his mother. But he had my eyes . . .

The Golden edged closer, his own liquid eyes filled with sorrow.

"Fifteen years without my beautiful boy, Yev. If you were still here, you'd tell me that I keep trying to save my son, even though I know I can't. That Sam is the reason I've tried to save all these kids over the years, all these green children who should be holding a baseball or a girl's hand, not an M16. Not dying alone in some godforsaken place."

Beckett raised his eyes to the stars, searching for comfort. For answers. But Cassiopeia had no answers for him tonight. Just a sky full of memories and pain. He took another swallow of the Jack. Another.

Beckett poured the final inch of bourbon on the base of the stone wall, held the cold flask to his forehead in salute. Black pain engulfed him.

"You saved my life in 'Nam," he muttered. "Somehow you got me out of that river and carried me out of hell." He rubbed a hand across his eyes. "I still see that river, Yev. It crashes into my dreams, shining like black ice. That damned wooden boat breaking apart, all those drowning faces disappearing into the water. I see that father, going under, but holding his little boy high over his head, out of the stinking water. Christ! I remember running toward them, swimming against the current, my damned gear pulling me down, trying to get to that kid before the water swallowed him . . ."

"I wanted like hell to save that little boy." He squeezed his eyes shut, gripped Shiloh closer. "My nightmares are filled with the faces of the dead," he whispered.

Beckett shook his head, touched the name etched on the cold stone. "You and I know that my son, Sam, is the real reason I'm here tonight. I couldn't save him, Yev, just like I couldn't save that little

Vietnamese kid from drowning in a river. But maybe I can find your grandson for you. Save your beautiful boy . . ."

He swiped at the tears, hot and unexpected, that coursed down his cheeks. How many years was it since he had cried?

"Irina named your grandson Yevgeny, after you," he said thickly. "He has your eyes, I'm told. Thought you'd like to know."

Beckett's breath caught. His son was long gone. But now there was another boy in trouble. Beckett squinted into the darkness. "What we did mattered, Yev. And I know you would tell me that what I do still matters."

His gaze dropped to the Golden. "They had me at the kid," he murmured.

Shifting his body, Beckett placed the flat of his palm on his friend's name. "You get very close to the guy who carried you out of the jungle on his back," he said softly. "I miss you, man, every damn day. I lost part of myself when you died. I'll find out what happened to your daughter, Yev. And I'll find your grandson, Dov, for you. Count on it."

CHAPTER SEVEN

BEACON HILL, BOSTON

Almost midnight.

In the shadowed music shop, Maggie sat curled on the sofa, her bare feet tucked up beneath her, wineglass empty on the table. Gracie was nowhere to be seen.

Finally, tired enough to sleep, Maggie slipped on the tortoise glasses and glanced at her phone once more. One new message. Smiling, she clicked on the numbers, expecting to hear Michael's rusty voice. But it was Yuri Belankov's rumbling baritone, inviting her to dinner in London. How had he gotten her cell?

Her eyes scanned the tiny print on her phone once more. Still no message from Michael. Something was definitely wrong.

She texted, *Everything okay? Call me, I'm awake.*

Maggie rose and began the familiar ritual of turning off the lamps in the music shop. One pool of soft light vanished, then another, until there was only the glow of the tiny bulb that lit the étagère against the far wall.

Finger on the switch, she stilled for a moment to appreciate the beautiful, luminous blown glass pieces set on the shelves. Three swirling bowls, a sphere, a ruby goblet, a tall vase that twisted like grape vines, its radiant colors reminding her of the artist Chihuly. And in the center, her favorite—a slender, curving figure of a woman, her long blue gown swirling gracefully around her legs, her gold-streaked hair flowing like an iridescent banner behind her.

Each piece ethereal, dreamlike. All designed and hand-blown by her husband's grandmother.

My granny was a glass blower, Maggie. She ran off with an English bloke when I was just a wee boyo and settled in a small village called Boscastle in North Cornwall. She created beauty, like you.

Johnny's words flew into her mind. Maggie's fingers brushed the case, remembering a night just before he had left for Europe. When he had come up behind her, pushed her hair to the side so that he could kiss her neck . . .

Do you ever wonder what you would do, Maggie, if you could no longer play music?

I've never wanted to do anything else, Johnny. I've loved the piano since before I could walk. You know that.

Humor me, Lass.

If I had to . . . I would move to the cottage on the Vineyard. Read books by the fire. Take long winter walks on the beach. Listen to the wind and the waves and the call of the seabirds—and I would compose music in my head! And you, Johnny, if you could no longer be a journalist? What would you do?

I would learn to make beautiful glass sculptures, like my Granny. To create beauty, like you.

He had lifted the small figure of the woman and held it to the light, then turned to touch a tendril of Maggie's hair. *But my figurine would be wearing a green dress, the color of your eyes. And her hair would be like yours. Black as onyx, the color of night.*

Would you move to Cornwall, then, to blow your glass?

Aye. As a boy, I spent all my summers there, in a land of legends and knights. My granny taught me to blow the glass in her hot shop. And she told me the tales of King Arthur. I played by those cliffs, learned to sail in that sea. I had my first pint in The Black Cobweb Pub. And I stole my first kiss in a Circle of Stones on the moor nearby. So I think I would go back to those roots and open my shop near Tintagel.

Tintagel? What is that?

It's pronounced Tin-TAH-jel, Lass. A jagged, rocky headland, shrouded in mists, spilling into the Cornish Sea, just beyond my village. You've seen the drawings in my office—the Castle, the Stones, and Merlin's cave. Legend has it that King Arthur was born in Tintagel. I would go to Merlin's cave in the mornings, when the beach was empty, to listen. And sometimes I would hear the Sorcerer's music in the shadows . . .

Johnny had a book, she remembered suddenly. A beautiful tooled-leather first edition of King Arthur, usually resting on the table by his favorite chair. She glanced toward the wingback, realized she hadn't seen the book in a long time. Where was it?

With one last glance at the now darkened blown glass, she turned toward the stairs. The memory had slipped in, out of nowhere. She could see the moment so clearly, Johnny's eyes shining electric-blue as he'd told her of the cliffs and caves, of a Circle of Stones in a land shrouded in fog and legends. And a sorcerer's music in the shadows. *Tintagel.*

CHAPTER EIGHT

THE BLUE RIDGE MOUNTAINS, VIRGINIA

HE'D TAKEN AN Uber back to the cabin, and now Beckett sat on the deck above the lake, heedless of the cold, staring at the dark mountains etched against the sky. Miss Lucile, his guitar, was still in its case beside him—it was no night for music.

"Happy Birthday, Sam," whispered Beckett.

Maybe, Sam, I can do some good tomorrow. There's this missing kid, name of Yevgeny Davidov . . .

His old friend Simon Sugarman, an agent with Justice, had gotten back to him just after he'd made it home. No information on Irina or her son yet. But Sugar had tracked down the mob friend of Irina's, listed in her lawyer's papers. Lev Vronsky was in Hazelton Federal Prison in West Virginia. *Be careful, Mike, those Ruskies are a bad lot. Dangerous, I oughta know. They're making my life miserable. Let me know what you find out. Maybe something will help my Russian operation.*

Okay, he had a place to start. He'd drive to the prison first thing, pay it forward for Yev and his family. Shaking his head, he ran a gentle hand over Shiloh's scars. "Can't take you with me this time. Prison's no place for a good guy like you. But Sally will take you for a long walk and bring you biscuits."

Shiloh, his head resting against Beckett's thigh, raised his eyes with a forlorn, knowing expression.

"Yeah, you're right. Some nights are worse than others," he muttered.

On the bad nights, Beckett tried to find a quiet place to go in his mind. A place without dark, fetid jungle leaves and a little kid disappearing into a raging river. A place without body bags and flag-draped coffins, where the final notes of "Taps" didn't haunt the air. *Christ.*

Think of something else. Something good. He closed his eyes, took a ragged breath.

And pictured Maggie's face. All he wanted to do was talk to her. Hear her voice. Tell her about Yev. And Sam. But he couldn't talk about Sam's birthday on the phone. He'd tell her Friday night, when she got to the cabin. When he could look into her eyes. Eyes a man could fall into, eyes that refused to let him drown, that lit the darkest parts of him . . .

An image of Maggie slipped into his mind. The last time he'd seen her, just two weeks earlier. She'd been standing right here on the cabin's deck, the sky glowing in tangerine streaks behind her, her dark hair escaping from its pins and blowing across her eyes. The way her dress, the color of mist, had fallen to the redwood floor. The shadow of her body, etched against the darkness of the night.

When he closed his eyes, he could hear her music in his head. He even owned a few classical music CDs now. Played them when he was missing her. Okay, maybe Chopin was no B. B. King, but the music helped him feel even closer to her.

He thought of the tiny jewelry box he'd brought home last week and hidden beneath his socks in the chest of drawers in the bedroom. Just like a damned teenager.

I need your light, Maggie. I love you like air.

CHAPTER NINE

Inhale. Exhale. Inhale. Exhale.

Maggie ran along Beacon Street, her Nikes hitting the cobblestones with the steady beat of a metronome. Right at Arlington Street, up the spiral pedestrian ramp to the Arthur Fiedler footbridge that crossed over Storrow Drive's traffic, then down onto the leafy three-mile esplanade that ran along the Charles River.

Inhale. Exhale. Inhale. Exhale.

She'd learned after her husband died that when she exhausted her body and mind, nothing could get inside her head to haunt her. Running kept the ghosts away.

If she ran fast enough.

This early in the morning, a soft mist drifted like wisps of smoke around her legs. The cobwebs on the bushes glinted with silver dew in the new sunlight. Today the river was a deep, metallic blue, already dotted with all the bobbing white sails of the BU sailing team and the long, sleek sculls crewed by students from Harvard and MIT.

She'd risen before dawn and struggled for two hours to reconnect with the first movement of Rachmaninoff's concerto. She had studied the music many years earlier, before she was emotionally or physically ready to play it, but her mind and body still remembered most of the notes and chords. Too bad technique was only the beginning. The challenge now was to honor Rachmaninoff, to find a way to transform her technical knowledge into music that was sensitive, passionate, and beautiful. To find its soul.

But she'd forgotten all those changing keys and dissonant chords. And those damned arpeggios flying between two hands were impossible. Rachmaninoff had huge hands able to span twelve keys. What was she thinking?

Finally, she'd just closed the score, pulled on her sweat clothes, and headed out into the new day. In rhythm with her steps, she squeezed the small pink balls held in each hand to strengthen the muscles in her wrists and fingers. Rachmaninoff demanded strength.

She'd turned off her phone and now the morning's silence surrounded her. No voices or traffic, just the ghostly whisper of the river, the breath of the leaves overhead.

Then sudden footsteps running behind her. Fast and hard.

She slowed, glanced over her shoulder. Only shadows.

No! There. A man, tall and sinewy, in black running clothes, dark blue aviator glasses, and wool hat pulled low over his face. Gaining on her.

His body so familiar . . .

Then he took a path to the right and disappeared beyond the trees.

Okay. Just breathe.

Turning right, she ran along the path beneath just-ready-to-burst cherry blossoms. She dodged early bicyclists and a scattering of other runners. Ahead, through the swaying willow branches, she could see the slanted rooftops and chimney pots of Beacon Hill, the towers of Government Center, and there—just a glimpse of the bright gold State House dome. She usually ran a loop of three to four miles, crossing to the Cambridge side of the river and returning past the imposing white buildings of MIT. But today she had a destination.

And that destination was just up ahead. She ran faster.

The text had been on her phone when she awakened. *Can you meet me first thing at the Hatch Shell?*

Sure, she'd replied. *If you bring the coffee.*

Now the Shell took shape beyond the tree branches. The Hatch Memorial Shell, the beautiful outdoor concert half-dome where she had played so often over the years with the Boston Pops.

At this hour of the morning, empty except for the squirrels and the dark figure of a tall, motionless man. Watching her.

Simon Sugarman, Michael's friend from their war days. *Agent* Simon Sugarman, now of the U.S. Department of Justice. Intense dark eyes and jet hair buzzed very close to his scalp, the sheen of a beard against his ebony skin. Fit and muscular as a basketball player. Smart as hell and the diamond in his ear just quirky enough to be interesting. Still looking like Michael Jordan in a suit...

She shook her head. Sugar was a charmer for sure. But whatever he wants, she cautioned herself again, whatever he promises you—*just say no.*

* * *

Simon Sugarman stood in the shade of a large cherry tree just ready to bloom, watching Maggie O'Shea jog toward him.

She slowed to a walk, hips swinging. Cloud of black hair caught up beneath a Red Sox cap. Slender dancer's body in the narrow leggings and black fitted tee. Today her shirt said, *Don't Look at the Trombones, It Only Encourages Them.* Chuckling, he stepped toward her.

In the morning light the huge green eyes were questioning and guarded. Well, she had good reason, given their history together. But a smart, fine-looking woman if ever there was one. His pal Beckett was a damned lucky man.

He grinned. Beckett was probably meeting with that Ruskie at the prison right this moment. Good luck with that.

Slipping his Ray-Bans to the top of his head, Sugarman raised a hand in welcome. "Yo, Doc, long time no see." He knew Maggie held two doctorates in music and was amused that the nickname Doc pushed her buttons. In his business, knowing the right buttons was a good thing.

Breathless, she bent at the waist, hands on knees, and gasped in air. After a moment she straightened, moved closer, and looked up into his eyes.

He gestured to the steps that led up to the Shell stage, where he'd set two tall Starbucks containers beside his folded *Times*. "Here, have a cup of java and catch your breath."

"No."

"What, no coffee?"

Maggie held out her hand. "Coffee, yes. But no, whatever you want from me, Simon, the answer is no. Just no."

He pulled her close into a huge bear hug. "Aw, c'mon, Doc," he said against her cheek. "I thought we were friends. And I haven't even asked yet."

Hugging him back, she gazed up at him and laughed. "You can save that innocent choirboy act, Simon. Friends, yes. But you are not good for my health or my peace of mind."

"Ouch. Hey, Doc, I'm a changed man since I found love." He smiled as he pictured his fianceé, Hannah, a cellist currently on tour with the National Symphony Orchestra.

"You and Michael will never change."

"Yeah, my pal Mike will always be the same old Sir Galahad. A white hat who doesn't suffer fools gladly."

"Doesn't suffer fools *at all*," she murmured.

"Bingo. Mike's not like the guys I know. He thinks that *how* we do something is even more important than what we do." *No need to tell her about the Russian Mob problem, let Mike do that.* He grinned at her. "But me, I'm here about the 'what.'"

Maggie sank to the broad, curving white step and took a slow sip of her coffee. Her eyes locked on his, wary but determined. "I know it has to be important if you've come all the way to Boston from D.C. Again. Third time in ten months . . . Wouldn't it just be easier if you moved into my extra bedroom?"

"Can I help it if you always have something I need?"

"I'm a pianist, Simon. Not a missing art specialist. I cannot play Lady to your Macbeth skullduggery again."

"Good one. Okay, sure, I'm still searching for missing art. Only this time, well . . ." He let his breath out. "Maggie, do you still have your husband's articles? His research?"

Surprised eyes flew to his face. "This is about *Johnny*?"

"Only sort of."

She took a deep, steadying breath. "Your agents stole most of my husband's files, Simon, just after he died. So what story of Johnny's is suddenly 'sort of' so important now?"

He gestured at the newspaper he'd set on the step, folded open to the *Times* crossword. "Give me a five-letter word for 'fixed luminous points in the night sky.'" He grinned. "Stars, Doc. A story about lost stars. And the woman who might know where to find them." Sugarman leaned toward her. "Did your husband ever mention a Hungarian woman named Donata Kardos?"

CHAPTER TEN

HAZELTON FEDERAL PRISON, WEST VIRGINIA

BECKETT FOLLOWED THE beefy, pug-faced guard down a barren, green-tinted hallway that smelled of sweat, disinfectant, and fear. Somewhere in the distance, cell doors clanged shut. Locked.

Beckett stared past the steel bars into an eleven-by-eight cell. An inmate sat on the bed, very still, head bowed. Not a damned moment of privacy, thought Beckett, but I'll bet he's never felt so totally alone.

The guard stopped, gestured toward a closed door. "In there, Colonel Beckett. Secure room, nice and private. Buzz when you're done."

Beckett opened the door.

The prisoner named Vronsky sat at a bare table, his left wrist cuffed to a metal ring. His face was narrow and pointed as a fox and his body was thin, prison thin, with a white swath of hair at the temple and a rose wrapped around a dagger tattooed across his neck. He had a purpling eye and a red bruise on his cheekbone. His eyes were blank. Dead.

The prison suit was baggy, too big. Too orange.

Beckett leaned forward, elbows on the table. "I'm Colonel Mike Beckett. I've got some questions for you, Vronsky."

The Russian gangster exhaled slowly. "Got any cigarettes?"

Beckett stood up, turned toward the door. "I didn't come here for you to waste my time, *amigo*."

Vronsky's cuffs rattled. "I got nothing but time in this hellhole now."

Beckett turned back. "You did the crime, Vronsky, you and your gang buddies. But you were collateral damage, caught up in the net. Justice was after bigger fish than you."

"And you guys got them. Or some of them . . . So I figure you're here because you need something else. But if I do something for you, you do something for me."

Beckett shrugged. "What do you want, Vronsky?"

"First you gotta agree to get me out of here. I got no friends inside this place. The gang members here hate my guts." He touched his bruised cheek gently. "Nasty sons of bitches."

"Your brotherhood did that to you? Your *Bratva*?"

"*Bratva? Nyet!*" Vronsky spit of the floor. "Those three, they are not my brothers. They called me a snitch, a stoolie, worse. Say I broke the code, sold them out."

Beckett frowned. "Why you? Five of you were sent here, Vronsky."

"The oldest guy didn't make it. Strangled in the shower, last month. Blood everywhere. They used piano wire! I can still hear the screams." He pointed an accusing finger at Beckett. "And they say I'll be next. You being here is dangerous for me, Beckett. The *Bratva* will assume I'm cooperating. You've got to protect me."

Piano wire. Beckett leaned closer. "If you want to stay alive, Vronsky, then you'd better tell me what you know about Irina Davidov's death."

"Irina? She's dead?" Vronsky's eyes widened with shock. "You're here because Irina Davidov is *dead*? Fuck, man! I . . . what happened to her?"

"That's what I want to know, Vronsky. Tell me about her."

The Russian licked his lips. "Gorgeous. Blond, curvy. Likes—liked—to go to the nightclubs. But classy, you know? And smart as hell. She was a corporate accountant, way out of my league." He shook his head back and forth. "Dead . . . holy crap."

"You two stay in touch?"

"I been here for seven months, man. The last time I saw Irina she was *alive*! Alone, sitting at an outdoor café, with a martini glass in her hand. Smoking a cigarette. The sign in the window had Cyrillic letters, the name began with a V. Vanya, Volga, Volna . . . shit, all I remember is tables with striped cloths. But that's it."

"Café Volna," said Beckett. "Brighton Beach."

He'd been there twice, once with Yev in their Army days and then again right after Yev's death to talk to his wife and meet his young daughter, Irina. It was summer, and the men at the next table, all in short-sleeved tees, had shown off red rose tattoos on their necks and chests. *A symbol of their membership in the Red Mafiya.* The Russian Mafia.

"Brighton Beach, yeah, Little Odessa." Vronsky touched the rose tattoo on his neck, shrugged. "If you say so, man."

"She said you were her friend."

"Did she? Okay, so maybe we were friends, helped each other out, but I never messed with her, I swear. Like I said, she was way above my paygrade, someone *else's lisichka*, if you know what I mean."

Now we're getting to it. "What someone? The name, Vronsky."

Vronsky cast a furtive glance over his shoulder, then he lowered his voice. "You will help me with the gang?"

Beckett shrugged. "First I need a name."

The Russian swallowed, light eyes darting back and forth. Then he leaned forward, lowering his voice to a raspy whisper. "Okay, okay. Maybe I got the guys you want."

"Guys?" *More than one? Stay calm.* Beckett waited, his glare locked on the Russian.

"A *troika*, we would call it in Russia. Three powerful Russians working together, deep in the shadows. Friends from their Army days, I think. They run everything. One of them, they call him Maestro. Another one is The Prince."

Beckett leaned closer, cocked a brow in impatience. "They knew Irina?"

A shrug. "All I know is, Irina was in over her head." Small, watery eyes squinted at him. "Way over. Something to do with smuggling art. Stolen art. You know, Picasso, those weird guys."

"I'm listening. What about the third man?"

"This one guy, he's bigger than the mob. *Much* bigger. He was the one with Irina. She wanted to leave him, but . . ."

"Tick tock, Vronsky."

"She has a kid, man. She was worried about her kid."

And here we go. "Okay, tell me about the kid."

"I know nothin' about him, man! Zip, zilch, nada. Why would I?" Vronsky's eyes twitched. Something was off, something he wasn't saying.

"Who was Irina so afraid of, Vronsky?"

"You sure you want to know? If you take this guy on, Beckett, you'd better watch your back."

"The name, Vronsky. Give me the damned name."

Fear bloomed in the dead eyes. "I don't *know*, man! I never met him. But he called me with a burner phone about a job—a hit—a month before I landed here. Quiet, raspy voice, like he was talking through water or something."

"What did he say?"

"Ordered me to whack a guy. He used an old Russian saying, from the Breshnev days. *Nyet cheloveka, nyet problem.* If there is no person, then there is no problem."

CHAPTER ELEVEN

THE CHARLES RIVER ESPLANADE, BOSTON

THE RISING SUN slanted through the spring-green leaves on the esplanade trees, casting quivering patterns of light and shadow across Simon Sugarman's face.

"Stars?" Maggie looked at him with disbelief. "I cannot imagine my journalist husband writing an investigative piece about stars."

"Hear me out, Maggie. For the last few months, I've been working with the ROC team at Justice. Russian Organized Crime. The Russians are involved up to their bee-hinds in art and antiquities smuggling. Big money. Real big." He looked up at the sky. "You know it; you read about it every day. Money funneled from Russian oligarchs into our politics—our elections, our leaders, our international relationships. Yeah, they've set their sights on us. Not to mention cyberattacks, funding for weapons, oil, reasserting their influence across Asia and the Middle East . . . Hey, it's the challenge of a new, very different Cold War now."

Sugarman stopped, shaking his head. "Hell, it's all about Russia these days, isn't it? Can't turn on the news without a breaking story out of Moscow Central. Got my eye on three Russians right now, maybe working together. Best I can hope for is a circular firing squad."

She laughed in spite of herself. "You're saying Johnny was writing a story on Russian Organized Crime?"

Simon grinned. "Nope. Actually, he was doing a piece on a Van Gogh painting that vanished after the Cold War. Tracking back the clues, the provenance."

"A painting of stars? You can't be talking about Van Gogh's *Starry Night*, Simon. Even I know it's not missing. The original is in the Museum of Modern Art. I saw it the last time I was in New York."

"Turns out four of Van Gogh's paintings feature stars. Who knew? But rumors of a lost *fifth* painting of stars have been flying around the underground art world for years. It would be the find of the century." He shook his head back and forth. "Your husband was writing about the search. And . . . as luck would have it, his research led him into a major Russian connection, as well. *Voila!* So he called me, off the record, to fill me in."

Maggie leaned in. "The three Russians you have in your sights?"

"Yeah, the Ruskies want that missing Van Gogh. Most of his works are worth eighty million at auction. *Starry Night* is valued at over one hundred million! We can only imagine what a long-lost Van Gogh would be worth. So I'm playing a three-dimensional chess game."

"But that was almost two years ago, Simon," said Maggie. "I don't see how I can help you now."

Sugarman stood, began to pace. Maggie leaned back against the stage steps, drank her coffee, and gave him her full attention.

"Johnny O'Shea was a great investigative journalist, Doc. Hey, he brought down two senators and a governor! And he was one hell of a storyteller. But you know, better than anyone, that your husband was also a history buff and an art lover."

She smiled with memory. "He was fascinated by any story about missing art. Always wanted to be the first to find those thirteen paintings stolen from the Gardner Museum in 1990."

"Yeah, he couldn't resist an art mystery. Me either. And one of the biggest mysteries of all is that rumor of a fifth Van Gogh painting of stars." He leaned closer. "When your husband called me two years ago, he told me that a Hungarian woman had contacted him with a story about a painting that's been missing from Budapest since the Cold War. A Roman Catholic nun, her given name was Donata Kardos. You sure he never mentioned her to you?"

Maggie thought for a moment, shook her head. "I don't think he— no, wait." She closed her eyes. "Not long before he died, I remember seeing Johnny talking very intently with a woman in his office," she said slowly. "Beautiful, about my age, maybe? She was very slender, dressed all in black, wearing a gold cross, that's all I can remember. I only saw her profile—high cheekbones and very short hair. She could have been a nun ... I had to leave for a rehearsal, and when I returned, she was gone. I never heard her name."

"Too bad. Your husband said that Ms. Kardos told him a story that began in Hungary, during the last years of the Cold War. Guessing you've heard of Anton Janos?"

Maggie's eyes widened. "The Hungarian composer? He taught at the Budapest Conservatory. He was passionate about his homeland, his concertos were compared to Franz Liszt. But the Iron Curtain closed off more than borders, you know that. It didn't only end religious freedom, voting rights, human rights—it ended art, dance, *music*. Janos was arrested one night and just disappeared." She stiffened. "Oh, God. Did Johnny find out what happened to him?"

"Janos died in a Hungarian prison, far as I know. But this nun, Donata, was a friend of the Janos family. She told your husband that when the soldiers came for him, Janos left behind his violin, letters and music, and a priceless piece of art—all hidden beneath a false floor next door in Donata's apartment. Brave neighbors, huh? Donata was the Janos daughter's best friend. She fled Hungary in the last years of the Cold War, with her friend's baby—Anton Janos' granddaughter. She and the baby vanished into thin air."

"Until she appeared on Johnny's doorstep? A Cold War escape from behind the Iron Curtain, a nun, a composer's music, missing art, and a vanished child... now I can see why Johnny was intrigued."

"Right? You know he was following the trail of stolen art. It was one of the reasons he went to France." He leaned in. "The provenance of a painting is its known chain of ownership. If you want to find a painting, Doc, you look at where it's been."

Maggie set down her empty coffee cup and gazed up at the trees. "Okay, Johnny was working on this story just before he died. And you know all about it because he called you to fill you in. But why now, Simon? Why is his story so important *now*?"

"Your husband never published that story, Maggie, he was never able to tell me what he found out. How it all ended." Sugarman's dark eyes looked down at her. "But now, I need to know. Because the Russians have upped their game. Someone in the New Russian Symphony is neck deep in stolen art smuggling. And everyone and his brother is looking for that Van Gogh."

The New Russian Symphony. Once more a frisson of warning skimmed down her spine like an arpeggio across a keyboard. "Smuggling? An *orchestra*? What on earth makes you think so?"

"A Justice agent, one of mine, planted in the inner circle of the orchestra. She's a flautist as well, a good one—and she overheard some damning conversations backstage. Discussions about missing art, including the search for a lost Van Gogh. She texted me two days ago, said she had proof that someone connected to the orchestra is dealing in high-end stolen art."

"What proof? I fail to see the connection between the orchestra and stolen art."

Sugarman shrugged. "She didn't give me specifics. I'm flying to London to meet with her. We've known for months that the Russians have a new source of millions of dollars, Maggie. Even *more* money to disrupt our elections, bribe our leaders, finance terrorist- and cyberattacks. So now I'm thinking this orchestra might be caught up in the international smuggling of stolen art treasures. As I said, big money in art. Billions." He hesitated. "There's just one more thing."

Maggie went rigid as Sugarman's implications hit her. "Oh God. You think the New Russian Symphony is connected to Johnny's story? His *last* story?"

Dark eyes gleamed at her. "One of those conversations my agent overheard mentioned your husband specifically—that information on the missing Van Gogh was in John O'Shea's last unpublished piece. So I've got to find Donata Kardos. She could be in danger. So could her kid. Lots of moving parts here."

Maggie was very still. "Okay," she said finally. "You're looking for information on Donata Kardos and a missing child—a girl who would be a woman, now, in her thirties. You think the information is still in Johnny's research notes. You want me to find the story Johnny was working on just before he died."

A breeze blew through the Esplanade trees, scattering dark pink-tinged shadows across Sugarman's face.

"We do what we gotta do, Doc."

CHAPTER TWELVE

HOTEL TAJ, BOSTON

NIKOLAI KIROV STOOD by the tall curtained window in the bar at the Taj Hotel, overlooking Boston's Public Gardens. Below him, the white Swan Boats drifted across the lagoon, scattering the ducks. He'd run past those boats less than an hour earlier—just after seeing the pianist meet with the tall stranger at the music shell. Who was he? He would know the man's identity soon—he'd taken photos of them together.

Now, after a quick shower and a change of clothes, he waited for Yuri Belankov in the Taj's dark, wood-paneled bar. Fireplace, lamps, mirrors, a gathering of aging white men in deep-cushioned chairs drinking one-hundred-dollar-a-glass aged whiskey in heavy crystal snifters. As always, he had opted for a Grey Goose, on ice. Smooth and cold. A shimmering bubble above the edge of the crystal. Yes. Vodka suited him.

His thoughts turned once more to the beautiful pianist. Yuri had told him that she had said he reminded her of a Romanov Prince. He smiled. Magdalena O'Shea was an intriguing woman.

And with her husband dead, she could be key to finding the Van Gogh.

You have your secrets, Malen'kya, he thought.

And I will know them.

As he waved a hand in the air, signaling for another vodka, he heard a woman's laughter. The sound, like soft music, reminded him of his mother.

The bar and its patrons faded away. He was in his family's Moscow apartment, his mother's artwork lighting the thin, drab walls, draping them in color. Voices in the kitchen. His mother, paintbrush in hand, her long dark hair framing her face, was smiling at his father.

His father's hand reached for her shoulder in a loving gesture. He was home on leave, his officer's jacket tossed over a chair, the medals on the shoulder gleaming in the light from the window.

His father turned to him.

Come, Niki, your Mamushka needs to paint. Let's go to the Zoo, it's a beautiful afternoon. We'll visit the tigers, see how Old Stepan is doing.

A fresh glass of Grey Goose was set in front of him, drawing him back to the present.

He remembered the day so clearly. He'd stood with his father in the Moscow Zoo, amid some of the original, intricate wooden buildings, and together they had watched the old tiger pace back and forth, his faded stripes shifting beneath hunched muscles. Kirov closed his eyes and pictured the aging tiger, suddenly halting in front of them. Old Stepan had stood very still, staring at him through the bars with amber eyes burning . . .

"The Siberian tiger—the Amur tiger—is a symbol of Russian pride," his father had said. "Like our people, he is dominant, strong, and agile, a survivor from our far east who has clawed his way back from poaching and frozen forests. He is a powerful, solitary predator, feared for his sharp teeth and ferocity."

But look at his eyes, Father. The anger in them. He longs to be free. No living thing should be caged. He should be back in his home, free to roam his snow-covered forests in the north . . .

"But freedom comes with a price, my son. Sometimes it comes only with death."

The next time they had gone to the zoo, just before his father returned to his regiment, a new, younger tiger roamed the confines of the cage. Old Stepan was no longer there. Kirov never saw him again. Many months later, he learned that the aging tiger had attacked a zookeeper and had been shot. Old Stepan had been trying to escape.

His eyes, thought Kirov, remembering. The old tiger's eyes, staring into his, burning with rage. Freedom had come only with death.

Kirov raised his glass. *Tebe, Stepan.*

He downed the vodka in one long swallow and put the memories of the old tiger behind him.

It was time to focus. Next stop, the pianist's music shop. The tiny, state-of-the-art electronic chip was in his vest pocket, the Russian Makarov pistol tucked into his Italian leather boot. And the mask was in his briefcase. Just in case . . .

With any luck, the bug would be planted in the next few hours, and tell him what he needed to know. So much was riding on finding that painting. There still was no trace of Donata Kardos or the baby girl she'd carried across the border so long ago. Now Magdalena O'Shea was their best hope.

Then, later today, he'd visit the Hazelton Penitentiary in West Virginia. He'd been told that one of the prisoners, a Russian gang member from Brooklyn, had information that could lead to the boy— the Russian boy Yuri needed to find.

No one dared cross Yuri Belankov. What did his old friend always say?

If there is no person, there is no problem.

His cell buzzed. Pushing his empty glass away, he slipped his phone from his suit jacket and read the message. The Russian mobster at Hazelton Penitentiary, Lev Vronsky, had just had an unexpected visitor.

"Timing is everything," murmured Kirov. He clicked more buttons, found the photograph he wanted. The face of a man in his sixties appeared, lined and serious, with strong bones, stone-colored eyes, bushy salt-and-pepper brows.

Colonel Michael Jefferson Beckett, Retired.

Why did you want to see Vronsky, he asked the man in the photograph silently. Did he tell you where the boy is hiding?

He would find out, in just a few hours. And then . . .

It was going to be a long day. A long week.

But worth it. He was so close to getting what he wanted.

Kirov closed his eyes, wondering what face he would see if he looked into a mirror. Suddenly afraid that he would see the burning eyes of Old Stepan staring back at him.

CHAPTER THIRTEEN

HAZELTON FEDERAL PRISON, WEST VIRGINIA

BECKETT CLOSED THE prison's security room door behind him with a sharp click.

"Get anything from the Ruskie?" asked the guard.

Oh, yeah. But not what I needed. "Waste of gas," was all he said.

He followed the pug-faced guard down the hallway. Through a barred window, he glimpsed the yard where the prisoners from C-Block were getting their daily dose of fresh air and thin, cool sunshine.

Beckett shook his head. Dammit. Something he'd said must have unnerved Vronsky—because all of a sudden, the Russian had pressed his lips together and refused to say another word.

It was when I mentioned Irina's kid, thought Beckett. Something was off.

I know zip, zilch, nada. Vronsky had protested too much; he knew something more about that kid. Beckett stopped. "I need to see the prisoner again," he said.

Before the guard could answer, his phone buzzed. "What? Okay, okay. I'll be right there." The guard clicked off, stared at Beckett. "Got a small incident in the yard. Wait here for me."

The guard turned toward a steel door. Beckett watched as he punched the keys on each corner of an electronic keypad and disappeared into the courtyard. Beckett squinted at the lock. Yep, one of the most common codes. One, three, nine, seven. He shook his head and moved to a small barred window.

Even with the sun shining, the huge prison yard was brightly lit by overhead searchlights. High double security fences edged by barbed wire surrounded the space, which was nothing more than cracked concrete and weeds, with a scattering of hard plastic lawn chairs, litter, and two rusted basketball hoops.

No balls to be seen. So much for daily exercise.

His gaze swept the two towers, the coils of razor wire, the patrolling guards with their pellet shotguns. The orange sea of inmates. The faces he was interested in, the men Vronsky feared, were . . . there, in the center of the yard.

Three thick-shouldered football types, all smoking. Sugar had described them. Winken, Blinken, and Nod, he'd called them. All three, Beckett knew, had a single rose tattooed on their chests. Gang membership. *The Red Mafiya.*

He knew they would be speaking Russian. He kept his eyes on their cigarettes, burning red arcs in the shadows. They looked like mob thugs, but he knew better than to underestimate them. They were smart, educated, loyal. *Lethal.* Doing time for narcotics, heroin trafficking, money laundering, weapons. Kidnapping, theft, smuggling, second degree murder. Nasty bastards. Sugarman had put five of them behind bars. But Sugar said there were at least a dozen more who had disappeared into the shadows.

A narrow side door swung open. A deputy stepped into the yard, followed by a slight, stumbling figure. Vronsky.

Vronsky blinked, pressed back against the cement wall, pushed his hands into his pockets, and kept his head down.

Beckett glanced at the door lock. *One, three, nine, seven.* Not my problem, he thought. And yet.

Irina had a kid, man. She was worried about her kid.

Vronsky's words echoed in his head. I should have pushed him about the kid. He was holding something back, I'm sure of it. What? And why?

The Russians stopped speaking, turned to stare at the pale, clearly nervous prisoner. Not good.

I promised Yev I'd find his grandson, thought Beckett.

The Russians began to cross the yard toward Vronsky.

Beckett looked toward the guards, but they were huddled together by the far fence, their backs to the yard. No help there.

The Russians approached Vronsky.

Vronsky paled, turned to run.

Take it easy, Vronsky, thought Beckett.

The biggest Russian moved fast. His hand shot out, grabbing Vronsky by the loose uniform, swinging him around. The three men closed around him, laughing.

A beefy arm raised, coming down.

The kid, thought Beckett again, as prisoners shouted and hurried to gather in a circle around the men. *Vronsky knows something about that kid.* They don't want him telling what he knows.

Vronsky crashed to the cement. A knife appeared, flashed silver in the spotlights.

Damn. So much for the bad knee.

One, three, nine, seven. Beckett punched in the numbers, burst into the courtyard, and launched himself at the man with the knife.

CHAPTER FOURTEEN

BEACON HILL, BOSTON

JUST BREATHE.

Maggie stood outside the closed door of her husband's office, located in the back of the music shop, next to her own. It had been at least a month since she'd been inside his room. She stood very still in the afternoon shadows. Waiting. For what, she wasn't sure.

Oh, good God, just do it. Open the door. Her hand reached out, stopped in midair.

Not yet.

Maggie gazed around the shadowed hallway. It was too damned quiet. Johnny had always listened to violin music when he was working. Paganini, Menuhin, Heifetz. She rested her forehead against the closed door. The heartbreaking melody of a violin concerto filled her head, spun her back to an early fall day, the air sharp and scented with chrysanthemums . . .

Johnny's office, bathed in twilight shadows. She was walking by, stopped right here, in the doorway. His door was half open, the chords of a concerto drifting on the air. Unfamiliar, haunting. What piece was it? Johnny sat on the edge of his stuffed blue chair, well worn and sagging in the center. An angular woman sat on the bench beside him. Their heads close, talking quietly. She lifted her face to his. Beautiful, sculpted profile, very short, silvered hair. A gold cross glittered against the severe, high-necked black sweater she wore. In her hands were several letter-sized pages.

Maggie opened her eyes. *Was she the woman Simon Sugarman was searching for? Donata Kardos?*

Taking a deep breath, she grasped the doorknob. Okay, Johnny, I need your research on Donata Kardos' story. Simon needs to know about the Van Gogh. And I want to know if Anton Janos' composed more music.

Just do it.

She pushed open the door.

A cold breeze touched her. Her mind registered that the sliding glass door to the tiny patio and garden was wide open. *Why?*

Confused, her eyes found the wall safe, now open and empty.

She stopped, froze. Bare bookcases. Dozens of books tossed on the floor. The drawers in her husband's huge, secondhand desk were hanging open, papers scattered. His framed prints and photographs, ripped from the wall. The green-shaded lamp on its side, its glass jagged and broken. The old typewriter, upside down.

Panic iced down her spine as realization dawned.

Oh God, Michael, I need you . . . She reached for her cell phone.

A sound behind her!

She spun around.

A figure stepped out from behind the door, dressed all in black, his face covered by a terrifying ski mask.

Without warning, he hit her.

The pain was intense, the fear paralyzing.

She cried out, raised her hands to protect herself. The phone flew from her grasp. Fingers closed like iron around her arm. Spun her against the desk.

Don't hurt my arm! Please, please.

The eyes staring down at her through the slits in the ski mask were like a shark's eyes. Empty, flat. Not a flicker.

She fell back, hard, the desk surface knocking the breath from her lungs. Iron fingers closed around her neck. Fighting for breath, kicking, clawing at the hand around her throat.

Her vision was spinning, going dark. Drowning in fear, she flung out her left hand, searching for a weapon, any weapon. Sudden pain as a sharp splinter sliced into her skin. A jagged piece of glass from the broken lamp . . .

She gripped, swung the shard toward her assailant with all her strength. Felt it pierce his shoulder muscle, heard his grunt of pain. She struck again, pushing deeper, felt blood hot on her palm. All she could hear was his harsh breathing.

His fingers loosened, dropped from her throat.

She wrenched away, fell to the floor. Running footsteps toward the garden door, and then he was gone. Sobbing, gasping for air, she folded herself into a tight ball on the carpet. From across the room, she heard the endless ringing of her phone.

* * *

The Hazelton Prison Infirmary smelled of disinfectant. Walking down the sterile hallway, Beckett stopped in mid-stride as if he'd been punched in the stomach. Why, suddenly, this inexplicable feeling of menace? His instincts for danger were rarely wrong. *Christ.* He dialed Maggie's number. It rang and rang.

He waited, eyes on the phone, then texted, *R U OK?* Nothing. He forced himself forward.

Vronsky sat on a cot in a curtained area, holding a thick blood-stained bandage to his upper arm. The fight in the prison yard had ended almost before it began. Beckett had given a punch, taken two, and then the guards had been all over them.

"Why the hell are you still here?" muttered Vronsky.

"Play nice," said Beckett. "Could have been a lot worse." He rubbed his throbbing jaw. "For both of us."

Vronsky shook his head, defeated. "My so-called fucking brothers."

"Listen, Vronsky, I spoke with the warden. They're going to move you to someplace safer."

The Russian's head snapped up. "Why the fuck do you care?"

Beckett frowned. "Beats me. But you've been straight with me. I just need one more thing from you."

"My dance card is booked, Beckett."

"Funny man. I need to know about Irina's kid—and I think you know where he is. Tell me how I can find Yevgeny Davidov."

Vronsky was staring at him, his eyes red-rimmed. "I can't remember what I had for breakfast."

"I'd hate to go back to the warden, Vronsky. You like it here that much?"

Vronsky glanced over his shoulder, shook his head.

"You're afraid of something. Someone. Let me help you."

"Okay, okay. Maybe I know something. But you—"

"Just tell me where I can find the boy and you're good to go. I keep my word."

A long moment. Beckett waited, his eyes on the Russian. The only sound in the cubicle was the whirr of the air conditioner.

"Last time I saw Irina's kid," said Vronsky finally, "was maybe a year ago, just before I was locked up. They were standing on a boardwalk, a huge Ferris wheel behind them. She had the kid by the hand. He was fair, too, like her. Had some kind of birthmark on his cheek. Like a bird's wings. Irina said it was his favorite place. Coney Island, maybe?"

"And his father?"

"How the fuck would I know?"

"But there's something else, Vronsky, isn't there? Do the right thing, for once."

Silence.

Beckett stood up. "Okay, Vronsky. Enjoy your new digs." He moved toward the door, reached for his phone. Still no word from Maggie...

"Beckett."

Beckett stopped, turned.

"Rumor is, the kid knows something he shouldn't," said the Russian. "They're looking for him. Find him fast, Beckett. He's a dead guy if you don't."

CHAPTER FIFTEEN

BEACON HILL, BOSTON

MAGGIE SAT CURLED in her husband's old easy chair. The EMTs and Boston's Finest had just left, leaving extra bandages, Tylenol, and an admonition to lock the doors.

Damned slider *was* locked, Detective.

Maggie sighed, rubbed a hand gingerly across her bandaged cheek. She'd have a shiner for sure. At least she hadn't needed stitches, only the butterfly bandages. Her left hand was wrapped in gauze as well— the glass from the broken lamp had sliced her palm when she struck the intruder. She wiggled her fingers. Superficial, thank God.

She'd seen Michael's messages and called him before calling the police. Told him she'd surprised a thief, nothing more. She'd just needed to hear his voice. She would tell him everything Friday night, at the cabin. There was nothing he could do now—except worry. But, oh, he was going to lose it when he saw her.

But I never saw his face, Michael. And he never spoke a word. All I can remember are those eyes, shark's eyes, gray and cold as a frozen sea.

She looked around the room, pulled the throw closer around her body. God, she hated feeling so anxious. So violated. I have to do something, she thought. Music. Play music. Music slows the whole world down.

But first, she had to set things right. Rising slowly, painfully, from the chair, she drew the curtains, righted the old typewriter, set the upended desk chair back into place, swept the shards from the lamp into a dustpan.

I hope I hurt him, whoever he was.

One by one, she lifted her husband's three large, brooding pen and ink drawings, centering them once more on his wall. Sheer rocks above a dark cave on the edge of a stormy, swirling ocean. A medieval castle, balanced high on a cliff overlooking a black sea. Johnny had told her about the drawings—*Tintagel*, King Arthur's birthplace. The last was the most unsettling—a brooding Circle of Stones, the rocks hunched like tall hooded men against a dark and starless sky.

The title of each piece was written in ornate, penciled script across the bottom of each matte. *Merlin's Cave. Tintagel Castle. Bodmin Moor, near Boscastle.*

Something caught her eye and she bent closer, squinting at the drawing of Bodmin Moor. Was that a figure, standing in the deep shadow of the stones?

She couldn't be sure and turned away.

Finally, Maggie turned to her husband's books, scattered all over the carpet. The last place she might find Johnny's research. Of course, his notes could still be on *The Green-Eyed Lass*, his sailboat now in the Vineyard dry dock. But her husband had been working right here, in this office, in the months before he died.

Balancing carefully on a metal folding ladder, she began, one at a time, to set the books back on the bookcase shelves. History, Biographies, Politics, Art . . .

A familiar name caught her eye. Yuri Belankov? The book was titled, *Art, Music and Culture: U.S.-Russian Relations in the 21st Century.* Of course, Johnny had been writing a piece on Belankov. Naturally he would have read Yuri's book. She flipped the first pages, saw the simple dedication. *For my daughter.*

Yuri Belankov had a daughter. There has to be a story there, she thought. She slipped the book back on the shelf and reached for another.

Half an hour later, reaching far back on the top shelf of the case, Maggie's fingers found the heavy red leather book lying on its side. Lifting it toward her, she gazed down at the beautifully tooled cover and heard, as if from a great distance, her husband's soft whisper in her head. *Have you seen my book, Lass? My First Edition of King Arthur's Tales. I can still hear the ancient music in the shadows of Tintagel.*

Maggie found her reading glasses, slipped them on. Very slowly, she opened the book. Several photographs and typed pages of notes drifted like leaves to the floor. And then—three pages of a musical score, smudged and scribbled in pencil.

Oh, Johnny. Score one for the good guys.

Settling once more into the old blue chair, Maggie pulled Johnny's woven Irish wool blanket over her lap. Music first. She lifted the score to the light. Photocopies of a violin concerto. The title was written in pencil across the top of the first page. *Amélie's Theme.* Who was Amélie?

She began to hum the chords. Beautiful, lyrical, emotional—and familiar. She had heard this music before. The day she walked by her husband's office . . .

In the garden beyond his open office door, the breathtaking notes of a violin. A lone figure of a woman, playing the most beautiful, haunting music. A piece Maggie had never heard.

The memory surprised her. Someone else was there that day with Johnny and Donata Kardos, thought Maggie. In the courtyard. A violinist.

But she stood in shadows. I couldn't see her face.

Maggie closed her eyes, trying to remember more. But all she could see was the figure of the violinist, shrouded in shadows. Maybe those answers, too, were in her husband's research.

She gazed down at the score in her hands, hummed the notes softly. Yes, it was the music the woman had been playing, that day in the garden. She examined the notes more carefully, page by page—and realized with a jolt that the final pages were missing.

No, please. She set the score aside. *Okay, don't panic.* Maybe the missing pages of music were in Johnny's notes.

Opening his research, her breath caught at her husband's familiar handwriting, the dark, strong scrawl in the margins of the pages and between the typed words.

She began to read.

CHAPTER SIXTEEN

BEACON HILL, BOSTON

Research notes gathered by John O'Shea from first meeting and discussion with Donata Kardos.

Now a Roman Catholic nun with a religious name protecting her identity, Donata Kardos is a Hungarian woman who escaped from behind the Iron Curtain in 1985, at age fifteen, with a six-month-old baby girl.

Ms. Kardos sought me out on the recommendation of my wife's old friend Father Robert Brennan. She came to me late this afternoon for advice, claiming to have knowledge of a priceless Van Gogh that disappeared during World War II.

She was accompanied by a violinist in her mid-thirties, a woman she introduced only as "my companion." There was obvious tension between the two women, and the musician immediately disappeared into the back garden. I spoke with Ms. Kardos alone.

She said that the missing Van Gogh, painted at Saint-Rémy, depicted a lone woman beneath a night sky filled with stars. It vanished in 1942, then resurfaced in Budapest during the Cold War in the possession of her neighbor, a Hungarian composer named Anton Janos. When he disappeared, the painting remained in the care of his daughter and granddaughter.

Ms. Kardos says that the baby left in her care was Janos' granddaughter. She insists that when she escaped from Hungary with the child, she had the Van Gogh and Janos' violin with her. They lived in Europe for several years before immigrating to the United States in the nineties. In all that time, she says she kept the Van Gogh safely hidden, in trust for the child. Now, for reasons Ms. Kardos was not ready to reveal, she wants to have the painting and its ownership authenticated.

Illegible words, written across the next sentence. Then—

Background needed here. Van Gogh was a Dutch Post-Impressionist who suffered from mental illness most of his life and committed suicide at age thirty-seven. At least four of his over nine hundred oil paintings feature stars—those four painted within the last two years of his life when he was a patient at Saint-Rémy. Stark and visually powerful works that celebrate the night sky. Worth billions. Every schoolkid knows *Starry Night*.

Maggie touched the words on the paper. *Stars.* The memories rolled at her in waves.

"Van Gogh painted *Starry Night* while he was in a psychiatric asylum," she murmured to herself. She knew because she had been there, at the asylum in France, just months earlier. St. Paul de Mausole, a former monastery in Saint-Rémy, where Van Gogh had spent his final days.

I've been in those gardens. She shuddered with memory. The place where she had accused a man of murdering her husband. An accusation the man denied, just before he died.

I will never know the truth.

She forced her eyes back to her husband's research.

Van Gogh was in Saint-Rémy in 1889, the year before he died. He often painted the night views from his bedroom window. The shadowed wheat fields, the dark pines, the stars. Van Gogh was fascinated by color, by the night sky, by the effects of light in darkness. He painted four known canvases with stars over a period of time while at Saint-Rémy and Arles—*Starry Night*; *Portrait of Eugene Boch*, with a night sky behind him; *Café Terrace at Night*; and the 4th painting—for me by far the most moving—*Starry Night Over the Rhône*.

Maggie had never heard of that painting before. She searched through the small photographs forgotten on her lap. A portrait, a café, the familiar *Starry Night* . . .

The last one showed a bay of dark water, reflecting the gas lights of the town. Glimmering. Two figures walked, hunched, in the shadows by the banks of the river. They seemed old, full of sorrow. Something stirred inside her.

She ran her fingers gently over the photograph. What was it that had moved Johnny so? She would never know.

She turned back to the research, her husband's notes running like tangled vines across the page.

We know about these four "Stars Paintings"; they are well documented and in museums and collections around the world. But, according to the nun's story, there was a FIFTH painting featuring stars—the one in her possession now.

Johnny had underlined the words with a thick dark pen.

Donata Kardos insists that she saw the Van Gogh for the first time on the night before she left Hungary—it was un-rolled for a moment before being wrapped and hidden in her friend's duffel bag, along with a rare Guarneri violin. The friend's father was Anton Janos, the composer. Note: Ask Maggie about him, she will know more.

I asked Ms. Kardos if she could prove the Van Gogh's ownership or authenticity. She admitted that the painting, which belonged to Anton Janos and was now in the possession of his granddaughter, had never been authenticated. Her only proof of ownership was a handwritten letter from Janos, which she found hidden inside the violin case beneath the Guarneri. It described how the Van Gogh came to be in his possession.

She also found two other items tucked into the violin case—a thick sheaf of Janos' music, and a journal. She brought three photocopied pages from his handwritten musical score as proof. The journal, she said, was written in French, but she believed it included more information on the Van Gogh—the all-important provenance, the history. *If I'm going to believe her story, if I'm going to help her, I need to get my hands on that journal!*

Maggie sat back on her heels, feeling the shiver run down her spine. "And I want to see that music, Johnny," she told her husband. My God, if Anton Janos had smuggled his original scores out of Hungary . . . She remembered, suddenly, reading that, during World War II, Gustave Mahler's widow had smuggled his music across the Pyrenees in her suitcase.

Her eyes sought the yellowed, penciled score on the table beside her. Was it possible? It would be like finding music by Franz Liszt. *What had happened to those last pages of his music?*

Once more her eyes dropped to her husband's notes.

Of course I asked Ms. Kardos why she had hidden the painting for so long. And the obvious corollary—why suddenly reveal it to the world now? After all the years of hiding the painting, what changed? She said only that it has always been about protecting her daughter.

And then her cell phone rang, ending our discussion abruptly. Agitated, she insisted she had to leave. I asked her to meet again in the morning and she agreed.

As of now I have more questions than answers.

Where is Anton Janos' granddaughter—a grown woman now? Logic says she is the young violinist who accompanied Ms. Kardos today. Why the secrecy? Why does she need to be protected?

What information is in Janos' letter?

What information is in the journal?

Who has the Van Gogh? Where is Janos' music?

Why reveal her story NOW?

And #6, perhaps the most important question of all. Handwritten across the top of that first page of music was a title. "*Amélie's Theme*."

According to my research, Van Gogh painted mostly landscapes— only rarely did he paint his fellow inmates at the asylum in Saint-Rémy. But old records show one of the patients was a young woman named Amélie. Perhaps his lover? All my journalist's instincts tell me that this woman, Amélie, is the key to finding the Van Gogh.

I believe Donata Kardos' story rings true. There have been rumors for years in the art world, stories of a lost Van Gogh and a baby girl that vanished on the same night during the Cold War.

Before she left, I asked Ms. Kardos to describe in more detail the painting she'd seen. Instead she offered me her cellphone with a photograph she'd taken of the Van Gogh.

It's a night scene, set in the asylum's garden. A woman stands beneath a tall pine, her face in shadow, playing the violin. Above her, the cobalt night sky is lit by huge chromium-yellow stars. Ms. Kardos says Van Gogh called his painting *Musique d'Ombre*.

Shadow Music.

CHAPTER SEVENTEEN

BEACON HILL, BOSTON

"DAMMIT, DOC, YOU should have called me right away!"

Simon Sugarman's voice vibrated with anger as he stormed past Maggie into the music shop. She had called to tell him about the break-in, the attack, and the research notes she had found. Now, not fifteen minutes later, he was on her doorstep.

"There's nothing you could have done, Simon. The police are taking care of it. I'll make copies of Johnny's notes for you, then you'll have everything."

Except the musical score. Amélie's Theme. *I'm not letting that out of my sight until I have to.*

"Tell that to Beckett. Thank God you're all right. He's ready to set the hounds of hell on me!"

"Calm down, I spoke with him. And I'm fine, really. Now, I just want to know who was so interested in my husband's research." She touched her throbbing cheek, winced. "I have a score to settle." She shook her head. "Tea?"

"Do you know me? Whiskey. Make it a double." He began to pace. "The music and your husband's notes were all you found? Donata Kardos said she'd return the next day."

"I have no idea if she came back. But those notes were the only ones I found." She walked to a cabinet, poured two glasses of Maker's Mark, and handed the double to Sugarman.

He took a long swallow. "We'll find the bastard who hurt you, Maggie. And the rest of the answers as well. Your husband's notes are a huge help." He hesitated. "There's just one more thing..."

"I know that look, Simon," she murmured, resigned. "What else do you want?"

He shot her his choirboy smile. "Nothing dangerous, Doc. No boats, no water. Your friend—that priest in New York, the Cardinal. I need to get in touch with him."

"Robbie Brennan?"

"Yeah, that's the guy. Father Handsome. He was a friend of your husband's, too, right?"

"Yes, they were close. They shared a love of art and music, met for scotch and chess whenever they could. I introduced them. But Robbie has gone off the radar, Simon. He refuses to see anyone."

Sugarman let out a long breath. "The Cardinal and I, we made a deal, after everything that happened in New York. He was very helpful—for a priest, he sure knows his way around the art world. His knowledge could be a real help to me. Before I came here today, I tried to track him down. But seems he vanished faster than an art thief with a hot Monet."

Maggie shook her head. "Robbie Brennan is simply Father Brennan these days. He needed to disappear, Simon. To heal, to come to terms with what happened. He'll be in a wheelchair for the rest of his life. So he's taken a sabbatical. He's in D.C. now, lecturing at Georgetown. Why do you—Oh." She nodded with sudden understanding. "It's the nun. You want Robbie's help finding the nun who contacted my husband, so you can question her yourself. Donata Kardos."

"I've searched everywhere for a Donata Kardos but there's no record anywhere, in more than thirty years. Nuns don't use their given names. It's Sister Joseph Maureen this, Sister Mary Catherine that." Sugarman moved his palms up and down as if balancing. "Priest, nun. Six degrees of religious separation and all that. The good father has to have a better chance of finding her than I do."

"Don't count on it, Simon."

"We had a deal, Doc. He owes me. And—" She heard the amusement in his voice. "He'd be a fool not to. You're headed to D.C. this weekend to see Beckett, right? I'm thinking maybe you need a little spiritual guidance first? Time for Father Handsome to pay the piper."

When Sugarman slowed for a breath, she interrupted. "There's something else, Simon, something I should have told you this morning when you told me about your Russian investigation. I have a feeling it may have a bearing on all that's happened."

Sugarman became very still, listening.

"I met a man yesterday," said Maggie, "a Russian who is arranging a U.S. tour for the New Russian Symphony."

"A Russian." She heard the change in his voice, the barely disguised interest. "Tell me his name, Doc."

"Yuri Belankov."

"Belankov!"

"You know him?"

"Let's just say I know *of* him. An oligarch from St. Pete—Russia, not Florida." His grin flashed. "A Russian billionaire who still has close ties to the Kremlin, we suspect. A flashy patron of the arts, made his money in telecommunications and oil. He has global connections, runs an international think tank these days."

"Yes, The Red Star Group. He gave me his business card."

A dark eyebrow came up. "The plot thickens. Yeah, he's a big-time mover and shaker in D.C., a powerful man with powerful friends. Plays golf with Potus . . . and still somehow manages to stay in the shadows." He took a long swallow of whiskey. "I've had my eye on him for several months. How'd you two meet?"

"The Fine Arts museum, yesterday, after my concert." She hesitated. "He introduced himself, mentioned an article Johnny wrote last year about his business. I thought it was just an odd coincidence, but now . . ."

She heard the sharp intake of breath. "With Yuri Belankov, Doc, there are no coincidences. His interest in you is no accident, believe me."

"I get into trouble when I believe you, Simon," said Maggie dryly. She grew silent for a moment, thinking. Then she said, "You think he's been watching me, was already aware that I was Johnny's wife."

Sugarman shrugged. "If what he told you is true, he was one of the last people to see your husband alive, Doc. Makes sense. At least in my world."

"Your world of shadowy Russian criminals and stolen art and secret meetings in dark alleys," she murmured.

"Can't argue with that one." He chuckled. "Okay, cards on the table. I told you I've been following a lead for a few months—several powerful Russians have found an ingenious way of smuggling art into the country. Thanks to the information from my agent, now I've got the New Russian Symphony—and one Maestro Valentin Zharkov—in my sights. And you've given me a direct link between Yuri Belankov and that symphony."

"Yuri Belankov—a smuggler? That's hard to believe." She gestured toward a vase of deep red roses that had been delivered that morning. "He asked me to have dinner with him while I'm in London, Simon. I'm in a unique position to—"

"You're kidding, right?" interrupted Sugarman, holding up his hands. "Not your wheelhouse, Maggie. Stay away from him. You think this guy is safe because he likes classical music? But he's not safe, he's dangerous. Belankov is bad news, Doc, no way I want you anywhere near him."

She shook her head. "I wouldn't be in any danger in a restaurant. I could find out what Yuri knows about the Van Gogh. Ask him about the New Russian Symphony. Find out why Johnny wrote about him." Her eyes found Sugarman's. "This is the part where you always ask me to help you out, Simon."

"Not this time, Doc. Listen to me. Yeah, Belankov is a deadly combination of charm, wealth, good looks, and intelligence. He's also immoral as hell. But the operative word here is 'deadly.' He's caught up in a Russian house of cards, Maggie. No matter how this story twists and turns, it always comes back to Russia. And the Russians. This is way too dangerous for you. Beckett would throw me to the wolves if I involved you. Or worse." He shook his head at her. "Here's how it's gonna play out. I'm headed to London, too, to meet with my DOJ agent. So I'll take it from here."

Maggie nodded. "You've given me a lot to think about," was all she said.

* * *

Standing in the light of the Tiffany lamp in her music shop, Maggie looked down at the text from Michael.

You sure you are okay? I can be there in 3 hours. Your call. Otherwise, tomorrow morning Shiloh and I will be on train to NYC, doing a favor for a friend. Back by Friday night for sure. Will see you at cabin. I'll cook.

She smiled. She knew that her healthy diet drove him crazy—and knew he didn't trust her not to burn down his kitchen. Her breath came out slowly. Helping out a friend—that was Michael. One more reason she loved him.

Smiling as she imagined his horrified expression in her mind, she texted, *YES I am ok. Simon came to make sure. Let's have dinner outside under the stars on Friday. I'll cook. I have a new Kale recipe. Xo*

His text came back in seconds. *Can you fry kale?*

Laughing, she clicked off her phone, remembering, suddenly, the first time she had cooked dinner for Michael at the cabin. So aware of his stony eyes on her as she moved, reaching and stirring and bending.

And then the smell of burned chicken, the swirling smoke, the shriek of the fire alarm. She shook her head. Damned dinner would have been just fine if he hadn't come up behind her, pushing aside her hair to kiss the back of her neck . . .

They had eaten peanut butter sandwiches by candlelight and made love on an old quilt on the floor in front of the fire, surrounded by the fluid blues chords of B.B. King.

B.B. King and Rachmaninoff . . . She and Michael were as different as their music. But you needed both black and white keys to make music. And all music was full of passion, wasn't it? It stirred the soul.

Their relationship had been complicated from the beginning. In the ten months she had known him, he had been shot, caught up in an explosion, and been in a fiery car accident. Then she had been stalked, shot, and almost drowned. He was the professional, the rational one. She led with her chin and her emotions. Not exactly your star-crossed lovers. *And yet* . . .

Maggie put a hand to her lips. She would be with him again in less than forty-eight hours. But until then . . .

Her eyes found the red roses sent by Belankov, and she flashed on the stark fear she'd felt when Dane had sent hundreds of bloodred roses to her rehearsal room last fall. But Dane was gone now. He had to be.

She took a deep, shuddering breath, retrieved Yuri Belankov's business card from her pocket, and dialed his number.

It was just a dinner in London. There was no reason to be afraid.

* * *

Just five miles to the east, the Arrivals area at Boston's Logan Airport was crowded with travelers arriving from Rome, Amsterdam, and New York.

The tall, slender young woman made her way slowly through the customs line, smiling at the guard as she passed through the passport checkpoint. No one had discovered, or asked her about, the knife hidden inside a book in her luggage.

She emerged into the evening and hailed a taxi.

CHAPTER EIGHTEEN

UNION STATION, WASHINGTON, D.C.
THURSDAY

At Union Station, Beckett and Shiloh boarded the 8:00 a.m. Amtrak Express train bound for New York City.

Beckett found the Quiet Car, tossed his duffle bag in the overhead bin, and settled back into the worn seat with a sigh. "Remember," he said in a low voice to the Golden, "you're supposed to be my emotional support animal. Try to look supportive."

The Golden gave him a withering look that acknowledged the irony, then climbed awkwardly into the window seat and turned away to press his nose to the glass.

So much for support. Beckett shook his head in amusement. Then, eyes on the filthy, rain-streaked window, he thought about everything Vronsky had told him about Irina Davidov and her son. Beckett was determined to find the answers before the day was over. And Vronsky had given him the place to start. Café Volna.

Brighton Beach was a well-known center for the Russian Mafia. The first time he'd gone there, on leave from Fort Drum before heading to 'Nam, he'd spent a day roaming the streets with his buddy Yev. They'd bought caviar at the small boardwalk kiosks, danced under the mirrored ceiling at Café Arbat, and drunk vodka at the Café Volna on the boardwalk—honey peppered vodka, he remembered, suddenly feeling the sharp, bright taste on his tongue.

Oh, yeah, he remembered the vodka. And the striped cloths on the tables at Café Volna.

So now in less than four hours he would be at the Brighton Beach café once again, looking for Irina Davidov's son, Yevgeny.

His cell buzzed. Sugarman.

"Hey, Sugar, Vronsky gave me info on three Russians who—what did you just say? Oh, God *damn* it to hell!"

Lev Vronsky had been found dead in the prison showers, just hours before he was scheduled to transfer to a safer prison. *He'd been strangled by a noose of piano wire.*

A mob execution? Or something more?

Had the Russians known he and Vronsky had talked? It always came back to the Russians. Christ. Was it his fault that Vronsky was dead? Beckett closed his eyes, listening to the rushing clatter of train wheels speeding north on wet steel tracks.

* * *

It was raining hard in Boston as well, the drops running like tears down the glass of the music shop's huge bow window.

Maggie had been sitting at the Steinway for hours, lost in a passage of Rachmaninoff's concerto.

A tiny timer on the table beside her pinged, startling her, bringing her back to earth, letting her know that The Piano Cat Music Shop would open its doors in an hour.

Where had the morning gone? Maggie's breath came out slowly as she sat back and stretched her aching fingers. The cut on her palm was healing, and the first section, the Moderato, was finally coming together. She was finding the shape, the themes, the feeling…

She heard her father's voice in her head. *Music tells our stories, sprite.*

Yes. For her, it was true. Especially with Rachmaninoff. It was as if he'd written the music for her to play, music that would tell her story. From the opening bell-like tolls that built tension, through the first theme's piano accompaniment to the more lyrical second theme—she felt as if she were living her own life through the music. And now, as she worked on the agitated and unstable closing of the first section, the wildly scaling arpeggios and changing keys were slowly forming a new musical idea in her head.

Yes, Rachmaninoff understood pain, and healing. Maggie knew he had suffered from deep clinical depression for most of his life and found himself unable to compose—just as she had lost her music after losing her husband. Rachmaninoff was finally able to write his gorgeous, stirring concerto only after many months of psychotherapy. He'd been so grateful to have his music return that, when he finished the concerto, he dedicated it to the doctor who healed him.

Maggie smiled softly. Kindred spirits. Like Rachmaninoff, she was finding her way through loss, and her life was slowly changing . . .

Her cell phone rang, scattering her thoughts. She glanced at the screen. Simon Sugarman. Her hands came to rest on the piano keys. She took a breath and clicked on her phone.

"Good morning, Simon. Last-minute instructions before I leave for London?"

"You're sure I can't change your mind about meeting with Zharkov, Doc?"

"Valentin Zharkov is the conductor of the New Russian Symphony. I am a soloist. This is about music, nothing more."

"There's a brutal new Russian underworld out there now, Maggie, black market crime lords who are as complex and dangerous as modern Russia. I don't want you anywhere near them."

"You're the agent, Simon, but I'm the musician."

"I wish it were that simple, Doc. The thing of it is, I read all of your husband's notes. They gave me a lot of good intel. But—"

"But what?"

"I still have more questions than answers. We still don't know where the Van Gogh is. Or Anton Janos' music, the letter and journal. Does Donata Kardos know where the Van Gogh is hidden? And what about the baby girl who vanished? She's a grown woman now. Does *she* have it? And what if . . ." A hesitation.

She knew, of course she knew, what he was going to say. "What if my husband knew."

A harsh breath in her ear. "Bingo. What if Donata Kardos told your husband where the painting was hidden? Or, worse—what if she *gave* the Van Gogh to your husband for safekeeping? *What the hell did he do with it?*"

* * *

Did you know where the Van Gogh was hidden, Johnny?

Maggie stood in her husband's office, trying to face the cascade of emotions. The room was set to rights once more. Everything the same, except for the shattered, missing lamp.

But right now, she just wanted answers. Someone wanted the Van Gogh. She'd thought the break-in was to find Johnny's research. Or Anton Janos' letter, which was sure to offer more information on the missing painting. But what if Simon was right? What if her attacker believed Johnny had known where the Van Gogh was hidden?

Oh, God. What if someone thought Johnny had told *her* where the Van Gogh could be found?

She gazed thoughtfully around the crowded office. There was no hiding spot for a large rolled canvas here, unless there was a false wall, a hidden door . . .

No. Johnny would have told her.

Wouldn't he?

She moved to the sliding door, checked the lock. Leaned her forehead against the cool glass. Gazed at her shimmering, ghostly reflection, blurred now by ribbons of silver rain.

She froze. A sudden movement in the garden. A shadow, darker than the trees.

She straightened, strained to see through the rain-washed glass.

A slender form. A glimpse of a pale face.

No. Nothing. Now.

But . . . she had seen something. Some *one*? Not a man. A woman.

Someone had been out there, watching her.

CHAPTER NINETEEN

CONEY ISLAND, BROOKLYN

IT HAD BEEN a long, exhausting day. Beckett was matching the Golden's limp by the time he eased down onto an ancient bench on Coney Island's famed Boardwalk. Shiloh settled close, his head on Beckett's thigh. The sun had just set through thick ocean mist, and now long gray shadows fell across the Boardwalk's splintered planks of wood.

Beckett closed his eyes. As soon as they'd arrived in Brooklyn, they had gone to the Brighton Beach Courthouse, and the words of the harried social worker still echoed in his head.

Yes, I remember Irina Davidov. A regular at the Tatiana Club. Beautiful woman, well educated, had a good job . . . but trouble just seemed to find her. Sent to prison for almost a year. She died recently, I'm told, found in an alley just behind the nightclub. Strangled, I think . . . Who knows what happened. Her son? Yevgeny is almost sixteen now, in and out of Juvie. Arrested for theft, possession of a weapon. Hated foster care, kept running away. Homeless now, I imagine, unless someone took him in. If he's arrested again, he'll be technically an adult—could be sent to Rikers. No, I don't know where he is. He doesn't check in with me, and I have sixty-seven clients to keep track of. Okay, okay, maybe some of the boys like to play basketball. They hang out at the community centers and the parks. Or the Boardwalk at Coney Island, you could try there. Sorry, I have another appointment waiting . . .

His eyes on the misty, empty Boardwalk, Beckett reached down to touch the Golden's sleek head, so still by his side. "No wonder the kid ran off," he said softly.

The Brighton Beach Police detective assigned to Irina Davidov's case—a jaded, cynical, seen-it-all, soon-to-be-retired grandpa—had no new leads on her murder. Death by strangulation. Empty alley, no prints, no witnesses, no answers. No sign of her kid. Case closed.

No witnesses . . .

Squinting up at the gray, threatening sky, Beckett pictured his old friend. "I'm sorry, Yev, so sorry that your daughter is gone."

At least I still have a chance to find your boy.

Over the last six hours, he and the Golden had searched the streets of Brighton Beach. Three local parks and two community centers, a quick lunch at Café Volnya. *Nyet, nyet, we know nothing about Irina Davidov and her son. What do you want to order? The borscht is good today.*

They'd visited Irina's rented rooms, talked to the bartender at Club Tatiana. Stood silently in a dark and dirty alley before leaving a single red rose on the cracked pavement.

No one knew anything—there was no sign of the boy. So they'd headed west to Coney Island.

Now, sitting on the old Boardwalk bench, Beckett's eyes fastened on the heart of Coney Island—the fifteen-stories-high Wonder Wheel, a huge dark circle wavering against a gray and fog-laced sky. The wind was picking up, cold and wet, blowing in off the roaring Atlantic behind him, sending newspapers and empty coffee cups skittering across the deserted, weathered planks of the Boardwalk.

"Rides don't open 'til Easter," said Beckett to the Golden. His eyes were on the boarded-up shops across the forsaken boardwalk. "But you should see it in the summer. Music, cafés, the smell of fried donuts. Fun Houses and jugglers and huge crowds of families in too-tight t-shirts." He grinned down at the dog. "But at least we've got a dry, dog-friendly room for tonight, just down the Boardwalk, and two more gyms to try in the morning before we catch our train. What say I text Maggie, then we get ourselves a couple of Nathan's Famous hot dogs? Kid has to eat, right?"

With a "good luck with that" look, Shiloh lumbered to his feet.

The crash of waves against the beach echoed around them. It was just beginning to rain.

CHAPTER TWENTY

BEACON HILL, BOSTON

THE STREAMS OF rain running down the bowed windowpanes of The Piano Cat were silver in the lamplight. Standing in the shadows, Maggie smiled with relief. She'd just read Beckett's text. He was hoping to catch a train in the morning. *Crazy day, I have a lot to tell you Maggie. Just please, no kale tomorrow night.*

I have quite a lot to tell you, too, Michael.

She'd be with him this time tomorrow. Her breath came out. He challenged her, drove her crazy, worried about her too much. But he made her feel so safe. And so loved.

She would pack that silk nightgown he liked, the one with the black lace—

A sharp rap on the door. Another.

Startled, Maggie looked down at her watch. After six. The shop was closed. And it was still raining, hard. An image of the frightening figure in her garden flew into her head. Okay, the front door was locked.

Just be careful.

She moved to the door, clicked on the outside lamp, checked the peephole.

A young woman, black hair glistening with rain. Dark, troubled eyes. So familiar.

Maggie unlocked the door, pulled it open.

The woman stepped toward her, into the light, bringing the scent of cold rain into the room. Maggie caught her breath.

The last time she had looked into those frightened eyes, both women had been covered in blood.

"Beatrice?" whispered Maggie.

*   *   *

Across Charles Street, Nikolai Kirov stood under an oversized black umbrella, just beyond the penumbra of the streetlamp's wavering light. His eyes were on the door of The Piano Cat. He'd seen the taxi stop, watched as a woman in a long, dark coat emerged. Seen her knock, then step back and shade her eyes as the overhead light switched on. Watched as the door slowly opened.

Magdalena O'Shea stood in the doorway, her beautiful, shocked face illuminated in the rain-washed light of the lamp.

She reached out, guided the woman into the shop. Then the door closed and the front light went out.

Kirov sensed that something important was happening. The conversation he would hear on the listening device could change everything. His instincts were rarely wrong.

He shook his head, tilted his umbrella, and headed across Charles Street toward the music shop.

CHAPTER TWENTY-ONE

BEACON HILL, BOSTON

"MY GOD, IS it really you?" Maggie reached out to grasp the young woman's arm. "Come in from the rain. I've been wondering what happened to you for months."

The woman entered, her eyes on Maggie. Makeup was blurred around the huge black eyes as if from recent tears, giving her a hollow look.

Maggie lit a lamp and locked the door, then turned back to the silent figure standing so still in front of her.

Something was off, like a wrong note played.

Maggie took a step toward the woman. "You *are* Beatrice, aren't you? Come, take off that wet coat, sit down. Are you in trouble?"

"I am Beatrice, yes. You remember. I've come a long way to find you. All the way from Greece."

All the way from Greece? Maggie gestured to one of Johnny's leather chairs. "You must be exhausted. Please, sit down."

Setting her large shoulder bag on the floor, Beatrice pushed her right hand deep into the pocket of her coat and sank into the wingchair.

Again, Maggie felt the wariness wash over her. What was in Beatrice's pocket? A weapon? She glanced around the room. *What could I use to protect myself?*

She forced herself to sit down. "Why are you here? Has something happened?"

Beatrice gazed around the room, her eyes stopping first on the framed photographs, then staying longer on the cabinet that displayed Johnny's blown glass collection. Finally, she took a deep breath and said, "I never thanked you for saving me that night. You tried to save my baby, too." She put a hand on her stomach and turned away.

Tried? Maggie heard the words and felt a chill pass over her. *The baby* . . . "You were hurt. Anyone would have helped you." She held out a hand. "Can you tell me what happened?"

Beatrice closed her eyes. "It was a terrible night, the worst of my life. I'll never forget it."

"Neither will I," said Maggie. The images of two men falling in slow motion through the air still haunted her dreams. "Surely you must know that Dane threatened and terrified me for months. And yet—I know you loved him. No woman should have to watch the man she loves die in such a terrible way."

There was a strange light in Beatrice's eyes. "We have more in common than you know," she said softly. And then, "Hurt people hurt people. I did love him, once—when I thought his name was Dante. It seems like another lifetime now." Beatrice's head came up. "You know he was my baby's father. We planned to be married."

"I'm sorry you've had to suffer." Maggie's voice was gentle. "And your baby?"

"I lost the baby that night."

"Oh, Beatrice, no."

Beatrice leaned forward. "For a long time, I blamed you for what happened. I made excuses for Dante's violence, his cruelty. I thought I could change him. Until that night . . ."

"And now?"

"Now, I feel as if I need to make things right. For my child's memory."

"I don't understand," said Maggie. "What things?"

Beatrice stood abruptly and walked toward the framed photographs set on the long table. Her right hand stayed in her coat pocket.

She stopped in front of Johnny's photo. "This man was your husband?"

Maggie rose and came to stand next to her. "Yes. His name was John O'Shea." *Did Beatrice know that Dane had arranged Johnny's death?*

"My husband suffered a violent death almost two years ago," said Maggie slowly. "It broke my heart. You and I have loss in common. I know how you must feel."

Beatrice turned to stare at Maggie. "No. I don't think you do."

Her right hand came slowly up from the deep coat pocket. Maggie caught a glimpse of something dark, heavy, clutched in her fingers.

Jesus God, a gun?

Maggie took a step back, reached for the solid silver frame on the table. *Could she hit another woman?*

But the object Beatrice held out was not a gun. She set a gray velvet pouch down on the table in front of Maggie.

Thank God, thought Maggie, her eyes locked on the pouch. "What is this?" Her voice sounded too low and scratchy in her ears.

"After that night, I returned to Dante's home, in Greece. I found this in the safe, among his things."

Maggie swallowed, felt the nerves skitter like arpeggios along her spine.

Once more Beatrice reached into the deep pocket. "I found these in the safe as well." She held out two small black-and-white photographs.

Maggie took the first in her hand, gazed down. It was badly water-damaged, but she could just make out the old photo of herself, taken on a Vineyard beach.

It was suddenly hard to breathe. Johnny had carried a photo like this in his wallet since the day they'd met.

The second photo had serious water-damage as well. Blurred and dark, all she could see was the figure of a man, his face lost in the shadows, standing in a circle of ancient standing stones. The stones hunched around him like cloaked giants.

Like the drawing in Johnny's office.

"Who is this?" whispered Maggie.

Without speaking, Beatrice handed Maggie the small velvet pouch. Not more than eight inches in length, it was heavy, smooth in her palm.

Maggie slipped off the velvet. And felt as if she'd been hit by a sledgehammer.

The blown-glass figurine caught the lamplight. It was a slender, curving figure of a woman, long gown swirling gracefully around her legs, her hair flowing like an iridescent banner behind her.

The twin of the figurine in her glass étagère. But this figure's dress was deep green, her hair the color of a glowing night sky.

Her husband's words flew into her head with the force of a thunderstorm.

If I couldn't write, Lass, I would make beautiful glass sculptures, like my Granny. But my figurine would have a dress the color of your eyes, and hair like yours. Black as onyx, the color of night.

Something else was tucked into the velvet pouch. Maggie withdrew a scrap of paper and unfolded it slowly, unable to stop the shaking of her hands. The handwriting was heavy, stark. Dane's writing?

She felt faint, suddenly, as the words blurred in front of her.

He is alive.

PART II

"BECKETT"

"I know nothing with any certainty
but the sight of stars makes me dream."

Vincent Van Gogh

CHAPTER TWENTY-TWO

BRIGHTON BEACH, BROOKLYN
FRIDAY

YOU ARE NOW IN THE WAR ZONE

Beckett stood outside the gym at the community center on Ocean Avenue, staring at the red and black graffiti. This was the last place on his list. He dropped his eyes to the litter of trash, broken bottles, and bricks on the gym steps and reached down to touch the Golden. Together they climbed the cracked steps and entered the gym.

The gymnasium was old, overheated, and smelled of sweat and old sneakers. It was still early in the morning, but the place was already teeming. Several teens were working with weights, others just hanging out. At the far end of the gym, five kids dressed in torn t-shirts were shooting hoops, running, guarding, shouting at each other.

The boys like to play basketball. Beckett settled on a bleacher, his eyes scanning the boys.

A photo would have helped, Irina.

One of them, the tall, bony one wearing scarlet high-tops and a Mets cap set backwards on his head, had flaxen-blond hair like Irina. It was long, unruly, kept falling across his eyes. Looked about sixteen. Just a few years younger than his own son would have been . . .

The kid stole the ball, dribbled, took a shot. Score! Someone shouted something in Russian, high-fived one of the girls standing nearby.

Good moves, kid.

As if he'd heard him, the boy glanced toward Beckett. A thin, jagged white scar in the shape of a V marked his right cheek.

Yevgeny Davidov.

I've got him, Yev! I've found your grandson.

The rear gym door slammed open with a bang. Two older teens walked in, one's head shaved bald as a cue ball, the other with tangled, grimy hair. Slavic faces, thickset, muscular shoulders in tight jackets. Faded blue tatts climbed up their necks. Russian gang members. Punks.

Cue Ball stared at the boys for a moment, then stepped closer. "Allo, Yevgeny."

Uh-oh. Beckett stood slowly.

At the sound of his name, the blond kid froze. Then he murmured something to his teammates and sauntered toward the Russians, hands in his gym short pockets, chin up. Bold. Cocky.

Not a good idea, kid.

"We've been looking for you." Cue Ball made a kissing sound with his lips. "*Sladkiy mal'chick*, eh?"

He'd heard Yev use that expression—Russian words for "sweet boy." Yeah, not good. Beckett edged closer. Two against one.

He felt the Golden tense beside him.

The kid in the Mets cap squared his shoulders, shook his head. Flipped his fingers and uttered something in Russian as he turned away.

"Time we even the odds," Beckett muttered to Shiloh. "But no more prison brawls. It's time for age and treachery to overcome youth and skill. So how about we resurrect our 'Good Cop Bad Dog' routine?"

The sweet-faced Golden came to attention, soft ears perked in anticipation.

"Can't make an omelet without breaking a few eggs," said Beckett to his dog. Together, they limped across the gym floor toward the group of youngsters.

"Hey, fellas," said Beckett in his best good-old-boy voice. "What's the problem? Me and my dog were enjoying the game."

"Beat it," said Cue Ball.

"Well now, I'd like to do that, son, I really would, but I'm here to take pictures for our Police Benevolent Association." He waved his iPhone in the air.

Out of the corner of his eyes, he saw the kid in the Mets cap step forward, grinning. "Hey, Officer Krupke," the boy said loudly, "long time no see."

Cue Ball looked at his friend and said something under his breath. Ignoring Beckett, they moved toward the kid in the cap.

Beckett took tight hold of Shiloh's leash, knowing what was about to happen.

"Hey, guys," he said softly, "I'd leave now if I were you. I don't want any trouble, but my dog, here, well, he doesn't like bullies. Like his father. *Who was a wolf.*"

On cue, Shiloh growled, deep and low in his throat. Baring his sharp fangs, looking for all the world like a fierce golden wolf, he lunged, snarling and snapping his jaws at the two Russian punks.

Cue Ball jerked away, then narrowed his eyes and pointed a warning finger at the boy as if to say, we're not done with you. Then they turned and headed for the door.

"Works every time," murmured Beckett, rubbing his shoulder where the dog had strained the leash. "You can be one scary badass, dude," he murmured to the Golden, who now sat with a gentle and satisfied expression, his liquid eyes on the tall, bony boy in the cap.

As the echo of the slammed door faded, Beckett turned to the kid.

"Officer *Krupke*?" he said to the boy. "Seriously? That's all you got?"

CHAPTER TWENTY-THREE

GEORGETOWN UNIVERSITY, WASHINGTON, D.C.

THE SMALL, TREE-LINED quad hidden behind Georgetown University's Healy Hall was quiet, the ancient brick glowing in the late morning sun. Only a few students sat on the benches, absorbed in textbooks or their phones. New spring blossoms scattered across the stones, swirling like pink confetti in the round fountain in front of the historic heart of the campus—Dahlgren Chapel.

A silver-wheeled electric chair appeared from an archway, whirred across the courtyard toward the chapel. Up the ramp, through the open vaulted doors.

Father Robert Brennan halted the chair in the foyer, one hand dropping to press hard on the black cassock that covered his legs. He felt nothing through the fabric.

Raising his head, he scanned the lovely old chapel. Spare and narrow, barely able to hold a few hundred visitors, it was his favorite place on the Georgetown campus. He came every morning, just before his first seminar, to read and think. To be alone in the quiet.

This morning, sunlight flowed through the intricate stained-glass window above the altar, setting the organ's copper pipes on fire. He often stopped in to listen to the organist practice, especially if she was playing Bach.

Someone had set white lilies on the simple altar. He shook his head to dispel the scent. The lilies reminded him of death. He much preferred the spice of incense.

The chapel was almost always empty. Except for today . . .

His eyes rested on a still, seated figure in a front pew. Not in the mood for company, he shifted aside the heavy book he'd brought with him, pressed a steel lever. His chair turned, rolled back toward the exit.

"Robbie?"

Robbie Brennan stopped his wheelchair, turned it slowly.

The woman in the front pew stood, smiling at him.

"Maggs!" He spun his wheels toward her. "What on earth are you doing here?"

"My old friend wouldn't return my calls," said Maggie. "So the mountain came to Mohammed."

He shook his head. "Mohammed needed some time," he said simply.

"You look the same," she said softly. "Handsome as ever. Well, except for . . ."

"For my white hair. Yes. Apparently not unusual following a traumatic experience, I'm told. Look what eight years in office did to Barack Obama." He gave a faint smile. "My female students call me 'Father Silver Fox'—behind my back, of course. I wonder what St. Francis would say?"

Maggie laughed. "Think of your silver streaks as strands of glitter."

"I prefer highlights of wisdom."

"You would!"

He spread his arms wide. "Get over here, Maggs. My God, I've missed you!"

She bent, let herself be enveloped in his safe, strong arms. Stronger now, she realized, with months of wheelchair use.

"I've missed you, too, Robbie," she whispered against the silvery wisps of his hair. "And I'm sorry I showed up on your doorstep unannounced."

"Sit," he told her, gesturing toward the closest pew. "I always want you in my life. And I know you have a good reason. My friend Thomas

Aquinas always said that 'Reason in man is kind of like God in the world.' There is always a reason for the choices we make, Maggs. Although I admit your reasons are more complicated than most."

She grinned at him as she settled in the pew and slipped her jacket off her shoulders.

The words on her t-shirt said, *Honor Thy Music*, and he gazed at her with sudden pleasure. "You're wearing the present I gave you. You know, I listen to your recording of Rachmaninoff's Rhapsody all the time. Glorious. What can top that?"

"Rachmaninoff is not finished with me just yet. I'm working on his Concerto No. 2."

"The Rach 2! By God, woman, you take no prisoners. Are you here because of your music?"

"I actually have two reasons for coming, Robbie. You are sitting next to one of them." She gestured at the heavy research book against his thigh on the wheelchair seat. "Still interested in art, I see."

"You can remove the priest from the art," murmured Robbie Brennan, "but you can't take the art from the priest . . ." Then his head came up with surprise. "You are here because of 19th Century Art?"

Maggie leaned forward. "Have you ever heard of a Van Gogh painting called *Shadow Music*?"

"The Holy Grail!" Robbie touched his book with reverence. "All serious art lovers have heard the rumor—that there is a *fifth* painting in Van Gogh's so-called star series, painted during his stay at the asylum in Saint-Rémy. It vanished under mysterious circumstances decades ago."

"That's the one."

"*You*—a classical pianist—have information about a lost Van Gogh?" He shook his head, smiling. "God never ceases to surprise me."

"Or me, apparently. My husband, Johnny, discovered the information, just before his death. I found his research, brought it here for you to read. You remember Agent Simon Sugarman, Robbie. He asked me to come see you."

"Ah. The agent who looks like Michael Jordan and tracks down all those bad guys who steal great art. How could I forget him?" His expression was rueful as he tapped his paralyzed legs. "He spoke up for me at the trial, warned me I would owe him one day."

"Apparently that day has come. Simon needs a favor. A big one."

"Never a dull moment with you, Maggie O'Shea. Yes, I owe Sugar, big-time. He's the reason I'm here at Georgetown and not in some godforsaken prison. And I pay my debts." He held up a hand. "But I'm not looking for redemption, Maggs."

She smiled at him. "Unless God just thinks redemption is the right way to go. Are you and God back on good terms again?"

"Not yet."

"Then maybe this is your chance."

Robbie Brennan glanced toward the altar. "Okay, then. *Heads-up, God,* we're about to raid the sacramental wine. And then you can tell me everything you know."

*   *   *

Sunlight flowed through the tall stained-glass windows, scattering shards of bright jewel colors across Maggie's uplifted face. She was silent, pensive, waiting for his decision.

Father Robbie Brennan gazed at her, a woman as beautiful and passionate today as she'd been that day so many years ago when she'd walked into his music workshop for kids from the Harlem projects.

In the last thirty minutes, Maggie had told him what she knew of the story of Donata Kardos and the infant girl in her care. About Kardos' secret visit to her husband—his old friend John O'Shea—and about John's research. He had read all of her husband's notes, growing more and more intrigued.

Good God, a lost painting by Van Gogh. For the first time in months, he felt a thrill of purpose. A long dormant stirring of life. Of hope. Stay calm, he told himself. *God has not forgiven you yet . . .*

"Johnny wrote that you sent Donata Kardos to see him," said Maggie, her low voice scattering his thoughts.

"Yes, I met her when she first became a nun—after her daughter went to college. She's one of those women you can't take your eyes off of." He smiled. "She contacted me two years ago, in need of advice on authenticating a piece of art. I had no idea it was a Van Gogh. I sent her to your husband."

"Simon Sugarman would like to talk with her. But he couldn't find anyone named Donata Kardos, and has no idea what religious name she chose. He's hoping you can tell him how to find her."

Robbie rested a hand on Maggie's forearm. "I haven't heard from her since she saw your husband, but I'll do what I can," he said softly. "I know people from my days as the Archbishop, they could find her. I'll make those calls just as soon as my first seminar ends. I'd be a fool to turn down a second chance to find my better angels."

"You never lost them," said Maggie.

"Ah, my darling Maggs. Always my biggest fan. Let's just say you had me at 'Redemption.'" He raised a gentle finger to her chin, tipped her face toward his. "But, when I look into those deep green eyes, I still see confusion, conflict. Hurt, and pain. You said you had *two* reasons for coming, Maggie. So talk to me. What else is troubling you so?"

"I don't want to tell you, Robbie. It will bring back terrible memories for you." She waved a hand around the peaceful chapel. "Memories you've come here to escape."

His breath came out. "When something horrific happened to my parishioners, Maggie, I'd always tell them not to ask 'why did this happen to me,' but 'how will it help me go on?'" He gazed down at his still legs. "I'm not the man I was, Maggs. But I'm stronger in different ways. I can take the bad memories. For you. Maybe I can help. I'm thinking you need to talk about everything that happened with Dane?"

"That moment when he lay dying plays over and over in my mind, Robbie. I didn't want to help him; he was so damned evil. But you insisted . . ."

"Think of what Steinbeck wrote, in *East of Eden*. Humans are caught—in their lives, their thoughts, their hungers and ambitions, in their avarice and cruelty, and in their kindness and generosity—in a net of good and evil. It is the only story we have, Maggie, our true moral dilemma. Do we want to do good, or harm, in this life?"

"Do you *always* know the right thing to say, Robbie Brennan?"

"With a little help from Steinbeck. And on occasion, Elvis. Does it help?"

"I don't know." She shook her head back and forth, her dark hair shifting like a cloak across her face. "You and I weren't the only ones there that night. Do you remember the woman Dane loved? Beatrice."

"The young pregnant woman? So much happened that day, I barely remember her."

"She came to see me last night. Beatrice lost the baby, Robbie."

A moment of silence. "Why did she come to you?"

"To give me a beautiful blown-glass figurine and two water-damaged photographs, one of me, and one of a man in the shadow of Standing Stones. She said she found them in Dane's safe. Dane's proof, she said . . ." Her face was as pale and fragile as an angel's wing.

"What are you saying, Maggs? Proof of what?"

"Oh, God, Robbie. She said it was proof that my husband is still alive."

CHAPTER TWENTY-FOUR

BRIGHTON BEACH, BROOKLYN

"Hey, man, I don't need your bull crap."

Beckett and the boy called Yevgeny were sitting in a back booth in a diner just off the boardwalk. The Golden was curled under the table against Beckett's boots, satisfied with a warm beef bone.

The waitress arrived, set their meals on the table. The kid began to wolf down his double cheeseburger, greasy fries, and supersized Coke.

Beckett stared across the chipped Formica table into the boy's bright blue eyes. *His grandfather Yev's eyes.* "I don't do bull crap, kid. You need a place to stay, and I've got a place to stay."

"I don't need nothin' from you, and I sure ain't going nowhere with you, man. What are you, some kind of a sex creep?"

"You come out swinging, I'll give you that." Beckett tried to cover his laughter with a cough. "Not the way I roll, kid, believe me. I told you, your Grandpa Yev and I were buddies. *Best* buds. In 'Nam he carried me straight out of hell, on his back. Couldn't tell my blood from his..." He gazed out the window at the traffic. "You don't steal horses from your friend's barn."

"That's supposed to make me feel better? I don't know nothing about horses, Beckett, but I know about 'uncles.' My foster care mamas brought them home all the time." The boy turned away to stare out the grimed window at a bus stopped in traffic.

"I'm not anyone's uncle, never have been," said Beckett. "You don't trust me, I get that. I've got no reason to trust you, either." Beckett raised a brow, shook his head. "But I met your mama when she was a girl. Stayed in touch. Before she died, she asked me to make sure you were okay. I've got a nice cabin in the mountains with an extra room, food, a shower, clean sheets—and this really sweet old Golden." He ruffled Shiloh's fur. "Right, Shy?"

Shiloh gazed up at him with superb indifference.

"He doesn't say much," said Beckett, "but he's a really deep thinker."

The kid's mouth began to quirk in a smile, but he pressed his lips together, shook his head, and took another huge bite of his burger.

"He's forlorn this month," said Beckett into the silence. "Missing his lady friend, a beautiful greyhound service dog who's traveling with her person."

"Your dog has a *girlfriend*?" The words were muffled by a mouth full of fries.

"We all need friends. When's the last time you ate, kid?"

A shrug. "Maybe two days."

Christ. No wonder his clothes were too big for him. "Look, I know I'm not good with kids. But I heard what those Russians in the gym said to you. If you stay here, Yevgeny, those thugs are going to come back for you. Is that what you want?"

The boy glanced over his shoulder, searching the faces of the diners, then turned back to scowl at him. "I can take care of myself."

"Yeah, I saw that today. If Shiloh here hadn't helped us run them off, you and I would *both* be in the ER. Or worse." He waited a moment, then said, "Why were they looking for you, Yevgeny?"

The boy stared down at his burger, shrugged. "They were just a coupla hoods." And then, "You gonna eat those fries?"

Nice change of subject. The kid was lying.

Beckett passed the side of fries to the boy, took a bite of his eggs, swallowed. "Hoods," he repeated. "As in, Russian gang members?"

A lift of bony shoulders. "I owed them some money, okay? No big deal, just drop it, man." Out on the street, a car backfired and the boy flinched, bit his lower lip as he slumped down in the booth. Something flashed in the bright blue eyes. *Fear.*

"You sure no one's looking for you, kid?"

"I'm outta here." Yevgeny reached for his backpack, on the seat beside him, and pulled it against his thigh. It was big, beaten, and looked to be very heavy. Something inside shifted, thudded.

He caught Beckett's gaze. "What are you lookin' at?"

"Your backpack. You got a weapon in there, kid?"

"Shit, man, no way. Well, a box cutter, maybe. You know, for protection. Nothin' else."

"Must be a rock collection, then? Where's the rest of your stuff?" asked Beckett.

"You're lookin' at it," said the boy, tapping the backpack with a bony finger. "All that I need."

"That's *it*? Where have you been living?"

"What is it with you, man? Why are you all up in my business?" The boy pulled the stained warm-up hoodie tightly around his thin frame, as if to put a wall between them. *Ready to bolt?*

"Maybe because I need your help. And if you stay here, if you keep getting arrested, you're no good to anyone. Then you're just another punk kid who loses his way to drugs, or worse."

"Hey, man—Beckett, is it?—I won't do drugs. My mama always told me to stay away from—shit, it doesn't matter anymore. She's . . . not here."

"Your mama was murdered, Yevgeny. At least that's what I was told yesterday morning by the detectives. If you want to know what happened, I can help you."

The boy paled, looked away, pushed his fingers through his long, filthy hair.

"I know what happened," he said finally. "Someone wrapped a wire around her neck. Just because—" He shook his head as if to banish an image too terrible to remember. "I just have to find him."

Him.

"You saw it happen?"

The boy dropped his burger to the plate. "You sure you ain't a cop, man?"

Beckett locked eyes with the boy. "I can help you, kid."

"Heard that one before."

"Just give me a few days. Maybe we can help each other." Beckett leaned across the table. "Look, I run a ranch. I could use some help with the horses. And there's Shiloh . . . He's afraid of the dark."

The Golden stirred at the sound of his name. The boy looked down at the Golden, his expression unreadable.

"Why?" he said finally.

"Why is he afraid? He was in Afghanistan, has PTSD. Post-traumatic—"

"—stress syndrome," the boy finished for him. "You don't grow up in my world and not know about that. He scared of loud noises, too?"

"We both are. And don't get me started on Rizzo, the kamikaze cat who just moved in next door."

Another almost-smile.

"Shiloh, here, is a military dog. In the Army, that means he's one rank higher than I am. It's a sign of respect. I'm a Colonel, so he's a Brigadier."

The boy nodded slowly, his eyes on the dog.

"The Brigadier's father isn't *really* a wolf, is he?"

Beckett just smiled. Then he leaned down and gave the Golden the remaining half of his egg sandwich. "There's an old Army saying,

'I've got your six.' It means that I have his back, and he has mine. Right, Shiloh?"

The Golden ignored him, choosing to focus on his sandwich.

"Well, most of the time," muttered Beckett. He fixed his eyes on the kid. "Just a few days, a week," he said. "Give yourself some time to breathe. Help me around the ranch. Then I'll help you do whatever you want to do. School, or—whatever."

Yevgeny jerked as if he'd been punched. "No way I'm going back to child services! I'm almost sixteen, man, I'm no child. I'll run away again, I swear I will!"

Beckett held up his hands in a peacekeeping gesture. "Take it easy, kid, no one is sending you anywhere you don't want to go. But you'll have to trust me."

Beckett signaled for the check, reached into his jacket for his wallet. Froze. Narrowed cold eyes on the boy. "Speaking of trust . . . Seems *someone* has picked my pocket. You've decided to pay for our lunch?"

Yevgeny looked away. Several moments passed. Then, with a sheepish grin, he slipped Beckett's wallet from his hoodie pocket and slid it across the table. "Gee," he said, "you must've lost it in the gym. I forgot that I found it for you."

Beckett, counting silently to ten, gave the kid a stare. "Okay, you've got to do what you can to survive. Everybody gets one second chance with me, kid. But that's it. Try anything like this again and you're gone faster than a bad toupee in a windstorm." He took a deep breath, feeling as if he were about to jump off a cliff. "I've got to get back to D.C. There's an extra train ticket in my pocket, if you want it. No strings." *And no looking over your shoulder every five minutes.*

The boy stared back at him, assessing.

"Hell of a dilemma, huh, kid?"

The boy blinked, swallowed the last of the burger, pushed his empty plate away, and swiped a hand across his ketchup-stained mouth. "You say you need help with horses?"

"Yeah, Yevgeny, I do."

Scowling down at the Golden, the boy stood up and reached for his backpack. "It's Dov, everyone calls me Dov. I owe you for the meal, so okay. But just for the record, I hate dogs." Another quirk of thin lips. "Even the deep-thinking ones."

CHAPTER TWENTY-FIVE

GEORGETOWN UNIVERSITY, WASHINGTON, D.C.

MAGGIE FOUND HER way to the university's Gaston Hall after Robbie left her to teach a graduate seminar on Thomas Aquinas. He had suggested she come here. He knew her life was spiraling out of control, understood her need for solace.

Music was her quiet place. Whenever she was troubled, she sought out a place of music, where she felt safe, centered. Where she could think. Where she could tell the piano her secrets. And this ornate, mural-decorated hall was a beautiful space for music.

She thought of the photograph in her office in Boston, of a lone musician playing his cello in a bombed-out square during World War II. *Music gives us our humanity.*

A Yamaha Grand Piano was set in a shadowed corner of the stage at the front of the auditorium. Maggie climbed the steps, sat down on the leather piano bench, and let the grace and beauty of the hall wash over her. Calm at last, she found her phone and reached out to the people she loved—her son, her godson, her father.

But she could not bring herself to call Michael. They would be together tonight. How do you say, *my husband might be alive, I have to know the truth.* The last thing in the world she wanted was to hurt him. To bring the darkness back to those rain-colored eyes.

She gazed down at the keyboard, her fingers aching. She would talk to Michael in her music.

Maggie set her fingers on the keys, closed her eyes, and began to play. The tragic, emotional C minor chords of Beethoven's Sonata No. 8—his haunting *Pathetique*—spilled like tears into the dark, empty hall.

* * *

"Where the devil are you, Maggie?"

Michael Beckett stood at the kitchen door. They'd arrived back at the cabin hours ago, and now it was almost five. He'd thought she might already be here, waiting for him, on the deck.

In fact, where the devil was *everyone*? The cabin was too quiet. Setting the two grocery bags on the wide oak table, he moved to the window and squinted at the setting sun, then checked his cell once more for new messages. Nothing.

His thoughts turned to the kid. When they'd gotten to the cabin, the boy had gone off by himself, staying in the guest room, not talking. Giving Shiloh a wide berth.

Just keep your dog away from me, man.

Whatever you say, kid. He'd made a quick run to Target, bought jeans, a few tees, socks, a warm hoodie. Had to guess at the sizes, but they looked about right. Crammed it all into a new navy canvas duffel. The duffel was still there, on the table where he'd left it. One more bad idea.

His cell phone buzzed with a text. *So sorry, delayed. Will tell you everything when I get there. By 8, I hope. Love you.*

He texted, *Love you back, darlin'. You are worth the wait.*

Okay, then, not long now. Dinner at nine. For two. Civilized, with candles, she liked candles. He'd give the kid and Shiloh an early dinner and—where had Shiloh disappeared to, anyway? He stepped out onto the deck. April was still cold in the mountains, especially when the sun went down. The kid would need that down jacket he'd bought . . .

"Shiloh! Dov! Chow time. Dinner is here, come and get it." He stopped and leaned his elbows on the railing, listening. The high cry of an eagle swooping across the sky, the soft whoosh of the pines in the late-day breeze.

He scanned the lake, the small empty beach, the wooden steps winding down through the purpling pines. The small shed, where he stored—*damn*. His old bike was gone from its stand.

The kid had bolted.

CHAPTER TWENTY-SIX

THE BLUE RIDGE MOUNTAINS, VIRGINIA

A SHARP BARK. Beckett raised his head, swept by relief as he saw Shiloh lurching toward him from the dirt road that cut through the firs behind the cabin. The kid was pedaling behind on the rusty old bike, slowed by the heavy backpack slung across his narrow shoulder. Got to get some meat on those bones, kid.

Shiloh hesitated at the low stone wall, the arthritis in his hind legs obviously painful. Beckett reached out to ease him over the stones, then watched in surprise as the Golden turned to wait expectantly for the boy, tail thumping. Dov set the bike down and stood in the driveway, gazing at them with an inexplicable expression.

Finally, he said, "I didn't steal the bike, Beckett. I just—"

"Hey, kid." Beckett held out a hand. "Good to see you out and about. Toss me your backpack and we'll have some dinner."

The boy laid a hand protectively over the canvas bag and shook his head. "I can manage." He leaped easily across the stone wall and stared at Beckett, his eyes bright with belligerence. "How did your dog lose his leg? Hit by a car?"

"He was hit, all right. Firefight, Afghanistan. He was trying to save a boy about your age when the bullets hit."

The kid paled, gazing down at the Golden, and murmured something in Russian under his breath. Then, "You think he remembers?"

"Yeah, I do. He has nightmares, hides from folks. Even scared of cats, like I told you." Beckett shook his head. "But he's got a home now, kid, with me. He's safe." He bent closer. "He knows I've got his six. This is a safe place."

The boy shook his head, his eyes stricken, too bright.

Beckett reached out. "C'mon, let me help you with—"

Dov jerked away. "I said leave it, Beckett!"

Shiloh tensed, bristled as Beckett held his hands out with a calming gesture. "Sure, sure, Dov. No harm meant. Where have you two been?" *And what the hell is in that bag?*

"Around."

Beckett slipped his Ray-Bans to the top of his head. "Around where?"

"What's it to you? We went down to the town." A shake of long, stringy hair. "Hick place, isn't it? I was just checking things out. You know."

"I know you didn't need your backpack for that. You sure you weren't planning to just keep going? Maybe you were looking for the Greyhound station?"

The boy flashed a guilty look. "Fat chance. Shiloh was with me."

Beckett smiled to lessen his suspicion. "Didn't think you and Shiloh got along. You being a dog-hater and all."

The kid frowned. "I told him to stay, but he just followed me anyway."

"Doesn't listen to me, either." A heartbeat. "Sorry, kid, but I think he likes you."

A moment of silence, and then Dov grinned.

"I don't really hate dogs, man, I just—don't want any attachments, you know? They slow you down."

"I know. So where were you headed? I thought we were planning to go to the ranch tomorrow."

"I wasn't running." Defensive. "Exactly..." He glanced over a bony shoulder.

"You wanted an escape route."

The boy shrugged. "Always good to know."

Beckett squinted at the last of the sunlight, sparking low on the water. "Smart kid. I'd do the same." He gazed at the boy's torn sweatpants, too long and frayed at the cuffs. "I got some new clothes for you."

The kid stiffened. "Sorry not to be all lit up by joy, Beckett, but I ain't no charity case."

"Didn't say you were. I thought you could use a change of clothes, a toothbrush. A warm jacket. It gets cold here in the mountains at night. No big deal." He smiled, brushing his own ragged jeans. "I'm not exactly 'the man' when it comes to fashion."

Shiloh barked as if in total agreement.

"It's not that." The kid looked down at his own jeans, too long and baggy. "I lifted these clothes from an all-night laundromat in the Bronx." His words were low, embarrassed.

"Desperate times and all that. Yeah, well, I've been known to borrow a few things in my time."

The boy's eyes dropped to his scuffed sneaker. "I had stuff, once. But I didn't want to drag it around in a black trash bag, you know? Like the other kids in foster care. So . . . now I'm on my own. I just take what I need, when I need it."

"Well, now you have a duffel bag for your stuff. When you need it. Is that so terrible?"

The boy glanced at the bag with an odd expression. "No one's given me anything in a real long time."

"Then it's time for a change, kid." Beckett glanced at Shiloh, winked. "Shiloh has a better fashion sense than I do. See what he thinks."

The Golden gave a soft woof in agreement.

The boy looked down at Shiloh, unable to hide his smile. "What's that, Brigadier? He thinks maybe a Mets t-shirt would be okay."

Score one for the good guys. "I'm a Yankees guy myself, but okay then," said Beckett. "Almost sundown, but we still have an hour or two before my friend gets here. What say we watch a movie or . . ." What did teenage boys like? "Or maybe we take the boat out, catch us a fish or two?"

"No boats." The boy glanced down at the darkening lake and frowned. "Don't know how to swim."

"A swing and a miss!" muttered Beckett. "You're not alone, kid. My lady friend hates the water even more than you do."

The kid's brows flew up. "Your friend is a *girl*? You have a *girlfriend*?"

Beckett stared at him. "Well, she's a *woman*, not a girl, but—yeah. A pianist from Boston. What, you can't picture a brilliant, beautiful woman with someone like me? I've been known to have a good line or two. Right, Shiloh?"

The boy looked at the dog and shook his head in disbelief. Beckett could have sworn Shiloh gave a smirk in agreement.

He scowled at the boy and the dog, then relented. "Okay, so maybe I don't get it either. But we were talking about you and me, kid. You like sports, right? So how about we go a few rounds with the gloves?" Give the kid some skills. Some muscle.

A hand nervously pushing through long hair. "Box? Here? On the deck?"

"Yes, yes, and yes." He smiled. "Why not? Got something better to do?"

The kid backed away. "B-ball is my game."

"Hoops are good, but boxing . . . you don't know what you're missing. I can teach you a few moves." Beckett tried to bounce from side to side on the balls of his feet, fists up and out in front of him. Damn, his body didn't move that way anymore. So he stopped, offered, "Feint, left jab, inside hook, bolo punch. Good for protecting yourself. You know, *float like a butterfly, sting like a bee.*"

Shiloh made a disrespectful sound and the boy grinned. Having this kid around was good for the Golden.

"Don't you have a job, Colonel? What about all those bad guys?"

Beckett chuckled. "I'm thinking the bad guys will have to wait. My woman is coming for dinner." *And I have a special gift for her hidden in my sock drawer.*

"Beckett? Hello, earth to Beckett? What's with you, man?"

Beckett gazed out over the lake, now shadowed with purple streaks, and reached for the grocery bag. "So, mac and cheese? Or mac and cheese?"

CHAPTER TWENTY-SEVEN

Nikolai Kirov stood very still in front of the painting—a huge acrylic, some ten-by-seven feet, filling the wall. Every shade of pink, rose, and lavender, it seemed to glow from within.

A long time since he had visited the East Building of the National Gallery of Art. But now, thanks to the listening device he had planted near Magdalena O'Shea's desk, he'd known she was coming to D.C. sometime today. He'd been unable to determine her plans for the afternoon, but he knew she would be at Colonel Michael Beckett's cabin for the night. And—she was flying to London tomorrow.

The pianist was definitely intriguing, worth following. She had been married to John O'Shea, after all. If you want the Van Gogh, he thought, you follow the woman who would know her husband's secrets.

And now her colonel was a person of interest as well. Because Michael Beckett had shown up at Hazelton Prison, just hours before he himself had arrived, and met with Lev Vronsky. How much had the Russian told him? Too bad for Vronsky.

So many questions that needed to be answered. And he *would* answer them.

But now, for this moment, he could simply enjoy the art. Contemporary art was his preference by far, and these gorgeous, soaring, sky-lit galleries held over five hundred pieces of modern and contemporary art. Everything from Kruger and de Kooning to Calder, Picasso, and Rothko. This sleek, I. M. Pei-designed East Wing—just a glassed fountain away from the centuries-old European Masters in the West Wing Building—reflected a huge cultural shift in art *and* society, thought Kirov.

His favorite artist was the abstract expressionist Mark Rothko, a Lithuanian who changed his name from Rothkowitz. Kirov shook his head. Who could not respond to those rich fields of color in his *White Center*? Or his breathtaking *Four Darks in Red*? But here, now, this painting in front of him . . .

Pink Alert, by Jules Olitski. An American artist, born in the Soviet Union. Another Russian, he thought. Deceased in 2007. My God, what a loss to the abstract art world. The colors shimmered, beckoned. Melted around him. He thought of his mother, adding wide, glorious swaths of color to her canvases in the small Moscow apartment. She would have loved Olitski.

What he wouldn't give to have just *one* of these paintings in his gallery in New York. Or, better yet, in his East Side condo.

A dream, for another time. But if they found the Van Gogh, it would sell for millions. Many, many millions. More than enough for him to purchase one or two of the abstracts he loved. *As long as they could prove the ownership.*

He frowned. Too many of the big museums still played fast and loose with the true ownership of their masterpieces—often refusing to return looted art to the rightful country or owner. But the times were changing. He'd just read in the *New York Times* that, for the first time since 1945, the Louvre had appointed a historian to investigate its own collections for any presence of looted works, with a view toward possible restitution. Good for you, he thought. So many world class museums were feeling the heat now—and the law—to behave more ethically when it came to their dubious acquisitions.

And yet. "Easier said than done," he murmured.

With one last, longing glance at *Pink Alert*, Kirov turned away. Entering the open atrium, his eyes found Alexander Calder's kinetic chandelier quivering high above him. Calder's last sculpture was called *Untitled*, because he'd died before he could name it.

Another one gone too soon, thought Kirov. All that brilliance.

And then—*I don't want to die Untitled.*

He had too much yet to do. Find the painting. Find the boy. And then there was the most important quest of all. His *raison d'être*.

At the coat check desk, he glanced at his watch, realized he'd lost track of time, and shoved his arm into the jacket sleeve. The wound on his shoulder blade began to throb painfully, reminding him of the moment Magdalena O'Shea had surprised him with the stabbing shard of glass. It was going to be an ugly scar. He grimaced, rotating his shoulder to ease the searing ache.

He had just meant to scare her. He would not take her for granted again.

Ignoring the pain, he grasped the suitcase handle and hurried out onto Pennsylvania Avenue to hail a cab. It was almost dark.

And it was going to be a long night.

CHAPTER TWENTY-EIGHT

THE BLUE RIDGE MOUNTAINS, VIRGINIA

IT WAS ALMOST eight p.m.

Beckett stood with his elbows on the deck railing, his eyes on the unsettled dark blue lake below, his thoughts on Maggie.

She would be here any minute. He raised his head, listening for the crunch of tires on crushed stone. Only the soft brush of leaves, the whisper of night animals.

His thoughts circled back to the boy sitting alone inside the cabin.

He had eaten quickly and in silence, head bent, jaws pumping. Then, telling Shiloh sharply to 'Stay,' he'd disappeared into his room. Damn. The kid was suffering, keeping secrets. How do I get through to him?

With a shake of his head, Beckett rose and entered the cabin.

The boy had emerged, was hunched in an easy chair by the fire, absorbed in punching buttons on his phone. Shiloh slept on the floor in a bright pool of lamplight near the kid's left foot, snoring. The new clothes were scattered across the sofa, price tags still dangling.

Moonlight fell in shifting bars through the window over the boy's shoulder, lighting the pale blond hair with bands of bright gold. He looked young, innocent. Vulnerable. Beckett felt something tighten in his chest. What would his son, Sam, have looked like if he had lived?

The boy looked up at Beckett's approach. "This your old lady?"

"Excuse me?"

Shiloh, knowing that tone of voice, raised his head.

"Your chickee? Your *Lyubushka*?" The boy cocked his chin at the framed photograph of Maggie on the side table.

Beckett looked down at the Golden. "Got to set this kid straight," he said softly. Turning to the boy, he said, "We treat women with respect around here, kid. Same way I'm trying to treat you. Magdalena O'Shea is not mine; I don't own her. This *woman* is my friend."

A shrug of narrow shoulders. "Didn't mean anything by it. She's"— Dov caught Beckett's scowl. "I mean—she's pretty. All that soft hair, like a cloud. I used to brush my mama's hair for her sometimes..."

The boy turned away, but not before Beckett had seen the lost look fill his eyes. *Get him to talk about his mother.* "Yes, Maggie is beautiful. Like your mother was."

Silence.

Beckett lifted the silver frame. "Maggie is impulsive, infuriating. Heck, she *inspires* exasperation. Complex, full of contradictions. Radiates intelligence—but they're still looking for the guy who asked her for directions to the concert hall."

The kid chuckled in spite of himself. "I hope she's not an Uber driver."

Beckett laughed. "She's a concert pianist. Crazy talented. Music falls from her hands like magic." He shook his head, touching the face in the photograph with gentle fingers. "There's just something about her. She couldn't knock the salt off a margarita, but she is strong and fierce and brave as hell. Her eyes are full of thoughts—and she makes me laugh. The only person I know who can fold a fitted sheet."

Dov held up his hands. "Time-out, man, way more than I wanted to know."

"I saw her run into five lanes of French traffic to rescue Shiloh." Beckett squinted into the distance. "And she's petrified of the water, like you. But she jumped into a stormy sea to save a little boy. She's like no other woman I've ever met."

Dov tilted his head. "Sure sounds like she's *your* safe place, Beckett."

He stared at the boy. "Yes," he admitted. "She lights up the dark places."

"The dark places . . ." Dov gazed at Maggie's photo, his expression unreadable. "So where is Wonder Woman?"

"Trouble has a way of finding her," Beckett said with a scowl. *Just like your mother, kid.* "She's running late as usual. But she'll be here."

"My mom played piano, too. I like music. Mom and I used to dance around the living room to Cardi B, Jay-Z, 50 Cent."

"She was an accountant, right? Good for helping with the math homework."

"She always used to say that numbers danced for her. Not for me, but . . ." His voice trailed off.

"It's okay to miss your mama, Dov."

The boy stood quickly, turned. He pulled out his cell phone and stared down once more at the video game on the screen.

"Where'd you get that snazzy phone?"

"Found it." Defiant, without looking up from the screen. "What's it to you?"

Beckett reached out to lay a hand on the boy's shoulder. It felt thin and brittle as a tree branch beneath his fingers. Dov stiffened, pulled away too quickly, and tripped over the chair behind him. He went down hard.

Beckett reached down to give him a hand.

Dov shoved his hand away. "Don't touch me!" he shouted, panic searing his voice.

Beckett dropped his hand quickly, jolted by understanding. "You think I was going to *hit* you? I don't hit kids. *Christ*, Dov."

The boy cringed back against the chair, looking at him with wide, frightened eyes.

Beckett took a step back as he shoved his hands into his jeans pockets. "You're gonna have to tell me some time, kid."

The boy rose slowly to his feet. "Sorry, Beckett. *No comprende.*"

"You're in trouble, kid. I can smell it. You in a gang?"

A quick shake of the head.

"Those Russian punks at the gym. Why were they looking for you, Dov?"

"No one's looking for me." The eyes slid away, sullen and angry. *Scared.*

"Wrong answer. Try again. Door number two this time. Why are you hiding, Dov? What did they want? What did you see? What do you *know*, damnit?"

"Fucking nothing, man! Get off my case!"

"You talk a good game, kid, I'll give you that. But me and Shiloh, we don't want to be worrying about you."

"Seems like I've been on my own for my whole life, Beckett. You said this was a safe place, right?"

"Yes. Count on it."

"So okay. Have dinner with your woman. Shiloh and me, we'll be fine. Right, Brigadier?"

Shiloh lifted his chin in agreement, his gold fur fluffed with pleasure.

Beckett stared at the boy as he disappeared down the hallway, closed the door hard. Beckett heard the angry click of a lock.

Something, some unfamiliar, inexplicable feeling, told him not to walk away. Beckett followed slowly down the hallway. As he neared the door, he heard the muffled, choking sounds from within.

Then a single raw, desperate sob.

* * *

At last, Maggie could see the lights of the cabin through the dense black pines. Just a few miles more, up the hill and around to the left. And then she would be with Michael. In his arms. *Home.*

Her headlights speared the darkness. She felt as if she could hear her heart hammering against her ribs. He would understand. Please God. He *had* to . . .

"Grief is not done with me yet," she murmured.

CHAPTER TWENTY-NINE

THE BLUE RIDGE MOUNTAINS, VIRGINIA

STILL NO SIGN of Maggie.

Or the kid. Better check. Beckett walked quietly down the hall, knocked softly on the guest room door.

No answer, no sound.

He tested the knob. Not locked now. He pushed the door open, very slowly, not sure if the kid would even be there. Half expecting the bed to be empty . . .

But the boy was sound asleep on the sofa bed, moonlight falling across his pale skin, his hand flung across his eyes in a young, innocent gesture. His sunken cheeks were streaked by tears.

Curled next to him on the mattress, the Golden raised his head and gazed at Beckett as if to say, "Don't even think about asking me to leave him."

Beckett raised an eyebrow, then smiled and nodded. "He's going to be okay, boy. He's worn down by the streets. He's lost so much. He needs to mourn. I'm counting on you to watch over him."

Then he saw the kid's backpack. It had fallen to the floor with its top flap open.

Beckett stared at it, then made his decision. *Sorry, kid. I don't like invading your privacy, but you're in a whole world of trouble. I won't touch anything, but I've got to know. It's for your own good.*

Stepping closer, ignoring his guilt, he bent down, angled his head to see the contents.

"Well, I'll be damned," he murmured.

The titles were jumbled together, one on top of the other. *Seabiscuit,* by Laura Hillenbrand. *Moby Dick,* and Jack London's *The Call of the Wild. The Revolutionary War. A Biography of Baryshnikov.* D'Aulaire's *The Greek Myths. The Constellations. The Art of Photography.*

Books.

* * *

Beckett stood at the window, full on dark out there now, his thoughts on the boy. Just gotta give the kid some space.

Headlamps pierced the pines.

Maggie.

His breath whooshed out. Damn, he hadn't realized he'd been holding it. What was the matter with him? Acting like a kid on a first date.

He thought of the small jewelry box hidden upstairs in his sock drawer. Shaking his head, he moved to the door, swung it open.

Hurried down the steps.

She was standing very still in the driveway, bathed in spinning smoky beams from the car's headlamps. The sight of her in the soft light, as beautiful and arresting as the first time he'd laid eyes on her, caught him off guard.

I'm happy, he thought.

Her car's engine was still running. He could hear the Righteous Brothers on the radio. His favorite, "Unchained Melody."

He grinned, reached out, folded her in his arms, began to sway with the music. "I've never danced with you in the light of headlamps, Maggie," he whispered, as he began to murmur the words of the song. "Oh, my love, my darling, I've hungered for your touch . . ." His lips brushed her hair as he sang. But—

Something was wrong.

She was too stiff, too rigid. He leaned back, held her away from him, looked down at her. Her face was as white as moonlight. There was a purple bruise on her cheek. And her eyes, those speaking eyes, were the color of dark forest shadows . . .

Good Christ. He felt his heart grow cold.

Once more he drew her against his chest. Wrapped his arms more tightly around her.

A long, lonely time . . . Now the words of the song echoed darkly in the night air. Fear brushed at him.

"Maggie? What is it, darlin'? What's happened?"

CHAPTER THIRTY

THE BLUE RIDGE MOUNTAINS, VIRGINIA

"HOLD ON TO me, Michael. Hold on tight. Don't let me go."

Beckett held Maggie close, tighter. Felt the rigid tension, the uncontrollable shuddering of her body. And knew, suddenly, that tonight was going to change them.

Just love her.

He stopped the dance, took the car keys from her shaking hand, and turned off the engine. "Come on, darlin', come in from the cold. The dance will wait for another night, another driveway." He took her large suitcase, then led her into the warm, firelit cabin. "Whatever it is, we'll deal with it."

Easing her coat off stiff shoulders, he settled her onto the deep sofa in front of the fire. The green eyes he loved were huge and full of confusion. And pain.

"Michael . . . Something impossible has happened."

"If that's not a conversation starter, I don't know what is." He tried to smile but it hurt his face. He held up a hand. "Not yet, Maggie. I know there is something you need to tell me." *Something bad.* He'd seen the bruised skin, the bandage on her hand. The fear in her eyes. "Just take a moment to breathe. I'm not going anywhere."

He found glasses, poured wine for her, a stiff bourbon for himself, and returned to the sofa. She held up a bright red high-top with a questioning look and tilted her head at him. "Do we have company?"

"A street kid from New York, lost his mom last week. He's damaged, Maggie, alone and hurting. But I have to admire his 'test-the-boundaries' style. His name is Dov. He's asleep in the guest room. Shiloh's with him."

"Opening your home to a stray child . . . that was the favor for your old friend."

"A debt of honor," he said softly.

"Honor is in your bones, Michael. It's who you are."

"You always see me as better than I am. But what matters is that you're home now, Maggie, that we're together." He gestured at her bandaged hand, brushed the dark bruise below her eye. "You've been hurt. Talk to me."

"The bruises will heal. But now there's something more." She set her glass on the table and stood to face him.

"I think my husband, Johnny, might be alive."

Time slowed. They stood perfectly still, staring at each other, while her words trembled like smoke in the air between them.

Christ. *He was caught on a train, out of control, swooping down a mountainside at an impossibly high speed into the darkness.*

Finally, he said, "I'm gonna need more words, Maggie."

"I know." She turned restlessly, moved to the staircase, dropped down to sit on the third step. He forced his body to follow, settled next to her.

They leaned toward each other, drawn by an invisible thread.

He took her hand, brought it to his lips. "The last time we sat on a staircase together," he said, remembering a theater in Paris, "was the day I fell in love with you. What I felt that day will never change."

She smiled. "It was love at first *fight*."

"Funny. I just know you made the first move." He waited a heartbeat. "Tell me what's happened, darlin'. There's nothing we can't handle together."

She took a deep breath. "Last night, Beatrice Falconi, the woman who was pregnant with Dane's baby, came to see me. I don't know if you remember her. She lost the baby."

He felt the shock run through him, forced a calmness to his words. "How could I not remember everything about that night? It was the night you were shot. *The night you almost died*. But Dane is gone. Why did she come?"

Maggie shook her head back and forth. "You know I blamed Dane for my husband's death; he arranged for Johnny's boat to explode that day in France..."

"I know the French searched for weeks. You said they found the remains of his boat in the sea off Hyères."

"Yes. I was there, waiting. For weeks." Her head came up, her eyes searching his. "Search and Rescue became Search and Recovery. But they never found Johnny's body, only his wallet. Beatrice brought me four things that she discovered in Dane's safe in Greece. Two water-damaged photographs—one of me, and one of a man who could be Johnny, standing in a Circle of Stones. A small blown-glass figurine with flowing black hair. And a note, handwritten by Dane, that says, 'He is alive.'"

He stared at her incredulously as she reached into her purse, offered the photographs, the note.

"So now what? What are you saying, Maggie?"

"My husband drowned, Michael. They never found him. I never got to say goodbye. So I ... Well, I ..." She held out her hands helplessly.

"You're gonna have to narrow that down, darlin'."

"I'm going to look for him, Michael. When I go to London. I'm going to try to find my husband."

Feeling as if he were swimming through viscous, dark water, he stood slowly and looked down at her. "Seriously? For fuck's sake, Maggie! Are you *serious* right now? You believe this woman? *Dane's* woman? He almost killed you. You think he wrote this damned note? I'm not buyin' it!"

She rose to face him, stunned by his fierce anger. He saw the hurt flash like lightning in the deep green eyes.

"It's not your call this time, Michael. It's mine."

"Like hell it is!"

"I'm going," she said.

His breath came out, his face softened. "I know you are, because I know *you*."

Emotion sparked like electric current between them.

Her breath caught, raw and scraping. "Don't you see, Michael? I have to know. I have to look for him, find out if my husband is alive. *How can I not?*"

She faced him—radiating intensity, vibrating with pain.

Fear gripped him. Losing her was unthinkable. He wanted to turn away, just walk away from her and not look back. Get away from the pain. But he stayed—of course he stayed, *how could he not*—and, wrapping her in his arms, he held on tight.

"I know you're angry," she whispered.

"I am not angry!"

"The air is throbbing with your fury, Michael. I didn't know I could make you so angry."

"I didn't know it, either."

He took a breath, shook his head. "Truth is, it's not you I'm angry at. You're right, it's not my decision to make. I learned a long time ago that you can't live someone else's life for them. But—there's an edge to this cliff, Maggie."

She just pressed against his chest. He rested his forehead against hers, and they stayed locked together, not speaking, for a long time.

Until, at the very same moment, they both whispered, "I'm sorry."

Beckett looked down at her. "I guess Socrates was the only guy who could ever make an argument sound noble."

She began to laugh, shaking against his chest. "Oh, Michael, how can I be mad at a man who reads Socrates?"

He tilted her chin up, until he was looking into her eyes.

"This is way too big for sorry, isn't it? But I love you more than I have ever loved another woman, Maggie O'Shea," he told her. "You do what you have to do. I won't stop you—couldn't if I tried, right?" He smiled into her eyes. "All I can do is trust you to be careful. And I'll be here waiting for you. Count on it."

She locked her gaze on his. "I want so badly to say, 'Come with me,' but I know you need to stay here. Because of the boy. Because of who you are."

"I want to, darlin', you don't know how much. Would in a heartbeat. But, yes—there's this kid, now, Maggie. In trouble. Danger, maybe. Caught between boy and man. He needs my help. Hell, I *need* to help him. And I said I would be here for him." He turned away. "Kid doesn't even want to be here. What was I thinking?"

"You weren't thinking, you were just being you. Something about him got to you. Your instincts always will choose to save kids."

"He reminds me of me, Maggie, when my mom died. I was just a kid—hurt, scared, so alone. And I see the same thing in his eyes."

She touched his face. "My noble soldier."

"I don't have a sword and shield and a big round table, Maggie. I'm just a guy who wants to be with his woman tonight." His fingers brushed across her lips. "Nothing noble about the way I'm feeling right now." His hand caught her neck, pulled her toward him. His kiss was slow, long, and deep.

"Come upstairs with me, Maggie. Let me show you how much I love you. Tomorrow will come soon enough. Now I just want to kiss you until the morning light."

She smiled into his eyes. Together they climbed the twisting stairs to his bedroom.

CHAPTER THIRTY-ONE

THE BLUE RIDGE MOUNTAINS, VIRGINIA
SATURDAY

MAGGIE OPENED HER eyes.

Daybreak. Pale gray light streamed through billowing white curtains, skimming her skin with soft, wavering shadows. She was naked, tangled in a thick blue blanket. She blinked, shifted. Found herself looking into Michael Beckett's silvery eyes.

"Sleep well?" he murmured. He brushed a strand of hair from her cheek. "There's nothing like your gorgeous morning-after hair."

"How did we end up on the floor?"

He chuckled. "I think it had something to do with chocolate." Very slowly, his thumb traced the angle of her chin.

God, she loved that crooked, knee-weakening smile. And the way he looked at her. "You do have a way about you," she whispered. "Is there coffee?"

"Depends. Which answer will get me what I want?" he said against her skin. "Christ, you smell good." He thrust the blanket aside, pulled her against him. "Is there any chocolate left?"

"Keep your eyes open, Michael," she whispered. "Look at me."

Then his mouth closed on hers and she wrapped her legs around him and forgot all about the coffee.

An hour later she was sitting on the small terrace off his bedroom, enveloped in his heavy woolen robe, her fingers folded around a steaming cup of French press. The line of pines was dark green against the sky. Far below her, the light was pewter, and mist swirled in ghostly ribbons over the dark lake.

Beckett came to stand behind her, setting his hands on her shoulders.

"Your coffee is always so much better than mine," she told him, smiling up at him.

"Not a hard thing to do," he said against her hair. "After you're dressed, I'll make breakfast, and you can meet Dov. I see something in this kid, Maggie. There's just something about him."

"I can tell." She rose. "I'll help make breakfast."

"Funny." He pushed her gently back into her seat and settled in the deck chair close to hers. "This is the part where you say, 'Last night was all a dream.'"

She reached out, put her hand on his cheek. "I don't know how to do this, I really don't. I don't want to hurt you."

He gazed out over the lake. "What time is your flight to London?"

"Seven tonight." When he remained quiet, she said, "I know what I'm doing, Michael."

"I'm glad one of us does. I did a lot of thinking last night, while you were asleep. I'm smart enough to realize you can never really get over a person you loved. I know about grieving, Maggie. Grief is just love with nowhere to go."

Her hand rested on his heart. "You're talking about your son," she said softly. "I know it was Sam's birthday this week, can only imagine how much you must miss him."

"The way I see it," said Beckett, "grief is a circle filled with sorrow. It doesn't shrink over time—life just grows around it in a bigger circle. *Love* grows around it. Sam will always be in my circle. Just like I'm in your circle now. But it seems we have a flashing neon elephant in the circle with us all of a sudden."

Their eyes connected, held.

"If you want to walk away from me, Michael, and not look back, I wouldn't blame you."

"All I know is, I'm not going anywhere, Maggie. I won't lose you. Feelings don't just shut off; my love for you hasn't changed. If anything, after last night, it's deeper." He wagged his spiky silver brows at her. "As long as I am breathing, I will love you."

She wanted to say, *Oh my darling, I feel the same way*—but she was afraid she would burst into tears. So she said, "I'm glad. I don't want to leave you, Michael, but I loved my husband. I have to do the right thing."

"I get that you've got to ride this train. You loved him, still do. Whether you are still grieving or moving on, either way the ghosts stay with you."

The ghosts . . . "Yes. I owe it to Johnny to find out the truth."

"But where the devil will you look for him?"

"Beatrice said Johnny was last seen in Calais. That's where you catch the ferry to England. And the photo—the circle of stones . . ."

"There have to be hundreds, thousands, of stone circles in Great Britain."

"Johnny told me, once, about a place he loved as a child. Cornwall. I'll start there."

"But what if you *find* him, Maggie? Then what? *What about us?*"

"Don't go there, Michael. Just—don't."

"*So* not an answer. We have to face the fact that your husband might be alive." He stood up. "If he is, then we will deal with it. Somehow." He hesitated, gazing up at the brightening pink sky. "For a long time, I didn't think I had a future. Until now—it's so easy with you, so right. But we can't think about a future together until we know. So for now, let's get you some breakfast. We're going to enjoy every hour we have together today."

"Every hour," she whispered, caressing his face. She watched him disappear through the doorway, then lifted her face toward the sun-lit window.

Her phone pinged. A text from Robbie. *Found Donata Kardos, meeting her today.* Good. Hopefully she would have more information about Johnny and the Van Gogh and they could—

No. She wouldn't think about Johnny, or Robbie's meeting in D.C. with the mysterious nun, or what was waiting for her in London.

Today was all about Michael.

CHAPTER THIRTY-TWO

WASHINGTON NATIONAL CATHEDRAL, D.C.

Donata Kardos sat alone on a wooden bench in The Bishop's Garden, the walled garden in the shadow of Washington's National Cathedral, watching the late afternoon light spill across the towers of the beautiful Gothic church.

Where was he? She would need a Plan B if he—The whisper of wheels on stone.

"Sister?" A resonant voice, behind her. She stood to face him. He was wearing a simple black collared shirt and warm jacket. No cross, no priest's white Roman collar. And yet—he has the face of an apostle, she thought.

Dropping the scarf that covered her hair, she held out her hand. "Yes. It's me, Robbie."

"Holy Christ," muttered the priest. He raised a brow in disbelief.

She grinned. "You sound surprised."

"It's just . . . I'd forgotten that you are not at all what the nuns I know look like." And then, "Sorry. You look wonderful. Thank you for coming."

"You're welcome." Her smile was soft. "It's good to see you again, too. Though I might add that nothing about *you* suggests piety, either, Father."

His laughter was full and sonorous. "How long has it been, Sister, since our days together in New York?"

"Too long." She watched him maneuver his wheelchair toward her. "When you mentioned the wheelchair, I thought it would be easier for me to drive to you. I'm often in Annapolis, not that far. Thank you for suggesting this beautiful garden. The boxwoods, the fragrance, the medieval sculptures . . . I had no idea it existed."

He nodded, sweeping a hand toward the ancient gray stones and thick, flowering bushes. "I love to come here. It's quiet, peaceful. A good place for reflection, a place to escape the stress and craziness of campus life." He shook his head. "I feel closer to God in this garden. And . . . no one knows me here."

Something in his eyes. Regret. Sorrow? And something more.

"If we meet no Gods, it is because we harbor none," she said into the stillness.

He raised a pale brow. "You always liked Emerson. A nun *and* a scholar."

"Surely we should be both. I teach Graduate Literature at St. John's College now."

"That's how I found you," he said.

"I live at the St. Cecilia by the Bay Retreat House just north of Annapolis. The Chesapeake Bay is just steps from my window. It's a solitary life." She gazed at the new vines climbing ancient stone walls. "The Bishop's Garden . . ." she said softly. "Do you miss the Archbishop's life you had in New York?"

He gestured to the stone bench. "Please, sit. And I must remind you that I'm the *Ex*-Archbishop now."

She dropped to the bench. "I could care less what title you used to hold, Robbie."

He squinted up at the sky. "It's funny, what you miss. I miss sitting alone in a tiny church off-Broadway, late at night, with only the candles burning. I miss my old parishioners, the scent of incense lingering on my fingers. But the power?" He shook his head. "It seems, like you,

I prefer the solitary life. Isolation is my church now. Life is nothing if unpredictable. As you well know."

"I must admit, I was intrigued by your call. I cannot imagine what the *Ex*-Archbishop of New York wants to discuss with a nun from a small retreat house in Maryland." She glanced at the book in his lap. "Russian Art? You are a Professor of Art History at Georgetown now?"

"Let's just say I am still an 'admirer' of art. I teach seminars on the great Catholic philosophers and theologians."

"That's the Robbie I remember." She leaned toward him. "What is so important that you could not tell me over the phone?"

"Some twenty months back, you came to me seeking advice about authenticating a piece of art. And I sent you to John O'Shea."

"John?" The sharp shock of surprise. "You asked to see me because of John O'Shea? But you must know he died shortly after I met with him."

"Yes. As you know," he murmured, "in another lifetime, John and I were friends. Close ones, I like to think. I met him through his wife."

"I was so sorry to hear of his death," Donata said quietly. "His story was far from done." She set her dark eyes on his. "You're like him—one of the good guys."

"Ah, but that was before my fall from grace." Robbie Brennan closed his eyes, as if to shut out a terrible memory. "My very literal fall from grace," he added ruefully, tapping his rigid, motionless thighs. "My fatal sin was to choose passion over reason."

Donata shook her head in denial. "We all let passion rule reason at some time in our lives, don't we? Maybe your—intensity—is why I've come. Tell me what you need."

He smiled. "Agent Simon Sugarman, from the Department of Justice, asked me to find you. He has found John O'Shea's notes on his conversation with you, your story of a missing Van Gogh . . ."

She felt her stomach tighten. "But the notes are incomplete," she whispered. "I never went back to see John as I promised. You are hoping I can fill in the blanks?"

The priest shrugged. "Thomas Aquinas said that hope has to do with things that are not at hand."

"And St. Francis said, 'It's in giving that we receive.' So I will try to help you."

Robbie smiled. "Even I cannot argue with St. Francis. So. I, too, have read John's notes on his meeting with you. There are still so many questions."

She hesitated, her huge eyes dark in the pale face. "It's all so complicated . . ."

"Life is not complicated, Sister. People are."

She ran a hand through her short hair and nodded. "There's a reason I haven't come forward. I'm scared, Robbie. I've been protecting my daughter all this time. From the day we escaped, someone has been hunting for her."

* * *

Robbie Brennan moved his chair closer to the woman who sat before him.

Just shy of fifty, perhaps, but she looked much younger. She was tall for a woman, very slender in a black turtleneck and slacks, and had sharply defined cheekbones and close-cropped dark hair shot with silver. The eyes that found his were huge, black, and startling. In a word, she was beautiful. Even more so now.

"Where do I begin?" the nun said into the silence.

He smiled. "When my parishioners asked me that question in the confessional, I always told them what Plato said. 'The beginning is the most important part of the work.' Tell me in your own words."

She raised her eyes to the clouds, lost in memory. Her voice, when she began to speak, was low and rich in timbre.

"My birth name is Donata Kardos," said Sister Terese Rozsa into the quiet of the Bishop's Garden. "I escaped from Hungary in 1985, toward the end of the Cold War, when I was just fifteen. I never wanted to leave my country, Robbie. I wanted to stay and fight. But . . ." With a shrug of shoulders, her voice fell away.

"But God had other plans for you," said Robbie Brennan. "Tell me what happened."

"Not a what, but a who. My best friend, Tereza Janos. I chose her name when I took my vows." Her gaze fixed on the treetops, turned gold by the afternoon's sun. "I was born at the height of the Cold War," she continued finally. "For years I was too young to understand how living behind the Iron Curtain would control my life. As I grew older, I studied, desperate to take my vows. But the Russians had shut down the churches."

She shifted on the stone bench, waved a slender ringless hand in the air. "My friend, Tereza, had to leave Hungary. I was helping her cross the border."

"I thought the borders were more open by the eighties."

"You are right. It should have been easy to leave, via the border crossings. But Tereza had a baby, you see. The father was a Russian soldier . . ."

"Ahh. And he wanted his child."

"He wanted—something. When Tereza disappeared with the baby, he set extra patrols at the borders. And then, on the night we planned her escape . . ." Tears filled her huge eyes.

"I know your friend did not make it. I'm so sorry."

The nun shook her head, her gaze inward, remembering. "It all happened so fast. One minute we were running down the hill toward the border, the next... Oh, God. The soldiers, the gunfire. A terrible flash, and Tereza was just—gone. I took the baby, and I ran."

"You'd think God would know better." Robbie Brennan looked down at his legs. "What we do for love," he murmured. "Of course you raised the child as your own."

"A baby girl, yes. Gemma Rozsa. I call her Rose. We lived with my cousin for over a year, then made our way from Austria to London, eventually here to America."

He leaned toward her. "The child would be in her thirties now. You said someone has been hunting her since she disappeared from Hungary?"

A flash of fear in the dark eyes. "Her father is Russian; he was stationed in Hungary during the Cold War. Tereza never told me his name. I never met him; I only heard his voice. But he would be at least in his mid-fifties by now, maybe a bit older. I believe he has been searching for Rose all these years. But I don't know if he wants to find her because she is his daughter—or because he wants the Van Gogh that belonged to her grandfather."

She shuddered and pulled her jacket closer.

Robbie Brennan looked up at the purpling sky. "It's getting dark, and colder. What would you say to continuing this conversation back in my apartment near the campus? It's five o'clock, the sun is almost over the yardarm, and I make a mean Rob Roy. And I've got a fireplace and a box of pasta."

"You had me at Rob Roy." She stood up, tightening her scarf around her neck. "I just hope you have plenty of maraschino cherries."

CHAPTER THIRTY-THREE

THE BLUE RIDGE MOUNTAINS, VIRGINIA

MICHAEL WAS IN the shower. Maggie sat at the old, scarred upright he had bought for her just months earlier—a surprise, the first time she'd come to the cabin. She smiled, remembering. The battered Yamaha still had a good, true sound. She would take the next hour to work on the Rachmaninoff—she was now deep into the second movement, the *Adagio Sostenuto*. Technically, she was ready. But she hadn't yet found the emotion she wanted. Needed. The passion that would transform the music, give it *life*. The heart. The *soul*.

Her favorite pianist, Horowitz, had advised, *Play Chopin like Mozart and play Mozart like Chopin, because Chopin needs clarity and Mozart needs drama.* Okay.

This morning, she would work on the second movement—the piano entering with those arpeggios, the slow build to a climax, and then her favorite section, the cadenza. She loved the improvisation, the freedom.

She tried not to think of the final, third section of the *Adagio*, still to be faced. The music would just die away, finishing with the piano—all alone—in E major. And she thought about leaving Michael behind, in just a few hours, to go on—*alone*—to England to search for her husband. You are a soloist, she reminded herself. Music tells our stories.

But please, Rachmaninoff, don't let this leaving be my story . . .

Her thoughts slipped to the four items Beatrice had given to her back in Boston, now packed securely in her carry-on bag.

The water-damaged photographs of herself, and a man in the shadow of huge Standing Stones—almost exactly like the framed black-and-white drawing in her husband's office. The small blown-glass figurine of a woman in a fluid emerald dress and long, ebony hair. And the note from Dane, its three words etched in her brain.

He is alive.

Proof that her husband was still alive? Or one last cruel joke from Dane, the man who still haunted her nightmares. Maggie shook her head to dispel the thoughts, set her fingers firmly on the keys, and began to play.

She was deep into the improv section when she caught a movement out of the corner of her eye. A changing of the light.

Stilling her fingers, she looked up. A tall, thin boy of about fifteen stood in the open doorway, with late afternoon light behind him, turning his tangled pale hair to silver and casting a long shadow across the carpet. He was dressed in baggy jeans, a Mets sweatshirt, and red high-tops.

"Hello," said Maggie. "You must be Yevgeny. Michael told me about you. He said everyone calls you Dov. I'm Maggie. We missed you at breakfast." She grinned. "Did someone warn you that my pancakes can be used for hockey pucks?"

The boy remained silent, staring at her. The bright blue eyes held suspicion—and something more. Then, "My mama used to play the piano."

"Did she?" Maggie gave a small wave of her hand. "Come in. Did she play classical music?"

"No. She liked John Denver. Simon and Garfunkel, Elton John. The Beatles."

Maggie smiled. "Your mom had good taste. Did she teach you to play?"

"She always said she was going to, but . . ." He shook his head, gave a shrug of bony shoulders. "Beckett told me about you, too. I like your sound."

Maggie shifted, making space on the bench. "You can thank Rachmaninoff for the sound. Want to sit down?"

He stood very still, then gave a short nod and sat on the edge of the piano bench, careful not to touch her. He held up the cell phone in his hand. "I have a picture of her."

"Your mother? Will you show me?"

He thumbed through several photographs, then held the phone toward her. "Her name was Irina. Her hair was even longer than yours."

Maggie found herself looking down at a striking woman in a gauzy, flowing dress, standing barefoot on a beach, the waves unfurling behind her. The light caught her hair as it blew across her eyes, turning it to gold. She was smiling, gazing at the person behind the camera.

The boy's fiercely blue eyes held a telltale brightness.

"Your mother was very beautiful. And this photograph is beautiful as well—the light, the shadows, the composition . . . It's like music. It tells a story. You're a good photographer."

"I like to take pictures." He took the phone, thumbed through the shots, held it out once more. "The cat's name is Big Red. I think they're becoming friends."

There was Shiloh, his sleek head lifted toward a huge, thick-furred cat sitting on a stone wall washed by sunlight.

Maggie laughed. "That's our Shiloh, just like Ferdinand! You've captured him perfectly. How did you get him to pose for you?"

The boy scowled. "Beckett says he likes me."

"Sorry to tell you, Dov, but I think I like you, too."

The boy stood up suddenly, his expression unreadable, and headed for the door.

"Dov, wait . . ." Her cell phone beeped. Robbie.

The boy disappeared through the doorway without a backward glance.

"That went well." Maggie sighed, and gazed down at the text.

Meeting now with Donata Kardos. She has an adopted daughter who was fathered by a Russian soldier in Hungary. Russian still looking for his daughter—but is it because he really wants the Van Gogh? Much more to story, TBC.

Maggie thought of the striking woman she'd seen in Johnny's office that long-ago afternoon—and the shadowed figure playing an unknown, haunting violin concerto in the garden.

The daughter? Of course.

Yes, much, *much* more to the story, Robbie. To be continued is right.

She turned back to her keyboard and Rachmaninoff, as light—bright and then darkening—spun through the high windows.

CHAPTER THIRTY-FOUR

GEORGETOWN, WASHINGTON, D.C.

FATHER ROBERT BRENNAN'S apartment was on the first floor of a narrow row house on the corner of 35th and O Street, close to the Georgetown campus. The ramp constructed just before he'd moved in had made access relatively easy, as had the added safety bars and other changes made to accommodate his wheelchair and needs.

"I live alone here," he told Donata Kardos as he unlocked the door. "Not easy, but I prefer the solitude."

She gazed around at the simple furniture, the unadorned walls. "It's . . . uncluttered." She smiled. "No worldly temptations for you, Father."

"Those worldly temptations are what landed me in this chair, Sister. I decided that if I couldn't have original art on my walls, I would do without. But I admit it is a penance of significant magnitude." He gestured to a low chair by the gas fireplace as he rolled toward the open kitchen. "Just turn on the fire and get warm."

In moments, he returned with two Rob Roy cocktails and a shaker, on a small tray that balanced on his lap.

"Extra maraschinos." He smiled as they clinked glasses. "To your courage."

She glanced around at the bare white walls. "And to yours."

"You know about my accident?" He tilted his head at her. "Ah. You googled me."

"I'd have been a fool not to."

"And still you came." He smiled, pressed a hidden button, and the soft chords of a Bach Brandenburg Concerto filled the room.

"I have my reasons. And *you* still have good taste in music, Father."

He sat back in his chair with a sigh. "So now you know all my fatal flaws. I'm afraid that not having Bach in my life would be a penance too great to bear. So. You were about to tell me about your daughter's father. The Russian."

Donata closed her eyes, remembering. "He would come to see her at her apartment, sometimes with two of his friends. I never saw them, but I heard their voices, more than once, lifted in laughter or song. One night he came alone. It was the night we knew Tereza had to get away from him . . ."

*   *   *

It was dark beyond the windows of the small apartment. She was fifteen and still afraid of the dark, but the sounds of the violin, seeping through the thin walls and heating grates from the apartment next door, always calmed her.

Every night, since his wife had died, Tereza's father played his violin for hours.

Tonight, he was playing something so beautiful, the notes making her think of moonlight on water, shimmering like black diamonds.

And then a door slammed.

The music stopped. The visions of moonlight and diamonds disappeared like smoke in the wind.

A man's voice, deep and shouting. Angry . . .

"Where is it? What did you do with the painting?" It was Tereza's boyfriend—the one she met secretly, late at night. She had heard the timbre of his voice, through the thin wall, when he was alone with Tereza.

Tereza's father answered, his words too quiet to understand. Donata pressed up against the wall, suddenly, inexplicably afraid.

A thud. The sound of something shattering. A muffled cry.

"You will be sorry, old man! I will have it, and my daughter, too—my Rizhaya. One way or another. You will not stop me."

* * *

"The soldiers came for Tereza's father the next day," said Donata Kardos. "We never saw him again."

"And the painting?"

"They tore Tereza's home apart. But her father had hidden the Van Gogh and his violin with my family. They never thought to search our apartment."

"You didn't know the painting's value?"

"I did not even know it was a Van Gogh for many years. Tereza and I began to plan her escape because we were afraid they would return for her baby."

Robbie Brennan nodded slowly. "You could not know what would happen."

Donata swiped at the tears on her cheeks. "I miss Tereza still, so much. But I had Gemma Rozsa to take care of, to protect. All I knew was that I had to keep her from her father. That's why I brought her to America, changed her name."

"Tell me about your daughter."

The nun took a slow sip of her drink and gazed into the firelight. "As soon as we arrived in Austria, I took my mother's maiden name for us—Vasary—to keep Gemma Rozsa safe, to hide her from her father." She smiled gently. "Rozsa means 'Rose' in Hungarian. She had hair the color of bright copper roses, you see, highly unusual for a Jewish child but not unheard of."

"You said her Russian father called her '*Rizhaya*.'"

"Yes, it's Russian for 'Red-Haired.' Gemma Rozsa became Rose Vasary. My daughter."

"Rose Vasary . . . Why is that name familiar to me?"

For the first time, her smile was real. "Rose's grandfather, Anton Janos, was a wonderful musician. A composer, a violinist. Like Liszt. She inherited his talent and his Guarneri. Now she is a fine violinist in her own right. She's playing in London tonight."

Robbie's head came up. "Good God, of course! Rose Vasary. The violinist. No one plays Vivaldi's *Winter* the way she does."

The nun smiled. "I agree. But—" She shook her head back and forth in frustration. "Not long ago she was offered a chair with the New Russian Symphony Orchestra, on tour. I was against it, for obvious reasons. But my Rose is a grown woman now, as fiery as her hair and as headstrong as her mother was."

"You love her very much," said the priest.

"Yes. All I want is to keep Rose safe." Donata Kardos locked eyes with his. "I can still see those three soldiers, standing frozen, their silhouettes black against the sky. The flash of the rifle. A shout of agony. And I can't help wondering if it was all planned that day. Did someone *want* Tereza to try to escape? Or—want her to die?"

Robbie leaned toward her. "Because of the Van Gogh?"

She shrugged. "I trusted John O'Shea, and I trust you. I'll tell you what I know."

She looked across at the high windows, now black with night. "Anton Janos left his Guarneri violin and the Van Gogh for his daughter. They were packed in her duffel bag on the day she was shot. When Rose was old enough, I told her about her mother's love and courage, that she gave her life to protect her child. That her father was a Russian soldier. I told her about her grandfather and gave her the violin. Hidden in the case, beneath the Guarneri, we found a thin journal, a rolled sheaf of music, and a letter from her grandfather. I left all of it—the Van Gogh, the journal, sheet music, and letter—hidden in a bank vault in London for many years."

"Is the painting still there?"

"When Rose turned eighteen, I showed her the Van Gogh. I told her I was afraid her father wanted to take it from her. So we agreed I would keep it hidden until we felt safe. She does not know where it is."

"And you never authenticated the painting."

"No. I hoped John O'Shea would help me do that. But I never had any reason to doubt it was a Van Gogh. The colors, the strokes, the signature . . ."

"What about ownership, Sister? A bill of sale, a deed?"

"There is nothing but Anton Janos' word, in his letter."

Robbie shook his head. "How did a Van Gogh, painted in France, come into the possession of a Hungarian composer?"

"The letter we found hidden in the violin case tells the story of Van Gogh's provenance. Anton Janos writes that Van Gogh painted the piece in 1889 while at the asylum in Saint-Rémy. He called it *Shadow Music*. It was in a private collection for years—and then came into his possession when he was in France, during World War II."

"I'm afraid we'll need more than that, Donata."

"I know. But I only read that letter once, so many years ago. I do remember it was star-crossed." She smiled. "Pun intended. But you need to read the provenance in Janos' own words."

"I'm no stranger to the moral dilemma," Robbie said wryly. "But I must ask you this, Sister. Is it possible the Van Gogh does *not* belong to Rose?"

"If I knew that to be true, I would have returned it long ago. I believe the Van Gogh belongs to Rose. She wants it to go to a museum." Donata touched the small gold cross in the hollow of her neck, frowned. "No, my sin is that I have insisted the Van Gogh should stay hidden. I didn't want to hide it, but I thought I was protecting Rose's identity. But dangerous people will do anything to have this painting. And now the search for the Van Gogh will lead them directly to my daughter."

"You're afraid that the people who think Rose knows the painting's location will come after her."

"They already are. All we've done is argue. I no longer know what is right or wrong." Donata Kardos shook her head. "Rose is fearless. She insists on doing the right thing. Loan the Van Gogh to MOMA. Honor her grandfather's legacy by playing his music for all the world. Find her father."

"Grace comes in many forms." He took her hand. "But what do *you* want?"

"I want to keep her safe. My best friend gave her life to save her daughter. It's up to me to protect Rose now. But she no longer wants my protection."

"Perhaps there is a way to do both," said Robbie. "Although what you need is not in my wheelhouse, so to speak." He flashed an ironic grin at her as he ran a hand over the silver wheel of his chair. "But I can tell when someone is in pain. It's still my job to take away pain, Sister. So. You have given me a divine clout over the head by reminding me what I'm here for. Of course, I will help you."

"A prosecutor I know says that conspiracies hatched in hell don't have angels as witnesses."

"Ah. But angels have no memory, I'm told." He poured another Rob Roy into her glass. "Let's begin with the hundred-million-dollar question. Literally. Who else knows where the Van Gogh is now?"

"Not even Rose knows. I've shared the secret with only one other person. John O'Shea. I didn't tell him, but he figured it out, just before he left for Europe two years ago. He told me he knew. But then he disappeared..."

Robbie closed his eyes, thought of Maggie. "They say that two can keep a secret only if one of them is dead."

"That's what I'm afraid of."

"Okay. I need to read Anton Janos' letter. Where is it now?"

"My daughter Rose has it."

CHAPTER THIRTY-FIVE

ROYAL FESTIVAL HALL, LONDON

"The Maestro is out of his bloomin' mind!"

Two female musicians in their thirties were hurrying down the rear staircase of the Royal Festival Hall in London, their high heels clicking a staccato beat on the hard steps. The concert had ended some twenty minutes earlier, and now the members of the orchestra, too energized to sleep, were scattering to the hotels, coffee shops, pubs, and dance halls that filled London's popular South Bank neighborhood.

The woman in the lead, a tall, attractive brunette, waved an arm as she kept venting. "Whatever possessed him to speed up the Prokofiev tempo that way? My God, I wanted to take my flute and crash it across that gorgeous Russian face of his!" Her laughter didn't quite hide the fact that she meant every angry word.

"Slow down, Cara!" Breathless, the woman behind her gripped her violin case closer to her chest. "I would never risk my grandfather's beloved Guarneri against those granite cheekbones!"

Cara Schumann slowed, came to a stop by the gray metal stage door, and turned to look up at her friend. "Well, of course you wouldn't, Rose—but only because there are less than two hundred Guarneri del Gesu violins left in the world."

"Okay—but there are other ways to take our revenge." Rose Vasary shook her head, laughing. "Did you see that arrogant down-the-nose look he threw at the strings during the Dance of the Knights? Well, there is always poison, isn't there? It's very Russian. Maybe a very slow poison. Prolong his suffering..."

"One more reason you are my friend." Cara took a deep breath, let it out, and smiled. "Okay, tantrum over. You know I would never risk my flute either. But if anyone deserves to suffer, it's that *insufferable* Valentin Zharkov!" She pushed the artist's entrance door open and cold night air flooded over them.

Rose followed her friend out into the darkness. "You've been crushing on him for weeks, Cara. What's changed?"

The flautist slowed, shrugged. "He's not who I thought he was. Let's go have a glass of wine. Or three. Half price tonight for musicians at The Walrus Pub. I'll tell you everything. And we can plot the Maestro's demise."

Rose Vasary returned the smile as she slipped the strap of her violin case over her neck and shoulder like a backpack and followed her friend out onto Belvedere Street, which ran behind the Festival Hall. The night was dark and moonless, but, as they turned toward Hungerford Bridge and the beckoning glow of the Thames Promenade, she could see the spinning lights of The Eye against the starless sky. London's Millennium Wheel, the over-four-hundred-foot-high observation Ferris wheel above the Thames River, never failed to thrill her.

Chatting about music and the night's performance, the women turned into a narrow, cobbled side street. Passing a darkened storefront window, Rose caught a glimpse of her reflection—a slender woman bundled in a blue coat and scarf, her spiked, deep coppery hair turned to fire in the halo of a lone streetlamp. Up ahead, darkness.

In some recess of her mind, Rose registered the only car parked ahead of them on the deserted street, a large black SUV. She saw the last three letters of the rear plate—SMR, black against yellow metal. Then a shift in the dim light, a darker shape moving beyond the car. Some instinct warned her of danger, and she thrust a hand on her friend's arm to stop her.

A sound, and two men dressed all in black stepped out of the shadows.

Rose saw the glint of a knife. "Run!" she whispered to her friend. Cara whirled.

Too late.

It all happened in slow motion. The man closest to Cara grabbed her arm and slammed her brutally against the SUV. Rose heard Cara cry out in pain, saw the flute case crash to the stones.

"No!" Rose ran toward her friend, knowing only that she couldn't leave her. For a split second, their eyes met. "Get help," shouted Cara.

But now the second man sprang toward Rose, spun her around, wrenched her right arm behind her. Pain rocked through her, sharp as an ice pick.

Jesus, not my arm . . .

A rough hand clamped hard over her mouth.

She couldn't breathe!

She felt her violin case thump against her back. *Please, please don't let him get my violin . . .*

Get away.

Think!

She struggled, terrified, but could not break his grip. Panicked, unable to breathe, she raised her knee and somehow was able to wrench off her stiletto shoe with her left arm. Twisting around, she smashed the sharp heel into his face. Felt the heel sink into flesh.

He grunted in pain.

She pushed harder.

"*Tyolka!*" he whispered in Russian. His hands fell away as he stumbled back.

Kicking off her other shoe, she turned and ran, sobbing, toward the lights of the giant spinning wheel.

The pound of running feet followed her.

CHAPTER THIRTY-SIX

THE BLUE RIDGE MOUNTAINS, VIRGINIA

THE TAXI WAS pulling into the driveway.

The day had flown by. Maggie had decided to leave her car at the cabin, and now Beckett stood on the dusky deck with Maggie, Dov, and Shiloh, all eyes on the faded red cab.

A beginning. And an ending.

John Denver's lyrics floated into his head. *Taxi's waitin', he's blowin' his horn. Already I'm so lonesome I could die."*

Maggie turned to the boy, her eyes soft. "I'm so glad we had a chance to meet, Dov. It's good that you're here. These two need someone to keep them in line while I'm gone." She winked. "I'll practice the Russian you taught me. And don't forget you promised to send me your photographs of the ranch. You are going to love it there. Especially the horses."

The kid just stood there, his expression mesmerized, staring at Maggie as if she were some exotic bird. Beckett shook his head. In a few short hours she had learned more about Yevgeny Davidov than he had learned in two days. *Who knew the kid liked to take photographs?*

Beckett watched as Maggie bent to wrap her arms around Shiloh, unconsciously graceful, burying her face in the soft gold fur of his neck. The Golden's fluid eyes glistened with love as he nuzzled against her.

Yeah, she's got us all wrapped around her little finger, boy. Just walks into a room and sets everyone back on their heels. Bam! Even managed to charm this sullen, uncommunicative kid. How the devil does she do it?

Today her t-shirt said: *Instant Pianist. Just Add Coffee.*

Beckett smiled, remembering the morning's interrupted coffee, and rested a hand on Maggie's shoulder. Too thin, the bones sharp. "It's time, darlin'. You don't want to miss your flight." *Please miss your flight.* "You're *sure* you don't want us to drive you to the airport? You know I want to, the Jeep has a full tank of gas . . ."

She looked up at him, the huge emerald eyes swimming in mist. "It's much easier this way. For both of us."

He waved to the kid. "Give us a hand with the luggage, son?"

The boy threw him an icy, belligerent scowl. *Ouch, right, sorry. Not my son.*

Dov pressed his lips together and carried the luggage without comment down the steps to the taxi, Shiloh lurching along by his side with his ungainly gait.

Beckett turned to Maggie, took her in his arms.

"You're sure about this, Maggie? You really want to put all your chips on that one tiny red square?"

"No. But I've got to go. You know I do."

"I know. Sometimes we clash heads, sure, but we *get* each other."

"More than anything," she said softly, her hands against his chest. Over his heart.

He bent to her, held her tighter. "I'm better with you. You make me know what's possible. Just come home to me."

"I promise. The only truth I know is you, Michael. *You* are my home now."

"Maggie . . ." Christ, he wanted so badly to say, *Don't go.* Would she stay? He pressed his lips together and said nothing.

Maggie framed his face in her hands, her fingers brushing his eyes, his cheeks. "You would know it if I didn't love you, Michael," she whispered. "Trust in us."

A tap of the taxi horn broke the moment. Beckett smiled as casually as he could manage. "Go, now. Before I make a fool of myself. But know this. I'm not giving up on us. I'll be waiting here for you."

"I know. I'll call you as soon as I land at Heathrow."

He took her hand, raised it to his lips. Held it there for a heartbeat. Then he said, "*Mes hommages.*"

They looked at each other for an endless, silent moment. Too much to say. He pulled her against him, wrapped his arms around her, held her as if he'd never let her go.

But he did. He had to. He stepped back. He knew he could ask her to stay. But he said nothing.

One more look. Then she turned and ran quickly down the steps.

All too fast, the taxi door slammed shut. The sound of wheels spinning on gravel, her face a pale oval in the window, and then she was gone, vanishing into the melting twilight.

* * *

It was growing late, the scent of pine and spruce sharp in the air, the high cobalt night like a velvet cloak pierced by stars. Thousands of them, scattered across the sky like diamonds.

Beckett sat on the deck, his guitar in his hands, his eyes on the glimmering sparks of light that surrounded a pale crescent of moon. So many nights over the years, he'd gazed up at the star-struck heavens, searching for answers. Searching for his soul. The endless shining vault over the Afghan desert, the dark sliver of night sky through 'Nam's wet jungle leaves . . .

He didn't know a damn thing about the stars. Except that they made him question. They made him dream. Maybe the kid knew something about the constellations, but he was inside the cabin, totally absorbed in some video game. What the devil was *Fortnite*?

Beckett shook his head. Just two nights ago, he had gazed up at this mountain sky, the sight of all those stars making him feel that his future was waiting for him. Dreaming about a future with Maggie. "All I want is a home, family," he said to the stars. "This woman, with a ring on her finger . . ."

But maybe being happy was not in his stars after all. He could feel her slipping away. Now, his world just felt hollow.

He pictured Maggie's face, pale and tear-streaked, gazing back at him as the taxi pulled away. He reached down, touched Shiloh's smooth head, and murmured, "What in holy hell just happened?"

Shiloh shifted closer, his expression forlorn.

"Guess we finally know what 'gobsmacked' means." Beckett lifted the guitar, closed his eyes, began to sing Brett Young's "Mercy." His voice was low, the words spilling raw and searing from his heart.

If you're gonna break my heart, just break it . . .

If you ever loved me, have mercy . . .

Beckett stopped playing, frowned down at Shiloh.

"Do you believe in happy endings, boy?"

The Golden gazed at him as if he'd just been asked if he loved broccoli.

"Yeah. Me neither. Not anymore." Beckett shook his head. "I'm such a damned fool. Why the hell did I let her go? I should have listened to you."

He had a flash of the first moment he'd laid eyes on her, standing in violet light in a cemetery in Paris. That shocking, stunning sense of recognition.

Oh. There you are. I've been waiting for you . . .

He thought about the small jewelry box, still hidden beneath his socks in the bedroom. "She's like no one else, boy. She slipped into my soul—and I let her in. She changed me, she opened me up to life again. She took the darkness away. And now . . ."

He looked down at the Golden. "All I wanted was to say, 'Stay with me, don't go.' But you and I both know I couldn't. John Glenn's wife didn't tell him, *'Don't Go,'* right?"

Shiloh lifted his head, gave a plaintive wolf's howl.

"Yeah, that's us, all right. Two lonely guys barking at the moon."

She had told him, *The only truth I know is you.* But Beckett knew that there was her truth, and his truth—and the real truth. And the real truth could be that her husband was still alive somewhere. She could still be married to another man. A man she had really, really loved.

Christ. He ruffled the Golden's soft fur. "Damn, Shiloh, she's still in love with a ghost. On a scale of one to ten, with ten being 'I'm totally screwed'—what do you think?"

Shiloh gave a short, pained whimper, his eyes shining in the darkness.

"That's what I was afraid of. All my angels have left the building."

Beckett gazed up at the swirls of starlight, but they held no answers. And now great black clouds were rolling in. If only he could shake the feeling that Maggie was in some kind of danger. Whole damned 'he's alive thing' just didn't feel right.

"The ink on this story will never dry," he muttered.

At least the day couldn't get any worse. His cell phone buzzed; his heart leaped. Maggie?

Sugarman. Good. "Listen, Sugar, I need a cell phone number for Beatrice Falconi and—what?"

Sugar's words tumbling like sharp nails into his ear. *Has Maggie left yet? Don't let her go. Stop her!*

What the devil? "She left for Dulles hours ago. She's on her plane by now. What's happened?"

He listened as Sugarman told of a vicious attack in London on two musicians. "Mike, they disappeared from backstage following a performance at the Royal Festival Hall—by the New Russian Symphony."

The New Russian Symphony. A warning bell clanged in his head. "God damn it, Sugar! Maggie is meeting with the conductor of that orchestra tomorrow. You're saying she's in danger."

"You're not gonna like this," said Sugarman. "They discovered the flautist's body early this morning, floating in the Thames. Her name was Cara Schumann, one of my DOJ agents, my source in the orchestra's inner circle." A raw breath. "It was a brutal death, Mike. She was strangled by a noose of piano wire."

Piano wire. Beckett closed his eyes. Fear embedded in his chest like splinters of glass. A death just like Vronksy's, in prison. Just like Dov's mother, Irina, in a dirty Brooklyn alley. No getting around the connection. A *Russian* connection.

He took a hurting breath. "And the other woman?"

"The missing violinist is a woman named Rose Vasary."

"Never heard of her," said Beckett. "Dammit, Sugar, in what universe is it okay to send Maggie into a world of vicious murderers?"

"I told her not to get involved, Mike. But you know Maggie. She's gonna do what she thinks is right. And for the record, I admire her."

"*Admire* her? God damn it, Sugar, one musician is missing, another one is dead! Vronsky and Dov's mother both strangled. What the hell are you—"

"I'm on the next flight to London," interrupted Sugarman. "I'll make sure the Doc is okay."

Beckett punched the disconnect button and looked back up at the vast night sky. The moon was gone. The stars were vanishing one by one, swallowed by blooming black clouds. Then—the tiny blinking red lights of a plane, turning northeast.

Maggie?

Just come home to me, darlin'.

The huge dark clouds billowed across the plane's tiny lights. He watched as, one by one, the last stars blinked out. Until he was back in the darkness.

CHAPTER THIRTY-SEVEN

DULLES AIRPORT, VIRGINIA

MAGGIE SETTLED INTO the British Airways Business Class seat 5A, by the window. The seat next to her was still empty.

Please God, no overly friendly seat-mates tonight. She just wanted to close her eyes and forget her last glimpse of Michael, standing against his beloved blue mountains. The look on his face when her taxi pulled away. What she'd seen in his stricken eyes—the turbulence, the pain. The darkness. Her throat ached with unshed tears.

Dear Lord, what was she doing? What had she done?

She'd called Michael from the airport lounge, left a message. *I love you. Are you okay?* Damn, damn, why had she said that? Of course, he wasn't okay. Neither was she.

Maybe she'd never be okay again. You made this choice, she told herself. You have to go. There's no turning back. You have to *know* if your husband is alive.

She accepted a glass of water from the attendant and tried to slow her breathing. She needed to focus, to think about the coming days—a Master Class, her talk at the Royal Academy of London, the meeting with the Russian conductor Zharkov.

And dinner with Yuri Belankov. She needed to understand his connection to her husband. And what he really wanted from her. Was Simon right?

The eyes that stared back at her from the pale reflection in the oval window were dark and troubled.

A flurry of movement in the aisle, the faint scrape of luggage stored in the overhead, a wisp of subtle, expensive cologne—a tall figure folding himself into the chair beside her.

"I hope you will allow me to buy a beautiful woman a glass of champagne."

The voice was low, slightly accented. Intimate. She turned to her right, and her eyes widened. Dark, close beard, sculpted face, blue-tinted sunglasses. The look of a prince. She knew this man . . .

He smiled, leaned toward her. "Magdalena O'Shea, yes? I heard you play in Boston last week." He tilted up the sunglasses, looked at her with pale gray eyes that seemed colorless in the dim light. "I am Yuri Belankov's friend—Nikolai Kirov."

* * *

The cell phone rang and rang. Beckett was just about to disconnect when a woman's voice answered. "Yes?"

There was loudspeaker noise in the background.

"Hello?" Beckett raised his voice. "Beatrice Falconi?"

"Who is this?"

"This is Colonel Mike Beckett, Maggie O'Shea's friend." Again, the jarring, loud announcements, somewhere close to her phone. "Sorry, it's hard to hear above the noise."

"I'm at Logan Airport. I'm . . ." A hesitation. "I'm flying back to Greece tonight. I only have a few moments. Why are you calling?"

"You and Dane just disappeared after that night," he began.

He heard her sharp intake of breath. "What do you want, Colonel?"

"I'll cut to the chase, ma'am. You told Maggie O'Shea that her husband is alive. She believes you, but I don't. At least—well, let's just say I don't think you told her the whole truth. So I need to know what you left out. And what you really want."

"I told Maggie what I believe to be the truth about her husband. I owed it to her."

In the background, a final call for American Airlines Flight 7091 to Madrid. Beckett pressed the phone closer against his ear, trying to hear. "I just don't get it, Beatrice. You came all the way from Greece. Feels to me as if there's something more going on here."

"You're wrong."

"Well, here's the thing. Maybe you think if you could find that Van Gogh before anyone else—"

"I have money," she interrupted. "I don't need the Van Gogh."

"Then maybe someone came to you, paid you to tell Maggie this story of yours? Send her off on a wild goose chase to God knows where?"

Another announcement, closer, louder than the others. "They're calling my flight. I have to go."

"Just one more question, ma'am, please. Maggie was there with you that night, when Dane died. I have to wonder if it's vengeance you want, Beatrice. Against Maggie?"

The phone went dead.

Christ. I knew it.

Beckett sat back, felt the cold whisper down his spine. His instincts were right. Beatrice was lying.

That last loudspeaker message he'd heard was not an announcement for a flight to Greece.

Beatrice was flying to London.

PART III

"I will endure the darkness because it shows me the stars."

O. Mandino

CHAPTER THIRTY-EIGHT

THE FIRE GLOWED hot, casting shifting shadows of light and dark across the man's sweating face and clear protective glasses as he bent over the golden glob of molten glass that twirled on the end of the four-foot metal tube.

He puffed gently, shaping the glass. Paused. Puffed again, moving fast, turning fire into glass. The sound of his breaths was like bursts of muted music set against the roar of the oven. Sometimes he felt as if his breaths were trapped forever in the vessels he created.

Against the wall behind him, shelves of luminous vases, goblets, bowls, ornaments, beads, and figurines shimmered in the shadows, curved and translucent, as magic as Aladdin's cave. High above his dark head, delicate glass butterflies, sparkling chandeliers, and a mobile of stars swayed in the waves of heat that rose around him.

He blew into the tube once more and watched the golden bubble of liquid glass expand on the tip of the pipe. He spun toward the furnace, just feet away, and reheated the bubble. Then more blowing, turning, and rolling the glass on the flat stone slab. Over and over, until he lost count of the number of times he'd dashed between bench and furnace, shaping and reshaping the soft, honey-like glass.

Beneath his fingers, the curving shape of a woman's long skirt slowly emerged from the drop of molten sun, catching the light like a bronze mirror.

Damn, it was hot. He glanced toward the glory hole—the glowing chamber where he had heated the molten glass over and over—knowing it registered a blistering 2,200 degrees. He rubbed gloved hands on the stained, heavy apron. Looking down at the gleaming figure taking shape, he shook his head. *Just sand and heat and alchemy.*

Today, he was beginning work on a new figurine—a woman in a red dress, dancing, slender arms above her head, long dress billowing and floating around her. She had been appearing to him every night for the last week, in his dreams. Spinning, her head thrown back, her laughter spilling like music. Beautiful, mysterious, graceful. Who was she?

Why did he feel as if he knew her?

Why did he have the feeling he had heard that laughter before?

No. Just a dream. This was his life now. The heat, the glass. He gazed down at the bit of glass in his gloved hands. Finally, it was ready to cool and harden in the annealing oven.

When it was set, he straightened, leaning against the scarred wooden work bench, and took a deep breath. Wiping his forehead with an old cloth, he removed his glasses and gloves, smeared lip balm across his blistered mouth.

He glanced toward the windows, noted with surprise that the light outside the shop was changing, turning pink with dawn. The flames of his fire danced across the windows of the hot shop. He turned down the oven and removed the heavy apron.

Time for a shower. Tomorrow, he would begin to mold the woman. He would use copper and gold chloride to color her dress a deep, flaring red. And for her hair—cobalt oxide. He needed to find the color of a night sky.

CHAPTER THIRTY-NINE

BRITISH AIRWAYS—SOMEWHERE OVER THE
ATLANTIC OCEAN

MAGGIE LEANED BACK against the padded headrest, her eyes on the eastern horizon framed in the small oval window. The faintest red ribbon of color was spilling from the dark sky. Dawn in Europe. She would land at Heathrow in just a few hours.

Too emotional and spent to sleep, she had eaten only the small dinner salad, sipped one glass of Pinot, and tried not to see Michael's face when she closed her eyes. Looking for all the world as if he wanted to find a punching bag and beat the hell out of it.

One night not too long ago, she had awakened to see him staring up at the stars through the cabin's bedroom window. She had risen, gone to him, wrapped him in her arms.

"What's wrong, Michael?" she had whispered against his skin.

"Just dreams, darlin'. Go back to bed. I'll be along soon."

"I'm not leaving you this way. Can you talk to me?"

"It's the darkness," he said in a low voice. "You know I don't talk much about the past, Maggie. But in my dreams, I can still smell the hot, dark leaves of 'Nam. See the cold, silent night stars over the Afghan desert. I dream of going back into the darkness."

How often had she seen the darkness hovering behind those silver, stony eyes.

Last night, at the cabin, she, too, felt herself spinning back to that dark place where she had lived so long after her husband had died. The grief, the sorrow, the pain. The nightmares.

There had been that moment, as they'd climbed the stairs to the bedroom, when she'd been struck by an unsettling wave of confusion. Guilt. If her husband was alive, was she betraying him? But then she had looked at Michael's face in the shadows. It's okay to love someone again, she told herself. Love is never wrong.

Oh, Michael, I wish you were here with me now.

For one crazy moment of madness, back at the cabin, she had almost pleaded, *Come with me!* But he needed to stay with Dov—she knew he did—and her words would just have added more complications.

"It was easier when I thought Johnny was dead," she murmured. The man asleep beside her stirred at her words.

Maggie glanced toward him. His eyes remained closed.

Nikolai Kirov had made small talk during dinner, finished two vodka martinis, then set headphones on his head, leaned back, and closed his eyes.

What did she know about him from their conversation?

In his mid-fifties now, he'd told her he had come to the U.S. from St. Petersburg in the late eighties to study Russian and Eastern European History and Modern Art at Princeton. His mother had been an artist.

He'd never married; played chess and soccer. He liked poetry, and enjoyed listening to opera, especially Boris Gudenov and Eugene Onegin. His art gallery was located on Madison Avenue in New York. Paris was his favorite city—but he was traveling to London as an old friend of Yuri Belankov, to attend an auction at Sotheby's in search of several rare pieces for Yuri's new art collection.

Maggie shook her head. A Renaissance man who was totally at home in the international art world and looked like a Russian prince. Not to mention Yuri Belankov's friend. Surely it was no coincidence that he was seated next to her. But what did it mean?

She sighed. Let Simon deal with it. With all of it.

She had to be honest, face the real reason she was going to England now. Of course, she would honor all her musical commitments and promises. But the truth was, her purpose had become more personal, driven by her heart. She had to know if her husband was alive. It was all she could think about. And the only place she knew to begin was with Beatrice's story.

Maggie closed her eyes. Willed herself back to the night Beatrice had come to see her at The Piano Cat. Every word, every gesture, could be important. Beatrice had said that Dane had told her of Johnny's fate. Dane. The man who had terrorized Maggie just months ago. The man whom she believed had caused her husband's death.

But Beatrice hadn't known Dane as a killer. She'd known him as Dante, the man she loved. Maggie let her mind spin down into the soft cadence of Beatrice's voice . . .

* * *

"I met Dante last September, in Tuscany," Beatrice had said into the shadows of the music shop. *"Dante was still healing from the plastic surgery my father had performed. We became lovers. One night we were sitting on a terrace, high above the vineyards. The stars were glittering and falling all around us.*

"For such a long time, Dante's gaze was locked on those stars. Finally, he turned to me, and said, 'It is not in the stars to hold our destiny, but in ourselves.' Dante was always quoting Shakespeare—I think the words were from Julius Caesar.

"I told him that I didn't understand.

"'There is a painting, my Bella Beatrice,' he said, 'of stars so bright they will take your breath away. Van Gogh called it Shadow Music. *It disappeared during World War II. Many people have been searching for it—including myself. And a man named John O'Shea.'*

"*Your husband, Maggie, although I did not know it at the time.*

"*He told me that John O'Shea, in the course of his search for* Shadow Music, *had discovered Dante's connection to millions of dollars of stolen art.*

"'*I could not allow him to ruin my life, to send me to prison,' Dante told me. I knew Dante was deathly afraid of small spaces, I understood his fear. He confessed that he arranged for John O'Shea to have a sailing accident, in the Mediterranean near the Îles d'Or. He paid a local criminal to set explosives on the boat.*

"*But something went terribly wrong. Your husband washed up on the shore of Porquerolles, seriously injured, but* alive. *A fisherman found him, brought him to his cousin—a nurse. The man who set the bomb eventually found out that John O'Shea was still alive, and contacted Dante. Dante sent him to find your husband and finish the job.*

"*But his cousin said that your husband remembered nothing of the accident. Or of his life before. Your husband had no ID or passport when they found him on the beach. Only some Euros and two old photographs, zippered into a waterproof pocket of his windbreaker. Even so, the photos were badly water-damaged. One was a photograph of a woman on a beach, the other appeared to be a Circle of Stones.*

"*Your husband suffered from nightmares, every night. Once he told the cousin that he dreamed of a haunting painting filled with stars.*

"*Dante knew that John O'Shea had been searching for Van Gogh's* Shadow Music—*and he thought your husband might have found it. And so, he paid off the cousin, and allowed your husband to live, with the hope that one day he would lead Dante to the painting.*

"*Your husband found work in a local glass shop, and, when he grew stronger, asked for a small kiln. He began to create blown glass in the shed behind the cottage. The figurine I found in Dante's safe in Greece was one of those pieces. Dante had saved it in a box, along with the photographs and his message for you.*

"But then one night, John O'Shea stole a boat and disappeared. They tracked him to Marseilles, and then as far as Calais, before he vanished into thin air.

"We never found your husband. Or the missing Van Gogh."

* * *

Maggie opened her eyes. The sky framed in the oval window was bright blue with morning light, the green meadows of Ireland flashing by far below. Their final descent was beginning.

She felt as if she were caught in deep water, being relentlessly swept toward jagged rocks.

Was her husband really alive? Where was he, how would she find him?

Beatrice's words . . . *He was last seen in Calais.*

She thought of the photographs Beatrice had given her. His favorite picture of her—and a dark figure in a Circle of Stones. And she remembered the conversation she had had with Johnny, late one night in the music shop, when he had spoken to her of childhood summers in Cornwall. A place with stones like hooded men, just a few miles from his village. Ancient castle ruins high on a cliff. And a sorcerer's music in the shadows of the caves.

He'd taken the ferry from Calais to England, she was sure of it.

Tintagel, thought Maggie. Johnny went to Tintagel.

CHAPTER FORTY

THE RATTLE OF turbulence jolted him awake.

Nikolai Kirov's eyes flew open, heart pounding. Where was he? He took a slow breath, willing himself out of the dream. The whine of the Boeing's engines throbbed, changed. The oval window was filled with watery light. They were descending.

He turned his head slowly to the left. Magdalena O'Shea was very still, her head tilted toward the window, eyes closed. Touched by the light, she was quite beautiful in profile, reminding him of a medieval Rubens Madonna. He saw the shine of a single tear trapped under dark lashes. A long wisp of silken hair, the color of a raven's wing, had escaped its clasp and curled against her pale cheek.

He raised a hand, then halted in midair, realizing with surprise that he wanted to reach out and smooth her hair back from her face.

He shook his head wryly. Not like him at all.

He felt the throb of the deep gash on his shoulder blade, where she had stabbed him. She was his adversary, a means to an end, nothing more. The woman who could lead him to John O'Shea. Because he was convinced that John O'Shea was alive. Somewhere. And that he knew where the Van Gogh was hidden.

And yet. There was definitely something about Magdalena O'Shea...

He signaled the attendant for coffee and opened the book of poetry he'd brought with him. Byron, Shelley, Blake, Wordsworth, Keats. He preferred the imagery of the Romantic Poets to the Russian writers, saw himself as a modern-day Lord Byron, brilliant and restless—"mad, bad, and dangerous to know," as one of Byron's many lovers had described him.

His eyes fell on the words of Blake's "The Tyger."

Tyger Tyger Burning Bright. Yes, he thought, I am a fearsome creature, molded by fire. Not for the first time, he wondered why an all-loving God would create such a dangerous, frightening beast.

His eyes lingered on the line, *When the stars threw down their spears.*

Even the stars themselves surrendered their weapons rather than face the dreaded Tyger. Or perhaps Blake, too, saw his destiny in the stars?

Stars. And now his thoughts had come full circle. He closed his book and turned toward the window.

Beside him, Magdalena's eyes were closed. Suddenly her body tensed as she murmured in her sleep. Her tone was anxious, fearful.

Kirov gazed down at her, could not stop himself from resettling the thin blanket gently across her shoulders. What was haunting her dreams?

Or who?

"Tyger Tyger burning bright," he whispered. "In the forests of the night..."

* * *

She was lost.

It was foggy and very dark. The wind whipped her cape around her body, caught her hair and tossed it behind her like a banner.

Where was she?

One by one, the stones appeared out of the mist, towering over her. They looked like old men, hunched and wrapped in long cloaks, as they circled around her.

Closer, closer.
A soft sound, not more than a breath.
A dark figure, his face hooded, stepped from the shadows.
A hand reached for her . . .

* * *

Maggie jolted awake.

Good God. She turned her face toward the window, tried to slow her breathing.

She'd dreamed of the stones in the photograph Beatrice had given her. The same stones in the pen and ink drawing framed in her husband's office. The drawing was titled *Bodmin Moor, near Boscastle.*

Where she would begin her search for her husband.

CHAPTER FORTY-ONE

THE BLUE RIDGE MOUNTAINS, VIRGINIA

"PICK UP THE damned phone, Maggie!"

Beckett stood by the bedroom window, staring down at the lake. The water glowed like a warrior's shield in the morning's first light.

The cell phone in his hand was ominously silent. He'd tried three times to reach Maggie in the last hour, but only heard static and the endless ringing in his ear. Couldn't even leave a message. He was ready to pitch the damned phone into the lake.

Seven a.m. Just noon in London. What the devil was Maggie doing? She was scheduled to give an interview on music at the Royal Academy tonight. So why couldn't he reach her now? The only messages from Maggie, left while he was still asleep, had been *Landed!* and *Are you okay?*

Dammit, Maggie, he thought, *nothing* about this is okay.

He felt as if he suddenly was lugging around a box of rocks where his heart should be. Face it, old man, he told himself. You are just so damned scared you're going to lose her. If her husband is alive—what will she do? Hell of a choice.

And if he isn't . . . then someone was going to a whole effling-lot of trouble to make Maggie *think* John O'Shea was alive. Beatrice had to be in London by now. Nothing good about that, he hadn't trusted Dane's woman from the get-go. And if she lied to him about where she was headed, what else had she lied about? He had a sick feeling about this one. What did Sugar always say? *JDFR*. Just didn't feel right. And if his suspicions were true . . .

Just let me be wrong on this one.

The only easy day was yesterday, he thought, turning away from the lake. Okay, call Sugar, get his help on this one. Then coffee, strong and black. Wake the kid and Shiloh, get over to the ranch to check on his Vets, the dogs and horses.

But first—try Maggie once more. He dialed. *You've reached Maggie. Please leave a message.*

"It's me. I just needed to hear your voice." He gripped the phone. "This is important, Maggie. I think Beatrice has gone to London. No idea why, but you need to be very careful." He took a deep breath and spoke the lie. "I'm okay, darlin'. Just stay safe for me."

As he clicked off the phone, his eyes touched the bureau, lingered. Ambushed by a wave of intense longing for the woman he loved, Beckett reached out, opened the sock drawer, and slipped the small black velvet box from its hiding place.

Don't open it.

He opened it.

The antique emerald—its color the heart of a forest—shimmered at him, as intense and deep as Maggie's eyes. He'd found it in a small Parisian jewelry shop on the Left Bank, because he wanted the ring to come from the place where he had fallen in love with her. But now—

"So, Beckett, what's for breakfast?"

The boy stood in the doorway, slouching against the jamb with a "who-gives-a-damn" attitude.

"Ever heard of knocking, kid?"

"Ever heard of keeping your door closed if you want privacy?"

Beckett grinned. "Okay, points. Pancakes before we head to the ranch?"

At the mention of pancakes, Shiloh stirred, lifted his head expectantly.

The kid laughed in spite of himself. "We won't say no, right, Brigadier? Hey, what you got there in your hand?"

Beckett sighed, gestured the kid to come in. "A ring. For Maggie."

The boy moved closer, whistled. "Dude! It's . . ."

"Beautiful. Yeah." *I wanted it to be the story of us.*

Dov rolled his eyes. "You got it bad, man. Shoulda gone with her."

Beckett leaned toward the boy, spoke slowly. "I made a commitment to an old friend to be *here*. I mean what I say, kid. I keep my promises." *Most of the time.*

Dov stared at him. Finally, he said, "So, you engaged or what?"

"It's what. Didn't get to make the offer. Turns out her ex might be alive."

"*Shlya-ha!* Very Russian-folk-tale."

"Yeah," said Beckett. "That's what worries me."

*　*　*

It was cold and gray in the small Georgetown University courtyard. Father Robbie Brennan had just exited the chapel following early Mass when the woman ran toward him across the stones.

"Father!"

He stiffened, warned by the frantic voice. "Sister?" He reached out to her. "Good God, Donata! What's happened?"

She fell to her knees in front of him, her hands gripping the arms of his chair, so that they were eye to eye. She was white as an altar cloth, her eyes huge and black in the carved face.

"It's my daughter," she whispered. "The Mother House just called. My daughter was attacked in London last night. Rose is missing!"

He gripped her cold hands in his. "Breathe, Donata. Come inside with me. I'll call Simon Sugarman. We'll find your daughter, I promise you."

Standing quickly, she wrenched away from him, shaking her silvered head back and forth. "No! Oh, God, I didn't protect her! I have to get to London, I have to—"

He reached out, grasped her arm. "You're a strong woman. Find strength in your faith. Find strength in *me*."

"You! But you—"

"Never argue with an Archbishop. Just come with me."

She locked eyes with his, saw what she needed to see. Took a deep, shuddering breath. Finally nodded. "Ex," she murmured. "*Ex* Archbishop. How do we even know you're still in God's good graces?"

The priest tapped his motionless thighs. "I may still be in penance mode but I have to believe God has a soft spot for black sheep. And I'm thinking he owes me one, Sister."

Robbie Brennan was already dialing Simon Sugarman's number when she followed him up the ramp into Healy Hall.

CHAPTER FORTY-TWO

THE BLUE ELEPHANT, LONDON

IT WAS NOT yet six p.m. when the maître'd led Maggie and Yuri Belankov to a corner table in The Blue Elephant's intimate, elegant dining room.

"I lived in London when I first left St. Petersburg," said Yuri, taking in the dark wood and Thai antiques with an appreciative glance. "I surrounded myself by beauty and culture to be less homesick."

Maggie slipped off her dark glasses. "It must have been hard to leave St. Petersburg."

"Ah, Magdalena. The radiant white nights, the Winter Palace, the rolling Neva . . . the city that gave us Dostoyevsky, Nureyev—and your Rachmaninoff, eh?"

"And now Putin is drawing your remarkable country back into its repressive past."

Belankov fixed his appraising, sable eyes on her, making her think of wild bears deep in a Siberian forest. "*Da.* Now my beloved St. Petersburg is like a beautiful woman with diamonds in her ears and a noose around her neck." He shook his head. "For me, life is safer in the States."

Unable to read his expression, Maggie was not sure how to respond. Finally, she said, "Did something happen, to make you leave?"

"I spent my younger years there as a student, a violinist; some might have called me a dissident." He grinned at her. "In 1979, all I could think about was getting hold of American blue jeans. I spent some time in prison, don't ask . . . And then I was conscripted into the Army." He shrugged. "Well. The Soviets were losing control over the Eastern Bloc, yes? Mother Russia needed me. After that—upheaval, chaos, Glasnost. I found my way into telecommunications, and was quite successful. Too successful for some, it turns out."

"Were you forced to leave Russia?"

"Let us just say that the wise choice for me was to come to Washington. But lately—I find that all I want is to find a quiet place, away from the secrets and lies."

She nodded. "Beacon Hill is a refuge for me."

"Yes, you understand. I want a place where I can disappear, be myself. I've just bought an estate in rural Maryland. The Catoctin Mountains—rolling fields, birch and oak forests that remind me of Russia. Quite beautiful." He smiled at her. "And isolated."

Maggie tilted her head in surprise. "But your business is in Washington."

He shrugged. "Yes, my life is there. I have an apartment, and an office, at the Watergate. Quite the power view of the Potomac and the Kennedy Center. But the estate is not far from D.C. And I am still a Russian in my soul, Magdalena. I brood. I need forests. Quiet."

She thought of the dedication she'd seen in the book he'd written, found in her husband's office. *For my daughter.*

"Do you have family in your life now, Yuri?"

The sable eyes clouded, darkened. "Not anymore," was all he said.

She waited a heartbeat. Then, "You radiate so much energy, I cannot imagine you sitting quietly. Or alone."

The dark eyes cleared and laughter rumbled. "Ah, my cover story is blown. A true Russian never acts as if he's having a good time, eh? The truth is, when a Russian smells flowers, he looks around for the coffin. Ha!"

She shook her head at him, not sure whether to be amused or wary.

"I have found my safe place, Magdalena. The new house has good light, many blank walls. Now I want to grow my art collection. I want to surround myself with color, with beauty. With interest. I want serious pieces. The kind that make me feel. Make me think. Like your music, eh?"

"Yes. From my first memories, music took my hands, my heart. My soul."

"Exactly!" Belankov leaned closer. "I will concentrate on the Russian artists at first, but I want it all. Old Masters, Impressionists and Post-Impressionists, the Modernists." He tapped thick fingers on the table. "Monet and Renoir, they are soft, hazy, gentle—they create peace for the soul. But Van Gogh—his madness screams from the canvas, *Da*? He lived in the border town between genius and insanity."

"I know several composers and musicians who live in that same border town as well," said Maggie.

The waiter set down a glass of *Belle Glos Pinot Noir* for her and an icy Grey Goose for him. Belankov raised his glass. "To art and music, Magdalena. Both have the power to make people *feel*. I know your husband believed that as well."

Her eyes locked on his over the wineglass. "Is that why he wrote an article about you?"

"One of the reasons, I think. But you know his passion was politics as well. I think he was intrigued by a Russian oligarch, quietly subversive and haunted by melancholy, who appreciates fine art. It was a good piece of writing."

Belankov stared down into his glass, as if gazing into a crystal ball. "Like your husband, I always have been fascinated by the history, the provenance, of a beautiful painting. Who painted it? Where, when? *Why?* What was the inspiration, the passion to create it? Every piece of art has a story behind it . . . violence and death, pain and sorrow, greed, passion and love. Did it hang in a cathedral, an attic, a museum, a villa? Did the painting stay in one place for centuries? Or was it passed, hand to hand, over the years, perhaps lost or forgotten for a time."

"I feel that way about music," said Maggie. "All the old scores, some lost for decades, some never played at all. Or the pieces written during wars. Prisoners found a way to paint and write beautiful music in the concentration camps. Music and art lift the human spirit. We express our pain and sorrow, but also our dignity, our hopes and dreams. My father always said, 'Music tells our stories.' And surely art does as well." She raised her glass. "To the future Belankov Collection."

"Windows to my Russian soul." Belankov swirled the clear vodka in his glass, took a long swallow.

Maggie's slender fingers played an arpeggio on her wineglass as Simon Sugarman's warning echoed in her head. *What does Yuri want from me?*

"You play like no one else I've ever heard," said Belankov, his eyes on her fingers. "How do you do it?"

"It's hard to explain—it's as if the music takes me, and it's just me and the piano." She gazed into the dark wine. "Eighty-eight black-and-white keys," she said, "but they create a thousand colors. I fall into the music, I become someone else. Then the music ends and the magic is over and I am just Maggie again."

"'Just Maggie' is a compelling thing to be, Magdalena." He leaned in, held her gaze. "I want you to solo with the New Russian Symphony Orchestra. Valentin Zharkov is a genius conductor. A wizard." He held up his hands. "I know, I know, he is a *dark* wizard—demanding, arrogant, belligerent, impossible. Ah, but the music he makes . . ."

Belankov put a hand on her arm. "I told you we are planning a festival featuring distinguished musicians from Russia and prominent American orchestras, working together to share our musical and historical cultures. From Russia, with love. Music transcends politics, eh?"

Laughter rumbled as he took a long swallow of his vodka. "Maestro Zharkov is planning quite a challenging program—Prokofiev, Tchaikovsky, Stravinsky's *Firebird Suite*—and, of course, Rachmaninoff. You told me, Magdalena, that you are preparing Rachmaninoff's Piano Concerto No. 2. Ah, those hauntingly beautiful melodies. The swelling of those opening chords. The sounds of the bells, heard from afar. The theme is so very Russian . . ."

Maggie heard the echo of distant bells in her head—knowing Rachmaninoff was tolling a warning of approaching danger. *Don't get in over your head.*

"I'm meeting Zharkov tomorrow morning. We can talk, see how it goes. But no promises, Yuri."

"Do not underestimate Russian pride, Magdalena. Everything I do, I do very intensely." He reached out, took her hand, brought it to his lips. "You know what they say about Russian fairy tales? No happy endings. Wolves, wicked grandmothers, evil sorcerers . . . Everyone dies violently. Even the children."

CHAPTER FORTY-THREE

THE BLUE RIDGE MOUNTAINS, VIRGINIA

THE MAN AND boy stood together by the slatted wooden fence, shoulders not touching, their eyes on the horses. Shiloh, his rocking gait endearing, was some yards away, exploring the brush warmed by late morning sun.

"Too bad you don't like the water," said Beckett into the silence. "Shiloh and I, sometimes we like to go fishing after a long day at the ranch."

Dov gazed at the words on Beckett's hat. "Do fish really fear you?"

Beckett grinned. "Let's just say the fish are entertained by us."

The boy shook his head and turned away.

"Maybe you should try it," said Beckett. "Smart guy named Thoreau said that many men go fishing all their lives without knowing that it's not the fish they are after."

"I know who Thoreau is, Beckett. And I don't need to fish to know what I want."

"Look, you've had a rough time," said Beckett. "But you're here now. So how about we find you some work boots in the stable? You can help muck the stalls, exercise the horses."

"Child labor," muttered the boy. But his dark eyes gleamed with—expectancy?

"I want to introduce you to the dogs, too. They're just as smart as the horses—Shiloh would say smarter." He chuckled, glancing toward the Golden. "Labs, retrievers, shepherds. A corgi named Emma who loves kids. We're training them to serve injured Vets. The dogs sense when a person is anxious and stay close. They're intuitive, notice the physical signs of panic attacks or nightmares before you do." Beckett waited a moment for his words to sink in, then waved a hand toward the wheelchair ramps, the low basketball hoops. "Almost everyone working here is a Vet."

The boy shrugged bony shoulders with a look that said, "no big deal," and turned away.

"Hey," said Beckett sharply. "You are way out over your skis, kid."

Dov's head came up. "Funny. You seriously think street kids know how to ski?"

"Fine, so you of all people should understand this. These Vets are *not invisible*. They are men and women who have given service above and beyond to this country, kid, and come home without arms or legs in the process, disabled in mind and body and spirit. Most of the folks here have scars you can't even see, most of them are still fighting a war. The least you can do is show some respect and *see* them."

Now the boy's eyes found his. "Sorry, Beckett," Dov mumbled. "Yeah, I know what it's like to feel invisible."

"Okay, then. Because I see them, Dov. And I see *you*, too. Count on it." He squinted toward the barn, where several Vets were training the new service dogs. "Every Vet has a story to tell, kid. Their lives are real, as real as yours and mine. They matter. Ask them sometime."

The boy nodded slowly. "I'll ask." A heartbeat. His eyes moved to the horses.

Beckett leaned closer, relenting. "They're beautiful, aren't they? We have seven horses now. Five mares here, two studs in the back pasture—all rescue. Some of them were overseas. They did their service and now deserve to live out their days in peace. Six of them are doing just fine, responding to the love and care, but one of them . . ."

Dov turned toward a sinewy, too-thin dark horse standing alone at the far end of the paddock. "That one. The lonely one."

Something in his voice.

Beckett raised a spiky brow. "Yes. That one. Her name is Lady in Black. She's afraid to get close, to man or beast. One eye gone, some terrible scars. Won't let anyone here approach her. She's almost fifteen hands, and strong. But skittish, spooks easy. She'll rear up, could hurt someone. The other horses know to stay away from her. So do I."

The boy nodded slowly, his eyes bright. "What happened to her?"

Beckett gazed at the boy, decided on honesty. "Found her being prodded up a ramp onto a kill truck last month, in West Virginia."

"Kill truck? Jeez, is that what it sounds like?"

"Afraid so. A truck with slatted sides, takes the horses no one wants to the slaughterhouse." Beckett blew out his breath. "The horses sense it; they smell the fear in the others. Hooves clanging, nostrils flaring. Christ."

"You took her?"

"Well . . . I jumped from the car, shouted, ran closer. She looked right at me. She was filthy, broken, open wounds across her flanks—but somehow there was still a light behind that one good eye. A spirit, something proud. There was just something about that horse. So, yeah, I took her." He gave a faint smile. "Guy didn't want to let her go, but Shiloh and I, well, we convinced him."

The kid chuckled. "I've seen your 'Good Cop, Bad Dog' routine."

"Something like that."

The boy nodded thoughtfully, his eyes back on the black horse. "Hey, lonely girl," he murmured.

Beckett put a hand on the boy's shoulder. "I know what it's like to lose someone, kid. To be alone. Maybe if we could—"

The boy jerked away.

"For chrissakes, Beckett, I'm fine. I'm a loner, that's all. I just want to be left alone."

"And I just want to be younger. Not gonna happen."

"I don't need anyone."

"If you say so, kid. But you remind me of me, when I was your age. The truth is, being a loner just means you're lonely."

Beckett stepped away, his left boot brushing his duffel bag on the ground. "Almost forgot. Got something for you." He bent, searched the canvas, held out a small black Canon camera. "It's old, but it still works. Maggie said you might like to take some photos of the ranch and—

The kid was slowly backing away, eyes bright, his hands held out in a stop position.

"What is it with you, man? I'm not your kid! I don't want *nothin'* from you! Except to be left alone."

He turned and loped toward the barn, disappearing through the open stable doors into the shadows.

Beckett stood very still. The kid was beaten down, wounded, haunted—just like the mare, but they were both survivors. Spirited. Both had that damned light behind the eyes.

"That went well," he said into the silence.

CHAPTER FORTY-FOUR

NORTH CORNWALL, ENGLAND

IN THE SHADOWED hot shop, the glass took on a life of its own as the man breathed into the molten shape that shimmered at the end of the rod.

He had turned the volume of the opera way up, and now the swooping, soaring notes of *Aida* seemed to breathe new life, pulsing energy into the swirling figurine.

Bold and delicate fluidity at the same time. Like the woman in his dreams.

The glass taking shape in the furnace burned with scarlet light. At moments like this, he felt like Prometheus, holding his stolen fire aloft.

A hard-drumming sound caught his attention. He turned, saw the rain slashing against the windows, running down the glass like tears.

* * *

Maggie hurried down Cheyne Walk in Chelsea, searching for her key. Rain spilled like silver ribbons from the black sky, beating against her umbrella with the soft thrum of a timpani drum. Just across the road, the River Thames ran swift and gunmetal gray. Gas lamps shined, blurred and golden, as if they were flames caught inside the tangled tree boughs. Thick wisteria, dripping with purple rain, arched over the high doorway and across old brick.

Chelsea in the rain. She felt as if she had stepped inside one of her husband's beloved Impressionist paintings.

Just think of the history, she thought. All the famous names who have lived on Cheyne Walk—T. S. Eliot, Swinburne, Ian Fleming, Ken Follett, Keith Richards. Even Mick Jagger.

She had spent the evening at a classical music fundraiser for St. Martin-in-the-Fields at the beautiful old church in Trafalgar Square and then called Simon Sugarman, who had just arrived in London.

"Yuri Belankov reminds me of Tony Soprano," she'd told him. "Brash, swaggering, a larger-than-life bon vivant with an easy arrogance. And with quite a quirky sense of humor. But he's also watchful, brooding. Intense. He did talk about Van Gogh, but not specifically the missing painting. He's a contradiction, surely, but he didn't strike me as dangerous, Simon."

The bad guys don't want you to know they're the bad guys, Doc.

Simon's words echoed in her head as she remembered Belankov's dark, assessing gaze.

She found her key just as she came to the beautiful old Queen Anne house she'd rented.

But something was off.

Maggie hesitated, confused. The windows of the ground-floor flat were dark. Surely, she had left several lamps on before she'd left for dinner?

A slender, indistinct shadow appeared, then moved quickly behind the rain-washed glass, disappearing into the darkness. A trick of the light?

Her eyes locked on the window, Maggie found her cellphone and dialed Simon Sugarman. No answer.

"Meet me at the Cheyne Walk flat," said Maggie. "Hurry."

She stood a moment longer in the cold rain, then made up her mind and hurried up the path, entered the foyer, pressed the four-button code. A moment's wait, and then the painted wooden door buzzed and swung open.

She stepped into the hallway. The security lighting was very dim, the far end near the building exit draped in black shadows. *Be careful.*

Folding her umbrella, she held it in her left hand like a weapon as she approached Flat #1, inserted the oversized iron key as quietly as she could. And kept the key between her fingers just in case. She thought of the terrifying masked intruder she had surprised in Johnny's office. *I won't be caught off guard again.*

The sudden, sharp clang of a door closing at the far end of the hallway.

She flinched.

Opening the door to the one-bedroom flat, she gazed around the deeply shadowed space. Dark wood, chintz, lamps, the scent of fresh roses. The baby grand Steinway in the corner by the window. Nothing out of order.

Rain smashed against the high windows and thunder rolled across the room as the storm intensified. Maggie moved slowly into the room, tense, ready to fight.

Thunder crashed; the rain lashed like pebbles against the tall windows. A flash of lightning illuminated an almost empty glass tumbler on the small kitchen island. Maggie froze.

Someone had been here.

She thought of the figure she'd seen hurrying past the window. The slam of a hallway door. Setting down the keys, she slipped her cell phone from her purse once more. Dialed.

A huge flash of lightning bloomed beyond the window, illuminating a hooded figure hidden by a black umbrella, running away from the house, toward the river. There was something about the slender shoulders, the way the body moved. *The way a woman moved.*

Her breath whooshed out. Certain now that she was alone in the flat, still Maggie forced herself to turn on lamps and search the bedroom, the closets, the bath. *Under the bed.*

She was alone.

Okay. She would make tea, calm her throbbing nerves. She clicked on the last lamp, illuminating the kitchen. And saw the huge bouquet of red roses in a vase on the counter.

Oh God.

Johnny had always given her red roses. But then, last fall, the brutal killer named Dane had filled her rehearsal room at Carnegie Hall with hundreds of roses the color of blood. Dane, who continued to haunt her dreams. She had watched him stop breathing. So why did she still feel as if she were his puppet, dancing on the end of his string?

She thought of the dark figure, disappearing into the storm.

No, it couldn't be . . .

CHAPTER FORTY-FIVE

MAGGIE STOOD IN the darkened wings of the Royal Festival Hall, stage left, listening to the New Russian Symphony rehearse Alexander Scriabin's revolutionary *Prometheus, Poem of Fire*. She took a deep breath. Every stage had the same familiar scent—old wood, velvet, painted scenery, perfume and sweat, nerves. It was home.

Seating more than twenty-five hundred people, the renovated hall was modern, spacious, and luxurious, with beautiful woods, cantilevered boxes, and remarkable acoustics. The theater's spectacular organ, bathed in changing light, rose behind the orchestra. The organ's seven thousand pipes were the centerpiece of the auditorium.

But even the dazzling organ could not compete with the man conducting the orchestra. His fierce arm movements drew her eyes, captured her attention, pulled her in. Held her.

Looking much younger than a man in his fifties, Valentin Zharkov was tall, sharp-boned, and angular, with long, pewter-streaked hair that curled uncontrolled around the nape of his neck. A day-old beard, rough and scruffy, covered his jutting chin. She could not see his eyes from her position in the wings. Just as well, she thought.

He was dressed in jeans with torn knees, a tight black turtleneck, and Adidas sneakers. His expressive hands at once cajoling and demanding as the baton flew through the air. His movements were familiar and yet unfamiliar. She had played with many top-tier orchestras, both at home and abroad, and more recently with her father, the legendary conductor Finn Stewart, as well. She knew the dips and swirls, the plunges and boxing stance, the furious leaps and head snaps and arm movements meant to convey every human emotion—from beauty and joy to sorrow and agony, from loss, power, and betrayal to hope, love, and redemption.

And yet . . . Valentin Zharkov was in a category all his own.

Everything she had read about him—from the *New York Times* music critic, the *Times* of London, the erudite music publications—all seemed to be true. Possibly the most artistic musician in today's Russia, Zharkov defied convention—not simply conducting pieces, but conquering them, making them uniquely his own. Enigmatic, brazen, and flamboyant, with manic energy and naked ambition, he was a take-no-prisoners Maestro who somehow managed to translate every note and chord into his own musical language.

From the six dissonant opening chords—musicians called it the "mystic chord"—the *Prometheus* had taken her breath away. Zharkov had cast his spell over her.

Listening to the wondrous sonorities, she let her eyes wander over the members of the New Russian Symphony. They were mostly young Russian and Eastern European men and women, she thought, with a sprinkling of French, Spanish, British, and American musicians, just as Yuri Belankov had described.

Their faces were intense, eyes riveted on their scores, caught up in the grandeur and demands of the music. No hint of fear, or danger. No indication that two female musicians had disappeared from this orchestra just twenty-four hours earlier . . .

Except for the two empty chairs, one in the violin section and one next to the other flautists. Someone had left a single white rose on each of the seats.

Both Simon Sugarman and Michael had left messages on her cell, telling her of the missing musicians and now warning her to steer clear of Zharkov and his orchestra. Simon had cloaked his words in caution. *I don't need or want your help on this, Maggie. Don't do anything until I get there . . .*

But her blunt, beloved Michael had not stood on ceremony. *Stay the hell away from that bloody Russian and his orchestra, darlin'.*

But she was already inside the theater when she'd heard their warnings. Surely the man conducting this beautiful music could not—

Suddenly Zharkov's hands swooped down like hatchets and came to an abrupt halt. The music slid into silence.

"Ladies and gentlemen," he said in a guttural, deeply accented voice. "This music is humanity's epic journey. We are supposed to be storming heaven. Not strolling through Hyde Park on a Sunday afternoon. Where is your passion? Your *fury*?" He glared at the cellos. "And you. Catch up or leave."

He muttered something in Russian, shook his head, turned, and caught sight of Maggie standing in the wings.

She felt her stomach tighten.

"Tonight, we will play in honor of your colleagues Cara Schumann and Rose Vasary," he growled. "Curtain at 7:30 sharp. Find your fury before you return."

He dropped the baton to the music stand, leaped off the raised box, and strode toward her.

* * *

"The hardest thing in the world is to start an orchestra," said Valentin Zharkov. "The next hardest is to stop it!" Shaking his shaggy head, he took Maggie's hand, bent over it. His lips were thick, rough, hot against her skin. Then he raised his eyes to hers. An unsettling, intense black, they were heavy-lidded, secretive, and cold as a Moscow night.

He let go of her hand. "Magdalena O'Shea. I want to conduct you. Is your Rachmaninoff ready for me? We arrive in the U.S. next week."

Maggie held his eyes, willed herself not to step back. "I agreed to meet you, Maestro Zharkov, nothing more. As for the Rach 2 . . ." She thought about her search for the music's heart. Its *soul*. "It is not ready yet."

He raised a thick pewter brow as he lit a cigarette, inhaled. Smoke wreathed around them. "Learning a new piece is like moving from a familiar place to a totally different one. The Rach 2 has its own story to tell, yes? But I have no doubt you will find your way. Music is so much more than a conversation between two instruments—it is between the music and the listener. You know that music is not what you hear, Mrs. O'Shea. It's what you make others hear."

He reached for a metal ashtray set on the edge of the stage, ground out the unfinished cigarette. "I heard you play in Milan. Eckardt's *Echoes White Veil*. God Almighty! You dove right in, didn't you? No easy warm-up piece for you."

She shook her head, smiling. "*Dove* is right. *Way* over my head. I hope my hesitancy at the beginning wasn't too obvious."

"You covered. And then the music took off. It was a dizzying twelve minutes of stupefying difficulty. Ah, those cluster chords! Brilliant, modern madness. You are my *Valisisa*."

"The only Russian word I know is *Zvezda*. Star."

The dark eyes glinted at her. "Ah, you have been talking to my old friend Yuri. Valisisa is a heroine from our Russian folk tales. She was sent to find fire after all the candles went out. She was beautiful and strong and brave and, of course, after many dangerous adventures, returned with the burning coals. In a skull."

"How do Russian children sleep at night?" murmured Maggie.

"I never did." Zharkov grinned down at her. "So. Like Valisisa's tale, the *Prometheus* describes the gift of fire and light. What did you think of it?"

"I think *you* thought it was as beautiful and passionate as I did. And your cellists were perfectly on beat. Are you always so difficult on purpose?"

"Well. It never hurts to ask for a bit more fury, does it? They all will give it their best tonight, I assure you." He swept an arm toward the empty chairs. "A bad business. More to it than they are saying, not just a simple mugging. I was questioned by American agents this morning."

"Is there any word on Rose Vasary?"

He frowned, shrugged. "None. Are you sure you cannot attend tonight's performance?"

"I wish I could. But I'm attending an event at the Royal Academy."

"Yes, Yuri told me. My loss." Zharkov glanced at his jet-black Cartier watch. "A late lunch, then?"

"I have a master class scheduled for this afternoon."

"And I am not used to the word 'no.' So perhaps we could meet up with Yuri for drinks after the concert? The Beaufort Bar, at the Savoy. The champagne is excellent. Say eleven thirty, midnight?"

She gazed at him. "If I am not too jet-lagged, I will join you."

"Don't be too tired. I want to talk music with you, Valisisa. You will find your own fire and light for the Rachmaninoff, I have no doubt. Use the music to tell your own story."

Maggie turned toward the exit. "As long as there are no skulls involved," she said softly.

CHAPTER FORTY-SIX

THE SAVOY HOTEL, LONDON

IT WAS ALMOST eleven thirty when Maggie stood outside the Savoy's beautiful Beaufort Bar. She was exhausted, but after she met tonight with Valentin Zharkov and Yuri Belankov, she would be free to head to Cornwall in the morning and begin the search for her husband.

Slipping off her raincoat, she hesitated in the doorway to scan the room. Candlelight, dark wood, leather, a glowing chandelier, the soft clink of good crystal.

There. In a darkened corner, three men seated in chairs around a small table. Three men, not two . . .

Simon Sugarman's words echoed in her head. *Several people are looking for the Van Gogh, Maggie. At least three of them are Russians. They are all connected, somehow.*

She crossed the room toward the three Russians—Yuri Belankov, Maestro Valentin Zharkov—and Nikolai Kirov.

Yuri's voice boomed toward her through the shadows. "Kirov loves opera, I've never understood why. I always tell him what Shaw said. 'Opera is when a soprano and a tenor want to make love, but they are prevented from doing so by a baritone!' Ha."

Deep laughter, a seemingly genuine comradery. And then Zharkov saw Maggie and stood. "You came."

All eyes turned to her.

"I said I would try. Hello, everyone." She smiled at them, settled into the empty seat offered by Kirov and turned to him with a raised brow. "I didn't expect to see you again."

His gray eyes glinted at her. "Yuri invited me. And you know by now that I never miss a chance to be with a beautiful woman."

Maggie leaned back against the leather with an exhausted sigh and gazed at Zharkov. "Thank you for the invitation, Maestro. It's been a long night, and I'm afraid I turn into a pumpkin at midnight. But I am more than ready for one glass of the champagne you promised."

Zharkov was still in his tuxedo, now totally disheveled after the concert. His bow tie was unknotted, two dark ropes against his loosened white dress shirt. He waved an elegant hand in the air, and a server dressed in black appeared at his side.

"Bring us a bottle of *Dom Perignon*, 2009," said Zharkov, his eyes on Maggie. "I am hoping the champagne will help convince you to play the Rachmaninoff with me when we come to the States."

"It's an amazing orchestra," said Yuri. "A mirror of the old world, in the hands of a new generation. The average age is thirty, but these youngsters are graduates of Russia's great institutions, and have a remarkable maturity. And Zharkov has included many veteran musicians and soloists from around the world to bring their own intensity, insight, depth, sensitivity. To teach them how to stir the soul. Break the heart. That is why we want you, Magdalena."

"I'm intrigued," said Maggie, wondering how she was going to find the time to practice her music in the coming days. Gazing around the table at the three men, Sugarman's words flew once more into her mind. *Three Russians—all connected somehow.*

Somehow. She took a breath. "How do you all know each other?"

The men exchanged glances. "We met many years ago, as young, green soldiers." said Belankov. "*Spetsnaz*, with the Soviet Army. Mother Russia in her wisdom assigned us to the same regiment in

Eastern Europe. We were all amateur musicians—some more amateur than others—and we played together in a small band when we were not on patrol. Violin, piano, and Kirov's harmonica." He chuckled. "The three musketeers, eh?"

Maggie smiled. "More like Picasso's *Three Musicians*," she murmured. "All angles and shapes, complicated and not at all easy to understand."

"Very Russian," said Belankov. "Think of three men at an art museum, looking at a painting of the garden of Eden. The Englishman says, 'The garden of Eden must have been in England. Nowhere else will you find such beautiful flowers.' The Frenchman scoffs and says, 'No, it is France, they are nude and do not care.' The Russian just laughs and says, 'Clearly this is Russia. They have no clothes, no house, only an apple, and are being told it is paradise!' Ha!"

Genuinely amused, Maggie returned his smile.

The champagne arrived, was poured. Zharkov raised his glass. "To Yuri, for bringing all of us together tonight. And to Magdalena, whose Rach 2 will be—"

At that moment there was a click, a brief flash in the shadows. Maggie flinched, then saw the photographer lift his hand in a wave. She turned to Yuri with a questioning glance.

"Paparazzi," he muttered, adding what she assumed was a Russian oath. "Valentin Zharkov is big news here, especially if he is seen with a beautiful woman late at night, eh? That photo will be sold to the *Daily Mail* or the *Guardian* within the hour."

"It seems I am in the company of rogues," said Maggie, as she turned to Kirov with an amused look. "Since you seem to have chosen art over the harmonica . . . have you found a masterpiece for Yuri's new collection yet?"

"*Nyet*," interrupted Belankov. "I have very exacting demands. Post-Impressionist, a well-known artist, colors that jump off the canvas, an intriguing backstory."

"Is that all?" Maggie smiled. "Do you have a particular artist or piece in mind?" She felt Kirov's eyes on her in the dimness of the bar.

She turned away, her gaze finding the beautiful chandelier above them.

"Ah. You are thinking of Haydn and the Miracle," said Zharkov.

Maggie grinned, turning to both Kirov and Yuri to explain. "Haydn's Symphony No. 96 is called The Miracle Symphony because when it premiered in London, a huge chandelier fell from the concert hall ceiling and, miraculously, no one was hurt. Musicologists now say it happened during his Symphony No. 102, but it's a good story nonetheless."

Zharkov leaned back in his chair and grinned. "The perils of conducting. Dvorak fell asleep conducting his own work. Brahms forgot to button his suspenders and his pants fell down on the podium. Sir Landon Ronald began to conduct Mendelssohn, but his orchestra was playing Wagner. He fainted."

Belankov turned to Zharkov. "We laugh," he said softly, "but there is a very serious threat for your musicians now. Terrible news about the death of your flautist. A bad business. Is there any more news on your missing violinist?"

Zharkov shook his head. "I still can't believe Cara is gone. As for Rose Vasary—she is such a talent, not to mention a very determined and complex young woman. I have to believe that she will be found unharmed."

Maggie pictured the young woman she'd glimpsed playing the violin so passionately in the garden of the music shop in Boston. "Rose Vasary is a brilliant musician," said Maggie. "More than that, she is someone's daughter. We can't lose her. I have to believe she was smart enough, and strong enough, to get away, take cover until it's safe."

"Someone's daughter . . ." repeated Belankov, his dark eyes fathomless.

Maggie set her empty flute down, rose, and gazed at the three Russians. "I'm sorry, gentlemen, but the jet lag has won," she said softly, reaching for her coat.

Turning toward the door, her cell pinged. Michael? She glanced down, saw with shock that it was a message from the missing violinist they'd just been discussing.

My name is Rose Vasary. I know you are in London, and I need to talk with someone I can trust. Please meet me first thing in the morning at Westminster Abbey—The Lady Chapel, at the very back of the cathedral. For my safety, please tell no one and come alone.

* * *

It was almost two a.m. when the Russian entered his hotel room, dropped his coat on a chair, turned on the lamps. He moved slowly around the room, eyes alert and wary in spite of the several glasses of champagne. A search of the bath, the closet, beneath the bed. He was alone.

A quick check of the dresser. The drawers were as he'd left them— one not completely closed—his clothing undisturbed. No sign of an intruder.

He clicked on the radio, and the sounds of Tchaikovsky's Violin Concerto, one of his favorites, filled the room. If someone had indeed planted a listening device somewhere in the room, they would hear only the brilliance of Yehudi Menuhin.

With a long sigh, he dropped into the chair by the window. The drapes were open, the tall window filled with the deep blue of a night sky pierced by a spangle of stars above dark, angled rooftops.

She is someone's daughter. He heard Magdalena O'Shea's words like a haunting echo in his head.

It was on just such a night as this that he'd smoothed the soft down of ruby hair, and tucked the box with its tiny Russian cross under the pillow. The night he had seen his infant daughter for the last time.

CHAPTER FORTY-SEVEN

THE BLUE RIDGE MOUNTAINS, VIRGINIA

THE LAST OF the late day sun spilled across the ranch, touching the barns and fields and horses with apricot light.

Beckett sat in the Jeep, parked at the top of a ridge, his cell phone on the seat beside him. Late night in London for Maggie, he thought, hearing her words play once more in his head.

A midnight drink with three Russians at the Savoy . . . Rose Vasary is alive . . . Heading to Cornwall in the morning . . . How are Shiloh and Dov doing? . . . I miss you . . .

Christ, he missed her like crazy. Her friend Rachmaninoff surely understood that empty arms thing. But there was something in her voice, something troubled.

But right now, as much as he wanted to get on the first plane to London, he had a more pressing concern. He raised one hand to shade his eyes while he scanned the paddocks. Where the devil was Dov? His room at the cabin had been empty when Beckett checked, the old bike gone once again from the mudroom. Had the kid bolted for real this time?

Christ, let him be here.

"How's he gonna take the news?" he murmured to the Golden.

Shiloh, eyes thoughtful, stared down at the horses grazing in the paddocks. Beckett shook his head, set the Jeep in gear, and headed down the rutted road toward the ranch.

The Vets who worked for him were still busy, training the dogs in the north meadow, feeding and working the horses, mucking stalls, repairing fences, planting vegetables in the community garden. Several of the men and women, he knew, were working out in the gym specifically designed for the disabled Vets' needs.

But there was no sign of the kid. Wait. *There.* In the far paddock.

A tall, too-skinny figure. And the damaged new rescue mare, Lady in Black.

The mare pawed nervously at the ground, stamped, shook her beautiful head.

Uh-oh.

A sharp, frightened whinny as the horse reared up, front hooves flashing silver in the waning light.

Beckett swung the Jeep's wheel toward the distant white fences and stepped on the gas.

Moments later, he parked out of sight behind the barn. "Best we don't scare her," he said. "Hurry, but be quiet." He and Shiloh moved silently toward the paddock.

Then they heard the music begin, soft and beating in the cool evening air.

"What the devil?" muttered Beckett.

They rounded the corner of the barn and stopped short.

"Holy Christ."

Hip-hop music, a tune Beckett had never heard, throbbed from the boy's phone. Dov stood several yards in front of Lady in Black, gyrating to the beat. Baseball cap set backwards on his head, ignoring the horse, he moved his arms and legs in syncopated, stylized movements, bouncing from one foot to the other. Rocking hips, arms loose and swinging, bending knees. A look on his face that said, *Attitude.*

Lady in Black stood very still, watching the boy with her one good eye, nostrils flaring, her breath rising in a smoky stream. The deep scars across her chest and flank glowed like pewter swords in the light. Then, very slowly, her great ebony head came up. Her ears pricked forward. She took a tentative step toward the boy. Another.

Beckett tensed, his hand on Shiloh, ready to lunge forward. But something about the boy, and the mare, stopped him. *Neither one was afraid.*

The music pulsed into the air.

His eyes now on the mare, Dov kept dancing. Without missing a beat, he began to talk in a low, singsong voice. "Hey, Pretty Lady, we all feel alone. But you've got me, I've got you. Don't be afraid, come and dance, dance with me, Pretty Lady in Black . . ."

Her one huge dark eye glowing, the mare moved slowly toward the boy, until she was close enough for him to reach out and touch her.

But Dov just smiled and swayed to the music. One sneakered foot shooting forward, then the other. Back and forth.

A heartbeat. And then the mare put one hoof forward. Her breath, fluttering into the air. Then the other hoof, mimicking Dov.

"Good girl," whispered the boy. "Good beautiful girl."

Lady in Black responded by swinging her great dark head right and then left, as if she were dancing to the beat. Her tail swished in an arc; her long mane wafted across her single eye.

"Well, I'll be damned," murmured Beckett.

Beckett and Shiloh watched the boy dance with the horse for several moments. Suddenly, the mare stopped and stepped forward, resting her head on Dov's shoulder with a soft, blown breath. Dov stiffened. Then, very slowly, his thin arms came up to encircle the mare's neck and he held on for dear life.

The boy buried his face against the mare's sleek black head as the sky glimmered purple behind them. Watching, Beckett felt something tighten in his chest. He signaled Shiloh, and they turned and quietly disappeared behind the barn, leaving the boy and mare alone.

* * *

An hour later, Dov swaggered into the ranch office. "What's for dinner?"

Shiloh lumbered to his feet, moved in his ungainly hop to stand next to the teen. Beckett closed the financial report he'd been studying and eyed the boy. "I was worried about you, kid."

A shrug. "Just needed some space."

"I got nothing against space, need it myself. But I'd appreciate a heads-up next time so I don't worry."

"Next time?" The boy turned away, lifted up a small statue of a horse from the desk, twisted it in his hand.

"Child Services called this afternoon. There's this thing called school, kid. It's compulsory, you know? You're a minor, Dov. By law, you need foster care. Or a guardian."

The boy paled, stiffened, turned his head as if searching for an escape route. Then he turned on Beckett, his expression fierce and accusatory. "You *told* them I was here?"

Beckett held up a calming hand. "Hey, I don't need to be hauled off on kidnapping charges, Dov. Truth is, I had to check in with the Brighton Beach detective and your mom's lawyer, they needed to know you were safe."

The boy stared at him, betrayal shimmering in the bright blue eyes. "You sending me back, Colonel?"

Now or never, thought Beckett.

"Hell, Dov, what choice do we have? Unless, of course, you could accept me as your foster parent. Or guardian. Temporary, you know, just until you turn eighteen." He hesitated, his eyes on the kid. "Shiloh and I, we were hoping you might stay, help us with the horses. It's honest work, you could earn a paycheck."

"Look, man, no offense to you and your dog, but I gotta hit the road."

"You really want to do that to Shiloh? He'd miss you, Dov."

Dov looked down at the Golden. "Give me a break, man, he's a *dog*!"

Shiloh bristled and offered a low bark.

"I told you, kid, dogs are like FBI profilers. They are attuned to the people around them. Haven't you ever seen that video of the dog watching *The Lion King* and whimpering over the father lion's death? Dogs *feel*, kid! They love."

The boy squatted, put an arm around the Golden. "Sorry, Brigadier," he whispered.

"So what's the rush, s—" Beckett stopped himself. He'd almost said *son*. His breath came out. "What's the rush, Dov?"

"I don't need anyone to take care of me, Beckett."

"I get that you need to know you can take care of yourself. Take it from me, you can. But Virginia Child Services says different. If you stay here, you can have a home, go to the high school down the mountain. Work with the horses, earn some cash, save a bit for whatever's next."

"I got nothing to give, Beckett."

"Sure, you do. None of us do it all, most of us just do the best we can. Sometimes your best is just showing up."

"You don't get it, I got to find..." The boy's voice faded. He swiped the long flaxen hair back from his eyes, set his lips together with a desperate shake of his head.

"Got to find what?" Beckett stood up, came around the desk. "Or is it *who*? Talk to me, kid. This book of yours is missing a chapter. What's so important that you've got to leave? Who do you want to find? Let me help you."

"Nobody can help me, man. Maybe I should have stayed in New York. Maybe I was better off being invisible."

"Not gonna let that happen, kid. Get used to it."

Dov's eyes strayed to the window, locked on the lonely mare in the distance.

Beckett stepped closer. "I think Lady in Black needs you, kid." *And you need her.*

"Yeah." A sigh. "Maybe I could stay on to, you know, help out with the horses. Just a day or two. Figure stuff out."

"I'd appreciate the help, Dov. Especially now. Because I've got some personal business to take care of tomorrow."

"You finally found the stones to fly off to give that ring to your woman?"

Beckett chuckled. "I wish. No, but it does have to do with a woman. Her name's Beatrice. She's the reason Maggie's gone off to Cornwall, but I think she told Maggie a damn boatload of lies, and I want to know why. I need to know the truth."

Dov's head came up, his eyes anxious. "You think Maggie is in trouble? Danger?"

"I don't know. She called earlier. Asked if you've taken any pictures. Insisted she's fine, but there was just something in her voice. I think her nose is growing longer by the hour."

"Maggie—she's okay. Don't let anything happen to her, Beckett."

"Your lips to God's ears, Dov." He pictured Maggie, her beautiful face too pale when she'd left for the airport. What was she doing? He glanced at his watch once more, whistled to Shiloh, and then turned toward the Jeep. Waiting for the boy, he said, "Funny thing about not needing anyone, kid. When it comes to Maggie, sure sounds as if you've got her six."

CHAPTER FORTY-EIGHT

IT WAS JUST after nine thirty in the morning when Maggie entered the far end of Westminster Abbey, climbed several stairs, and stepped into the Lady Chapel. Separated from the rest of the abbey by elaborately carved brass gates, the small chapel glowed in the morning light. Maggie stood beneath the huge heraldic banners, totally still, caught up by the beauty. High above her, the vaulted ceiling was built in a series of carved stone fans that arched gracefully over the chapel. Sunlight fell through tall stained-glass windows, spilling across the statues, sculptures, and intricately tiled floor.

"So beautiful," she murmured, wishing, suddenly, that she could share the moment with Michael. But the chapel was empty. She glanced at her watch. Where was Rose Vasary?

Would she come?

Maggie walked slowly past the altar, stopping at the imposing tomb of Henry VII to gaze at the gilt bronze effigies of Henry and his wife. Reaching out, she ran a hand over the cool marble. "Thousands of years of history . . ."

"Just think of the coronations, the burials," said a low, musical voice behind her. "Henry VII, William the Conqueror. Mary, Queen of Scots, Elizabeth the First. Lady Di."

Maggie turned. A slight woman in her mid-thirties, wearing a Phillies baseball cap and a thick lavender scarf wrapped around her neck, stood in the slanted bars of jeweled light.

Maggie took a step toward her. "Rose? Rose Vasary?"

"Yes." The violinist tipped off the cap to show Maggie her trademark red hair. Very short, the pointy spikes were dyed with slashes of pink highlights, as bright as the stained glass high above her. Her skin was white as a first snow except for the angry purple bruises across her cheek and jaw.

Setting the cap back on her head, she said, "And of course you are the pianist, Magdalena O'Shea. I'd know you anywhere. Thank you for meeting me."

"My God," said Maggie, leaning closer to gaze at Rose's face. "You've been hurt. Do you need a doctor? Everyone has been crazy worried about you."

"I managed to get away from the men who attacked us," said Rose. She glanced around the chapel. "The bruises will heal. My friend was not so lucky. I've been hiding. I was afraid to trust anyone. But I'm so angry, Magdalena, I can't keep hiding. And this seemed like a safe place." The faintest of smiles. "As long as I keep my cap on."

"Call me Maggie. You can trust me, Rose. And Simon Sugarman. He's an American Department of Justice agent and a friend. He told me what he knows of your story. He's here in London now, too, searching for you. Your mother has been frantic with worry. You've called her?"

"Just before I came here."

"Good. How can we help you?"

Rose took a deep breath and gazed around the small chapel. "I know some of your story, too. One musician to another, Maggie—I'm scared."

Maggie put a hand on Rose's arm, drew her to a stone bench set behind a pillar. "Of course, you're scared. You were brutally attacked, Rose. So was I. That alone is terrifying. But not knowing the attacker, not knowing *why* . . . Simon just wants you to be safe. We all do."

"I know it. It's just . . . maybe I do know the 'why.' The newspapers said the attackers were after my friend Cara. But I think maybe they were after me."

"Because of the Van Gogh."

"Yes! You're not surprised?"

"Everyone I know seems to be searching for it. Do you know where it is?"

"No, only my mother knows. But someone surely thinks I know." She shook her head back and forth with vehemence. "I don't like being afraid, not being in control. It's not me. So here I am, taking control back on my terms. I refuse to be a victim, Maggie. I thought you would understand."

"Only too well. So, talk to me. Let's take back control together."

For the first time, Rose's smile was real. "I knew I'd like you. I met your husband, you know, about two years ago. Lovely man. My mother had a meeting with him, at your home in Boston."

"About the Van Gogh, yes. I found his research notes. I remember hearing you play the violin that day, in our garden. The most beautiful music. Transcendent. I'd never heard it before. It broke my heart."

Rose's eyes shined at her. "My grandfather composed it. No one has heard it but my mother, and now you. He called it *Amélie's Theme*."

"Amélie must have been important to him." Maggie smiled. "Your mother showed my husband the first three pages of the score. As a musician, I think finding Anton Janos' lost music, sharing it with the world, would mean more to me than finding that Van Gogh." She lowered her voice. "Do you have your grandfather's score with you?"

"Not here. Everything—his letter, his music, a small journal—is in a safe place." She checked her watch, a bracelet timepiece too big for her thin wrist. "I need to get to Heathrow. Somehow, I need to get on a flight for Washington. I want to go home, to be with my mom,

Donata. Donata Kardos. You said you know my story. So you know she's the only mother I've ever known."

"Yes. She and my friend Robbie Brennan are friends."

"I need to see her and retrieve my grandfather's papers. There is so much more to this story. And the missing Van Gogh." Rose shook her head. "But I'm sure my passport is flagged—and some very dangerous people are looking for me. I don't know who to trust."

"Let me put you in touch with Simon Sugarman," said Maggie. "As I said, he's a Justice agent and my friend, as well. He's been in touch with your mother; she trusts him. I know he'll get you home safely."

"Thank you." Rose looked at Maggie, leaned in. "There is something more you need to know, Maggie. I've been lying to my mother about something for months, and now I'm afraid it affects you, too."

"I can't imagine what . . ."

"It's quite a lie. My mother doesn't know that I've been searching for my father. To find out the whole truth. It's why I'm here in London."

Maggie felt her chest tighten. "You think your father is *here*?"

"Yes. I know that my father was a Russian soldier in his twenties, posted in Hungary at the end of the Cold War. Donata remembered hearing that he played a musical instrument with a local orchestra." She reached inside her blouse, held up a chain with a delicate rose-gold Russian Orthodox cross. It had three crossbars, the lowest one slanted, and glowed deep red in the light from the stained-glass windows.

The color of blood, thought Maggie with a sudden chill.

"This is the only thing I have from the father I never knew. I've been searching for him for a very long time. Maggie . . . I think I've found him. I think my father could be the man you just met. Maestro Valentin Zharkov."

CHAPTER FORTY-NINE

BODMIN MOOR, CORNWALL

"OH, GOOD LORD!"

Maggie jammed on the brake. The rented blue Renault jerked to a stop in the narrow, crooked lane as three sheep wandered slowly down the rutted path.

Four hours earlier, she had driven Rose Vasary to Heathrow and left her in Simon Sugarman's very capable hands, with the promise to reconnect with both of them in D.C. as soon as she returned.

She had been driving west ever since—on the left side of the road, no less. Thank God for the small red sign pasted to the rental's windshield that warned KEEP LEFT! Now it was getting dark. Shadows fell across the high hedges that lined the road and brushed against both sides of the car. The leaves were deep purple in the dusky light.

Impossible to pass the sheep. What were the Brits thinking?

"Shoo, damn you!" cried Maggie, rolling down her window and beeping the horn sharply. "Let me pass, or I promise, you will be woolen sweaters within the hour!"

Something in her voice must have convinced the sheep that her threat was real, and they turned as one and disappeared through a hidden gap in the hedgerows.

Maggie shook her head and edged the car forward into the dusk. She was somewhere in the far northwest corner of Bodmin Moor, just a few miles from the towns of Boscastle and Tintagel. *Bodmin*

Moor, near Boscastle was the title beneath the drawing of the Stone Circle in her husband's office.

Just take the lane behind the pub, luv, and follow it to the end. But mind the sheep.

The old woman at the village store had assured her that the stones were at the end of this road, but . . . was she lost? Was it even a road? She would just drive another five minutes, and then turn around. If she *could* turn around in the impossibly narrow lane. Damn, damn. She squinted through the shadowed windshield.

Ah. Maggie slowed the car. The woman in the village had been right after all. Just ahead, the lane opened onto a broad field cloaked in purple mist and shadows. The British called this time of day "the gloaming." A poetic word for twilight, the last glow. But soon now it would be dark. And then what?

Maggie pulled to the edge of the road. Now her only link to the modern world was the throb of the Mini's motor, the jounce and crunch of tires over the rutted lane. She turned off the engine.

The silence was complete. No birds, no wind sighing in the boughs. No lights flickering in the distance.

Talk about remote.

She shuddered, gathered her jacket more closely around her, and stepped from the car.

And then she saw them.

The stones appeared one by one out of the gray mist, tall and hunched, like cloaked elders wandering in a primeval land.

The Standing Stones.

Maggie's heart caught in her chest. She clicked on her phone's light, held it high, and forced herself to step closer.

Ancient and mystical, the silent stones took shape. More than a dozen vertical rocks, many almost eight feet tall, towered above her, circled around her. Drew her in. She had the impression that she suddenly had left her life behind and stepped back three thousand years in time, into a Celtic legend. She raised her head, listening, half expecting to hear the thunder of hooves, the clang of swords in the dying light.

In olden times, she thought, secret ceremonies and rituals had been held on altars in the center of the stones . . .

Don't go there. Holding her phone high to cast light, Maggie walked to the center, stopped, and turned slowly in a complete circle.

Yes, this was the place. The drawing on her husband's office wall and the Stones in the photograph given to her by Beatrice.

A sound, a breath behind her. A sudden movement.

Maggie spun around.

A figure, hooded and darker than the shadows, stepped from behind one of the stones.

She'd seen him in her dream. Maggie stood frozen as panic sliced through her.

The figure, hidden by a long, cowled monk's robe, walked slowly toward her through the mist.

"Don't come any closer!" She tried to shout, but the words rasped low with fear.

The figure stopped. She glimpsed a shard of a man's face beneath the hood, bony and pale in the darkness.

"Who are you?" she whispered.

Very slowly he raised his left hand. The sleeve of the robe fell back, and she glimpsed the sharp silver glint of steel.

Oh God, a knife . . .

For a long moment they stared at each other.

And then, without a word, the man turned and ran, disappearing into the stones and shadows.

CHAPTER FIFTY

BOSCASTLE, CORNWALL

SOMEHOW, SHE FOUND the old inn.

The village of Boscastle was only three miles north of the Standing Stones, but the drive on twisting, unmarked roads through the now pitch-black night was impossible. And all the while the man in the Standing Stones hovered on the edge of her mind. Who was he?

Even more unsettling, for the last two miles of the drive, headlights hovered in her rearview mirror. Sometimes closer, sometimes dropping back when she dared to speed up. Maggie couldn't help but wonder if she was being followed. By the stranger on the moor?

Sugarman's warnings echoed in her head. Just pretend you have no reason to be scared, she told herself over and over. Just keep going.

The last mile was a steep, narrow, hold-your-breath drop into the village of Boscastle. But now, finally, she was settled in The Bridge House, a two-hundred-year-old B and B in the charming Cornish fishing port nestled close to the coastal cliff path. The small cottage she'd rented, at the rear of the property, was warm and welcoming, scented by the peat fire in the hearth and a jar of spring flowers on a wooden table. A cat the color of oranges slept on a pillowed chair drawn up to the fire. And against the far wall, a small upright piano waited for her touch.

Maggie turned away to gaze out a mullioned window. It was full on dark now, too black to see the cliffs. But she could hear the roar of distant waves beyond the village, and knew that somewhere out there, just a few miles to the south along the coast, Tintagel was waiting.

The place her husband had loved as a boy.

It's a jagged, rocky headland, Lass. Shrouded in mists, spilling into the Cornish Sea. I have a photograph of it, in my office. Legend has it that King Arthur was born in Tintagel. It's said that Merlin's cave is hidden beneath the castle's ruins, at the base of the cliffs. I always imagined I could hear Merlin's music in the shadows . . .

Tintagel. She would find her way there, first thing in the morning.

But for now, the lights of the ancient stone buildings and arching footbridges in the village flickered beyond the window and reflected off the river. She would take a walk after she'd had the tea and light supper that the motherly innkeeper, Mrs. Whitcombe, had prepared. Maybe she would find the pub her husband had mentioned and show Johnny's photograph to the locals.

And then—Rachmaninoff. She'd chosen the inn because of the upright piano. Her fingers tingled as she thought about the music.

* * *

The furnace roared.

The man stood in the small workshop, sweating and breathing hard, surrounded by the familiar jumble of rods and pipes, chemicals and metal tools. Shelves of glass objects shimmered in the firelight. There was a sharp, burning smell in the air that mixed with the scent of the nearby sea.

His mind was whirling. Hard muscles tensed beneath his shirt.

He forced himself to slow his breathing, still his pulsing body, calm the nerves that skittered across his skin. Trying to slow his heartbeat, his eyes focused on the long, hooded robe that hung next to his blue jacket by the door.

He reached for the selenium, and watched the pale glass on the end of the rod turn to a deep, rich ruby. His hammer made a chiming sound. Waves of heat washed over him.

The glass spun, glowing like a garnet, taking on shape . . .

His hands stilled. It wasn't working. He couldn't get the woman's face, so pale against the Standing Stones, out of his mind. Beautiful, compelling. Familiar. He had a flash of huge eyes, dark green in the shadows, widening in fear.

Who was she? Why did he feel as if he knew her?

Damn the woman!

An image flew into his mind. *A dark room. A woman, naked, lying on a bed. Smiling at him. Long hair tousled, wild, the color of midnight. Eyes as green as the rolling moors in springtime. The soft strains of a Mozart sonata. Long curtains stirred, and she rose, crossing to the window. She stood awash in moonlight, her body glowing with gold and shadow. And then she turned to him . . .*

The glass in his hand crashed to the floor, scattering bright scarlet shards across the stones. He had to get out, into the night air. Maybe a pint or two at the pub. Voices, music, laughter.

Especially music. Somehow, he felt the need for music tonight.

Anything to get the woman's face out of his mind.

Who was she?

*   *   *

The Black Cobweb Pub, set on the edge of the river, was smoky, crowded, and pulsing with music. Maggie sat at a small, scarred wooden table, her back against a stone wall that had to be at least a century old, listening to three aging Irishmen sing "Whiskey in the Jar." Fiddle, Tin Whistle, Flute, Pipes. She smiled, shook her head when asked to dance, and sipped her Guinness. Just as good as Pinot, she thought, finally beginning to relax. Maybe better, here in Cornwall.

The old room was full of shadows, the air swirling with the scent of peat fires, tobacco, and dark beer. Above her, cracked mugs and pottery hung from rafters stained black by decades of smoke.

She gazed down at the photograph on the table. Her husband smiling at her, his beard red and wisping against his neck. Oh, Johnny . . . She'd shown his likeness to the bartender, the musicians, several of the guests.

No, luv, sorry, never seen this bloke.

Slipping the photo into her purse, her thoughts returned to the man in the Standing Stones. Oddly enough, as she thought about him now, he seemed less threatening. I intruded on his place, she told herself, taking another sip of the Guinness. He seemed just as shocked to see me . . . maybe more so. He meant me no harm, she thought.

And he was the first to run off.

If only Michael were here. He was always the levelheaded, rational soldier—choosing head over heart, not like she did—and he would have had a perfectly good explanation for the man in the stones.

She reached for her phone to call Michael just as a small ping caught her attention. Sent by Yuri Belankov, it was the paparazzi's photograph of Maggie with the three Russians in the Savoy bar. She grinned, and with a few clicks sent it on to Michael. *An oligarch, a Russian prince, and a maestro walk into a bar . . .* she texted. *Clearly, all is fine, but I would rather have been in the cabin with you in my arms.*

Another sip of the Guinness, and then she would go back to her room and Rachmaninoff. She would—

Ice tingled along her spine. A sudden sense of . . . something. As if someone was watching her. She searched the faces in the crowd gathered around the small stage. Wizened men in caps, women wrapped in scarves and bright woolens, clapping and swaying in time to the fiddles. No one interested in her. Imagination.

She pushed the half-finished glass of Guinness away with a sigh, dropped several pounds on the table, and gathered her jacket. The walk back to the inn was short; the night air would clear her head. And get her ready to take on Rachmaninoff once more.

Maggie stepped outside, hesitated in the sudden quiet. The air on her cheeks was cool, damp, and smelled of rain. Mist brushed the bushes, the pines, rising like ghosts in the night. She could see the blurred lamps of the inn, just across the river. Clicking on the small flashlight, she set off. Several cats darted through the shadows on the deserted path ahead of her.

After a few moments, the lane divided. Left or right? She couldn't remember which way she'd come.

Damn. Turning left, she walked for several yards, then heard the rushing murmur of water. Saw the narrow, one-car bridge that arched over the dark river.

Oh, no.

Maggie stopped. She had suffered from nightmares and a desperate, paralyzing fear of water since her childhood. And then her husband had drowned in a faraway sea. *God.* No wonder she refused to swim or even go near the water, wouldn't even board Michael's old rowboat on a calm day. The only time she'd ever *chosen* to go into the sea, it was to save a little boy.

She closed her eyes. That memory was still very much with her— the freezing cold, the darkness, the terrifying, crashing waves, pulling her down into the depths. Not being able to breathe . . .

Turn around. Find the main road.

Retrace her steps? Don't be ridiculous. It's just a small bridge, not the sea. Get on with it.

Maggie pulled her jacket more tightly around her, squared her shoulders, and stepped onto the narrow bridge. It was made of wood, clearly very old, and seemed to sway slightly under her weight. She hesitated, gripped the railing tightly, and found herself gazing down at the black water that tumbled and flowed swift as rapids beneath her. Swollen by spring rains, the river rushed under the bridge, deep and menacing. The innkeeper had told her that the village was built on land where three rivers met, and spring floods were not unusual.

Maybe she should have turned around, maybe she should have—

A sound.

A car engine, muffled, but louder than the water. Behind her. Coming closer.

She spun around. Just darkness.

Out of the corner of her eye, a blur, something darker than the night. Moving fast.

Time slowed.

Suddenly twin headlamps lit the night, blinding her.

The car appeared like an animal lunging out of the shadows, put on speed. Aimed right at her.

The sharp edge of panic sliced like a knife through her chest.

Doesn't he see me?

Too close, too fast. The car swerved, hurtling toward her.

Trapped by the low railing of the bridge, she turned and began to run.

A screech of tires. The car roared onto the bridge.

No room! She cried out, flung herself against the railing, felt her phone fly from her fingers. Saw the dark, hooded figure of the driver. Glimpsed a pale profile just as the railing cracked, gave way.

And then she was spinning, flying over the railing, falling into the blackness as the car rushed past.

CHAPTER FIFTY-ONE

BOSCASTLE, CORNWALL

MAGGIE HIT THE water hard.

The weight of her coat pulled her down, the black river closed over her head.

She couldn't breathe!

Cold, so cold.

The racing current took her, hurled her along, body spinning.

So dark.

Which way was up?

God, God, I can't breathe!

She kicked wildly, desperate. *Hold your breath, get out of this coat.*

She struggled with the jacket, clawed at the buttons.

Tumbling down, her shoulder striking something sharp.

Choking, the water pulling her into blackness.

Please, God.

Michael's voice calling to her. *Fight, darlin'!*

And then she was free of the jacket. Thrashing arms, kicking legs, lungs bursting.

Blind! Too dark, too dark . . .

No breath left.

Spinning down.

Arms around her, strong. Lifting her up.

Breaking the surface. Air! Great, gasping breaths.

A man, pulling her through the current to the shore.
Michael . . .
She felt herself lifted, settled gently on dry earth.
Coughing, gasping, choking up river water.
A warm hand on her cheek.
She opened her eyes.
Lights, flickering shadows. A man's blurred face above her.
I need you, Michael.
A whispered word.
Blackness.

* * *

Some thirty-five-hundred miles to the west, at the ranch in Virginia, shadows were beginning to lengthen as the sun began its spiral toward the horizon.

Michael Beckett squinted up at the sky. Just after four p.m. The day, and the longer night, stretched out ahead of him. What was Maggie doing? He glanced at his cell phone, uneasy. No new messages. Why was he so anxious?

He looked down at Shiloh and frowned. "You think she's okay, boy?"

A deep, baritone growl.

"Yeah. Me neither. I should have listened to you. I should have gone with her."

The Golden simply stared at him, his liquid eyes saying, *Got that right.*

Beckett reached down to ruffle the deep gold fur. "Yeah, okay, I know she loves me. But love is never that simple. Emotions don't play by the rules, you know that. She loved her husband, can't deny that. So if she finds him . . . there's no certainty who she'll choose. If only I . . ."

He stiffened as a menacing coldness washed over him. "Christ. Something's happened to Maggie. Something bad."

He fumbled with his phone, punched in her number.

Broken buzzing, static.

He dialed again. This time he called British Air.

*   *   *

He was on the long, winding security line at Dulles Airport, fuming and ready to jump the barriers, when she called.

"Michael? It's me."

"Maggie!" The relief washed through him, overwhelming. "Christ, darlin', are you okay? I knew something was wrong. I've been crazy with worry."

"I'm okay now. I'll tell you everything. I promise I'm all right."

Like hell you are.

Her voice, deceptively light. "Why do I think you're at the airport?"

"Where else would I be, Maggie?"

"Go home to the cabin, Michael. To Dov. I'm fine, I'm wrapped in one of those soft cotton hotel robes you love so much and I'll be safely asleep before my head hits the pillow."

He heard the forced amusement in her voice, pictured her in the robe.

"It's what's *under* the robe that I love," he murmured. "But you're distracting me on purpose, Maggie. Tell me what's happened to you."

"I fell into the river. Someone fished me out."

"You fell into a *river*?"

"The good news is, I dropped my purse and phone on the bridge before I fell. Can we talk about all this in the morning, please? Now, I just need to sleep."

"Come home to me, Maggie. Just get on a plane, first thing tomorrow."

"Just one more day, Michael. I'm going to Tintagel tomorrow. I have to know, you know I do, I've come this far. But I'll be in your arms Thursday night."

"Speaking of *arms* . . . I listened to your concerto last night. I had no idea Frank Sinatra stole "Full Moon and Empty Arms" from Rachmaninoff. Made me feel so close to you. But, Christ, Maggie, how do you play all those notes?"

She laughed. "Just two more days, Michael. Then no more empty arms for you."

"Maybe you could bring that robe home with you, darlin'."

He knew she was exhausted, he could hear it in her voice, and so he disconnected. Let her rest, they would talk tomorrow. But, Christ, a river? He knew how terrified she was of water. Had she fallen, as she'd said? Or been pushed.

He reached once more for his phone. All bets were off, now. Maggie was in danger, and where the hell was Sugar? Christ, he should have listened to his instincts, gone to England with her. The tigers were coming out of the forest, and Maggie was in the crosshairs.

What had Churchill said about the tigers? He closed his eyes, tried to remember the words. *Dictators riding to and fro, upon tigers which they dare not dismount. And the tigers are getting hungry.*

He dialed Sugar's number. Yeah, the tigers are getting hungry. I want Maggie out of there. Now. It's too damned dangerous.

Tapping his fingers with impatience, he listened to the distant ringing and tried not to think about Maggie, struggling in the river. His fingers stilled.

Someone fished me out.

Who the devil had saved her?

CHAPTER FIFTY-TWO

ST. JAMES PARK, LONDON
WEDNESDAY

SHE WAS ALIVE! No thanks to him.

Clicking off his cellphone, Kirov strode through St. James Park, heading toward the Thames. The idiot he'd hired to follow Magdalena O'Shea had lost her. And then someone had run her off the bridge. She could have drowned. And then where would they be?

He uttered a low Russian curse. Someone else was after her. Who? He would leave for Cornwall within the hour.

He left the park, turned toward Big Ben. Eight chimes boomed above him. He was late. His friends were not going to be pleased.

* * *

Warmth, sunlight on her face.

Maggie stirred. Opened her eyes.

It took a moment to realize that she was in the cottage, in a bed beneath a soft down comforter. Not—

The river!

She bolted up, looked around the room. Had she been dreaming? No. She'd been walking back to the B and B. Gotten lost. There was a narrow bridge. A car. A car that had aimed at her, grazed her, pushed her into the river. She couldn't breathe, she was drowning. And then . . . What?

The man. A man had rescued her. Not Michael. A stranger.

A jolt of fear. Her eyes swept the small cottage. She was alone.

Think, think what happened next.

The man had bent over her. She'd lost consciousness. And then...

Then she'd awakened to the voice of the innkeeper. Mrs. Whit-combe, fussing, murmuring, helping her into a warm nightgown and robe, calming her with hot tea. Her purse and phone had been found on the bridge. She had called Michael, needing to hear his voice. And then, finally, she had slept.

Maggie drew her knees to her chest and tried to calm the wild hammering of her heart.

A chill washed over her as she remembered the rain-blurred figure outside her Cheyne Walk apartment in Chelsea. The roses.

And then—the man hiding in the Circle of Stones, the headlamps that had followed her across the moor to Boscastle. The unnerving sense that someone was watching her later that evening at the pub. The roar of an engine as a car hurtled toward her on the narrow bridge. *Toward* her. Not imagination this time.

She closed her eyes. That glimpse of a pale face. A man? Or a woman?

She was in someone's sights. Time to call Simon and tell him everything.

Her thoughts returned to the moment she'd fallen into the river. The cold, the paralyzing fear, the heavy coat, pulling her down. She gripped her knees tighter and rocked back and forth, fighting for breath. You're okay, she told herself. You're okay.

I'm not okay.

Strong arms around her...

Maggie stiffened. What happened to the man who rescued her?

She would ask the innkeeper, as soon as she was dressed. She closed her eyes. Tried to remember, tried to see his face. All she could remember was a voice, low and desperate.

What had he said?

She wasn't sure, but—oh, God, it had sounded like . . .

Lass.

* * *

The wooden sign on the road leaving Boscastle said: TINTAGEL 3 Miles.

Maggie slowed, remembered at the last moment to bear left at the roundabout. It was almost noon, the sun flashing off the windshield. She adjusted her sunglasses and headed southwest.

She'd risen at dawn, played Rachmaninoff for almost three hours. The third movement was finally taking shape. Including Michael's "Full Moon and Empty Arms" melody. God, it was so beautiful. Then tea and breakfast scones with the innkeeper, who believed Maggie had accidentally fallen into the river. Maggie had shown her the photograph of Johnny. Now the conversation swirled once more in her head.

You saw the man who brought me home last night, Mrs. Whitcombe. Please, did he look like the man in this photograph?

Ach, wee one, 'twas well after dark when a booted foot kicked at me door, and there he was, himself so handsome and standing there in the candlelight, water dripping down his face, holding you in his arms. Like a Romance Hero from one of my books, he was. And you so lifeless and pale as my Ma's lace curtains. My goodness, I didna know what to think . . .

You took such good care of me, Mrs. Whitcombe. I'm forever grateful. Was my rescuer like the man in this photo? Did he give you a name? So I can find him, to thank him.

He was that tall, luv. But clean-shaven, his face a wall of bones, a strong chin like me Da. And not red hair, you see, but white—long hair the color of snow that curled around his neck. And eyes that were dark in the shadows, wild with worry. He carried you to the bed, he did, laid you down as gently as if you were a babe. Take care of her, he said. And when I turned, just like that, he was gone.

Long white hair . . . Maggie pictured her husband's dark red hair, the soft, curling beard. The intense blue of his eyes.

Another roundabout, another sign. Two miles to go.

Maggie knew where she wanted to go. Driving out of Boscastle, she'd stopped at the local glass shop on the cobblestoned High Street. The artist did not recognize Johnny's photo, but she'd offered, *I've heard tales of a new hot shop run by a talented bloke near Tintagel. I think the shop is called The Glass Blower . . .*

The Tintagel headland appeared in the distance, lit by sunlight.

CHAPTER FIFTY-THREE

TINTAGEL

MAGGIE DROVE INTO the village of Tintagel, a small and unremarkable town set on barren land just half a mile inland from the sea. The wide main street, Fore Street, was a jumble of fourteenth-century and modern homes and shops, stone churches and cemeteries, an old post office, a toy museum. Horses, their hooves clattering on cobblestones, pulled laden carts past tourist shops offering "everything King Arthur."

And the tourists were everywhere. Crowds and busloads of them, jostling and spilling off the narrow sidewalks into the streets. She was thankful she'd chosen to stay in nearby Boscastle.

Finally, she found a tight place to park in the gravel drive of the King Arthur's Arms, asked directions to The Glass Blower, was told to head up Vicarage Hill toward St. Materiana's Church and graveyard.

But the lane is too narrow for cars, Lass. 'Tis a hike you'll be doin', and surely not for the faint of heart.

Okay, at least she was wearing her Nikes. Shaking her head, she turned, saw the sign just steps away. *Merlin's Cave. Unsafe at high tide.*

A small arrow pointed toward a steep footpath that descended to the beach from the cliff path just beyond the village shops.

Merlin's cave . . . Her husband's words slipped into her head. *I always went to the caves in the morning, when the beach was empty, to listen to Merlin's music.*

A small detour wouldn't hurt.

The path, narrow and rocky, wound precariously down the side of the cliff. It was slow-going, but Maggie finally stepped onto the beach below Tintagel's cliffs.

She gazed at the stony crescent of sand. The air was cold and smelled of salt and seashells. The only sounds were the shush of the waves against the sand and the high cry of the gulls soaring along the cliffs above her. No tourists. She was alone.

Another sign at the edge of the sand warned that high tide closed off the small beach and filled the caves with rushing seawater. She gazed at the dark, restless sea, felt the thrum of fear along her nerves. A small wave crested, foamed close to her feet. She jumped back, out of reach.

No more close calls with water, she thought. Last night was more than enough. But the tide was coming in. Hurry.

Just down the beach, the mouth of Merlin's cave yawned darkly. She'd read that it passed right through the cliff beneath the castle, to the other side. Crossing the sand toward the cave, she suddenly felt another strum of nerves ice down her spine, as if someone had his eyes on her. She stopped, turned. No one behind her on the beach, but several people on the footpath just beyond the sand. A family, a teenaged couple, a lone man looking out to sea. A slender woman in a long dark coat.

No one seemed to be interested in her.

She turned back toward the cave, gave a sharp gasp as she found herself looking directly into Merlin's sightless eyes.

Stepping closer, Maggie saw that the sorcerer's bearded face, with its blank stone eyes, had been carved into the rock by a local sculptor. At that moment another wave broke across the sand, reaching for her Nikes.

Closer to the cave, the seawater broke against the rocks, echoing against the dark, shadowed walls of the cave like music. She hesitated, listening. Johnny had spoken of a sorcerer's music in the shadows.

She could almost see the robed wizard lifting a child from the frothing sea and carrying the once and future king deep into the cave, disappearing into the mists of legend.

She looked up, and saw a glimmering light reflecting gold against the rocks deep within the cave. A torch, a lamp, a flashlight . . . Someone was in there.

As she moved across the sand toward the flickering light, a wave surprised her, soaked her Nikes. Stay or go?

She heard Michael Beckett's voice so clearly in her head. *For once, darlin', choose head over heart!*

She pictured his face. She'd promised to be careful.

A wave frothed over her ankles, the water stinging like sharp ice. *Go.* With one last look at the quivering light deep inside the cave, she ran back across the sand toward the footpath. As she began the long climb, she swore she could hear the echo of Merlin's music, calling to her from the cave's shadows.

Shadow Music.

* * *

Half an hour later, Maggie was climbing Vicarage Hill, toward St. Materiana's Church and graveyard. The Glass Blower shop couldn't be too far now.

She gazed out at the bleak, ancient scenery. A lonely, brooding landscape. The towering cliffs, the distant castle ruins floating in the haze high above the village, the bare, rolling hills. Sheep and donkeys wandering among tilting, broken stones in a centuries-old graveyard. No tourists here, just a handful of hikers scattered over the hills, a shepherd in the distance, a family on the steps of the old church. Someone had left a bouquet of yellow flowers by an ancient grave.

Once again, Maggie felt as if she had dropped back in time.

A small turn-off, just ahead. A hand-painted wooden sign, *The Glass Blower*, pointing right. A road that disappeared over a low rise of open land.

She took a deep breath and turned to the right.

* * *

The hot shop was an ancient stone cottage not much larger than a garage, set in a stand of pines bent by the sea winds. The door was closed. There was no sound of a furnace, no sign of smoke curling above the sharp incline of roof. Only the distant thunder of surf and the call of seabirds under the high clear sky.

Maggie knocked, waited. Knocked again. Peered in the dusty front window.

The shop was dark, but she could make out a bench, tools, a long table, shelves lining the walls. The glint of glass, catching stray beams of sunlight that filtered through high windowpanes.

Was that a shadow, moving across the rear of the shop?

She took a step back, called "Hello!" Counted to ten.

Set her hand on the knob and eased open the door.

"Hello," she called again. "Anyone here?"

She stepped into the shop.

The air smelled of fire and smoke, sharp chemicals, sweat and coffee. Somewhere in the back, drifting on the shadows, the strains of classical music. Prokofiev. *Romeo and Juliet.*

Shadow Music, she thought, and smiled.

Her eyes adjusted to the darkness, and she gazed around the room, drawn to a wide shelf that held some of the most beautiful, intricate blown glass she had ever seen. A turreted castle, set high on a cliff. A crystal sword set in a faceted sphere. The kings, queens, and knights of a chess set, fashioned of glowing glass. A concert grand piano. A mobile of spinning chromium-yellow stars.

She lifted a necklace of teardrops from a metal stand, held it up. Even in the dimness, the heavy pieces of amethyst glass shined with an inner light.

A soft footstep behind her.

Maggie turned. A tall figure stepped out of the shadows. She gasped, backed up against the table. Before she could run, he crossed the room to her, wrapped strong arms around her, caught her against his chest, and bent his head to hers. She saw a flash of blue just as his mouth covered hers in a kiss that was long and slow and yearning.

* * *

Time seemed to stop. Their lips, locked together, became the spinning center of the world.

Her knees turned to water; her body vibrated against his. For a moment of electric shock, Maggie's arms went around his neck, her mouth answered his. And then reason returned, and she put her hands on the man's chest, pushed him away.

"What the hell do you think you're doing?"

She wrenched away, stumbled back against the table, heard the quick shattering of glass.

The man stood frozen. Very slowly, he tipped back the hood from his jacket. Maggie took a step forward, her eyes on his face.

And found herself looking into her husband's lightning-blue eyes.

CHAPTER FIFTY-FOUR

TINTAGEL

"Johnny?" whispered Maggie. She took a step closer, her hand coming up to touch his scarred cheek. "Johnny, oh God, is it you?"

The blue eyes gazed down at her, shining and unreadable.

"My name is Prospero," the man said slowly. "Folks around here call me Pros." He moved away from her hand, ran his fingers through the long white hair. "I didn't mean to frighten you, Lass. I don't know why I kissed you. Well, except who would *not* want to kiss you, you are that truly beautiful. But of course, that is no excuse. I . . ." He turned away to gather the shattered glass on the table. "I had no right to do that. But I meant no harm. Forgive me."

"You just called me *Lass*. Don't you know me?"

He stopped, turned to stare at her, finally shook his head. "The truth? You are as familiar to me as a breath. But . . . no. I don't know you. I've seen you only in my dreams."

* * *

"It was *you*, last night, by the river." Maggie sat on a wooden stool in the small kitchen, her eyes on the man who called himself Pros. "You pulled me from the water."

He handed her a mug of hot tea. "Aye," he acknowledged. "I couldn't let you drown, now, could I? A man can't lose the woman of his dreams . . ." He grinned, that cocky, devil-may-care grin she remembered so well. But his face was so much thinner, sharp-boned and scarred.

"Somehow, I knew it was you." She cupped her hands around the tea. "Were you following me?"

"Seems I could ask the same of you, Lass."

She nodded, chagrined. "*Touché*. At least I can say thank you for rescuing me."

The deep blue eyes fastened on hers. "There's an old Irish saying, Lass. If you save someone's life, it belongs to you forever."

Something stirred in her chest. "Be careful what you wish for," she said, not sure if she was talking to him or herself. And then, "It's true I came to Cornwall to find you." Her head came up. "Were you the man I saw at the Standing Stones?"

"That was *you*? I didn't realize. I go often. There are over one thousand stone circles in Britain, but these—I sense that they have some meaning to me, something to do with my past . . ." He shrugged. "I didn't mean to frighten you."

"But you had a knife."

"Holy Mary! A knife? No, Lass, it was a tool for blowing the glass."

"Of course," she murmured. Glancing at the bright, swirling pieces he'd set on the kitchen shelves, she said, "Your glass is so beautiful. It's sculpture, art."

He smiled at her. "I think of glass blowing as a dance between heat and gravity. And the occasional spark of madness."

She lifted a six-inch-tall figure of an angel, wings furled, on bended knee. One side of her body was bathed in gold light, as if illuminated from within. The other half was in shadow.

"She is exquisite." And then, looking closer, "Her left wing is broken."

"Aye. I fashioned her the way she appeared to me, in my dreams."

"The colors make me think of music."

"I'm glad my pieces please you."

She held out the angel, but he shook his head. "She's yours now. To protect you, if you need her."

"Oh, I couldn't . . ."

He waved a hand at her. "Too late." He smiled. "So, you like music, then, as well as the glass?"

Sudden tears filled her eyes, and he shook his head. "It seems we have much to say to each other, then, and not all of it easy. So come with me now. We'll sort out everything in the sunlight."

He handed her a silver helmet.

"What's this?"

He grinned. "I live on the edge of the world, Lass. The townspeople don't want my fires and chemicals too close, and I like being alone. How do you think I get around?"

He wrapped her angel in soft tissue, settled it in her purse, and then led her outside to a beaten-up motorbike of indeterminate age and color parked on the side of the cottage. Setting a black helmet on his head, he thrust a leg over the seat, turned on the engine, and waited for her.

Shoot me now, thought Maggie. Taking a deep breath, she settled onto the rear seat and slipped her arms around her husband's waist.

"Plus," he shouted over his shoulder, "you never see a motorbike parked outside of a psychiatrist's office, do you now." And with a roar of the Yamaha's engine, they raced off across the hills toward Tintagel Castle.

Maggie closed her eyes and held on, too aware of her husband's body pressed against hers. He's lost weight, she thought.

He parked in the carpark. "This way," said Johnny into the sudden silence, heading toward the castle ruins high above them. Maggie gazed up at him, this man beside her who was at once so familiar and yet no longer recognizable. She had no idea what to say. Where to begin.

And so they walked in silence, not touching, toward the cliff walk—each lost in their own thoughts and questions.

High above them, the wild geese flew in long, undulating skeins across the sky, their wings catching fire in the sunlight. Ahead of them, the Tintagel cliffs rose steeply, narrow steps winding up the rock toward the stone remains of the castle. Cats were everywhere, wandering over the harsh, moss-covered hills.

"You must have a name, Lass," said Pros finally.

"Maggie. Magdalena O'Shea." She waited, watching his face hopefully.

"Maggie. Aye, the name suits you. It's familiar to me . . ."

She held her breath.

"The classical pianist," he said suddenly. "Is it you?"

Her chest tightened. "Yes, I am that Maggie O'Shea," she said softly.

He nodded, smiled as he read aloud the words on the t-shirt she wore under her open coat. "'Eat, Piano, Sleep, Repeat.' I should have known. I love your music, Maggie O'Shea. You create magic out of air. Your emotion transports me to another place."

"I'm glad," was all she could manage. She thought she was going to faint.

They'd come to the first set of stone steps that climbed the cliffs— twisting like vines, irregular, narrow and steep. He took her elbow, his sudden touch sending shock waves rippling down her skin. "Mind the stones," he said in the low-timbred baritone she remembered. His bedroom voice . . . Oh, God.

"History runs deep here, Maggie," said Pros, his eyes raised to the high, stark promontory that jutted out into the crashing Cornish sea. "Layers and layers of it, wherever you look. A six-hour drive from London takes you back fifteen hundred years." He waved an arm toward the ruins high above them. "The Arthurian saga is especially fascinating. His castle, built on the most absurdly romantic headland one could imagine. Uther Pendragon seduced the Duke of Cornwall's wife there, and she gave birth to the once and future king. Legend has it that Merlin was standing on the rocky shore when the babe was borne inland on a fiery wave. The cave is down there, just below us. It's said Merlin raised Arthur in that crystal cave."

"I was there this morning, on the beach by the cave, looking for you. There was a lantern's light reflecting against the rock walls."

He grinned down at her. "Were you now? You're a brave one—it's barely reachable even in low tide. No, I wasn't there; it must have been someone else." He gazed toward the edge of the cliff. "But I hope you heard the music of the cave."

"Merlin's shadow music." She smiled. "I did."

He nodded, pleased. "But the story of Arthur isn't true, of course. This castle dates from the thirteenth century, almost seven hundred years after King Arthur is supposed to have ridden over these hills with his Knights."

"If King Arthur didn't live, he should have," said Maggie, remembering an evening when Michael had shared the Winston Churchill quote while they watched an old movie based on the Camelot legend. A sharp stab of guilt washed through her. Michael. What was she going to tell him?

The truth. Whatever that truth was . . .

She began to climb the steep, uneven steps. The staircase was irregular and precarious, without railings, demanding her full attention. The man called Pros was right behind her.

"Hundreds of steps, but I won't let you fall. And the view is worth it, I promise you," he said. "We'll talk at the top."

She tilted her head back to look up at the dizzying zigzag of stone steps and wooden bridges. "If we still have breath," huffed Maggie.

CHAPTER FIFTY-FIVE

TINTAGEL CASTLE

BREATHLESS, MAGGIE STOOD with Pros on the blustery headland, the stark, harsh landscape of sea and rocky cliffs spread before them for miles. Behind them, the ruins of a medieval castle, glinting silver in the light. Far below them, waves crashed against the shore. The haunting cry of the seabirds soared on the wind.

"It's beautiful," said Maggie softly. "So lonely and wild. Just the wind and the stones and the roar of the sea. It's music. You can really believe in the magic and legends of knights, sorcerers, a boy-king—all in a long-gone past."

"And yet it's surprisingly intimate, isn't it?" said Pros. "Come, Maggie, sit over here with me." He drew her to a high, flat stone. They sat, surrounded by wildflowers that grew from the crevices in the ancient rocks. A gray cat, clearly well fed, wandered over, curled in the grass at their feet.

Maggie looked up at the man next to her, staring at his face. Searching for the romantic, larger-than-life man she had known in this white-haired, thoughtful stranger. Somehow, he'd gone through fire and survived. And now, like his glass, he was chiseled, harder. Burned and reborn as someone else. His voice scattered her thoughts.

"So, Lass, you've come a long way to find me. And surely not because you have a love of blown glass. You have a story to tell, and a complicated one at that. I see the sadness in your eyes, like green glass trapped under water."

"You always were a poet," she murmured.

He stiffened. "Do we have a past together, then?"

She gave him a faint smile. "Yes," she said simply. "It's clear you don't remember me. I'll tell you everything you want to know. But first, will you tell me what you *do* remember? How you came to be here, what happened to you?"

His breath came out in a long sigh. "You're right about my memory loss, Lass. All I know now is this place, the name I gave myself, and the molten glass . . ."

"I'm a good listener," she told him. "And this is a good place to tell your story."

* * *

"I suspect I was a good sailor in my other life," he began with a grin and a lift of a snowy brow.

"You were. You had a beautiful forty-foot sailboat called *The Green-Eyed Lass*. It's in dry dock on Martha's Vineyard." She waited. "Any bells?"

He shook his head. "None. But—*The Green-Eyed Lass*? No doubt you were my inspiration."

"No doubt at all," she admitted. "Although I'm terrified of the water."

"More and more intriguing. Because the last thing I remember is water. Sailing a boat, alone, in the Mediterranean Sea off Hyères—it's a port town near Marseilles."

"I know it well. I spent two weeks in Hyères when you disappeared."

"Ah. I see. You thought I was dead. Drowned."

She felt the sharp, terrible grief rise in her throat. "Yes."

He put a gentle hand on her arm. "I'm sorry, Lass, for causing you such pain. There was a storm, you see. Lightning, thunder, black smashing rain, ten-foot swells. I remember that. And I remember a sudden, huge flash of light, a terrifying bang. An explosion, I think. Fire. I went spinning through the air, down into the darkness." He looked blindly out to sea. "I still dream of it. The cold. Fire on black water. The drowning."

"So do I. Sometimes I'm trying to find you in the water. Sometimes I'm the one under the sea, spinning down into darkness." She shuddered. "How did you survive?"

"A fisherman found me, washed up half-dead on the shore of an island just off the coast. Porquerolles. One of Les Îles d'Or."

"I took a ferry to all three of those islands when you went missing, searching for you."

"Did you now. But it's no wonder you didn't find me. The fisherman's cousin was a nurse. He brought me to her place, an out-of-the-way vineyard hidden in the island's wild interior. Pine forests, eucalyptus-scented paths, the hot beating sun, and only the click of the cicadas breaking the quiet." His eyes found her. "When I woke up, it was to a brutal fog of pain, and no memory. A head injury, they said. Retrograde amnesia." He swept the long white hair back from his face to expose an angry, four-inch scar that curved from the crown of his head down his right temple.

"Oh God."

"After the first month, I chose a name for myself."

Shaken, she tried to smile. "Prospero. From *The Tempest*?"

He nodded. "Shakespeare's Duke, sent in a small boat to die in a storm at sea, only to survive in exile on a tiny island." The grin, wider this time. "It seems I was a lover of Shakespeare in my other life as well."

"You were. All things literary, in fact. You are—were—a very successful investigative journalist, in Boston. You also loved chess, and lobster, abstract art, good scotch, and the Red Sox." She smiled. "Not necessarily in that order."

"This man from your past sounds like quite a fine bloke." Low laughter rumbled in his chest. "I do love chess and a wee splash of Macallan's single malt in the evening. And who doesn't love the Red Sox?" He saw the look on her face, and leaned in. "No, Lass. Not memories. Just . . . a knowing."

She closed her eyes. "But you never contacted the authorities, let them know you were alive?"

He looked away. "Losing your memory is a terrible thing, Maggie. It strips you down to nothing. You don't know who you are; there is no constant in your life. I was very sick for months. And then the nurse told me only that I'd been in some bad trouble . . . and more trouble was the last thing I wanted."

"And so you left the island."

"Not right away, no. When I got stronger, I found work at a small hot shop just outside of the town. I didn't know my own name, but somehow, I knew how to blow glass. As if I'd been born from fire."

The explosion, she thought. "Your grandmother taught you. Summers, when you were a boy, here in Cornwall."

"Did she now. That's a memory I surely want back. And it helps to explain why I'm here." He looked over at the ancient stones, then down at the sleeping cat. "I stayed on Porquerolles for eight months. Except for the sailboat and the storm, my only memories— or dreams?—before the accident were of Cornwall. The Stones, this place. Somehow, I knew it. And so I came, hoping it would bring my lost memories back." He shrugged. "Well, that didn't happen. But now, here you are. Will you tell me my name, Maggie, and what I meant to you? What we meant to each other?"

Her eyes locked on this stranger, looking at her with her husband's deep blue eyes. "Your name is John Patrick O'Shea. You and I were married for ten years." She reached out toward the long wisps of white hair. "Your hair was deep red then. And you had a beard." *But your eyes are still the same—the startling, astonishing blue I remember.* "You always brought me roses. You called me *Maggie-mine.*"

He nodded slowly. "And now I'm thinking we must have been truly, madly, deeply in love."

"Truly, madly, deeply doesn't begin to cover it."

He nodded, stood up. Held out his hand. "Then come with me, Maggie-mine. You have your own story to tell. And I am in dire need of a drink. We'll go to a place I know. I hope you like Indian food? God knows the only way to survive English food is to eat Indian whenever possible."

"Still the quirky sense of humor," she murmured.

This time she took his hand, and together they began the long descent down the ancient stone steps.

CHAPTER FIFTY-SIX

THE BLUE RIDGE MOUNTAINS, VIRGINIA

MICHAEL BECKETT DISCONNECTED his phone and moved to his ranch office window. His beloved mountains were dark blue against the dome of sky.

This was the fourth New York City hospital he'd called in the last three hours, after Sugar paved the way with their Administrations for his questions. The woman in the Records Department at Lenox Hill Hospital on East 77th had just confirmed his suspicions.

Yes, there were records of a Beatrice Falconi and a man named Dante admitted to the ER on October 30 of last year. *Two* admissions. Beatrice Falconi was discharged three days later. No other records for the man named Dante could be found. There was no death certificate.

Maggie's words, describing that night, spun through his head.

Dane stopped breathing. Then, within seconds, the EMTs arrived. It was chaos. We all were rushed to different hospitals . . .

Dane could have been resuscitated in the ambulance.

Christ, thought Beckett. I have to warn Maggie.

Had Dane survived?

* * *

"So, Maggie O'Shea, do we have any children, you and I?"

Maggie sat across from her husband in the crowded Indian restaurant on Tintagel's High Street. A basket full of hot naan was in the center of the table, the air fragrant with the scents of cardamom, nutmeg, cumin, and roasting chicken.

She set down her glass of Pinot and lifted her cell phone, thumbed through the photos until she found the picture she wanted, held the phone out to him.

"You have a stepson, Brian, and now an adorable grandson, Ben. I was a single mom when I met you. But Brian became your son in every way." She smiled. "They're in California, visiting the other grandparents."

John O'Shea gazed down at the photo, his expression bemused. "Imagine that," he said softly. "Two fine boyos. Now there's a memory a man doesn't want to lose."

He glanced away, swiped at his eyes, cleared his throat. Focused on a bright, contemporary painting framed above their booth.

"You always loved art," she said into the silence.

He turned back to her, his white brows raised. "Did I, now? Well, that explains it."

"Explains what?"

"Why I was so drawn to Fondation Carmignac." Seeing the blank look in her eyes, he added, "A French museum on Porquerolles that opened to great fanfare last year, with a world-class collection of contemporary art. Ruscha, Warhol, Lichtenstein—postwar giants. The gallery is built beneath a historic villa, the sculpture garden has a mirrored maze. Talk of it has been reverberating throughout the art world."

"Art is one of the reasons I'm here. Missing art."

"I see." He leaned toward her, across the table, eyes locked on hers. "And the other reasons?"

"For more than eighteen months, I've believed my husband was dead. Then last week, a woman named Beatrice came to see me. She brought me a small blown-glass figurine and two photographs she'd found in Greece, hidden in the safe of the man she loved. She told me you were still alive. His name was Dane." She waited.

No reaction, no hint of recognition.

He took a huge swallow of whiskey. "Was it the figurine with the night-black hair?"

"Yes."

"I wondered what happened to it." And then, the spark of realization. "It was *you . . .*" he murmured to himself. "I told you, Lass, that I've dreamt of you. Well, dreamt of a beautiful woman with wild black hair like yours. It's why I fashioned her from the glass. But I thought you existed only in my imagination. And now—perhaps they were not dreams at all, but memories."

Maggie nodded slowly. "Perhaps. But—" She took a deep breath. "That explosion you remember on your sailboat. It wasn't an accident or caused by the storm. You were writing a story about lost and stolen art worth millions of dollars and a vicious, murdering art thief named Dane. He thought you were going to expose him. He paid a local criminal to plant a bomb on your boat."

Her husband listened in silence, jaw clenched, blue eyes hooded.

Finally, he said, "So this man Dane tried to kill me." He turned away, but not before she saw the disbelief flash in his eyes. The fury. The pain. And something more. Something that frightened her.

"He succeeded, then, didn't he?" Pros said. "Because he surely took away my life."

"Oh, Johnny," she whispered, reaching a hand across the table toward him. Stopped when she saw him stiffen. "I'm sorry. Of course, you prefer Pros."

"It's the only name I know, Maggie. Your story is a world to take in, for sure." He tried to smile at her, failed. "Well, you have my attention, Lass. Just point me toward the bloody murdering bastard."

"He's dead, Johnny—I'm sorry, *Pros*. I saw him die myself."

The blue eyes darkened, stayed on hers, their expression unreadable. She registered the furrowed brow, the angry set of jaw and broad shoulders. "So I don't even get my revenge," was all he said. "Tell me about the missing art."

"In your old life, you were friends with a Department of Justice agent named Simon Sugarman. Sugar. He came to me last week, told me you were working on the story of a missing Van Gogh just before you disappeared. Another painting of stars. He asked me for your research notes."

"And did you find them?"

She thought of the stranger in his office, the brutal attack. "I found your notes, and more." She told him the story of a lost Van Gogh—another starry night—called *Shadow Music*, of a woman named Donata Kardos and an infant girl born in Cold War Hungary who grew up to be a brilliant violinist named Rose Vasary.

There was no spark of recognition when she mentioned the names.

"There are several men looking for the Van Gogh, Johnny. Dangerous men. Some of them might suspect you are alive, that you know where the painting is hidden—and that you can lead them to it. You've got to watch out for them."

"I can't tell them what I don't remember. But I'll heed your warning, Lass."

And then he surprised her.

"Van Gogh's stars," he said under his breath. "I've dreamed of stars as well, Maggie. Great bright yellow shapes swirling across a cobalt sky." He leaned toward her. "I fashioned a mobile of stars, back at the hot shop. I thought it was because of the dreams, but maybe it was because I saw that painting you describe. I'll show you the stars, before you leave."

Leave, she thought. *I've just found you again, and now you expect me to just—leave?*

CHAPTER FIFTY-SEVEN

TINTAGEL

"THIS CAN'T BE easy for you, Maggie."

It was after seven p.m. They stood in the shadows by her car, not far from the restaurant.

"Easy?" Maggie gazed at the night sky shimmering above them. "Grief tears you apart, Johnny, it strips you down to nothing. My life caved in when I thought you'd drowned. And now—everything I've believed to be real for these last eighteen months, well—it's not."

"Aye, unreal. Not unlike the way I'm feeling myself."

She put a palm against his chest. "I'm so sorry this happened to you. It's so damned unjust. So *wrong*."

His smile was gentle. "I chose quite an exceptional woman in my other life, it seems. But it was *another life*. I'm okay with this new life, Maggie. I'm comfortable in my skin here, it seems to suit me. I don't know what I lost. But you do. *You* are the one who has sorely grieved, who has carried all the pain for both of us. I see it in the way you look at me, the deep sadness in your eyes."

"The hardest thing about losing you was that I also lost *me*, Johnny. I lost both of us."

He reached out, touched her face. "But grief also exposes what's hidden inside. I see a brave and loving woman, Maggie. In spite of all that's happened to you—I don't think suffering has changed you so much as revealed your courage and grace."

Suddenly afraid of the storm of emotions, the feel of his very alive hand on her skin, she took a step back. "Johnny . . ."

He hesitated. "Come back with me to the hot shop. Will you stay, Maggie? I have an extra bed in the cottage. I won't bother you. I just feel as if we're not done. You feel it, too, Lass, I know you do."

He sees through me, she thought, *as if I'm made of one of his glass figurines.*

She shook her head. "Yes, I feel it, of course I do. But—" She reached out as if to touch him, then dropped her hand. "You and I, we've just had our worlds turned upside down. This is huge, life-changing—a roller coaster of emotions for both of us. We need time to breathe, to think about what comes next. Find some clarity. How will our decisions change us—change our *lives*—and the people who love us?"

"'Tis wise you are, Maggie O'Shea."

"Truthfully, what I need right now, more than anything, is music. My life is spiraling out of control. I just need to go, Johnny. I need to let all these feelings out, put them into the piano. Find some solace in all the chaos of my life."

He nodded slowly. "A back-from-the-dead husband who doesn't remember you is surely a bit of a shocker." And then, "There's something you haven't asked me yet, Lass."

She gazed up at him in the new darkness, her heart thudding like a hammer in her chest. "Will you think about coming home with me, Johnny? See our old life in Boston, your friends and colleagues? Meet your stepson, your grandson? You could be seen by a doctor there, a specialist in amnesia. Boston has a renowned medical community."

He gestured toward the open land behind them, the low hills disappearing into purple shadows. "This is the only home I know now, Lass. You were right, I need to think, for as long as it takes, about what is next for me. What I want."

"Yes, I understand. Of course you do. If you come to Boston, your life surely will change completely. And ..."

"And yours would as well." He leaned toward her. "I got on a sail-boat one night and woke up on a French island with no memory. But while I've been gone, your life went on." He took a step closer. "We haven't talked about the elephant standing here between us." He grinned. "Two elephants, actually."

He tilted his head down toward her. Even in the falling dark, his eyes still glowed that astonishing color of the sky. "You are a beautiful woman, Maggie. And you don't wear a wedding ring, so I'm thinking maybe you've found a way to move on with your life?"

She was very still. "I was so broken, Johnny," she whispered. "I lost you and my music. I could barely get out of bed. I didn't know how to go on. I just knew I had to find a way to pick up the shards of my life."

"And someone helped you gather those shards."

She stared at him. "Someone did, yes. A good and noble man. A man who wants to make the world a better place."

He nodded. "I thought so." He raised his hand, touched her cheek. "There is an amethyst glass necklace in the shop. Perhaps you saw it?"

"I did. It's beautiful." *And here comes the other elephant.*

"It's made by a woman who lives in the village. Her name is Kayla. She's an artist; she creates jewelry. And I, well, we ..."

"You've moved on as well," she said, her thoughts on the intricate necklace. *Of course he has.* A deep breath. And then, "Do you love her?"

"It's too soon to know for sure, but—aye, I think I do. And I think you might love this man—this good and noble man—back in America."

"I do."

"And yet," he whispered, "there is surely something between us, Lass. Something unfinished. Like a piece of music."

"And yet," she acknowledged.

"We will talk then, in the morning? I'll call you, early." He stopped, looked down at her. "Would your husband have wanted vengeance, Maggie, for all that was taken from him?"

She looked into his eyes. "I don't know," she said honestly. "But he would have fought for what was right."

"Fair enough. I will think on all of it, Maggie. Knowing the past would change my life, a life I've come to love. So the true question is—do I *want* to know my past?"

Unable to answer, she turned away, and disappeared into the black Cornwall night.

* * *

He watched her drive away, until the twin taillights vanished like dark water into the shadows. He stood for a long time, thinking about the beautiful woman with night-black hair who had suddenly dropped into his life.

Play for me, Lass. Tonight I want to hear Scarlatti.

The words flew into his head, drifted like smoke in the air. Bloody hell! Where had that come from?

From his past.

No, impossible. Oh, aye, she was beautiful enough. Smart, clearly gifted. Vulnerable. But he didn't remember her. And yet . . . there was just something about the woman. Something familiar, sensual. Tender. A connection he felt, just couldn't name.

He turned with an oath, revved the bike's engine, and roared into the night.

An image of fire on dark water smashed into his thoughts. The man I am now, he thought, the only man I know, was born in fire.

I need to turn on the fire, he thought. I need to blow the glass tonight. Pour a stiff Macallan's. Like Maggie O'Shea needs her music, I need—

He pulled up to the cottage, turned off the engine, looked up. The door to the hot shop was open.

He ran up the steps two at a time, through the door.

Glass crunched under his boots.

He clicked on the lamp. Froze.

Someone had been in the shop, searched through his things. Drawers and cabinets, opened, emptied. Benches upended; his tools flung to the floor. Sharp shards of brightly colored glass scattered like a terrible mosaic across the stones.

For a long time, he stood very still, his eyes on the broken glass. Thinking about his broken life. About everything taken away from him. About the stricken look in a beautiful pianist's eyes. And like a dam suddenly bursting, the need for vengeance thundered over him, icy and fierce, crushing everything in its path.

Finally, he took a harsh breath, reached for his cell phone.

"Game on," he murmured.

* * *

Ambushed by the intense rush of emotions, all at once, that crashed into her like ocean waves, Rachmaninoff's chords tumbled from Maggie's fingers. The third movement, *Allegro Scherzando*, was a monster to play. She felt as wild and troubled as the music, and threw her whole body—her whole being—into the notes.

He is alive. My husband is alive! But he doesn't know me.

The chords were ominous, lurching out of control. Like her life . . .

God, God, how did I not know he was alive? I let him down, I should have known . . .

She felt the fierce anger flowing through her arms, her fingertips, spilling onto the keys.

What could I have done? What should I have done to find him?

The music hurtled forward, mirroring her devastation.

Just hearing his voice, seeing those eyes . . . How do I deny the old feelings? The love.

The notes spilled out, burning the air around her.

Oh, God, what now?

Finally, she came to the beautiful, sensuous melody that music lovers around the world recognized as "Full Moon and Empty Arms." Moonlight flooded through the cottage window, surrounding her in a pool of trembling light and shadow.

Empty arms.

Emotion overwhelmed her, found its way into the music.

Now the face that took shape in her mind as she played the notes was Michael Beckett's, not her husband's. She felt Michael's nearness, so close that she could reach out and touch him. See those beautiful stone-dark eyes. He had that way of looking at her, so intensely, as if no one else was in the room . . .

Her fingers crashed to the keys, froze.

The echo of the music shimmered in the air. Then silence.

I'm finally finding the music, she thought. *But I'm losing myself.*

Her head dropped to her hands, now so still on the keyboard.

What am I going to do?

PART IV

"It is not in the Stars to hold our destiny, but in ourselves."

Shakespeare

PART IV

CHAPTER FIFTY-EIGHT

GEORGETOWN, D.C.
FRIDAY MORNING

MAGGIE HAD TRAVELED all day Thursday and fallen sound asleep on the sofa in front of the fire not ten minutes after arriving at the cabin. Michael must have carried her upstairs to the bedroom. When the morning sun woke her, he already had left for the ranch. But he'd left her hot coffee, muffins, and a single white lilac.

Now, exhausted and jet-lagged, Maggie stood by another fireplace, this one unlit, in Father Robbie Brennan's Georgetown brownstone. Behind her, Simon Sugarman paced and Donata Kardos sat on the small sofa, head bowed, reading while she waited for her daughter, Rose, to join them.

The soft whir of a wheelchair. "I'm thinking coffee will help," said Robbie, rolling to Maggie's side and holding up a steaming mug.

She took the coffee gratefully, wrapped cold hands around it. Gazing at the dark clouds spilling across the window, she said, "I'm not sure anything can help me right now."

"That's the jet-lag talking. I know this has been a tough trip for you, Maggs. But you'll be on your way back to Captain America within the hour. He's really what you need."

"That's *Colonel* America." Maggie smiled, then shook her head. "Michael is going to want answers, Robbie, and I still don't have any to give him. I don't want to keep hurting him." She waited, then gave the priest a faint grin. "Isn't this the moment when you always give me your Thomas Aquinas wisdom?"

Robbie narrowed his eyes and shot her his best apostle look. "How about, 'To love is to will the good of the other'?"

Maggie just stared at him.

"Okay, maybe not. I'm afraid that Tommy fell a bit short when it came to affairs of the heart. It happens to the best of priests, you know." His eyes found Donata, rested on her bowed head for a moment. "But there is always the chance for a miracle."

"The way things are going," muttered Maggie, "if my miracle happens, I'll probably be turned into a pillar of salt before the day is over."

The front door buzzed and swung open. Rose Vasary strode into the room carrying a bright azure-blue violin case. The short spikes of her hair burned hot pink in the late morning light.

Donata Kardos closed her book, stood, and wrapped her daughter in her arms. Watching the two women was like watching the final scenes of a silent movie. Maggie smiled as she texted Michael. *Rose arrived, now the pieces should come together. Will be with you as soon as I can. xo*

Simon Sugarman found a chair, set his elbows on his knees, and leaned toward the four people before him. "You all are one hell of a team," he said softly. "All committed to finding the truth. To doing the right thing. I'd want you on my side any day." He turned his gaze on Rose. "We've gotten you safely back to the States; you've reconnected with your mother. It's time we talk about your grandfather and the Van Gogh."

Rose nodded, gazing at the people gathered around her. "My grandfather Anton Janos left me four priceless gifts," she said. Lifting the blue case, she flicked the catches, released the protective leather straps, and withdrew a beautiful violin crafted of spruce and maple. "Most important to me, my grandfather gave me his love of music. This was his violin. It's a Guarneri del Gesu." She held it out, her fingers clasped around the instrument's graceful neck. "You see the small Roman cross on the wood? There are fewer than two hundred Guarneris in the world now. The sound is darker, more sonorous than a Strad. It suits the music I play."

Rose set the violin gently on the chair and removed two slender bows. "But you all are here because of my grandfather's story. The pages I have are copies, of course. The originals are in a safe deposit box."

Reaching into a padded accessory compartment at the rear of the case, she withdrew a thick sheaf of papers and held them toward Maggie with a soft smile. "For you, my friend, the scores for my grand-father's music."

Maggie caught her breath and turned pale. "Anton Janos' *music?*" she whispered. Accepting the papers, she gazed at the score, touched the penciled staffs and notes with reverence. She hummed a few chords, put a hand to her heart. "This is the music I heard you play in my garden in Boston."

"Yes." Rose turned to the others. "It's a gorgeous, haunting violin concerto. My grandfather called it *'Amélie's Theme.'*"

Maggie's head came up. Music tells our stories, she thought. "Who was she?"

Rose held out an envelope, nodding toward Sugarman. "This letter will explain everything. Of course it's written in Hungarian, but my mother taught me the language so I will translate into English for you. My grandfather wrote this in Budapest in 1985, just before he disappeared. It's his handwritten account of how he came to possess Van Gogh's painting *Shadow Music.*"

Rose sat down next to her mother, unfolded the letter, and began to read aloud.

My name is Anton Janos.

CHAPTER FIFTY-NINE

BUDAPEST
1985

THE LETTER BEGAN.

My name is Anton Janos.

I am a violinist, a composer, and a new grandfather. I survived a war.
And now I am the guardian of an exquisite Vincent van Gogh painting
titled, Shadow Music.

    This is the story of Shadow Music, *but it is my story as well.*

    I am a Hungarian Jew, born in Budapest in 1921. My mother taught
me to play the violin before I could talk. Music was my first language.
Even today, now in my sixties, I still dream in music.

    Toward the end of World War II, in 1944, almost 600,000 Hungar-
ian Jews were deported, most to Auschwitz, and murdered—including
my friends, neighbors, and my parents and two younger sisters. I survived
because my parents had sent me away years earlier, to study music in
Paris. It is a story I've never told.

    I am writing this now, some forty later—in March, 1985—because
over these last decades of the Cold War, the persecution of the Hungarian
people—my people—has persisted. Russian soldiers have continued to
quietly but systematically remove musicians, artists, poets, historians,
lawyers, doctors, and scholars from our universities and conservatories.
Very few of us are left now. I know that my days are running out as well.

Because one Russian soldier, a man who knows my daughter and her secrets, has threatened my life.

And so I write this for my beloved daughter, Tereza, and for my beautiful new granddaughter, Gemma Rozsa.

And for a young French girl they never knew, named Amélie.

I loved Tereza's mother dearly, but she was not my first love. This story begins long before I met my wife, on an early spring day in Budapest. It was 1934, a time when the cold winds of war and anti-Semitism were just beginning to sweep over the hills and rivers and rooftops of Europe.

I had just turned thirteen. My father and I stood on the sidewalk outside our synagogue, after prayer service. He told me that he and my mother wanted to send me to live with my Uncle Jacques, my mother's only brother, who lived in Paris and worked at the Louvre. My mother had given me French lessons over the years, and Jacques would arrange for me to study the violin at the École Normale de Musique Conservatoire. They had some money put aside—since my dream was theirs, as well.

I didn't want to leave them, but they insisted. And in the end, I agreed. Of course I planned to return. But when I finally was able to return home, just after the war, my family was gone. I never saw them again. I carry the guilt to this day.

But that spring of 1934, I was just a naïve teenaged boy who knew only music, a boy who could not begin to imagine the unimaginable atrocities of war. And so, on a cold April morning I kissed my parents and sisters and left Budapest by train for Paris, sitting for hours in a drafty coach seat. I had a small suitcase, a knapsack, and my violin, and a thin wallet of money and identity papers sewn into the inside of my jacket by my mother. My uncle was waiting for me in the Gare du Nord station.

For almost four years, I had a happy life. Yes, I missed my family dearly, but I was doing what I loved—studying music and history, learning new music and composers, playing the violin with my friends in the school's orchestra. And I loved living in the Marais—Paris' beautiful old Jewish community—with my Uncle Jacques in his small apartment just off the rue des Rosiers.

And then on a late November night in 1938, my Uncle sat me down and gave me a chilling message from my father.

Kristallnacht, the Night of Broken Glass, had taken place just weeks earlier, in Germany. The Nazis had torched synagogues, vandalized Jewish homes, murdered Jewish families. The thousands of shattered windows from that night were a turning point, my father said, a warning for the Jews of Europe. War was coming.

He spoke of the anti-Jewish policies in our beloved Hungary that were already in place or coming very soon, restricting work, study, and voting rights for Jews. My father promised me that he, my mother, and my sisters would be fine. He had arranged passage for them to Switzerland.

I trusted my father, but I cried myself to sleep that night.

Every day the news grew worse. Uncle Jacques was convinced that the Maginot Line would hold, and the people of France would be safe. But others insisted a wall of rocks would never stop Hitler, and so we began to gather food and supplies, and plan an escape route to the southern provinces—or perhaps Switzerland. Just in case.

By June of 1939, life was very different. Many of my music professors and fellow students were gone. Food, gasoline, coal, and clothing were rationed; theaters and schools were closing. The days were dark, and getting darker.

And then one night everything changed for me. As I biked home in the blackness through the Marais' ancient alleys, I heard the most beautiful violin music. I followed the sound to a tiny square behind the Église Saint-Gervais on the rue des Barres, where I found a girl in a flowing blue dress, playing Vivaldi's "Summer" on her violin beneath a leafy plane tree. She was swaying, lost in the music. The light from the single streetlamp fell through the branches, lighting her pale skin and dark fall of hair. The night breeze shifted the leaves, scattering ever-changing shadows across her body as she played. Light and dark, light and dark.

I could not breathe. Such gorgeous music, how she caught Vivaldi's chords of thunder, lightning, and wind . . . She was as tempestuous and beautiful as the music she played. I think I fell in love with her at that moment.

I stayed, listening, until she was done. Then somehow, I found the courage to introduce myself.

She told me she was just eighteen, studying nursing at the American Hospital of Paris. Passionate and headstrong and full of life, the fear of coming war fell away when I looked into her deep blue eyes.

Her name was Amélie.

* * *

Rose stopped reading, raised her head. "There is much more to this story, of course. It's star-crossed, in more ways than one, as you will see. But first, to understand how the Van Gogh came to my grandfather, you need to know what was written in the journal he gave me."

She reached into the back of the violin case, withdrew one last thin sheaf of pages clipped together. "Not a journal, really, but a diary. And not written by my grandfather. These copies are from the diary of the young woman he met that night in Paris. The original entries are in French, of course. This is the English translation. These are Amélie's words, written in her diary during World War II."

CHAPTER SIXTY

PARIS
1939

June 1939

I've met a man.

His name is Anton. We walk along the Seine for hours, talking end-lessly. Drink wine in small cafés, wander the museums, play music together, and dance on the cobblestones in the moonlight. He loves to see me in my blue dress and calls me "ma belle Amélie."

He lives with his uncle, who works at the Louvre, and of course I have my dear Grandmère, living near the Place des Vosges. Otherwise, we just have each other. I am totally, helplessly in love for the first time in my life. And I've never been happier . . .

August 25, 1939

Anton's uncle asked for our help. We went with him to the Louvre, which was closed for three days for repairs. But in reality, we, and hundreds of other volunteers, spent those days packing more than eighteen hun-dred waterproofed wooden cases with almost four thousand pieces of the world's most beautiful art. Art that will be shipped on two hundred trucks south to the Château de Chambord in the Loire Valley.

For protection from the Nazis, the crates were labeled only with symbols—yellow circles for "very valuable," green for major works of art, and red circles for World Treasures. We watched through a veil of tears as a weeping old Frenchman painted three red circles on Da Vinci's Mona Lisa.

The last piece to leave was the heart-stirring Winged Victory. *Anton took my hand and held it against his heart as we watched the huge marble sculpture eased down a wooden ramp built over the stairway. That day, to me, spoke more about the threat of the coming war than even the stories of Nazi atrocities we hear every day.*

When we left the Louvre that last night, so heartbroken but yet so proud of what we had saved, the greatest museum in the world was almost empty. Anton's uncle told us that those paintings will be moved secretly from château to château, then to castles and abbeys, always far away from the strategic targets most likely to be bombed. I can only pray that the Mona Lisa *will survive.*

Anton's uncle had to accompany his beloved art to the Loire Valley. He pleaded with Anton to go with him, but Anton refused to leave me. I still can see Jacques' face, pressed against the truck window, his eyes bright, his hand raised in farewell. We never saw him again.

May 1940

The days grow darker. Nazi Germany has invaded my beloved France. The Maginot Line crumpled, and France surrendered. My country is at war. I cannot sit by and do nothing. I am sickened by France's passivity. It's our moral obligation to fight. How can I not?

June 14, 1940

Today, in the early morning hours, the Nazis entered Paris and paraded down the Champs-Élysées. Now there is a giant swastika flying beneath the Arc de Triomphe. It is my nineteenth birthday. I went to see Grandmère, and we cried together.

July 1940

A young mother with two little children—a boy and a girl—have moved into the back room of the apartment next door. I think they are hiding from the Nazis. I met the children through the window on the rear fire escape—Phillipe and Colette. They were so quiet and shy. I gave them a bit of chocolate.

August 1940

Hitler is a monster. There have been arrests, interrogations, spying, retribution, deaths, and disappearances. The music conservatories, theaters, and restaurants are off limits to all but Germans. All French Jews are forced to wear a yellow Star of David. We try to go about our lives quietly and stay invisible.

But I am a French Jew to the core, proud and determined and patriotic. I have stored my violin and my blue dress safely in the closet and found an old schoolmate I trust, and together we have joined the Resistance. I nurse resistance fighters, take photographs, smuggle documents and medicine. I ride my bicycle into the countryside and change road signs. The danger is terrifying, increasingly perilous, and Anton and I argue endlessly. But I must do this.

My network meets at night, after curfew when all the lights are out, in a curtained basement near the Tuileries. We produce an underground press, relay messages, create false identity papers, help to hide or plan escape routes for Jewish families. We even plan acts of sabotage and attacks on German officers. I have lived here all my life. I know all the underground sewers and tunnels, the best alleys and ways to cross the rooftops.

The Nazis underestimate French women. One essential lesson I've learned is that it pays to listen. My code name is Violin.

I have only broken one rule so far—keeping this written record. But I won't use any last names. And to protect all those I care about, I keep this diary in a very safe place.

October 1940

Of course Anton is terrified that I will be caught. He just wants to survive the war and compose his beautiful music. I am afraid, too—fear of the unspeakable haunts my days. But I tell him that war makes some of us into people we didn't know we were.

Christmas 1940

Today I found a homeless kitten in the alley behind our apartment. I could not bear to leave her there alone. I brought her upstairs, gave her a bit of milk, then invited the children next door to play with her. Such joy on their little faces, such laughter. The kitten, the young ones, they do not understand war. Amid all the desolation and horror, a moment to step back and smile. And remember that there is still beauty and humanity in the world, like Grandmère always says. And then the sound of tanks rumbling by in the street, and the war was back.

Winter 1941

No one is who they used to be. Last night I helped to set a bomb on the railroad tracks north of Paris.

When I told Grandmère what I had done, she tossed her cane to the chair and hugged me close. I could smell the Guerlain perfume she loves on her neck. She said what she has always said to me, my whole life—"Je t'aime vers les étoiles et retour." I love you to the stars and back. Then she whispered, "Whatever happens, my darling Amélie, just remember to stay human."

Spring 1941

The round-up of Jews has begun. It is more dangerous for Anton, as a foreigner. He gave up his chance to escape, for love. This causes me sorrow, yes, but we both feel that the only worse regret would be not knowing our love.

As I write this, we are sitting around one small lamp and a candle. There is no heat, and we are wrapped in a blanket that we share. Today I was able to give the little ones next door an orange and an old book of fairy tales. And our extra blanket! Their smiles said it all. I think I have found a way to get them to safety.

Fall 1941

The Allies are not doing well. I spent the afternoon with Grandmère. She seems more frail these days, often out of breath. I found the cane she refuses to use—it's a beautiful antique walking stick—and insisted she use it. She took it to please me, climbed the stairs, and brought me to her bedroom, where she told me a story—and a secret—that astonished me. Then she asked me for a promise. I would do anything for her. Je t'aime vers les étoiles et retour. It has even more meaning for me now.

Grandmère does not want to leave Paris, but tonight, I will make arrangements with my network for her to move to Vichy next week. She will be safer there.

The New Year, 1942

My heart is broken. Today, the family living next door to us was taken away. My dear little Phillipe and Colette! I gave them berries just yesterday, and they kissed my cheek with sticky red lips. The cat is gone as well. The only thing left behind in the hallway was the broken book of fairy tales. I cannot bear it.

July 1942

So many months since I have been able to write my thoughts. But this night cannot go untold. Even with all the fear, all the arguments, all the hardship, all the loss—my dear Anton took me up to the roof of our tiny apartment building and asked to me to marry him.

I know I should have said no. But we all need love, to fight the horrors. I said yes.

We lay back against the hard roof deck, looking up at the stars. They swirled above all of Paris, like bright flames flickering beneath a deep blue sea. For those few moments, there was no war. Only us. The stars made us feel as if we had a future, as if we were a part of something much greater than our lives. As if we were glimpsing eternity.

"Je t'aime vers les étoiles et retour," I whispered, saying the words my grandmother loves.

We set the date for our wedding, just weeks away. July 20.

Tomorrow I will take him to the south, to meet my namesake, my Grandmère Amélie. Our news will bring her such joy. I will ask her to share her secret with him.

And then, perhaps, I can get up the courage to tell Anton my own secret.

I am with child.

* * *

The listeners in the Georgetown living room sat in shocked, frozen silence as Rose Vasary folded the papers in her hand. "That's all that was in the diary," she said. "Amélie never made another entry."

CHAPTER SIXTY-ONE

THE BLUE RIDGE MOUNTAINS, VIRGINIA

JUST SEVENTY MILES west of Georgetown, Beckett stood on his cabin deck gazing out at the mist, luminous as pearls, that swirled like a necklace through the treetops. All he could think about was Maggie.

She would be here in a few hours. She was barely able to speak last night, but he knew she'd found her husband, knew he didn't remember her. Knew she was in Georgetown now, with Sugarman and Rose Vasary. Knew she'd return to the cabin in just a few hours. But that was all he knew. No dancing in the end zone just yet. He didn't know how she *felt*, dammit. Didn't know what was going to happen next.

Well, he'd know soon enough.

Beckett scowled, shook his head in disbelief. How could anyone not remember Maggie O'Shea? But for now, she was back home, she was safe, that was what mattered. She'd been safe in his arms last night.

He reached down to touch Shiloh, felt only the emptiness of damp, misted air. A sense of loss washed over him. I need the dog more than he needs me, he thought. But right now, it was the kid and his night terrors who needed Shiloh the most. With a low oath, he turned and entered the cabin.

The boy was by the bookcase, staring at a small framed quote that said, "The mountains are calling and I must go." Shiloh was sprawled on his back in front of the fire, snoring.

Beckett chuckled. "I see you've met Brother Reclinata of the Order of Eternal Indifference." Won a smile. "So, you like poetry, kid?"

"Some. This guy's pretty cool."

"John Muir, he's a naturalist. 'Going to the woods is going home,' he says. He gets the way I feel." Beckett gestured toward the huge window that framed a line of pines wavering against the silvery sky. "Some nights, the wind sounds like a blues harmonica playing through the boughs. You should give it a listen."

Dov shrugged. "I miss the blare of sirens and taxi horns, the stink of cabbage and trash in the hallways. The broken concrete." He grinned. "But this place, this mountain . . . well, it's not so bad. Maybe I'll give your trees a listen."

"You won't be sorry. Muir said, 'The clearest way into the universe is through a forest wilderness.'" Beckett reached up, took a book off the shelf. "Muir's *Wilderness Essays*. Take a look."

The boy backed away. "Geez, Beckett, I can't . . ."

"Can't what? You like books. I got books." He swept a hand toward the filled bookcase.

The sapphire eyes narrowed, fixed on him with a hard, icy wariness. "What makes you think I like books?"

Uh-oh. Just tell the truth. Kid deserves it.

"I came into your room the other night, looking for Shiloh. You'd left your backpack unzipped. I might have seen a few books."

The boy stared at him, considered, finally shrugged. "You busting me for overdue library books?" He snorted dismissively, then gestured at the bookcase. "You've read all these books?"

"Almost all. I like Churchill a lot. And if you like mysteries, no one beats Dashiell Hammett. But this one's my favorite." Beckett searched the bookcase, reached for a slim volume. "Hemingway. *For Whom the Bell Tolls*. It's the story of a young American volunteer in the Spanish Civil War. Ever read it?"

"Must've missed that assignment."

Beckett raised an eyebrow, half exasperated, half amused. "The guy sees the world with all its corruption and cruelty, but against all odds he still believes it's worth fighting for."

Dov looked from Beckett to the Golden. "Like you and the Brigadier here."

Shiloh raised his sleek head, pleased to be recognized by his military rank.

"Doing the right thing matters, right, Shiloh?" said Beckett softly.

"Is that why you joined the Army?"

Beckett grinned. "I wanted to be a surgeon, but people would have died. So . . ."

"Funny man. But somehow I think you and the Brigadier were meant to be soldiers."

"Maybe. The truth is, kid, I've always admired men who stand up against wrongs. It's how your Grandpa Yev and I became friends." He hesitated. "You remind me of him. He loved books, too. His favorite was *All Quiet on the Western Front*, by a guy named Remarque. He wrote a World War I story through the eyes of a German soldier. Your grandfather used to say that most soldiers all worry about the same things—family, home, friends."

Dov was quiet, listening, his eyes on the trees beyond the window—eyes that were bright with yearning.

"Maybe your grandfather was right. But wars are brutal, too, Dov. They hurt all of us. There are physical injuries—and moral ones. One of my heroes was Senator John McCain. He said, 'I've fought in a war, and helped make a peace.' Me and Shiloh, that's us. Now we're just trying to make the future better than the past."

Beckett handed Hemingway's novel to the boy. "So. Speaking of the future. I have those papers for the Child Services folks. They keep calling. Okay with you if I sign them?"

"Damn, Beckett, I told you! *I can't stay here.*" The blue eyes were fierce, then softened. "Even if I wanted to—I've got something I gotta do."

Shiloh snorted.

"More fun than us?" Beckett grinned. "Well, Dov, the Brigadier says you are cutting the lawn in different directions. So how about we work together on this?"

The boy just shook his head, turned away.

"Now why do I think you know what's right but are trying to find a justification to do what's wrong?" said Beckett.

"Is this a trick question?"

Beckett laughed. "I'm just sayin', sometimes two plus two is four. And sometimes it's twenty-two. Sometimes there are no easy answers."

"Maybe so. But I've still got to do what I've got to do."

"You sound like my pal Sugarman," said Beckett. "Okay. I respect that. But how about you give us one more day? Maggie's coming, and Lady in Black needs a good workout. Hey, almost forgot. I took some photos of you and the mare—they're on my phone. I'm not the photographer you are, but have a look."

Dov stopped, turned back with a pleased light in his eyes. "Can't hurt," he mumbled.

Got to remember to play the horse card more often, thought Beckett. He tossed the boy his phone. "Just swipe through."

The boy moved to stand in the pearly light of the window and began to scroll through Beckett's photos. Beckett watched him, youthful blond head bent in concentration, bathed in wavering bars of light and shadow. And felt something stir inside him.

Oh, no. No way. Not this kid. He was turning away when he saw the kid jolt, then freeze, staring down at the photo in his hand.

What the devil?

Somehow sensing the boy's unease, Shiloh's ears came up, and he lumbered to stand, unbalanced, on his three legs.

The boy turned pale as a first snow and murmured something in Russian. His voice trembled with agony.

"Dov? What is it, son?" Both man and dog moved to the boy's side.

"Who are these men? Where did you get this picture?"

Beckett looked over the boy's bone-sharp shoulder.

"Ah. The three Russians. Maggie sent it. She had drinks with these guys in London; some journalist took the photo. She says one of the men is the symphony conductor, Valentin Zharkov. I don't know the others; Maggie will have to tell you." He hesitated, then put a comforting hand on the boy's arm. "What is it, Dov? What's wrong? Talk to me."

But the boy wrenched away, dropped the phone to the table, and ran down the hallway.

His door slammed.

"Do someone a favor and they'll never forgive you," muttered Beckett. He looked down at the Golden. "Easier to back up an eighteen-wheeler than reach this kid. You thinking what I'm thinking? He recognized one of the Russians."

The Brigadier gave a low growl of agreement.

CHAPTER SIXTY-TWO

GEORGETOWN, WASHINGTON, D.C.

IN THE FIRELIT living room in Georgetown, rain lashed like pebbles against the tall windows.

Maggie and the others sat frozen, still caught up in Anton and Amélie's story, coffee cold and forgotten on the table before them.

Donata Kardos was the first to break the silence. "I read Anton's letter so long ago," she told them, "but I don't speak French, I never read Amélie's diary. My God, it's harrowing. And yet . . ."

"For every child of war there is a story," said Robbie Brennan softly. "What this young woman did took extraordinary courage, resourcefulness, and love. She had to live in the shadows for years. I wish we could tell her, somehow, that what she did mattered." He smiled. "And that the *Mona Lisa* was finally returned to the Louvre after being moved and rehidden five times."

"I'm almost afraid to know what happened next," whispered Maggie. She was rigid, eyes closed, one hand fisted against her heart.

Simon Sugarman leaned toward Rose. "This is all very touching," he said, "but the agent in me still doesn't know who had the Van Gogh. Unless . . ."

Maggie turned to him. "Of course, we know," she said suddenly. "It was her grandmother. Grandmère Amélie must have owned *Shadow Music*."

* * *

Rose Vasary turned toward Maggie. "The rest of Amélie's story is told in the last pages of my grandfather's letter. He describes how, the day after their engagement, Amélie's Resistance network created false identity papers for her and my grandfather, and arranged for a vegetable truck packed with crates to get them to a small village in the Loire Valley . . ."

Once more she began to read from Anton Janos' letter, the words drawing the listeners back into a world of war.

Amélie and I sat, holding hands, in the rear of the shadowed truck . . .

Her hand was cold, the air stinking of rotten tomatoes and moldering root vegetables, the road beneath the thin tires rutted and jolting.

I put my arm around her shoulders, hugged her close. "Lean on me," I told her.

She smiled, contented. "Even the war can't hurt us today."

Her words caused a sudden shiver of ice down my spine, and I closed my eyes against an inexplicable fear. "Tell me about your grandmother," was all I said.

"She is smart and kind and beautiful," answered Amélie, her eyes on the tin roof of the truck. "And a brilliant musician. She raised me, taught me to play the violin. She needs a cane now, of course, and her once-dark hair is pure white. But her spirit is still so young, so bright. I love her with all my heart."

"Does she still play the violin?" I asked her.

"Yes. But only the pieces remembered from her youth. Achingly sad music."

"Why so sad?"

"For almost all of her life, she suffered bouts of depression. In 1889, Grandmère became pregnant and lost the baby. She was only seventeen.

Her depression was severe, the loss so terrible, that her family sent her to be treated at the asylum in Saint-Remy."

"The same place where Van Gogh was treated for his mental illness?" I was surprised. "He would have been there in 1889."

"Yes. They became friends, perhaps more. I know he painted my grandmother, playing her violin in the gardens."

"Good God, Amélie." I could not contain my shock. "Your grandmother was painted by Van Gogh . . ."

She touched my face. "You are the first person I've ever told."

"I can only imagine how beautiful the painting must be," I said. "Did you ever see it?"

"Growing up, it was always on the wall of her bedroom. My Grandmère Amélie is very young, alone in the garden of Saint-Rémy, a small figure lost in the shadows of the pines. She is playing the violin beneath a sky of swirling stars. Van Gogh always sent his paintings to his brother, Theo, she told me. But this one, he gave to my Grandmère. He called it, Shadow Music."

"Je t'aime vers les étoiles et retour." I nodded thoughtfully. "Van Gogh's stars. And now she wants you to have it."

"Yes. She wants me to share it with the world. I promised her that after the war I—"

The truck came to a sudden, jerking halt. We looked at each other in the dim light, gripped hands, and waited.

The metal door rolled open slowly, the sound loud in the stillness.

Pushing the crates aside, we crawled towards the light. I jumped down, reached for her.

And then the truck roared away and we were alone on the narrow country road in the dusk.

"The château is there, set back in that woods." She touched my shoulder, gestured. In the soft purple light, a small château appeared like a faded jewel behind a rusted iron gate.

But the gate was broken from its hinges.

The high front doors were wide open, the mullioned windows shat-
tered. Books were scattered like bright fallen birds across the lawn. A
single gray plume of smoke spiraled above the roof.

"Grandmère . . ." whispered Amélie. She ran toward the open doors.

* * *

"The Nazis raided the château," said Maggie into the silence.

"Yes," said Rose.

"What happened to Amélie's grandmother?" Maggie's voice shook
with concern. "And what happened to the painting?"

Rose shook her head, her eyes bright with emotion. "I don't know,"
she said, as the rain clattered against the windows. "These papers are
all I have."

Rose turned to her mother, took a deep breath.

"I told you I didn't know where the last pages of my grandfather's
letter are, but . . ."

Donata paled, stood to face her daughter. "You know?"

"Not for sure. But I've thought about it for years. You told me
that, just days before my grandfather disappeared, the three Russians
visited. I think my father must have taken the papers when he went
to see my grandfather the night they argued."

"It's possible," said Donata.

"I haven't been honest with you, Mama," said Rose, touching her
mother's arm. "For months I've been searching for my father, to get
the pages back. To find out the *whole* truth. It's why I went to London
to play music with Valentin Zharkov."

CHAPTER SIXTY-THREE

THE BLUE RIDGE MOUNTAINS, VIRGINIA

THE MIST HAD lifted and now a pale spring sun warmed the treetops when Maggie's car pulled into the driveway.

Shiloh barked happily and lurched ahead, his ungainly gait not stopping his headlong rush to Maggie and the treats she always brought. Beckett limped behind, cursing the knee that always ached more after a rain.

The slam of a door, running footsteps on gravel. And then she was in his arms.

She seemed to melt into him, and he held her for a long moment, letting the scent of wildflowers surround him, feeling her heart beating against his chest. Then he stepped back and gazed down at her. "How have you gotten even more beautiful in three days?"

She laughed, bent to Shiloh. "Oh, it's so good to be home." She rubbed the Golden's back, then looked toward the cabin. "Where's Dov?"

"With the horses. I dropped him at the ranch a few hours ago. We'll get him in a bit, he really wants to talk with you." He put his arm around her, pulled her close. "But for now, we need to say everything we haven't been able to say. Let's get you inside."

* * *

They sat close together before the fire, fingers linked. Shiloh sat beside her, his head pressed against her thigh.

She knew just where to begin.

Speaking into the flickering shadows, she told him about sitting with Kirov on the plane. Meeting Valentin Zharkov, in the theater. About dinner with Yuri Belankov and drinks with the three Russians. Rose Vasary alive, reaching out. Amélie's story in her diary.

He sat very still, head bowed, listening.

Then she told him about the roses left in her Cheyne Walk apartment. The Standing Stones in Cornwall, and being pushed into the river.

His grip tightened as he stared at her. "Dammit, Maggie, you were in danger, and I was four thousand miles away. Making mac and cheese while someone else saved you."

She brought his hand to her lips. "But it was your voice I heard in the river, Michael, willing me to fight."

She took a deep breath. Told him about Merlin's cave. The hot shop on the edge of the cliffs, finding her husband there. His injuries, his memory loss. His new life in Tintagel.

"I don't think he'll ever remember me," she finished. "He said it was like a curtain coming down. I think he'll stay in Cornwall, make his life there. But at least I know he's still alive in this world now. My heart's not broken for him anymore."

"Still leading with your heart," murmured Beckett. He thought about the look on her face when she'd told him about finding her husband. No, she hadn't told him everything...

"You're here, Maggie, but somehow still so far away. It feels like you're in two places at once. The past and the future. And it feels like you still hope he'll remember you."

"I don't know," she whispered.

"Yeah. You do."

"I'm here."

"But are you here because he didn't remember you and chose to stay behind? Would it have been different if he'd wanted to come home with you?"

"He's my past, Michael."

"Maybe. But your world has tilted, darlin'. You've got one foot in the present with me, one in the past with your husband."

"A past I can't pretend never happened."

"A ghost stepped out of the shadows for you, Maggie. I get that. I get the memories and being loyal. I get that love doesn't just go away. But I can't pretend it doesn't shake me to my core."

"You know I had to go, Michael. I had to do the right thing—even though I knew it would cause someone I loved pain."

Irony of ironies, he thought, that I just said those same damn words to Dov a few hours earlier. The universe just won't give me a break. He looked down at her.

"I know, darlin', it's who you are. I love you for it. I'll never stop." He thought about the small jewelry box hidden upstairs in his sock drawer, gave her his crooked grin. "Of all the reckless, crazy things I've done in my life, Maggie, the one thing I'll never regret is falling in love with you."

"Reckless?" She smiled for the first time. "*Crazy?*"

He couldn't win this one, so he just kept going. "But maybe the past can't stay in the past. You're still in danger, Maggie. Now more than ever."

"Because of the Van Gogh."

"Someone is willing to kill for it. That flute player is dead. So is a Russian gang member in federal prison who knew too much. Rose Vasary was attacked, and so were you. Twice." His breath came out, harsh and angry. "You didn't know anything about the painting when Sugar first came to you. But now . . ."

"Donata told Robbie that my husband figured out where the Van Gogh was hidden. But if Johnny knows where the painting is, Michael, he doesn't remember. And I surely don't know where it is. Anton and Amélie's story didn't tell us."

"Maybe you don't know, Maggie, but some very bad guys still think you do. And if your husband knew, he could have told you." His breath came out. "There's more. Brace yourself. I told you Beatrice lied to me, followed you to London. So I did some checking. *There is no death certificate for Dane*, Maggie."

Her face went white. "It's all beginning to make sense. I felt, sometimes, that I was being followed by a woman . . ." Her eyes locked on his. "And I've always had the feeling that Dane was still lurking on the edges of my life."

He leaned closer. "You need to think about going back to Cornwall. To your husband."

She opened her mouth to speak, but he put a gentle finger on her lips.

"You once asked me if I ever loved someone enough to do anything for them. I'd rather lose you to someone who loves you than risk losing you forever if you stay here."

"You want me to *leave*?" She leaned toward him. "Seriously? You're playing the 'far, far better thing I do' card? Then we have a problem. No way in hell I'm leaving you."

Unless your husband remembers you.

"Heart over head," was all he said, shaking his head as he pulled her closer.

CHAPTER SIXTY-FOUR

SUNRISE RANCH, HUME, VIRGINIA

"Hey, Pretty Lady."

The boy stood in the paddock, washing down Lady in Black with a hose while he sang to her. Her huge dark eye was on him, trusting and unwavering, as water sluiced over her mane, down her scarred but regal neck, across her still-too-thin flanks. Her black coat glistened, the deep scars sharp and white as blades in the slanting sunlight.

"How could anyone do that to you?" whispered the boy. And then, "Okay, so you have a coat of scars. But it doesn't matter. You are still the most beautiful horse I've ever seen." He grinned. "Beckett's okay. Yeah, he's got a weird sense of humor. And maybe he thinks too much, you know? But he loves books, he loves these mountains, and he loves animals. He'll make sure you get everything you need when I leave. You can trust him."

He stopped, surprised, hearing the echo of the words in his head. *You can trust him.*

He shook his head in denial, turned to gaze at the Vets who were exercising horses in the adjoining paddock. "Do you think you'll ever be able to let me up on your back, my beautiful?" He smoothed a gentle hand over her flank. "Hey! Not that I want to! I'm afraid, too. I've never ridden a horse in my life."

The sound of a car engine caught his attention, then silence. He looked over his shoulder to see Shiloh tumble out of the just-parked Jeep, followed by Beckett and Maggie O'Shea.

Beckett slipped an arm around her shoulders, bent to her. She raised her face to his. Even from a distance, he could see the way they looked at each other. Maybe someday, he thought.

If he survived. Because now he knew what he had to do.

He thought of the face in Maggie's photograph. It was him. The same face he'd seen in the Brooklyn alley the night his mother was murdered.

Now, he just needed the name.

"*Ya sobirayus' ubit' tebya*," he whispered.

* * *

Beckett and Maggie stood, shoulder to shoulder, by the white paddock fence, while Shiloh explored the bushes that lined the path behind them.

They watched as Lady in Black bent her massive head to Dov. The boy turned off the hose and put his arms tightly around the mare's neck. Held on. Then he gently toweled her dry and, with one final caress on her nose, he walked toward them across the paddock.

"Hey, Dov," said Maggie. "I see you're continuing to make friends. In spite of your determination not to." She grinned at him.

The boy blushed, glanced back at the mare. "Easier with animals," he mumbled. Then his thin shoulders straightened with determination. "Maggie, I'm guessing Beckett told you that he showed me a picture you sent him from London. You and three Russian men. I need to know who they are."

Beckett, arms folded across his chest, remained quiet. He already had filled her in on the boy's interest, and now she had her own phone ready, set to the photograph. Beckoning the boy closer, she held out her phone and said, "Sure. Have a look."

She felt Dov stiffen beside her, but he remained silent, staring down at the three Russians.

"The fair-haired man on my right," said Maggie, "is Valentin Zharkov. He's the conductor of the New Russian Symphony. On my left is Nikolai Kirov, a New York art gallery owner. The man on the far side of the table is Yuri Belankov, he runs a think tank out of D.C. called The Red Star Group."

Careful not to glance at Beckett, she only said, "They served in the Russian Army together in the eighties. What else do you want to know?"

Dov looked at her for a long moment, considering, the sapphire eyes darkened by some inexplicable emotion. Finally, he said, "Are these men still in London?"

She wanted to ask him why, but she said, "All three of them are flying to D.C. sometime tonight. Yuri Belankov arranged a U.S. tour for Zharkov's orchestra—an all-Russian classical music program. Their first performance is in D.C. next week. I've agreed to be a guest soloist on opening night. I'll be playing Rachmaninoff with the orchestra. It's in two days, at the Kennedy Center Concert Hall." She hesitated. "Would you like to go to the concert?"

"*Da*," said the boy slowly, his gaze on the mare at the far side of the paddock. "I would not miss it."

CHAPTER SIXTY-FIVE

SOMEWHERE OVER THE ATLANTIC OCEAN

ALL THREE OF the Russians sat apart from each other in the first-class section of the United Triple Seven aircraft. It was close to midnight, London time, and the night sky beyond the windows was black and moonless.

Each man had his own reasons for wanting to find the Van Gogh. But tonight, their thoughts were spinning elsewhere.

The Russian in Seat 1A had his eyes fixed on the reflection of blinking red lights against the thick plexiglass panes. Magdalena O'Shea had found her husband. She would do the right thing, he was sure, to protect the people she loved. And after they had the painting, they would find the boy. A pity, he thought, but such is life. And death. He swallowed the last of his Grey Goose and closed his eyes.

Two rows behind him, in Seat 3B, the second Russian stared down into the clear vodka trembling in the narrow flute glass. A round face took shape, tiny and beautiful, with wisps of hair the color of ripe cherries. His *Rizhaya*, whom he had sworn to protect. The child of his heart, whom he had only touched one time, so many years ago. Yet he could still feel the silken softness of her skin on his fingertips . . .

He pictured the necklace he'd tucked into the crib with her that night, the miniature Russian cross. Did she have it still? He fingered the heavy gold charm on the chain around his neck, a duplicate of the small cross but three times larger. He'd worn it since the last night he'd seen her, more than three decades ago. His only link to the child. *Until now.*

The third Russian sat in the fourth-row aisle seat on the opposite side of the aircraft. He slept soundly, snoring, his mouth slightly open. He dreamed of a white wolf slinking through a forest of birch trees and shadows, toward a beautiful woman playing a grand piano, her hair the color of night in the moonlight.

* * *

They were back in the cabin.

"You think Dov knows one of the Russians," said Beckett.

"I'm sure of it," said Maggie. "Not the name, but the face."

"I think you're right. And now he knows the name."

"What are you going to do?"

Beckett glanced toward the hallway to the bedrooms. "Talk to him, now."

"Good. I'm concerned by what I saw in his eyes." She gestured at the old piano set near the window. "But this is between the two of you. I'll take on Rachmaninoff while you take on your boy."

"I'd rather take on Rachmaninoff," muttered Beckett. "And he's not *my* boy, darlin'."

She just smiled sweetly at him as she sat down at the piano and began to play.

Beckett shook his head, then bent to build up the fire for her before he went to find the kid. The concerto she was playing really was beautiful. He stopped to listen, caught up in the music, as she repeated the same passage three times. To him, the first time had sounded perfect.

She had her eyes closed, head thrown back, caught up in the beauty of the melody. Looking as if she was made of music. Twilight streamed through the window, light and dark, changing the shadows on her face. It was a moment he wanted to hold on to forever, wanted to—

A high-pitched howl broke into his thoughts. Shiloh. Something was wrong. Where was he? Somewhere outside? He spun around.

At that moment, a sharp rap on the cabin door.

What the devil? A stranger, maybe, who had frightened the dog.

His eyes found Maggie, unaware, still caught up in the music.

He had to get to Shiloh. Hurry.

He swung open the door, felt the ambush of a crushing gut-punch.

The tall, gaunt stranger stared at him, his long hair white in the twilight, his eyes intensely blue.

"You're John O'Shea," said Beckett.

"I don't know who I am anymore," said the man, looking past Beckett toward the piano. "But I've come to talk to Maggie."

Another howl, more frantic now.

"You've found her," said Beckett, pushing past him. "But I've got to get to my dog."

As he ran across the clearing, calling Shiloh's name, he heard the music inside the cabin crash to silence.

No time to think about that now, not when Shiloh could be . . . There! Thank God. He was okay. But leashed, tied to a strong wooden post, thrashing and barking, frantic to free himself.

What the hell? He never tied up the Golden.

"Easy, boy, easy." He bent to unknot the leather, free his dog. "Who did this to you?" Could this damn day get any worse? And then realization struck.

Oh Christ. It just did.

Dov. The kid had tied up Shiloh so that the Golden wouldn't follow him.

Beckett closed his eyes, knowing, deep in his bones. The kid was gone.

PART V

"MAGGIE"

"The setting sun, and the music at the close . . .
Writ in remembrance
More than long things past."

Shakespeare

CHAPTER SIXTY-SIX

THE BLUE RIDGE MOUNTAINS, VIRGINIA
LATE DAY, FRIDAY

"HAVE YOUR MEMORIES returned, Johnny? Is that why you're here? Have you remembered our life together?"

When Maggie had seen her husband cross the room toward her, she'd risen from the piano so quickly that the bench toppled and crashed to the floor. Now, faint with shock and surprise, she faced her husband in front of the old upright, not sure what to expect. And not at all sure what she wanted his answers to be.

Behind her, the sudden, sharp bang of a door, and she sensed Michael had left the cabin.

John O'Shea looked down at her with his stranger's face.

"No, Lass. I haven't remembered. But it didn't seem right, leaving things the way they were between us. I haven't been able to get the look in your eyes out of my mind. And then there are the flashes. Of a word, a shadowed face, a feeling, a moment—fragments of memory, like a shard of colored glass. Sometimes I catch a whiff of perfume, or hear low laughter on the breeze. And I wonder . . . has it been you all along, Maggie O'Shea? Or just a trick of the mind. At the very least, I've found a good doctor in London to give things a chance."

"And if you *do* remember?"

"Then we take it as it comes, Maggie. One hour at a time."

"What about the woman back in Tintagel? Kayla, was it?"

"Aye. I told her everything. She wants what's best for me." Something sparking, deep in the electric-blue eyes.

"A strong woman," murmured Maggie, unsure what to say, suddenly feeling as if the ground was shifting beneath her feet.

Johnny took her cold hands in his. "There's something more, Maggie. After you left, someone trashed my hot shop. All the glass, shattered. A cruel and destructive thing." He shook his head back and forth, the long white strands of hair catching the evening light.

"Oh no, Johnny, not your beautiful glass! I must have led someone to you."

"I don't blame you, Lass. But too much has been taken from me. I won't have it." A lightning bolt of anger flashed across his eyes. "Do you know who would have done such a thing, Maggie? Who was following you?"

"No, Johnny. I never saw anyone. I just felt it . . . I don't even know if it was a man, or a woman."

"It's the real reason I'm here. I'm afraid you may be in danger as well."

"I'll be careful, Johnny. But please, don't put yourself in danger."

"The need for vengeance is strong, Lass. But I don't own a gun. My conscience is torn. What would your Johnny have done?"

"You were not a violent man. You believed in justice, not revenge. But you—"

The front door swung open, and Michael Beckett appeared, followed by a loping Shiloh. "Maggie! He's gone. Dov is gone!"

She ran to him, grabbed his arms. "You're sure?"

"His duffel is gone, so is the old bike. He leashed Shiloh so the dog wouldn't follow him. It was the photograph. By God, Maggie, he's gone to find one of those damned Russians. I never should have trusted—" He shook his head, his face ashen. "I've just come for the Jeep keys. I've got to find him."

"Okay," she said, thinking, trying to breathe. "He must be headed to D.C. But he can't have gone far."

Beckett grabbed his keys off a small hook, turned to her. "I'm going to the ranch. I think he'll go there first. He wouldn't leave without saying goodbye to Lady in Black. I know it."

She held his eyes. "Yes, you know him. You're right." She reached for her jacket. "I'm coming with you."

Beckett stared at her, then turned toward John O'Shea. "No, Maggie, not when you're—"

"I'm coming," she interrupted. "Just wait for me in the Jeep. One minute, I promise."

"One minute." He nodded, rushed from the room.

She turned to her husband, standing so silently by the old piano. "You heard," she said softly. "Dov is a teenaged boy, in trouble. I'm not letting Michael go after him alone."

John O'Shea smiled faintly. "And well you shouldn't, Lass. I have my own business to take care of in D.C. I'll text you my hotel. Good luck with the boy."

"Thank you," she whispered, and ran to the cabin door.

*　*　*

Beckett's breath came out in a long, harsh sigh. He hadn't realized he'd been holding it. Maggie and Shiloh caught up to him at the fence, and all three gazed across the paddock.

The boy was near the barn, his arms around the mare's neck. The last of the light touched them with gold and shadows.

After a long moment, Beckett climbed over the fencing and headed across the grass toward the boy. Maggie and Shiloh followed.

Dov heard the footsteps, turned. "Shoulda known," he murmured.

"Yeah, kid," said Beckett softly. "You shoulda known we wouldn't let you do this alone." He scowled down at the boy. "How the devil did you get here?"

"One of your Vets, Tim. He gave me a lift. You were right, Beckett, these are good guys."

They stared at each other in silence.

Finally, the boy said, "Something on your mind, Beckett?"

"No, kid. Something on yours."

Dov's eyes slid to his backpack. "I'm going after him. You can't stop me!"

Beckett stopped in front of the boy, careful not to get too close to the mare. Put a hand on the boy's shoulder. "It's time you tell us what's going on. The Brigadier will never forgive me if something happens to you on our watch."

"You won't believe me, Beckett."

"Try me, kid. I know it's one of the men in Maggie's photo."

The boy bit his lip, closed his eyes. Took a deep, hurting breath.

"That Russian, Yuri Belankov. I saw his face in the alley that night, standing under the streetlamp." Pain ripped through the young voice. "He killed my mother."

CHAPTER SIXTY-SEVEN

THE BLUE RIDGE MOUNTAINS, VIRGINIA

IT WAS LATE, almost midnight. They sat by the fire—man, woman, boy, and dog—eating grilled cheese, with a beef bone for Shiloh, and devising a plan.

Tomorrow Maggie would go to the theater for an early morning rehearsal with the New Russian Symphony Orchestra, as prearranged. Dov, mutinous but outvoted three to one, would stay with Shiloh and Beckett at the ranch. Simon Sugarman was out of town, flying back late tomorrow. As soon as he returned, he and Beckett would deal with Belankov.

Beckett's cell rang.

"That was Sugar," he said when he'd clicked off. "His team thinks Belankov is preparing to flee. He has the money and connections. But—"

"But we know he's headed here."

"We don't know what he's planning, kid. We don't even know if he knows you're staying with me." Beckett nodded, pressed his lips together. "So it's time for Plan B."

"Do we have a Plan B?"

"No. Not yet." He thought of the Glock in his ranch office, a second pistol locked in the cabin's upstairs closet. "But I'll be ready for him."

"You?" said Dov, gazing toward the pitch-black windows. "It's *me* he wants, Beckett. *Almost as much as I want him.*"

"Me and Shiloh, we've got your six, remember?" said Beckett. "I promised your mother, and your grandfather, that I would keep you safe. If Belankov is coming for you, son, he's going to go through me and Shiloh first."

"No! This is *my* fight. When I find him . . ." Dov shook his head, his anxious eyes on Shiloh. "Sometimes the right thing is to break the rules."

Beckett chuckled. "You sound like your grandfather. But if you want to honor him, honor your mother, you've got to live your best life. That's not revenge. Once you pull the trigger, kid, you can't take the bullet back."

Dov stared at him, eyes dark, his expression unreadable. Then he stood and motioned to Shiloh.

"It's going to be okay," said Beckett. "We'll find out what happened to your mother. We'll get the monster who killed her, find justice for her. I promised your grandfather."

Beckett watched as the boy and the Golden walked slowly down the hall together, toward the boy's room. Shiloh's ungainly hop, pressing him against the boy's hip, was oddly reassuring. "Shiloh is good for him," murmured Beckett. "The kid has night terrors, you know? I hear him cry out."

"You're *both* good for him," said Maggie against his shoulder.

"Not so sure. I just lied to him."

She turned him toward her, rested a hand on his chest. "About?"

"I *do* have a Plan B."

"How can I help?"

"Not your fight, Maggie. I don't want you involved."

"I'm already involved, just by loving you. If it's your fight, it's mine. I'm in."

He flashed his lopsided smile at her. "Always my light. Truth is, Maggie, I can't stop Dov from going after Belankov. And I can't stop

Belankov from going after Dov. All I can do is try to control where it happens. Where I can be prepared."

"That's where I can help. Belankov has no reason not to trust me. And he'll be at the rehearsal tomorrow . . ."

Ten minutes later, Beckett began to turn out the lights. "Yuri Belankov has some deeper reason than just finding Dov," he said. "It's all connected, and Belankov is the link. I just have to figure it out."

"This is a good plan, Michael," said Maggie into the shadows. "You'll keep your promise, and you'll keep Dov safe."

"Finding his mother's murderer won't be the end for him, darlin'. There's a huge breach between resolving a crime and repairing all the damage it caused."

"Breathe, Michael. Shiloh will stay with him tonight. And we're here. I think Dov is finally beginning to trust you. It's the first step toward healing his pain."

Beckett turned to her, the fire's embers catching the sharp planes of his face and turning the stony eyes to silver. "I don't know how it happened," he muttered. "Kid just kind of crept up on me, you know?"

He ran a hand through his too-long hair. "For so long I was unattached, alone. Didn't need anyone, didn't *want* anyone." He scowled. "I liked it that way. Then a year ago, along came Shiloh. Then you . . ."

"And you didn't want either one of us."

He looked down at her, tugged her hair gently. "But now I do. Just you, me, and Shiloh. Perfect, right? But an old friend's daughter gets murdered in an alley and I find myself with a traumatized teenage boy." He turned to frown down at her. "And now, I'm making him pancakes. Sharing my dog with him. Talking about *emotions*!"

"For the love of a boy . . ." she murmured.

He looked away, toward the dark purple mountains framed in the huge window. "Christ, Maggie. I want to take him camping in the high meadow, go to his high school graduation. I want to give him

Christmas. Question the stars with him at night. Be the one he calls when he's afraid."

"Just remember—you didn't want me, or Shiloh, in your life. But you don't get a say about falling head over heels." Maggie smiled as she slipped her hands around his neck, pulled him down until their foreheads were touching. "You've got this," she said, taking his hand and leading him toward the stairs.

* * *

"Couldn't sleep either?"

Beckett gazed at the boy, who was dressed in a jacket and black ski cap and headed with slow, furtive steps toward the back door. It was just after three a.m. The cabin was dark, the only light coming from the red glow of embers.

Dov jolted, spun to wave his hands in angry frustration. "For chrissakes, Beckett, you scared the frickin' crap out of me! How did you know?"

Beckett, who had stayed awake in case Belankov showed up, pushed his pistol deep between the sofa cushions, out of sight. "I was a reckless kid once, too. Where's Shiloh?"

"Asleep. But no way I'm sleeping, not when I know the Russian who murdered my mother is so close." The boy's eyes locked on his, watchful as a hawk. "I just want to—"

"Hold your horses, kid." Beckett stood up. A smile lit his face as Shiloh lumbered into the room and sat directly in front of the boy as if to bar his exit. "Seems like none of us can sleep tonight. Look, Dov, I know how you feel. I can't stop you. But your grandfather used to say, it's not about being strong enough to use force, it's about being strong enough *not* to. Violence ruins two lives, not one. And who knows, maybe the horse will sing."

The boy looked at Shiloh and rolled his eyes. "Do you know what he's talking about?"

The Golden gave a snort as he shook his head. "I take that as a no," said Dov.

"It means sometimes we just have to wait," said Beckett. "Your grandfather liked to tell this story of a medieval criminal who pleads with the king for his life by promising that if the king spares him for one year, he will teach the king's favorite horse to sing.

"The king agrees. The criminal's cellmate tells the man it will never happen, not in his lifetime. But the man says, 'I have a year now that I didn't have before. So much can happen in a year. The king might die. The horse might die. I might die. And who knows? *Maybe the horse will sing.*'"

The boy pressed his lips together, uncertain, his eyes on the dark hallway.

"Look, it's the middle of the night. We don't even know where Belankov is! Be smart, kid. If you won't do it for me, do it for your grandfather."

"Low jab, Beckett, even for you. Okay, I'll wait 'til morning. But if that horse doesn't sing, I'm outta here."

Shiloh gave a sharp bark of agreement.

"Tough crowd," murmured Beckett.

He settled back onto the sofa and reached once more for the pistol.

Damned horse had better sing.

CHAPTER SIXTY-EIGHT

THE KENNEDY CENTER, WASHINGTON, D.C.
SATURDAY

MAGGIE'S WATCH SAID 9:45 a.m. when she sat down in the red velvet seat next to Yuri Belankov in the Concert Hall. Her heart was hammering, her hands like ice, but Beckett was counting on her. She took a deep breath. *Be natural.* "Hello, Yuri," she said. "You're up early."

Low laughter rumbled. "Sleep comes naturally to me, Magdalena. I could do it with my eyes closed." His dark gaze swept the stage in front of them, now filling with intense young musicians. Sound surrounded them—the shift of metal chairs and music stands, instruments tuning to the long, familiar "A" note. "But I would give up even my sleep for Rachmaninoff."

She gestured a hand around the concert hall. "And in such a beautiful setting. The organ, the chandeliers, the balcony seats . . ."

"John Kennedy understood the importance of the arts. He said, '*Americans cannot be afraid of grace and beauty.*'"

"I agree." Maggie swallowed. "I was hoping to introduce you to my friend Michael Beckett this morning. He wanted to come to the rehearsal but now he needs to stay at the ranch."

"Ah, you mentioned his work with American Veterans. Somewhere in Virginia, yes?"

"Yes. A small town called Hume. But he's also been fostering a teenage boy."

"Really? That cannot be easy."

"It isn't. But Michael knew his mother. Dov is from Brighton Beach, you may know the area. He's a smart, sweet kid, but he's been traumatized by his mother's death. Working with the horses seems to help him. Michael doesn't want to leave him alone."

The obsidian eyes became opaque. "I see," murmured Belankov. "Another time, then."

Several sharp taps of a baton on a music stand broke the sudden silence. Valentin Zharkov had taken the stage.

"There's my cue," said Maggie, rising. "I hope you enjoy the Rachmaninoff."

She climbed the stairs to the stage, settled herself at the Steinway concert grand piano to Zharkov's left. Forced herself to sit quietly, looking down at the keys. When she finally glanced toward the audience, Belankov's seat was empty.

She slipped her phone from her pocket, texted, *He's on his way. Get Dov out of there. And don't get shot, Michael!*

Zharkov's voice broke into her thoughts. "If our soloist cares to join us?"

"Sorry," she murmured, turning her phone off and slipping it out of sight. She settled her hands on the keys, took a deep settling breath, and gave Zharkov her full attention.

His baton came down with a flourish.

Somehow Maggie's fingers found the notes, and Rachmaninoff's bell-like tolls echoed out across the concert hall.

* * *

Ninety minutes later, Yuri Belankov pulled the black SUV into a dark stand of trees at the side of the road and shut off the engine. The sign at the end of the lane read: SUNRISE RANCH.

Kirov had told him there was a connection between Dov Davidov and Colonel Beckett. Magdalena had just given him the last piece of the puzzle.

Now, in the silence, his fingers beat a tattoo on the wheel while his mind raced. He should have killed that unfaithful bitch Irina Davidov long before he did. He felt like a trapped animal in a snow-filled Russian forest.

But what were his options? Cut his losses. Take the paintings he already had, leave the country, start over. But to give up everything he'd built . . . No! Not without the Van Gogh.

Think. One thing at a time. He could make it work. He and Zharkov still had the smuggled art operation going strong. There was still a chance he could find the Van Gogh before the others. Magdalena had found her husband. She had to know where it was hidden.

Or—his daughter knew.

He glanced at the message on his cell. From Gemma Rozsa. His *Rizhaya.*

Oh, yes, he would join them all at the chapel.

It was time, once and for all, to look his daughter in the eye. To tell her the truth. To get the location of the Van Gogh.

But first . . . His eyes searched the shadowed road. The ranch was just up ahead. First, he had to get Irina's flash drive. Then eliminate his biggest problem. One final witness. The witness who could keep him from the Van Gogh. Send him to prison for life. Or worse.

Nyet cheloveka, nyet problem, eh?

The sound of tires on the road behind him, slowing for the ranch entrance. His team, the three men who would storm the main ranch building. Bring the boy to him.

Smiling, he started the SUV's engine and headed toward the ranch.

* * *

Beckett stood in the darkened ranch office, waiting in the shadows. Shiloh was okay, closed in the stable with the horses. He'd sent Dov into town with Tim an hour ago to buy horse feed. Tim was a good guy, a Vet. He'd make sure Dov was safe.

Four of his most trusted men, all Veterans, were stationed around the building. Each of them had a gun, courtesy of the U.S. Army and Afghanistan. Their orders were to stop Belankov, without violence if possible. Sugar would take it from there.

Belankov had to pay.

A moving shadow beyond the window. The whispered rasp of a boot.

Beckett gripped his pistol.

Showtime.

*　*　*

Belankov eased his SUV along the back trail, past the paddocks and stable. The main ranch house was half-a-football-field farther away, on a low rise. His men should be there by now. Should be—

Movement to his left. In the trees. A figure stepped out of the woods and ran toward the stables.

The Davidov boy. *Irina's son.*

Belankov glanced up at the ranch house. The boy had been in the woods. Alone. Not with Beckett. Had Magdalena lied to him?

He pulled the car to the side of the road, opened the locked glove compartment. Two pistols sparked in the light. He chose one, relocked the compartment, and quietly eased open the driver's door. He slipped the Makarov into his belt and stepped into the shadows.

CHAPTER SIXTY-NINE

SUNRISE RANCH, HUME, VIRGINIA

Dov stopped in the shadows, chin up, listening.

Only the horses, snuffing and restless in their stalls.

He moved to Lady in Black's stall, lifted the iron latch, and entered. The mare lifted her head, ears pricked, and pushed her nose against his shoulder. She whinnied, pawed at the sawdust.

"What is it, Pretty Lady? I'm here now, you don't have to be afraid. Old Tim's gonna be frosted that I ditched him, but I just had this feeling . . . Something just didn't feel right."

The mare raised her head as if listening. Her ears flicked back and forth, her tail swished, her lip curled.

The boy rested his hands on her neck, felt the tension in her body. "What is it, girl? What's scaring you?"

Another sound, just outside the stall. The mare's nostrils flared. The boy turned.

Yuri Belankov stepped from the shadows.

"You look like your mother," said the Russian.

Dov froze for an instant, then stepped in front of his horse. "Don't you dare talk about my mother," he said, his voice strange and deep in his ears. "I saw you, in the alley. The night you killed her."

"She knew too much about my private business, *Malen'kiy Chelovek*. She was planning to betray me. I had no choice. '*Nyet cheloveka, nyet problem*.'" Belankov circled the gun slowly, aiming at Dov's chest.

"And now *you* are the problem for me. Where did you hide the flash drive she gave you?"

Dov stepped forward, swallowing the fear in his throat, his hands balled into fists. What could he use? Rope? Harness? Metal pail? Pitchfork, too far away. Play for time.

"What flash drive?"

"The one your mother made from my private business. I know you have it."

The faint pop of gunshots, coming from the main house.

Dov spun around.

Belankov smiled. "Yes, they are gunshots. There is no escaping, little man. No colonel to come to your rescue now, eh?"

The boy stepped forward. "I don't need the colonel. I'll kill you myself."

Laughter rumbled in the Russian's chest. "You are brave for such a stick of a boy." His eyes moved to the mare. "Let's just see how brave you are. She is your friend, *da*? Tell me where the flash drive is, now. Or she will take a bullet for you." The pistol swung toward Lady's stall. The mare snorted, backed up, her rear hooves striking the wall.

"No!" cried the boy, throwing himself at Belankov.

Belankov raised his arm.

At that moment a snarling golden blur burst out of the shadows, knocking the boy off his feet, out of the line of fire. Belankov took aim at the boy.

The mare gave a high, fierce whinny and bolted forward, kicking and striking out. Belankov fired wildly, spun as the mare's left front hoof caught him in the shoulder. He shouted as the gun flew from his hand and skittered across the hay-strewn floor.

Belankov twisted toward the gun, but the mare lunged toward him again.

Dov crawled across the floor, grabbed the pistol, pulled it to him. Heavy.

Then he stood slowly and reached for the reins. "Easy, girl, easy."

He aimed the gun at Belankov's heart. Shiloh stood on guard beside him, snarling.

"Stay, Shiloh. This is my fight."

Very slowly, Belankov rose to his feet, clutching his right shoulder. "You won't shoot me, boy," he whispered. "You don't have it in you."

Dov dropped the reins and grasped the gun with both hands, his whole body shuddering. He heard Shiloh's low growl, the mare blowing harsh angry breaths behind him. Everything seemed to stand still.

His vision narrowed, blurred by thick black clouds that thundered in his head. He gripped the pistol tighter, his finger trembling against the trigger.

Do it! Shoot the man who killed your mother.

Then, cutting through the blackness, Beckett's voice. His Grandfather's words.

It's not about being strong enough to use force, it's about being strong enough not to. Violence ruins two lives, not one.

Very slowly, eyes locked on the Russian, Dov lowered the gun.

Belankov smiled. Then, without a word, he turned and disappeared through the stable doors like black water into darkness.

The mare snorted behind him, a deep, rasping sound.

Dov turned.

Blood on the floor. Shiloh gave a loud howl.

"Lady!"

CHAPTER SEVENTY

THE KENNEDY CENTER, WASHINGTON, D.C.

THE STAGE WAS quiet as a held breath.

Maggie sat at the concert grand piano, head down, her hands in her lap. Still lost in the music, although the rehearsal of Rachmaninoff's Concerto had ended moments earlier.

Then, as if from a great distance, the sound of steady clapping.

She lifted her eyes, saw Valentin Zharkov leap off his conductor's stand and stride toward her. "No. It wasn't enough," she whispered. "I'm still not ready."

"You are almost there," he said in his heavy accent as he stood in front of her. "Technically, you are perfect. Rachmaninoff is just out of reach, Magdalena, waiting for you."

He turned, swept a hand to encompass all the musicians, dressed in casual clothes, who sat in the half circle of rows before him. "Thank you, Ladies and Gentlemen. Well done. Two words I very rarely utter. I only wish we'd had an audience. Tomorrow night's performance will be remembered, I promise you."

Shocked by the unexpected praise, the members of the New Russian Symphony Orchestra rose to their feet as one, applauding Maggie and each other. Then, with a scrape of metal chairs and the snap of leather cases, they slowly gathered their instruments and scores and made their way into the darkened wings.

Maggie stayed seated. She reached for her phone, turned it on. Damn, damn, nothing from Michael. What had happened at the ranch? He won't let anything happen to Dov, she reassured herself. They'll be okay.

Just breathe.

Zharkov handed Maggie a bottle of Evian. "What is going on, Magdalena? It felt like part of you was somewhere far away this morning."

"I know," she whispered, thinking of Michael and the boy. "But I'll be there for you tomorrow night." Somehow. She shook her head, took a huge swallow of water, and looked down at the words on her damp t-shirt. *Hit the right keys at the right time and the piano plays itself.* Well, sometimes.

"You are so close," Zharkov said in his deep growl. "Sometimes creation occurs just when you let yourself trust your heart. Last night I dreamed of waves of sixteenth notes, tumbling over a cliff in a waterfall of music and crashing in intricate patterns on the rocks below. So I thought, what the hell."

He scowled down at her. "You are at the edge of that cliff now, Magdalena. Tomorrow night, you must trust yourself. What the hell, right? Just let yourself jump."

Maggie just shook her head at him. "So your secret for genius is 'what the hell,'" she murmured. *Don't let Zharkov know anything is wrong. Michael will call when he can. Change the subject.*

"Genius?"

She waited a moment, then stood. "I just wish I could understand . . ."

The dark eyes held hers, full of questions. But he remained silent. *Just say it.*

Maggie swept her hand to encompass all the now-empty metal chairs and music stands on the darkened stage. "All this," she said softly. "I didn't expect to like you, Valentin, but I do. You are *made* of music. You have taught and mentored these beautiful young musicians, built a remarkable world-class symphony orchestra to be proud of. And yet—"

"Ah," he said, "I see. You have heard the rumors."

"About the stolen art? The smuggling? Yes."

He ran a hand through his long, silvered curls, pushed the strands back from his high forehead. "Music and art are intertwined like vines, Magdalena, you know it. You can't separate one from the other."

"Not good enough," she said. "Not nearly."

"Okay, so maybe when we cross borders the occasional canvas is rolled into a trombone, a tuba. Or hidden in the back of a specially made cello case."

"But how do you—" Maggie stopped and stared at him. "Of course," she murmured. "Your friend Kirov. You deliver the art to his gallery in New York."

"It's a business arrangement, nothing more."

"A woman *died*, Valentin."

His eyes darkened. "I did not kill her, Magdalena. Nor did I order her death."

"But you know who did."

"I have my suspicions," he admitted. "But—"

"But you still want the Van Gogh. You all were hoping I would learn its location from my husband."

He smiled sadly at her. "We still might, yes? Do you know what millions of dollars would do for this orchestra? For other orchestras, other young Russian musicians just needing their chance? Think of the music I could make!"

"This won't end well, Valentin. Please. If you would only—"

"Listen to me, Magdalena. Sometimes we do the right thing for the wrong reasons. And sometimes we do the wrong thing for the right reasons."

At that moment, Zharkov's phone buzzed. He glanced at the message, his sharp face going pale. "I have to leave," he told her. "I will see you tomorrow, at the performance." He hesitated. "I will think about what you said, that's all I can promise."

Maggie watched him rush toward the exit.

Just for once, Zharkov, do the right thing. For the *right* reason.

A ping on her phone. Finally, Michael!

But a message from Rose Vasary appeared.

I'm done waiting for answers, Maggie. I want to know who my father is, I want my grandfather's music. I've asked the Russians to meet me at the Dahlgren Chapel at Georgetown University at 3 o'clock. I want you to be there.

Oh, no. Rose wasn't going to wait for Simon Sugarman's return. She was going to face the Russians on her own. I have to stop her, thought Maggie. *She has no idea how dangerous these men can be.*

She texted Rose, *DON'T DO THIS, TOO DANGEROUS.*

After two already. She had to hurry. She texted Michael as she ran from the concert hall.

What had happened at the ranch? Dear God, let them be okay.

CHAPTER SEVENTY-ONE

BECKETT STOOD BY the front door of the Main House and stared down the empty road toward the stables.

His breath came out. The ambulance and the Hume PD would be here any minute. Sugar was sending his team as well. Three Russians were under guard in the gymnasium. Injuries on both sides, sure, but minimal. One bullet-grazed temple, a flesh wound in the thigh, some bruised ribs, a probably-broken arm. His men were the best. And being prepared for the attack had made all the difference.

But there'd been no sign of Belankov.

Was that why he still had this feeling of unease, this unsettling foreboding?

He realized with a jolt that he should have heard from Maggie by now. Where was she? Suddenly anxious, he reached for his phone, turned it on. Christ! A message from Tim. Dov had disappeared from the feed store . . .

"Goddamn it to hell!" shouted Beckett.

His gut told him exactly where the kid had gone.

At that moment he heard the single gunshot, coming from the stables.

Belankov!

God, no, please, no. Not the kid. He set off toward the stables at a run.

* * *

Breathless, Beckett rushed through the high stable doors.

In the dark shadows, the smell of blood. Shiloh's frenzied barking. The horses in the stalls nervous, snorting, pawing the earth.

"Dov!" he shouted. "Dov, Shiloh, where are you?"

"Here, Beckett. Hurry!"

Dov's voice, low and desperate. Thank Christ, he was alive.

They were at the far end of the stable.

Lady in Black was down, Dov on the floor beside her, holding his shirt pressed against a nasty wound in the mare's shoulder. The shirt was bright red with blood. Shiloh, now whimpering softly, huddled against the mare's head. Belankov was nowhere to be seen.

"Call the vet!" shouted Dov. His eyes were wild with fear.

Beckett's cell already was in his hand. He shouted instructions as he threw himself on the floor next to the boy and tried to stop the bleeding.

"It was Belankov," sobbed the boy. "Why did he have to hurt her?"

Rage surged through Beckett, but all he said was, "Get the towels in the back room. Water. We're not going to lose her, son. She had your back, now we've got hers. Go!" He laid a hand on the mare's shuddering neck. "Stay with us, Lady," he whispered.

Several of the ranch Veterans, including a medic, thundered through the doors.

Somehow Beckett got to his feet, moving out of their way just as Dov returned.

"Let them do their jobs, son." For the first time ever, he put his arm around the kid, felt the shuddering of the thin bones, and felt his heart begin to crack.

The boy turned his face against Beckett's chest.

Beckett held tighter. "She's going to be fine," he whispered against the pale hair. "I've got you."

CHAPTER SEVENTY-TWO

DAHLGREN CHAPEL, GEORGETOWN UNIVERSITY, D.C.

GEORGETOWN UNIVERSITY'S DAHLGREN Chapel flickered with candlelight and midafternoon shadows that spilled through the stained-glass windows.

Donata Kardos stood behind a narrow door near the confessional, her eyes on the three Russians who stood together at the back of the small chapel. The third man—Yuri Belankov—had just arrived, and now they all waited for the woman they had last seen as a tiny baby.

Donata knew their identities now, from Maggie's photograph.

"I don't like it. Why did she ask to meet us here?" Belankov's voice was a low, suspicious rumble in his chest.

"Patience, Yuri," said Nikolai Kirov. "We are so close to having what we want."

"But why now? Why *here*?" Belankov gazed at the empty pews. "Something is off, Niki."

"I agree," said Zharkov, his eyes on the altar at the end of the aisle. "Something is—"

"Not quite right?" Donata Kardos stepped from the shadows into the light.

The men froze. "You?" Yuri Belankov's shocked voice echoed in the high, open space. He stepped closer, staring at her. "You were in the meadow that night. You are the girl who carried off my infant daughter?"

Donata walked toward them, regal and calm. Robbie Brennan followed close behind her, in his silver chair.

"Yes. I am Donata Kardos, the woman you've been searching for." She dipped her head toward Robbie. "And this is my friend, Father Robert Brennan. You all know of me, of course, but we've never actually met." She gazed at each Russian in turn, then settled her eyes on Yuri Belankov. "But I recognize your voice. It's very distinct. I heard it often, in the hallway, through the thin walls. You are the man Tereza was seeing in Budapest, the soldier who fathered her child."

Yuri stepped forward. "It's been a very long time. Where is Gemma Rozsa? My *Rizhaya*. She asked us to meet her here."

"She is here." Donata gestured past Robbie into the darkness. "The question is, Yuri, why are *you*? Why have you been searching for her all these years? Is it your daughter you want? Or the Van Gogh she has hidden?"

"Cannot a father want both?"

"A *father*? You murdered her mother. I saw it happen. The three of you, standing there together in the twilight. I can still hear the sound of the rifle shots echoing across the meadow."

"We were Russian soldiers, Donata," said Belankov. "Doing our duty during the occupation. A woman was fleeing, trying to escape across the border."

"That woman was my best friend, the mother of your child." Donata stepped closer, locked eyes with him. "I will never forgive you."

"I don't need your forgiveness, Donata. I did what I had to do. We all did. Now..." Belankov raised his voice. "Gemma Rozsa, where are you? Please, show yourself. I have been searching for you for so long."

A heartbeat of silence.

"My name is Rose Vasary now." Rose stepped through the doorway and stood next to her mother.

The three Russians stared at her. Valentin Zharkov was the first to speak.

"Rose? My God! *You* are the baby from the meadow in Budapest?" He moved toward her, his arms extended, dark eyes shining with confusion. "Of course." He gazed at her. "You have hair like a sunset. Our *Rizhaya*. Why didn't I see it? Thank God you are okay. Everyone in the orchestra has been so frightened for you. But I don't understand . . ."

"Hello, Valentin." Rose gave a faint smile, shrugged. "Yes, I'm the child Donata carried across the border to safety so long ago. I joined your orchestra because I wanted to find my father, to finally have the answers to my questions. I honestly thought you were my father, Maestro. The truth is, I wanted you to be. I'm sorry. Clearly, I was wrong."

Her gaze took in all three men. "I know you all are here because you want the Van Gogh. But for me, I want my grandfather's letters and music returned to me. I want to know who my father is. And I want to look my mother's murderer in the eye."

She turned to Yuri Belankov. "Did you plan to murder my mother all along?"

He held out his hands. "Please, *Rizhaya*, just let me talk to you privately."

"Don't call me that!" She took a step toward him. "I deserve the truth, Yuri. You said you loved my mother."

"And I did! You must believe me."

"Liar." Kirov, who had been silent since Donata's arrival, stepped from the shadows into the bars of light that fell from the high chapel windows.

Belankov turned burning eyes on him. "What the hell, Niki?"

"You never loved Tereza."

Belankov paled. "I had a child with her!"

"No," said Kirov. "You didn't." He turned gentle eyes on Rose. "I did. You are *my* daughter, Rose."

Rose took a step back, reached for her mother's hand. Everyone in the chapel stood in shocked silence.

Kirov was the first to speak, his eyes still on Rose. "Your mother was a beautiful, gentle young woman," he said softly. "Tereza never loved Yuri. He was abusive, a bully. He threatened her. She was lonely, afraid. She turned to me. We met in secret, in the park . . ."

Rose sank to the closest pew, her eyes locked on the Russian who said he was her father.

"But how . . ."

"When your mother found out she was pregnant, she told me the child was mine. We kept the secret, for her safety. And yours."

"A ridiculous lie!" spat Belankov.

Kirov turned to him. "Is it, Yuri? Do you deny that you *wanted* Tereza to try to escape, made it easy so that you could find them fleeing, take the child? Take her so you could have the Van Gogh?"

"*My* child, Niki!" roared Belankov.

"No. Tereza had a friend who was a nurse. She tested our blood types. There is proof."

Donata Kardos stepped forward for the first time. "That night," she said, her voice trembling with memory and pain, "the three of you stood on the grass, outlined against the sky. One of you raised a gun, aimed at Tereza. I saw it." She turned to Kirov. "And one of you cried out, you tried to stop it . . ."

"I wanted Tereza and our baby to be free," whispered Nikolai Kirov. "I promised to join her as soon as I could."

Rose stood slowly, to stand once more by her mother. "My father left me only one thing," she said. Reaching into the open neck of her blouse, she pulled out a gold chain, held it up. A small Russian cross spun, sparkling as it caught the light.

Kirov smiled, and, in a similar gesture, lifted the chain from around his neck to expose the matching cross.

CHAPTER SEVENTY-THREE

DAHLGREN CHAPEL, GEORGETOWN UNIVERSITY, D.C.

IN THE SHADOWED Georgetown chapel, Rose and her father stared at each other.

Robbie Brennan wheeled forward. "This is a huge shock for Rose," he said into the silence. "You both need time alone, to talk, to get to know one another."

Kirov gazed down at Rose. "He's right, *Rizhaya*. I will stay, when everyone else leaves. We will say what has to be said when it is just the two of us."

"Very wise," said Robbie. Then, addressing all three of the Russians, he said, "But Rose and Donata deserve other answers as well. Where are the missing papers that belonged to Anton Janos? How did you know about the Van Gogh?"

The men looked at each other. Belankov's face was twisted with shock and rage. It was Kirov who finally spoke. "The three of us were at Tereza's apartment late one night, drinking. I went down the hall to use the restroom. It was dark, no lights on. I stumbled into a small room by mistake. Not much bigger than a closet. Just a violin in the corner, and a table with a lamp and papers scattered over it—some pages of a handwritten letter, lined sheets with a musical score. It was Anton Janos' office, his work. I was turning to leave when I saw it."

Kirov glanced at Belankov, whose face had turned to stone. Belankov made a "to hell with you" gesture and turned away, backing into the dimness of the chapel.

Unfazed, Kirov continued. "The painting was on the rear wall, in the shadows. Just hanging there, in a cheap wooden frame. I knew it was a Van Gogh as soon as I laid eyes on it, my mother was an excellent teacher after all. The signature had been painted over with some dark oil paint, but I knew. I turned back to the table, looked more closely at the letter. The words 'Van Gogh' leaped out at me. So I seized all the papers, hid them in my jacket, and returned to the others. Later that night, when we were alone, I told Belankov and Zharkov of my suspicions. That was the night we decided to steal Anton Janos' Van Gogh."

"Which meant Janos would have to disappear." Robbie Brennan leaned forward. "You turned him in to the police. They arrested him."

"Yes. But when we returned to the apartment for the Van Gogh . . ."

"The painting was gone, hidden with his neighbors next door." Robbie glanced at Donata, whose face was now the color of candle wax. "And the letters, the music you stole that night? Where are *they*?"

Kirov reached into his jacket pocket. "I brought them with me. They belong to my daughter, after all."

He held a folded sheaf of papers out to Rose. "I've been searching for you, to return them. Your grandfather must have written these pages earlier that very night. I think they hold the answers you've been hoping for."

Rose unfolded the papers slowly. Her fingers touched the penciled notes. Her breath came out, and she smiled at Donata. "The missing score for my grandfather's violin concerto! At last, I can play *Amélie's Theme* for the world."

She set the score carefully on the pew beside her and opened the remaining pages. "Yes," she said softly, "it's the missing pages of my grandfather's letter—when he and Amélie arrived at her Grand-mother's château."

Rose refolded the letter and bowed her head, brushing at the tears that spilled from her eyes. "Thank you, Kirov." The faintest of smiles. "Father..."

Kirov stepped toward her, then stopped.

"Where is Yuri?" he said suddenly.

Robbie and Donata exchanged uneasy glances.

Zharkov spun around as Yuri Belankov stepped from the shadows. A Tokarev pistol was pointed at Rose's heart, the chamber locked into place. "Enough of this. We came for the Van Gogh, not your family's music. Where is the painting hidden? Give me that letter, *Rizhaya*."

Kirov stepped in front of Rose. "Don't do this, Yuri. Her grandfather's letter does not give the location of the Van Gogh. If it did, we would have found the painting decades ago."

Yuri Belankov spoke to Kirov without taking his eyes off Rose. "She's been playing all of us, you fool, they all have! It's time for the game to stop. I want the Van Gogh, *Rizhaya*." The pistol shifted, aimed at Donata. "You've lost one mother, Rose. Unless you want to lose another, you will tell me now!"

"I don't *know*!" cried Rose. "It's the truth! Please, Yuri..."

Belankov shook his head and took a step forward, the gun glinting silver as he took aim.

Donata moved quickly in front of Rose, holding up her hands. "No! She's telling you the truth! Only I know where the Van Gogh is hidden."

At that moment, the high arched doors were flung open. Everyone turned as Maggie ran into the chapel. Sunlight spilled in, illuminating them like a frozen tableau in a spotlight. For an instant, Maggie stopped, her eyes adjusting to the shifting shadows. Then she took in the scene before her, registering Rose's fear and the black pistol in Yuri Belankov's hand. She threw herself toward him.

"No, Yuri!"

It all happened very quickly.

Both Kirov and Zharkov launched their bodies at Belankov. As he fell back, directly into Maggie, he fired off five shots. Donata screamed and flung herself toward Rose. Robbie Brennan hurled his body from his chair to cover both women. A plaster statue exploded into pieces. Glass and cement shards shattered around them.

Two bullets found their mark.

Blood spilled, ran in small rivers across the chapel's stone floor. The sound of gunshots echoed in the air.

When the smoke cleared, Yuri Belankov and Maggie were no longer in the chapel.

CHAPTER SEVENTY-FOUR

THE STREETS OF WASHINGTON, D.C.

"Don't speed. Just follow Canal Road to the Whitehurst Freeway."

Yuri Belankov had forced Maggie into the driver's seat of his BMW at gunpoint. Now he sat in the passenger seat, his left hand pressing the hard barrel of the pistol into her side.

"You're hurting me!" Her hands gripped the wheel, heart hammering in her chest. "Please. You don't want to do this, Yuri."

The pressure of the gun did not ease. "I don't have a choice, Magdalena. I had to get away. Now give me your phone."

"It was in my purse; it must still be somewhere in the chapel." She eased the car onto the Whitehurst, heading northwest. "Where are we going? I won't get out of this car with you, Yuri. You'll have to shoot me first."

He pushed the pistol deeper into her side. "I don't want to hurt you. But I am running out of options. You betrayed me, Magdalena." He gestured toward the E Street Exit. The movement seemed to cause him pain, and he cursed in Russian. "Go there. Then take a right on Nineteenth."

She shook her head, slowed the car. Thought about just slamming the brakes, opening the door, and jumping. Thought better of it.

Her eyes found his in the mirror. "Yes, I betrayed you!" she said fiercely. "And I'd do it again. You killed Irina Davidov. You just tried to kill her son! My God, I liked you, Yuri, I made excuses for you. How could you do such a thing?"

"Ah. You've talked to your Colonel?"

She nodded. "He called when I was on my way to the chapel."

"So you know they are alive."

"No thanks to you, damn you." Her breath whooshed out. "Was it *all* a lie, Yuri? Did you plan to meet me, all along?"

"I found you to be a beautiful and madly talented woman, Magdalena. There is just something about you, that part is not a lie. But—yes, I arranged to meet you because I wanted to find the Van Gogh."

"You thought I knew where it was hidden?"

"I thought your husband knew and that he told you."

"You believed Johnny knew the location of the Van Gogh . . . You sought him out?"

"Yes." He glanced out the window. "Turn left onto Constitution."

"But why did you think that?"

"A terrible irony. I happened to read one of your husband's articles in the *New Yorker*, about his on-going search for priceless, missing art. He wrote of a Van Gogh rumored to have disappeared from Budapest during the Cold War. I thought he knew much more than he was saying."

The car swerved into the turn as comprehension dawned. "You arranged to meet my husband."

"He thought it was by chance. Of course, we talked art. I think at some point he suspected that my Dufy painting, *Red Orchestra*, was a black-market purchase. I always thought my accountant Irina told him. She'd learned too many of my secrets by then."

"Irina?" murmured Maggie. "Oh, my God. Irina *Davidov*? *She* was your accountant?"

"Yes. The boy's mother." He shook his head. "She betrayed me, too. Copied my secret financial records onto a flash drive. Art, betrayal, death. A very Russian tale, eh? But—"

"But then Johnny went to Europe and his boat blew up," she finished for him. "So I was the only link you had left to the Van Gogh."

"You, and Donata Kardos." His voice changed. "We did not expect her to be with Tereza that night, to take the baby. We searched for her for decades, but we could never find her. It was as if she just vanished into the Austrian twilight."

Maggie glanced out the window once more, searching for a police car. "The real irony," she said, "is that Johnny never told me anything about the Van Gogh. And now that he is alive, he has no memory of it. Please, Yuri, it's not too late, just talk to Simon Sugarman . . ."

"It *is* too late, Magdalena. I attacked the boy at the ranch, people were hurt at the chapel. It's all coming undone. The tide goes out slowly, but it is unstoppable. I am a Russian. We have more secrets than most. More sins. We all have a bit of Rasputin in us, eh?"

She risked a glance at him. The eyes locked on hers were black and flat as stones.

Her hands were shaking uncontrollably. The National Gallery was on their right, the Capitol building looming straight ahead.

"Bear left on Louisiana," he ordered.

And then she knew where he was going.

Maggie eased the car into the huge traffic circle that would take them to the entrance to Union Station, Washington's massive transportation hub. From there, she knew, Yuri could board an Amtrak train to almost anywhere in the country, or a local Metro to one of three airports. Or he could simply circle back for a taxi or private car.

Do something, her mind screamed. Hit another car, hit a barrier, lay on the horn, speed away . . .

As if he read her mind, the gun barrel pressed harder against her. "Stop here," he said suddenly. Favoring his right hand, he unlocked the glove compartment slowly and reached for a thick envelope.

"I'm not going with you," she said into the silence.

"I have done enough damage over the years," he said softly, and mercifully she felt the gun drop from her side. He opened the passenger door. "Turn off the engine and give me the keys."

She did as he asked. "What are you going to do?"

"I'll be sorry to miss your Rachmaninoff, Magdalena. But I told you when we met that all Russian tales end badly. The wolf always eats the innocent children."

And then Yuri Belankov bolted from the car and disappeared through the huge doors of the station like smoke vanishing in the shadows.

For a moment Maggie sat frozen, staring at the empty doorway. "Not this time, Yuri," she whispered. Thrusting open the car door, she ran toward the station.

The huge station was crowded with hundreds of streaming commuters and tourists. Rolling luggage and carts. Food courts and potted palms. Maggie stopped to scan the enormous, echoing hall. Yuri Belankov could be anywhere.

Where was he?

Think. Look for a tall man with broad shoulders. A clean-shaven, bullet-shaped head. Shouldn't be too hard to spot. She turned in a slow circle, her eyes searching the blur of hurrying faces. Nothing.

But she couldn't let him just *leave*. Not after what he'd done to Dov, taken from him. Heart over head, she thought.

Damn, damn, where would Yuri go? A train, a bus, the airport . . . Wait. He'd told her he'd bought a home in Maryland, in the mountains. And now he would need a car. She looked for the exit signs to cars, taxis, Ubers, rentals. There. Up the escalator.

A glint of light on a clean-shaven head, at the very top of the moving steps. She began to run. A steep stairway paralleled the escalator. She took the steps two at a time.

Just as she reached the landing, Yuri Belankov stepped out from behind a wide pillar to face her. He raised his arm. The last thing she saw before the pain and blackness were his furious sable eyes.

* * *

Michael Beckett spun the Jeep around the last curve of Massachusetts Avenue, slammed on the brakes in front of a huge stone barrier protecting the entrance to Union Station. The lamplights were just flickering on, illuminating the high glass doors. He parked illegally, right-front tire up on the curb, and jumped out.

A doctor had called him from the Amtrak Security office. Maggie was here somewhere.

All he knew was that she'd been taken hostage by Belankov. Ignoring the shout behind him, he climbed over another barricade, heedless of his bad leg. Through the heavy doors, into the cavernous station. Two football fields long, a great vaulted ceiling one hundred feet high. Three levels of restaurants, shops, and some twenty train gates. And a damned thick sea of moving bodies. Amtrak Police everywhere.

Christ. Where was she?

Just be okay, Maggie. I can't lose you.

He clamped his teeth together to keep from shouting her name and forced himself around a towering luggage cart. There had to be thousands of people pushing past him, going in every direction.

Where the devil was she?

And then, at the far end of the endless hall, a flash of night-black hair caught the light.

"Maggie!" he shouted. "Here!"

A glimpse of her pale face, raised. Then she disappeared. He stood still, searching, waiting. Fighting the panic.

Then she broke from the crowd, hair flying, emerald eyes locked on his. Beautiful and brave. Running toward him.

He ran toward her, his heart tripping. She flung herself against him and he was holding her so tightly, as if he'd never let her go. In that moment, he felt as if he'd been waiting for her all of his life.

"You found me," she whispered.

"I'll always find you, darlin'," he said against her hair.

She swayed against him. "I almost stopped him," she whispered against his shirt, "but he hit me."

"Heart over head," he murmured, touching the huge purpling bruise on her temple. Lifting her in his arms, he gathered her against his chest and turned toward the exit. "I am taking you home to the cabin," he said. "A hot bath, then soup in front of the fire. Then you are going to sleep for twelve hours wrapped in my arms. Dov and I will make you pancakes. Then we will get dressed to the nines and drive you to the Kennedy Center Concert Hall, where you will play the hell out of Rachmaninoff. Deal?"

She stirred against him. "Do you think you could put kale in the pancakes?" she whispered.

CHAPTER SEVENTY-FIVE

THE KENNEDY CENTER CONCERT HALL
WASHINGTON, D.C.
SUNDAY

SOME TWENTY-FOUR HOURS later, the last gorgeous chords of Rachmaninoff's Piano Concerto No. 2 echoed out over the Concert Hall.

Maggie bowed her head, her shaking hands dropped to her lap, finally stilled. A moment of silence, and then applause thundered over her in waves. Hot tears streamed down her cheeks, unstoppable, falling like stars onto the deep blue silk gown. She felt faint, disoriented. Grateful to Rachmaninoff.

Tonight, his concerto had brought her full circle. All the tragedy, all the joy. Pain and sadness, beauty and love, past and future—all had come together in one huge, swelling wave of music. The whole human experience—*her* whole human experience, *her* life's story—had come alive, spilling from her heart into the piano.

And then Zharkov's arms wrapped around her, breaking the spell, drawing her slowly to her feet. The stage lights were spinning. She was vaguely aware that the orchestra members around her were rising to their feet, a sea of black and white gowns and tuxedos.

"You did it, my Valisisa," whispered Zharkov. "You said 'what the hell' and leaped off the cliff! It was all there inside you, just waiting to be released. *You finally found the silences between the notes. That is where true art resides.*"

Still unable to catch her breath, Maggie just closed her eyes and let the emotions wash through her in waves. The silences, she thought.

A haunted, homeless boy had given her those silences. And Johnny. And Michael. And a courageous young French woman she had never met who had loved her country and her grandmother to the stars and back . . .

She felt Zharkov's strong hands on her shoulders, turning her to face the audience. The lights were bright, the blur of faces dazzling. She raised her eyes. There, in the box up to her left, Michael and Dov, Robbie and Simon Sugarman. She could see the flash of white lilacs in Michael's arms.

She turned to the Maestro, looked into his shining eyes. Nodded once.

We did it.

He took her hand, raised it to his lips. Shouts of "Brava!" filled the air.

And then she turned and walked off the stage, into the darkened wings. Into the waiting arms of her husband, John O'Shea.

*   *   *

Johnny took her hands, gazing down at her with those impossibly blue eyes. "Your performance broke open my heart, Lass," he whispered. "All that sorrow, all that healing. It was a mirror of your soul. I'll never hear a more beautiful thing."

And then he enveloped her in his arms.

For a moment she rested her cheek against his starched white shirt. Breathed in the faint cologne she loved, felt his still familiar heartbeat against her cheek. And then she raised her gaze to his.

"You've come to say goodbye."

"Aye, Lass. My flight leaves Dulles tomorrow. But I couldn't leave without one last moment with you." He drew her deeper into the darkness, beneath the ropes and pulleys that swayed from the rafters.

"I knew it had to be," he said softly. "Knew where your heart was, from the moment you left me behind in the cabin to go off with your colonel." He gave her a rueful smile. "And I have the glass-blowing—and a life—waiting for me in Cornwall."

"And will you try to find the person who destroyed your shop?"

"Life is too short, Lass, to be consumed by anger, or vengeance. I think it's a lesson remembered from my other self."

"There is still so much of my Johnny in you. He was a fighter, too, but he fought for what was right."

He smiled down at her. "I hope to know that other self someday, that man I was. So early this morning, at the suggestion of my new doctor, I went to Boston. Your music shop is as beautiful as you are, Maggie."

"I'm glad you went. Did you remember anything at all, Johnny?"

"Well, I surely had one hell of an antique chess set, now, didn't I?" He grinned down at her. "No real memories, Lass. Unless—for a moment I thought I saw your reflection, standing behind me, in the case where you keep my granny's blown glass. The doctor thinks that's how it will be for me. An unexpected image, slipping into my head when I least expect it." He held out a small velvet bag. "I made this for you before I left Cornwall. Another memory, I think."

Without speaking, she unwrapped the small, intricately blown-glass figurine, held it up. A woman, spinning joyously in a circle, neck arched, slender arms above her head, her long red dress swirling around her ankles. And her hair like an onyx banner flowing behind her.

Tears welled. "Oh, Johnny."

"She came to me, in my dreams," said Johnny. "*You* came to me. Did you ever spin in a long red dress, Lass? I wonder . . ." His eyes became distant, looking into the past. "Holy Mother. You *did*! It was after the opera, the first night I ever kissed you. It was snowing . . . I kissed you in the snow, Maggie!"

She put her hand over his heart. "Yes, you did. It's a happy, beautiful memory. Now, for the both of us." She smiled into the bright sea-blue eyes. "Stay well, Johnny. Stay in touch. Be happy."

"Aye, Lass. You as well."

He turned to leave, stopped. "Your music almost made me forget! It's possible I had a memory of the Van Gogh, Maggie."

Maggie stepped closer. "You've remembered knowing where it's hidden?"

He shook his head. "Not exactly. But I have a very strong feeling that I *did know*. I was thinking about the Van Gogh again this morning and suddenly I saw a stone angel with a broken wing."

"Like the one you gave me in Cornwall?"

"Yes, I've seen her in my mind before. But never connected to the Van Gogh. And, this time, I heard the sound of waves, crashing on rock." He shrugged. "Of course, it may be nothing."

"A stone angel," she murmured. "You think the Van Gogh could be hidden in a chapel? A monastery, or a cathedral? A *cemetery*?"

A shrug and a smile. "Could be anywhere. But let's hope it's not a cemetery, Lass. I prefer my art above the grass."

"I'll tell Simon Sugarman." She stilled, suddenly thoughtful. "And I think I may know where to start."

He turned away once more, lifted a hand in farewell. "I'll call you," he said.

Maggie stared at him. They were the same last words he'd spoken to her when he'd left for Europe that autumn night two years earlier. *I'll call you*. And then he was gone.

She watched him disappear into the darkness, knowing that now he belonged to the land of legends, boy-kings, and a sorcerer's music in the shadows.

CHAPTER SEVENTY-SIX

THE VIETNAM VETERANS MEMORIAL, WASHINGTON, D.C.
MONDAY MORNING

BECKETT, DOV, AND Shiloh stood beneath the ancient trees on the edge of Washington's National Mall. To their right, just behind them, the morning sun glistened on the white marble steps that led up to the Lincoln Memorial.

But all three of them were looking to their left, down a narrow sloping path, toward the Vietnam Veterans Memorial—the V-shaped, highly polished black granite Wall, etched with the names of the fallen, that began low to the ground, angled up to an apex, and then angled slowly back down to the grass once more.

"You sure you're okay with this?" asked Beckett. "You don't have to, if you're not ready. I can go on alone. It's just that I made a promise and I need to tell your grandfather about your mother, Irina. And about you." He squinted up at the high clouds scudding across the sky. "When you make a promise, kid, you keep it."

The boy gazed toward the Wall for a long moment, then reached down to touch Shiloh's sleek head. "I made a promise, too," he said finally. "I want to do this, Beckett. I want to touch my granddad's name. Maybe tell him about Lady in Black."

"Yev loved horses. He'd be glad to know she's doing so well."

"The vet says she can come home tomorrow."

Beckett smiled. "Home?"

"Well—she needs me, right, while she's healing? I have to have her six."

"Yeah, kid. She needs you all right."

"And you said your mountains mean home." The boy pulled something from his hoodie pocket. His eyes drifted to the Wall. "I read that people leave gifts for the soldiers, Colonel. I brought a picture of me and my mom, on the Boardwalk."

"Yev will like that."

"And, Beckett . . ." Dov held out a small blue envelope. "I want you to have this. Maybe give it to your friend Sugar."

Beckett took the envelope, glanced inside at the small flash drive. "What's this?"

"Justice for my mother."

Beckett blinked, swallowed. "You did the right thing, kid. Belankov will pay. Not you." He set a hand on the boy's shoulder. "Okay then. Let's go meet your grandfather."

Man, boy, and dog walked slowly through the shadows toward the Wall.

* * *

Maggie sat in the passenger seat of Robbie's Dodge Caravan mobility car, holding on for dear life as he sped along Route 50 toward Annapolis.

"How cool is this, Maggs. Who knew I could rent a van that would do everything for me but make French toast! Maybe God has finally decided to forgive me after all."

"And maybe he's just testing you." Maggie braced her hands on the dashboard as he whipped around another car. "You're *sure* you know how to drive this thing, Robbie?" But she smiled as she said it. She hadn't seen him this happy in—well, a long time.

"I used to run marathons," said Robbie, reluctantly slowing his speed to seventy-five. "This is the first time I've felt the joy—the rush—of speed again. It's almost like having my legs back."

"Music does that for me," said Maggie. "And now I see a road trip in your future."

"Never tell God your plans." He laughed, took a quick glance at her, reached over to grasp her hand. "Saturday was a hell of a day for us both. When I think of what could have happened with Yuri Belankov—or what could have happened to Dov Davidov...I don't know what I'd do without you, Maggie."

She closed her eyes. "For some reason, Yuri spared me. But all I can think about are the two women whose lives he took—Dov's mother, Irina, and Rose's mother, so long ago. He changed the course of so many lives."

"Perhaps he couldn't bring himself to destroy the music in you. No word on his whereabouts?"

"None. Simon Sugarman says he just disappeared, like one of his stolen paintings, into the shadows. And the thugs Yuri sent to the ranch—they're not talking; they'll never implicate their boss. The Red Mafia is quite a brotherhood, it seems."

"So it will be Dov's word against Yuri's as to what happened at the stables. If they ever find Yuri." Robbie shook his head. "On the better news front, I heard that Maestro Zharkov turned himself in after the concert last night?"

Maggie nodded. "I think he and Simon Sugarman have come to some sort of understanding."

"Mercy for information? Could be much worse. The music world needs the Zharkovs."

"I could not agree more."

A long sigh. "If only mercy were that easy for the rest of us. Two people were shot, Maggs. In *my* church. I was *there*! I could have stopped it." He looked at the sky. "Why didn't God just keep punishing me instead?"

"I can't speak for God, Robbie, but you weren't expecting violence. You couldn't have known Yuri had a gun."

"Distinctions drawn by the mind are not necessarily equivalent to distinctions in reality." He shrugged his shoulders. "At least no one died this time. Yet. How is Nikolai Kirov?"

"Still in ICU. Rose spent the night there."

She glanced down at the directions on her phone. "The first exit for Annapolis is just ahead. Donata's Retreat House is just a mile north of the city." She gazed out the window. "Do you think she asked to see us because she's finally ready to talk about the Van Gogh?"

He clicked on his blinker. "There's no reason to keep it a secret any longer. But whatever Donata's reasons, it will be good to see her. She and I are kindred spirits. For a moment Saturday, in the chapel . . ."

She smiled at him. "Did you see this morning's *Post*? The headline called you 'The Hero Priest.'"

"Holy Mother of God. All I did was fall out of my chair on top of two women." He grinned. "*They're* the heroes who cushioned my fall."

"The last time I checked, false humility was some kind of sin," said Maggie. "You could have been shot, Robbie. You protected Rose and her mother."

"Not good enough, Maggs. Donata took the bullet. I blame myself."

"The blame falls on Yuri. Donata's shoulder will heal. She's here, Robbie, she's alive. That's what matters."

"Who can answer why something does *not* happen?" he murmured.

They drove the last two miles in silence, each lost in their own thoughts, and what might have been.

*   *   *

St. Cecelia by the Bay Retreat House was a huge, rambling Victorian building with a faded red roof above walls weathered by salt air, set on a grassy rise overlooking the Chesapeake Bay. Maggie followed Robbie up the wheelchair ramp, and they stopped for a moment on the covered, wraparound veranda to absorb the view. Wooden rocking chairs lined the porch, swaying back and forth in the wind as if the ghosts of nuns past were enjoying the view.

The Chesapeake Bay spread out below them, gunmetal gray and whipped by whitecaps. Maggie's hair blew across her eyes as she listened to the wild, high cry of the seabirds and the water crashing against the shore. The sharp salt scent of the bay surrounded them. In the distance, the tolling chime of church bells.

"There are moments when you can hear God," said Robbie.

Maggie thought of the first chords of the concerto's tolling bells. "Or Rachmaninoff," she murmured.

But it was a soft woman's voice that they heard, speaking behind them. "Welcome to St. Cecilia's," the old nun said. "Sister Therese Rozsa is waiting for you around back, on the porch." She gestured toward the bay. "Just follow me."

*　*　*

Donata Kardos sat in one of the rocking chairs, her left arm in a heavy black sling. A book of poetry rested in her lap. She smiled and gestured to the chairs pulled up by a small table set with a thermos and coffee mugs. "Thank you for coming. It's good to see you both. Please, be comfortable. Have some coffee."

When Maggie and Robbie were settled, Donata leaned toward them. "Rose wanted to be here, but she's still with Kirov. She wants to be with her father when he wakes up."

"Of course she does," said Maggie, thinking of her own father. "What are his doctors saying?"

"They're hopeful." She shook her head. "Is there any word on Yuri Belankov?"

"Simon Sugarman thinks he's left the country," said Maggie. "I can't imagine what you must be feeling."

"A crisis of faith," said Donata quietly. "He aimed a gun at my daughter. He could have killed her. For the first time ever, I wish I'd owned a gun. I would have shot him to death without thinking twice, Maggie." She turned to flash a look at Robbie Brennan. "For me there is no understanding, no forgiveness. Perhaps it's time to leave this life I chose."

Robbie's eyes softened. "If anyone could carry off the gun-toting-nun thing," he said, "it would be you. But your faith isn't broken, Sister, it's just shaken."

Donata shrugged. "I never even kept fireflies in jars when I was young, for fear of hurting them . . ."

"Because you knew it would be a sin against the night," said Robbie. "I've sat on both sides of the confessional, Donata. I know all about crises of faith."

"I no longer know if I chose the religious life to go toward something," said the nun. "Now I wonder if I've just been hiding. Running away."

"Somehow I don't think God is done with either one of us yet, Donata," said Robbie.

She scowled and turned to Maggie. "Henry II must have been thinking of Robbie when he asked to be rid of this 'meddlesome priest.'"

Maggie laughed. "One more thing you and I have in common."

Donata exhaled, managed a faint smile, and reached for several papers on the table beside her. "You both are good for me. But I asked you here because Rose and I had a long talk last night. We want you to know how Amélie's story ended—what happened when Anton Janos and Amélie arrived at her grandmother's château in southern France. And . . . what became of the Van Gogh."

She held out the final pages of Anton Janos' letter.

CHAPTER SEVENTY-SEVEN

Amélie ran toward the open doors of the château, wrote Anton Janos, *crying out for her grandmother.*

We searched the house, floor by floor, but there was nothing left. No person, no books, no food or wine, no art ... Just vast, empty, echoing rooms.

Then a voice at the front door.

A tall figure, standing with the light behind him. There was no place to hide.

But it was a neighbor, telling us that Grandmère Amélie had been sheltering a Jewish family for several days—until the village grocer had turned them in. Amélie's grandmother, and the family, had been rounded up just hours earlier and taken, along with many others, to the train station in the village.

We ran all the way. When we got there, it was a madman's dream. Babies screaming, suitcases and clothing tossed everywhere, soldiers with guns and whips, dogs growling. People were being pushed and lifted into slatted cattle cars, like animals.

Half of the soldiers and some of the collaborators, as well, formed a human chain to keep the townspeople away. My Amélie ran along the line, shouting for her grandmother. So many agonized faces. And then a cry!

Her Grandmère Amélie was near the front of the train, in line to be boarded. She was hunched forward, her blue violin case over her shoulder, her cane pressed against her side.

"*Grandmère!*" *Amélie's voice, clear and true, rose above the crowd. Her grandmother stopped, lifted her head. My Amélie began to run. I grabbed her arm to stop her, but she tore away from me.*

I fought to get to her, but a thick-necked guard hit me across the back with a heavy stanchion. I fell to the ground, shouting for Amélie.

Somehow, in the commotion, Amélie managed to break through the human chain of soldiers. I could see her between the sea of uniformed legs and boots.

My heart stopped as the SS ran toward her, their dogs snarling. But Amélie reached her grandmother, wrapped her in her arms.

Everything happened in slow motion.

"*Schritt aus der reihe!*" *A soldier grabbed Amélie roughly, trying to pull her out of the line. I saw her pleading, the soldier's cold face twisting with hatred. Then the terrible understanding that dawned in her beautiful eyes. Shaking her head frantically back and forth, she kicked him, hit him with her fists, slashed at his face with her Grandmère's cane.*

Her grandmother pushed her away, eyes wild, shouting through her tears for Amélie to obey the Nazi. To leave the line.

But I knew.

She would not leave her grandmother. She would not leave the line.

Her arms wrapped around her grandmother as if they were one, their heads close, tears streaming down both their faces. I saw her Grandmère Amélie try to push her away one last time, to save her. Whisper something against her beloved granddaughter's hair . . .

But Amélie held on.

Now three soldiers surrounded them. Somehow, my Amélie twisted toward me. Our eyes locked. She smiled at me, and her lips whispered my name one final time.

And then in a blur she and her grandmother were lifted as one and thrown into the train car, disappearing into the darkness. It was the worst moment of my life.

The train began to move. Everyone around me was screaming in agony, crying, waving their arms, struggling to break through the lines to get to their loved ones. I will never forget it.

Somehow, I stumbled to my feet, ran after the train. But it went faster and faster. We all stood there, breathless and sobbing. I watched through a veil of tears until the train disappeared into the distant woods.

I turned. Something bright blue glinted in a pile of belongings still jumbled on the platform. It was Grandmère's violin case, shattered, the violin inside crushed to tangled black strings and splinters of spruce. Hidden just beneath it, her grandmother's thick wooden cane. I grasped the cane, held it against my heart. And then I ran from the station.

I made my way back to Paris, where I found my Amélie's diary in a tight gap behind the stove. Words cannot describe the unbearable pain I felt when I learned she was pregnant.

Of course, I did everything I could to find them. I finally learned that the train was headed to a camp called Auschwitz, in southern Poland. For months I tried to get word of Amélie and her grandmother, but there was nothing.

And so, the days passed. I held on to Amélie's diary and Grandmère's cane, my only links to the last moment I saw my beautiful Amélie. I read the diary over and over. As for the old cane—it was just an ordinary object, surely, but it symbolized an unforgettable journey of tragedy, courage, and enduring love. For me, that cane became my Amélie's story.

I continued to search for her long after the war ended. But it was as if she just vanished from the earth. I found out eventually that those terrible July roundups were called Vel'd'Hiv—when thousands of French Jews were rounded up in both the occupied and free zones, including some 5,000 women and 4,000 children, and sent on cattle cars to Auschwitz. It is still unimaginable.

Only eight hundred returned after the war. My Amélie was not among the survivors.

It wasn't until years later, after I returned to Budapest, that I twisted my ankle one evening and remembered the old cane still in the back of my closet. When I grasped it, the silver top was loose. I twisted it, and it came off in my hands. The cane was hollow. Something was inside.

Of course by now you have guessed what was so tightly rolled and secreted inside Grandmère Amélie's cane—Vincent Van Gogh's painting of her, with her violin, in the garden at Saint-Rémy beneath the stars. Shadow Music.

CHAPTER SEVENTY-EIGHT

ST. CECELIA'S BY THE BAY, ANNAPOLIS, MARYLAND

DONATA KARDOS FOLDED the pages of the letter. The only sound was the ceaseless whisper of the waves below them breaking on the narrow strip of rock.

"So much courage," said Maggie finally, swiping at hot tears. "So much love."

"But still no answers to where the Van Gogh is now," said Robbie, with a raised brow directed at Donata.

She smiled serenely and turned to Maggie. "Maggie, dear, I asked you to come here today for two reasons. First, to thank you for your friendship and support for my daughter. You were there for Rose when she needed you, and I cannot thank you enough."

"I feel very close to her," said Maggie.

"I'm glad. And I hope you will tell your husband how glad I am that he is alive and how grateful I am for his trust and friendship." She gestured toward Maggie's chair. "Did you know that he showed up here two years ago, not long after I met him, and sat right there where you are now?"

Maggie shook her head, surprised.

"He was leaving for Europe and wanted me to know that he had figured out where the Van Gogh was. To tell me that the secret would be safe with him, that the painting's location was Rose's to share, not his. Your husband's last words to me were, 'I only hope that someday you and Rose will feel safe enough to share your beautiful Van Gogh with the world.'"

"That doesn't surprise me." Magie smiled.

Donata Kardos leaned forward and held out the book of poetry from her lap. "Maggie, I need one more favor. Will you return my book to the library while I have a private word with Robbie? It's through those doors, all the way at the end of the hall."

"Of course."

Maggie accepted the book and passed through the French doors, light suddenly replaced by shadow. The hallway was long, winding, and badly lit, with a dozen doors opening into a warren of gloomy rooms. Somewhere ahead, voices singing a hymn.

"Gothic," she murmured, wandering slowly, stopping to glance behind half-open doors. A meeting room with an oversized conference table. A tiny chapel lit by a flickering candle. The music room, where the small choir of women sang. Then a room for crafts and a small breakfast room where two aging nuns in sweat suits sat enjoying their coffee. On the left, an office with several old desks and file cabinets crowded together.

And then Maggie stopped.

A single bar of light fell like a beckoning path through a half-open doorway at the end of the hallway. Maggie glanced in and saw the high, bright window, the book-lined shelves, several easy chairs. The library. She entered, searching for a place to leave Donata's book.

Then she saw the angel.

"Oh, my God," she whispered.

Some three feet in height, the kneeling stone angel was set on a thick pedestal. The left side of the angel, illuminated by the window, glowed as if lit from within. The side facing the doorway was concealed in deep shadow, but Maggie could see the broken wing.

Pushing the door open, she entered the library. And there it was.

On the wall behind the angel, barely visible in the gloom, was a large, simply-framed painting. Maggie stepped closer and caught her breath as she gazed at the young woman playing her violin in a dark garden, her face in deep shadow. Above her, the cobalt night sky was lit by swirling golden stars.

Vincent van Gogh's *Shadow Music*.

CHAPTER SEVENTY-NINE

WESTERN MARYLAND

THE GULFSTREAM G500 luxury jet sat on the private airfield in western Maryland.

Yuri Belankov, the only occupant in the cabin, sat in one of the ultra-modern leather seats listening to the low growl of powerful engines. The jet had a range of over five thousand miles. In just moments, he would be soaring toward Paris.

Well, a man had to eat, eh? It might as well be the best food in the world. And then there were the beautiful women, the art galleries, the museums . . .

He leaned back, sipped the smooth, icy Stolichnaya vodka and smiled as he suddenly remembered a quote by Will Rogers. *Nobody in the world knows what vodka is made out of, and the reason I tell you this is that the story of vodka is the story of Russia.*

I am still a Russian in my soul, he thought.

The jet's oval windows were filling with twilight. The end of day, the beginning of night. The in-between time. That's what this trip would be. The in-between time.

What had his father always said? Little thieves are hanged, but great thieves escape.

Another slow, thoughtful swallow of the Stoli. So far, he'd skated the charges related to the attack at the ranch, and the far more serious charge of a brutal murder in a Brighton Beach alley. But there was no physical evidence. Just his word—a successful entrepreneur, philanthropist, friend of presidents—against the word of a homeless, vengeful boy.

Unless the boy had the flash drive.

The gunshots, the injuries in the Georgetown Chapel might not go away so easily. Donata Kardos hated him, would not hesitate to throw him to the wolves. And Kirov—Kirov was still in Intensive Care. If he awakened, what would he say? Of course, Kirov had a long list of his own broken laws to deal with. He had to protect himself.

But the betrayal of Rose still scalded, even with the vodka icing his throat. All these years, he'd believed he was her father. Believed that Kirov was his friend.

I should have trusted my instincts, he thought. *I sensed something was wrong between us. You can no longer expect loyalty from Kirov*, he warned himself.

As for Zharkov, well, his knowledge did not extend past the stolen art and Kirov's laundering gallery in New York City. And the maestro would, after all, sell his soul to keep his music.

So, he thought. Give it time. Let things blow over. See who says what. His paintings, including his beloved *Red Orchestra*, were safe in the Maryland countryside, at his estate deep in the Catoctin Mountains.

It was time to disappear for a while. *There are worse things than a year of Coq au Vin, a Saint-Émilion Grand Cru, and the Musée d'Orsay*, he thought.

And after that . . . his thoughts returned to Irina's boy. And Colonel Beckett. And Magdalena O'Shea. She had nearly ruined everything by following him into the station. *We are not done*, he told them all silently. Russians have very long memories.

A rev of engines, the rush down the runway. The jet lifted into the air.

He drank the vodka and looked down at the lights just winking on in the dusk below.

So much still to do. And the Van Gogh was still out there, somewhere.

He gazed down at the tilting, rose-tinged horizon.

I will be back.

* * *

Over five thousand miles to the east, night was falling over the Greek island of Mykonos. The hillside was cloaked in shadows that spilled across the cubed houses and olive trees and the terrace high above the sea. In the last of the light, the Aegean was the color of plums. Stars sparked like tiny flames against the vault of dark sky.

Beatrice walked slowly across the terrace stones toward the man who sat motionless, his face lifted to the heavens.

She stopped behind him, rested her left hand on his shoulder. Her right hand, by her side, held his dagger. "I failed," she whispered. "I did not find the Van Gogh."

His strong, sharp shoulder shrugged beneath her fingers. "And Magdalena O'Shea?" The voice was low, silky, barely a whisper.

"I followed her," said Beatrice, her eyes on the glint of stars caught beneath the sea. "You were right. She led me to her husband. But I wanted more. I wanted her to suffer. My God, I pushed her off a bridge. But I . . ." She let out her breath, set the dagger on the table. The sharp blade gleamed silver in the light. "I have no rage left. Only sorrow."

"Vengeance is not in you, the way it is in me." His hand rose, grasped hers. "She is forever locked in my memory. I know where to find her."

He raised his eyes to the star-struck night sky. "*The skies are painted with unnumber'd sparks, They are all fire and every one doth shine, But there's but one in all doth hold his place.*"

CHAPTER EIGHTY

THE BLUE RIDGE MOUNTAINS, VIRGINIA

SHE WAS STANDING on the deck, gazing out over the lake toward the mountains. One by one, the trees were catching fire as the sun dropped from the sky and spilled into the water.

Beckett turned on the CD player and listened as the first notes of Rachmaninoff's Piano Concerto No. 2 spilled into the cabin. Then he moved outside to stand behind her, setting his hands on her shoulders without speaking. She leaned back against him. They stood together for a long time, watching twilight come to the mountains and listening to the music that swelled around them.

Finally, he said against her hair, "Listen. Only music. No gunshots, no explosions, no sirens, no hostages, no one throwing you off the deck into the lake. It's just the two of us tonight." He turned her around so he could gaze down into the deep green eyes. "We haven't had a quiet moment to really talk, Maggie."

"About Johnny."

His breath came out, warm, touching her cheek. "No doubts, darlin'?"

She smiled up into his eyes. "When I walked through your cabin door today, I knew I was making a choice. Johnny and I are no longer the same people. He's a lovely man, but in so many ways a stranger to me now, as I am to him. My past with Johnny will always be part of me, Michael. But I've accepted that my old life is gone. I'm ready to embrace a new one. My present, my future, is here, with you. I'm choosing love."

"Hey, Beckett, Maggie. What's for—" Dov had wandered out onto the terrace, Shiloh hopping beside him, and stopped short when he saw their faces. "I mean—uh, change of plans, the Brigadier and I are, um, going to order pizza and watch *Star Wars* in my room. If that's okay with you guys?"

Shiloh's golden ears pricked when Dov mentioned pizza.

"You know Shiloh's magic word," said Beckett with a smile. "Quick thinking, kid, you must really want that trip to Disneyland." He leaned closer, became serious. "But you're sure you don't want company, Dov? It's been a helluva few days for you."

The boy's eyes darkened. "Yeah, a lot to process, right? But going to the Wall was good. Feeling close to my grandfather . . . it meant something, felt like a door closing on the bad stuff, you know? So I think I want to just crash tonight." He grinned. "Maybe even sleep for a change."

He reached down, tugged softly on the Golden's ears. "And I've got my pal the Brigadier for company."

"I'm here, too, kid. If you need me."

Something flashed in Dov's eyes. He turned toward the hallway, then stopped. "Hey, Colonel Romance," he called. "I think maybe your horse just might sing tonight!"

And then he and Shiloh disappeared into the cabin.

Maggie looked at Beckett. "*Colonel Romance?*" She shook her head in amusement. "*A singing horse?*"

"Long story," murmured Beckett. "Kid's too cocky, but he's right about one thing. I have to get something for you, something I stashed in my sock drawer a while back."

"You are full of surprises."

"And more to come. Remember how you described jumping off a cliff to find the heart of Rachmaninoff's music? Well, this is my 'what-the-hell-just-jump-off-the-cliff' moment." He cupped her face in his palms and brushed his lips across her forehead, her eyes, her cheek. "That's so you don't forget me while I'm gone."

"Not a chance."

He turned toward the stairs, then stopped and looked back at her, standing before him in a black t-shirt that said *The Setting Sun, and Music at the Close* . . . with the twilight glowing gold behind her. "Will you wait right here for me, Maggie?"

"I'm not going anywhere."

* * *

Seriously, socks?

She watched him climb the stairs, overwhelmed by the love she felt for this crusty, rainy-eyed soldier.

Then she turned back to gaze at the lake. Rachmaninoff's chords swirled around her, filled her, past and present becoming one. The sky above the mountains shimmered with the last whisper of light, turning the lake to deep crimson. A single star appeared, a bright glint against the dark blue of nightfall. Like a promise.

She looked down at Shakespeare's words on her t-shirt, words that had touched her long ago, and stayed with her. *The setting sun, and music at the close.*

"Maggie."

Michael's voice behind her, deep with love. She turned. He was walking toward her, clutching something in his hand. He flashed his lopsided smile at her.

She'd never seen quite that look on his face before. She stepped toward him.

"The four of us," he said in a rusty voice, "we can't live without each other, right?"

"The four of us, Michael. You all make me feel the way I feel when I'm playing music. I'm where I should be." She touched his arm. "Now please tell me you're not giving me a pair of old socks to welcome me home?"

He took a deep breath, moved closer, held out the jewelry box. Grasped her hand.

And jumped off the cliff.

AUTHOR'S NOTES

Thank you for joining me in Maggie's world.

Once again, I wanted to create characters with depth, paint pictures with words, and invite readers to "fall into" Maggie's story. And, whenever possible, to make the reader *feel*.

With the publications of *The Lost Concerto* and *Dark Rhapsody*, I realized that Maggie's story was not yet done. And so *Shadow Music* was born.

I believe that the right setting can truly enrich a scene, and I included several places I love and want to share in *Shadow Music*.

Memorials, for me, are a source of deep emotion and remembrance. I wrote one of my most moving scenes after revisiting Washington's Vietnam Veteran's Memorial—The Wall.

Also inspiring—the Hatch Music Shell on Boston's Esplanade; The National Gallery of Art, the Kennedy Center and Georgetown University in D.C.; London's South Bank; and Cornwall, a place I've been blessed to visit twice. This land of cliffs and mists and legends, so moody and evocative, inspired many of *Shadow Music*'s most suspenseful chapters. When I climbed those narrow steps up the cliffs to Tintagel Castle, I knew Maggie would climb them one day as well.

I also believe that history matters, and, because my dad and uncles fought in World War II, I have a special interest in those years and events. For me, blending past and present in *Shadow Music* makes this story far more stirring and meaningful.

Over the centuries, thousands of priceless pieces of art, musical scores, and valuable instruments have been documented as stolen, destroyed accidentally or purposely, or simply disappeared. But Vincent van Gogh's oil painting *Shadow Music* exists only in my imagination.

You may be interested to know that, like *Firebird, The Lost Concerto,* and *Dark Rhapsody,* my net proceeds from *Shadow Music* will go to nonprofit organizations that benefit our most vulnerable women, children, and families, via the Helaine and Ronald Mario Fund. Royalties will support inner-city food banks, education, health, shelter, child protection, the arts, and economic development, with an emphasis on programs that promote dignity, independence, and safety. A list of these organizations is included on my website, HelaineMario.com.

If you have enjoyed getting to know Colonel Beckett and Shiloh and are interested in learning more about PTSD and animals helping veterans, here are several websites for more information:

https://www.ptsd.va.gov/public/ptsd-overview/basics/
    what-is-ptsd.asp
K9s for Warriors: www.k9sforwarriors.org
Paws for Veterans: www.pawsforveterans.com
Battle Buddy Foundation: www.tbbf.org

And finally—the music. As many of my readers know, my son, Sean, was the inspiration for Maggie's vocation and her beloved classical music pieces. Background and research on these pieces come from too many sources to list, but any musical errors are mine alone. I'm listing below several of "Maggie's favorites," several newly included in *Shadow Music,* for those of you who love classical music or simply want to discover new pieces:

Bach – Cello Suites (Yo Yo Ma)

Bach – Brandenburg Concertos

Beethoven – Moonlight Sonata and Piano Sonata No. 8, the *Pathetique*

Beethoven – Piano Concerto No. 1 in C major

Beethoven – Piano Concerto No. 5 in E flat (The Emperor)

Beethoven – Concerto in D major for Violin

Beethoven – Symphony No. 3 in E-flat major (The Eroica)

Chopin – Piano Concerto No. 2 in F minor

Chopin – Ballades, Nos. 1 – 4

Chopin – Heroic Polonaise

Dvorak – Cello Concerto in B minor

Grieg – Piano Concerto in A minor

Khachaturian – Toccata in E-Flat minor

Liszt – Hungarian Rhapsody No. 2, C-Sharp minor

Liszt – Consolation No. 3

Mozart – Piano Concerto No. 19 in F major

Mozart – Piano Concerto No. 21 in C (associated with Elvira Madigan)

Prokoviev – Piano Concerto No. 3

Rachmaninoff – Rhapsody on a Theme of Paganini

Rachmaninoff – Piano Concerto No. 2 in C minor

Tchaikovsky – Piano Concerto No. 1 in B-Flat minor

Tchaikovsky – Concerto in D major for Violin

Vivaldi – The Four Seasons

Dear Reader,

We hope that you enjoyed *Shadow Music* as much as we did. We find that Helaine Mario's writing flows with a beautiful rhythm that makes it feel like reading music. But the beauty of her prose does not detract from the stark terror that faces Maggie O'Shea, acclaimed classical pianist.

If you have not already, we suggest you read the first two novels in the Maggie O'Shea series and let Helaine Mario pull you deeper into Maggie's world.

In *The Lost Concerto*, the first in the series, a woman and her young son flee to a convent on a remote island off the coast of France. There, a tragedy occurs and a terrified child—Maggie O'Shea's godson—disappears into the mist. Maggie, grief-stricken from the recent loss of her husband, sets off on a collision course with criminal forces. Decades-old secrets, stolen art, and missing music abound—and in the face of horrific evil, Maggie finds a new love.

In *Dark Rhapsody*, the second in the series, Maggie O'Shea is putting her life back together, struggling to find the courage to return to the stage. Bizarre circumstances intervene and drive her to explore the mystery of her mother's death and her father's startling disappearance. Her treacherous search leads her into the crosshairs of a brutal killer, the discovery of a priceless Nazi-hidden treasure, and a terrible secret from World War II.

In each of these novels, Mario will pull you into Maggie's world, lull you with classical music, and stun you with horrific evil.

Sit back and enjoy the beauty and the thrills!

For more information, see Helaine Mario's website: HelaineMario.com.

Oceanview Publishing